Edge Of
BETRAYAL

The New Caporesso Chronicles
Book I
L. J. Noker

ISBN: 0615456375
ISBN 13: 9780615456379

Library of Congress Control Number: 2011924001
CreateSpace, North Charleston, SC

A journey of a thousand miles begins with a single step.
—ancient Chinese proverb—

Strength of swords, honor in victory.

To my Annie:
You give me my strength and motivation.
Thank you for the greatest gifts in my life.

Acknowledgments

Thank you to my family and friends who assured me this story didn't suck. Your encouragement kept me going when I doubted I'd ever finish.

Thanks to the people from CreateSpace.com; without you guys, I never would have been able to pull this off.

Also, when your tenth grade English teacher tries to give you some advice, listen to her; she just might know more than you realize.

Prologue

The Tu'nide formed their battle line, four hundred horsemen long. At the head of the attack was their newest commander, Prince Col. He was now their captain, a position normally reserved for the most deserving warrior, not the king's stepson. Centuries of tradition had been eradicated by a whimsical choice, infuriating some of these elite cavalry troopers.

Across the field sat the insurgents' version of a cavalry force. There were over eight hundred men on horses, with an additional five hundred infantrymen in support. The Tu'nide was outnumbered three to one; what chance would they have against such odds?

Plenty, thought Col.

At Col's signal, their horses lunged ahead. After a few strides, they picked up speed, breaking into a canter.

Likewise, the insurgents began their counterassault.

As the Tu'nide closed the gap between their enemies, their speed slowed. They were deliberately allowing Col to separate himself from the rest of them. He was going to engage the rebels before the rest of the battalion.

Let's see how the royal brat does now, thought Lieutenant Sed'la. The promotion to captain was supposed to be his. And it was until King Guan intervened on behalf of Col. Others had assured Sed'la that Col was worthy of the position, but he disagreed. After this engagement, everyone would know if Col had been the right choice or not.

We swore an oath before we were teens to stand beside each other, no matter the odds, no matter the enemy. Brothers in arms? Ha! I spit on that oath. Let's see Guan hand Col a victory in this battle. Let's see Col survive without his stepfather's intervention.

The unvoiced thoughts stirred something in Sed'la. *No…I can't leave him alone. What have I done?* "Forward! Attack! Attack!" he barked, and with renewed purpose, the Tu'nide raced to join their captain.

Onward, the Tu'nide galloped.

Even though his soldiers were outnumbered, Col knew they still had the advantage. He and his men were the best-trained warriors in New Caporesso. There was no greater fighting force anywhere in the country, and they rode against some half-trained horde of rebels.

Their horses thundered forward, fearlessly charging into battle.

Col heard each labored breath exhaled from his horse, Choa. The rhythmic sound of his muscular destrier comforted him. Anticipating contact, Col unleashed a blood-curdling war cry. His voice seemed muted and unfamiliar.

Then for an instant the world was silent…and then…*Crash!* Col's spear splintered the shield in front of him, piercing the man. As the rebel fell, Col lost hold of his weapon and immediately drew his willow-leaf-shaped broadsword. Riding through their ranks, he deflected the incoming blows, protecting himself.

Emerging unscathed on the other side of the rebels, he was breathing hard. Wheeling around, he realized his men were not with him. They had abandoned him in the heat of battle. *I thought they'd do that.* He searched the melee looking for Sed'la, but could not find him amongst the fray. *I told Guan not to promote me, that the Tu'nide wasn't ready to have me as their captain. Brothers to the end?* He shook his head, *I'll deal with Sed'la and the men later.* For now, he had a battle to survive.

Movement at his flank caught his attention. As he ducked his head, a spear thrust missed him by inches. Bringing his sword to bear, he deflected the next attack. He effortlessly moved Choa around his enemy, attacking the rebel from his offhand side. With a single swing of his sword, Col separated the man's head from his body. Twitching, the man fell from his horse.

Two more horsemen charged at Col. He spurred Choa towards the closest man, ducking under a wild slash while simultaneously removing the man's arm. Sitting upright in his saddle, Col parried the second man's attack. *Clang…clang*, their swords sounded on the grassy prairie, the chaos of battle all around. Col moved closer to his assailant and slipped under another undisciplined slash. Leaning away from the man, he grasped the reins tightly and braced a leg against the stirrup. With his other, he kicked the rebel in the face. The man fell from his horse with a shriek, breaking his neck.

Col observed the carnage around him, mesmerized by its hypnotic effect. His men were engaged with the enemy and holding their own. Their spears were long and accurate. With strong shields and swift swords, they hewed their way through the enemy's lines with little resistance. Choa blustered wildly, bringing Col back to his senses.

Looking around, he saw one of his soldiers faltering against four rebels. Without concern for his own safety, Col plunged into their midst, drawing attention away from his wounded comrade. He quickly dispatched the nearest man, slicing through his gullet. As he did so, he caught the man's broadsword with his free hand. Now with a sword in each hand, Col continued battling his enemies. He blocked and attacked with the skill of an expertly trained warrior. In a matter of seconds, the remaining three attackers were dead.

Turning his horse, Col saw a seven-man group of infantry charge him. Urging Choa forward, he picked up speed. When they were almost engaged, Col gracefully dismounted and honorably met his attackers. Brandishing two swords and uttering a primal cry, he attacked. With two slashes from each sword, three rebels fell at his feet. Before the other men could muster a unified defense, he cut them down where they stood.

Panting heavily, Col surveyed the scene. Now the rebels were in full retreat, their numbers reduced by over half. He threw down his rebel sword and inspected his men. Many of them were injured, only a handful had fallen in battle. *Victory is ours!*

The men cheered in unison, "Ah-ooh...ah-ooh...ah-ooh!"

Col issued orders to his troopers. "First and second squads...deploy sentries to secure the perimeter." He commanded with confidence. "We need to be on alert in case they regroup and resume the attack."

On the open plains east of Cenkin, their location did not offer the most defensible of positions, but they had a commanding view of the surrounding area. No one could approach without first revealing themselves. For now, they were out of danger.

The remainder of the Tu'nide dismounted to tend to their wounded comrades. They wrapped bandages around open wounds on their friends' arms and heads. Surgeons treated the more serious abdominal injuries. Within a matter of minutes, the injured were being attended with expert care.

"Thank you, sir," someone said to Col.

Turning his head, he realized it was Sed'la. He scoffed, asking, "For what, Lieutenant?"

"For saving my life, sir."

With fire in his eyes, Col nodded his head.

Sed'la had a bandage tied around his upper arm. Blood had already soaked through the thick material, leaving a track running down his arm. Cuts on his face leaked blood, and with a scarf, he wiped away what he could.

Col spoke through clenched teeth, "Of course, Lieutenant." He cleaned the blood from his own sword and sheathed it. Choa approached, nuzzling his shoulder. Col patted the steady horse, whispering words of praise. He mounted the young stallion and moved next to Sed'la. "I'm sure any one of you would have done the same for me," he added, glaring into Sed'la's eyes.

Sed'la nervously laughed and looked away. "That's just it, sir. You *know* we wouldn't have done the same for you." He motioned at the other men, "We deserted you, sir." Ashamed, he lowered his head. "Some of us didn't feel you deserved your promotion, and we...I mean I, let you charge into battle without us." Stealing a glance at Col, he confessed, "I've broken my vow to the Tu'nide, sir. I've dishonored the other warriors who have fallen before us in battle. I don't deserve to be your lieutenant any longer. Sir—"

"The contempt you and the other men showed me today was repulsive, bordering on mutinous, you miserable bastard. You left me to die at the hands of those less-than-worthy hungry peasants." He pointed a finger at Sed'la and growled, "Don't ever act that way again, Lieutenant. Do you understand?"

"Yes, sir. I owe—"

"Silence!" he yelled. Several of the nearby soldiers watched them attentively. "Sed'la, I'm your captain...and you're my lieutenant. Guan is responsible for that arrangement, not me." Col seethed with anger. "I know you were next in line for this promotion, but you are a soldier and will obey my orders next time, or I'll have you drawn and quartered. Your head will stay in Cenkin, while your arms and legs visit Norkin, Werlo, Sokin, and Drador! Do you understand me, soldier?" he yelled.

Sed'la snapped to attention while still in his saddle, staring straight ahead. "Yes, sir. I understand you perfectly, sir." His horse sidestepped away from Choa. Forlorn, he looked at Col. "Sir—"

Col reprimanded him again. "Be silent, Sed'la, before I change my mind about ending your life." He nudged Choa closer. "I don't want to talk about today's actions again, do you understand? We went into battle together and emerged victorious. Period. The report will say that and only that." With a wave of his hand, he said, "Guan was testing me and my ability to lead men on a battlefield. He was hoping I would fail, and he was hoping you would abandon me." Raising an eyebrow, he leaned forward in his saddle and added. "Let's prove him wrong, shall we?"

"Yes, sir." Sed'la saluted. "But, sir, why would your stepfather want you to fail?"

"To prevent me from winning the support of the citizens of New Caporesso. He wants to keep me from becoming a celebrated warrior like my father...my real father. He also wants to hold my military career in check, preventing me from gaining your respect," he gestured at the Tu'nide. Choa neighed and bobbed his head.

Sed'la's horse skittered away from Col, circling around to the other side. "Sir? What about my actions today? You have every right to have me removed from duty and punished...even killed."

"I know I do, Sed'la." He let the statement hang. "That's why I will do nothing of the sort." Surveying the bloody field, he recalled, "We were friends as children, swearing silly oaths that boys do, but after Guan became king following the coup, he prevented us from associating together."

Half grinning, Sed'la said, "And I still remember your little sister beating you up. But as we got older, Guan kept you away from your friends...and I resented *you* for it. Somehow, I blamed you for his actions. Then when he promoted you to captain of our battalion, I was angry. I told the others you had not earned that privilege yet. It's my fault for what happened today, the men are blameless. Forgive me, my prince." He bowed his head.

Col sighed, "Sed'la, there is nothing to forgive."

Sed'la raised his head, a blank expression on his face.

"We survived the battle; that's all that's important. Nothing else matters anymore." He moved closer and put a hand on Sed'la's shoulder. "At one time, we were the best of friends, Sed'la. Our battle today is over; let us be friends once more."

Smiling, Sed'la put his hand on Col's arm, adding, "And nothing will ever come between us again, Col. No matter what, we'll resolve our differences before they stand in the way of our friendship or duties."

Sensing the tension slipping away, some of the Tu'nide gathered around their captain. Col looked from face to face; the men were not sure how Col would react to their momentary betrayal.

"Troopers, today we've triumphed over our rebel enemy." He drew his sword, brandishing it above his head. "We are victorious!"

His men thrust their fists in the air three times, chanting, "Ah-ooh... ah-ooh...ah-ooh!"

"Let today be the first day of our service together. You are mine to command, and I am yours, a man on whom you can rely. Let history show that we began the day as uneasy friends, but end it as brothers bathed in the blood of our enemies. We are one with each other." He shouted, "Strength of swords, honor in victory!"

Again, Col's troopers hollered. "Ah-ooh...ah-ooh...ah-ooh!" They boomed for all to hear, their voices echoing on the open prairie.

Col smiled to himself. Not only was he captain of the Tu'nide, but he was also the accepted commander of the elite unit. Never again would he stand alone in battle. His brothers would always be with him, and support him no matter the consequences...no matter the enemy.

Looking skyward, he moved a fist to his shoulder and saluted. *This is for you, Father. I'll find out what truly happened and avenge your death, this I swear. Your name has almost been erased from New Caporesso's history. I don't know why, but it has. I won't let you, or what you accomplished be forgotten. I'll make the people remember who you truly were. Your legacy will be living on as a hero of the people. No matter how long it takes, you'll have your vengeance, and your soul can finally be at peace.*

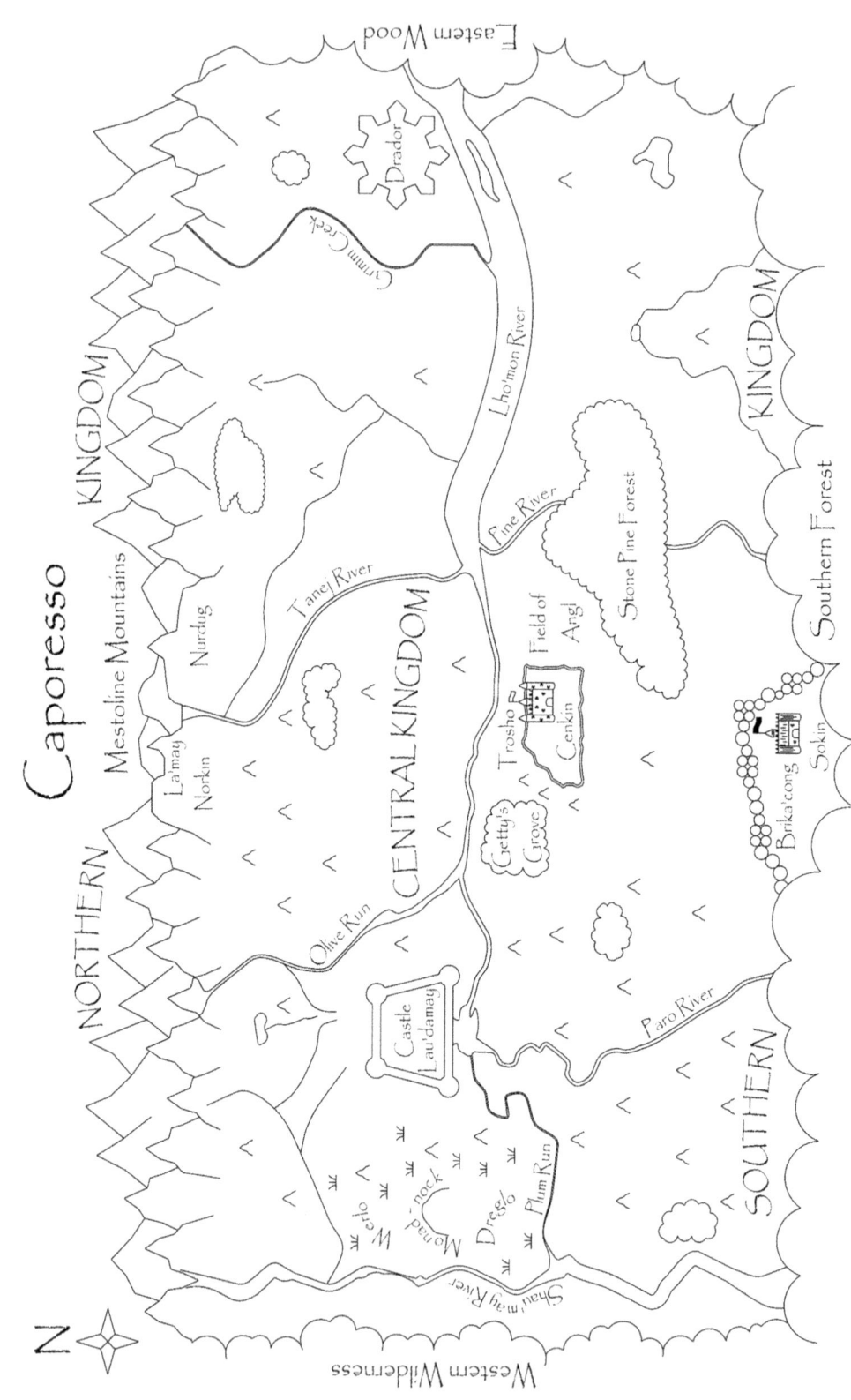

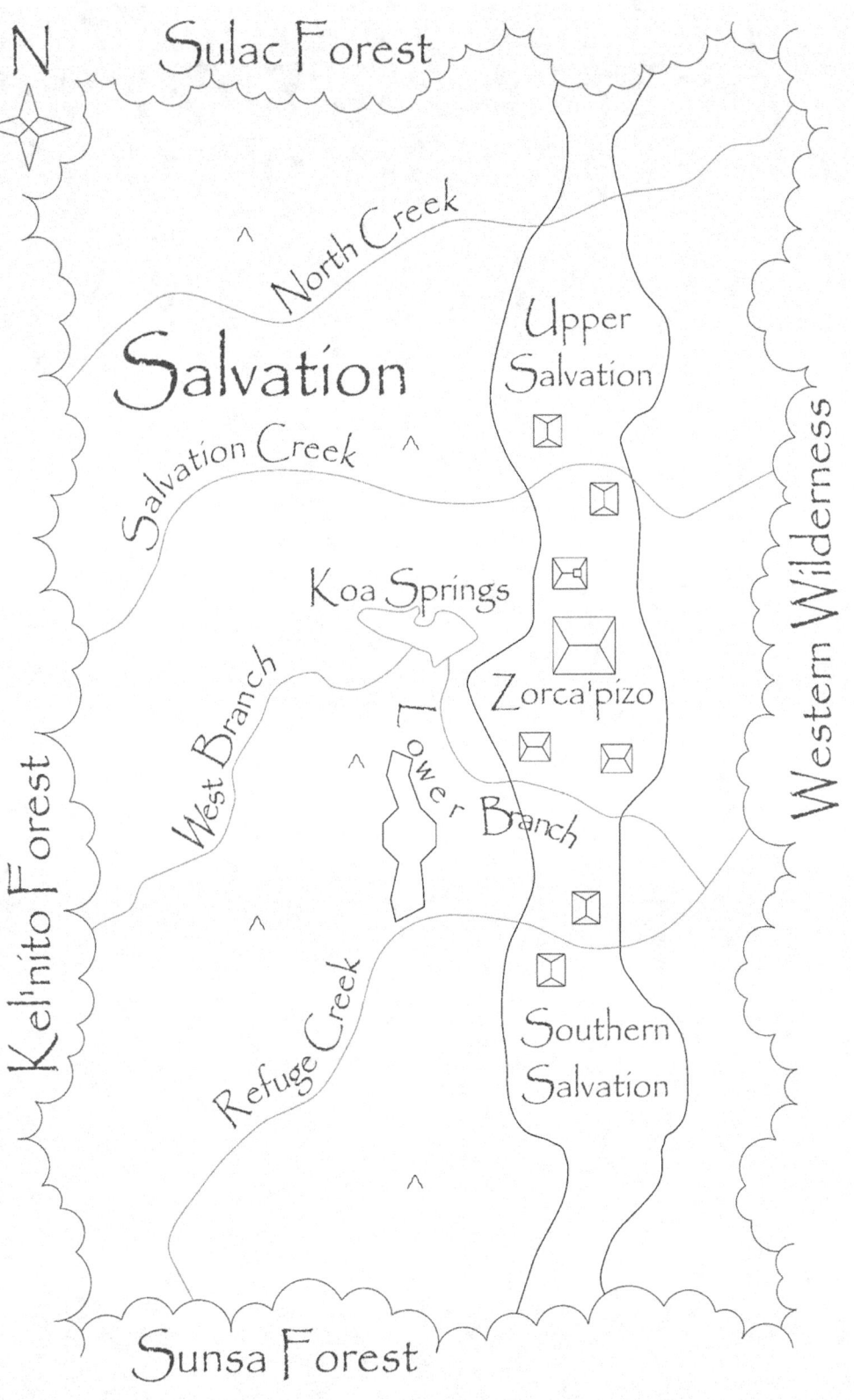

Chapter 1

With his eyes closed, he took a deep breath through his nose. Momentarily holding it, he cleared his mind and exhaled through his mouth. He opened his eyes and stared at his opponent. A steady spring breeze blew against his back. Both men held their swords in defensive positions, ready for the inevitable conflict. Holding his sword with two hands, Kellen glided forward...and engaged.

The metallic *clang* of swords rang clear on the rolling fields around the village of Salvation. The blades hit high and then low. Kellen pushed forward with his attack as his opponent backpedalled. He attacked with an underhand upswing, then a horizontal cut, followed by alternating slashes. His strikes were powerful, knocking his foe backwards with every blow.

The stocky man smirked as he deflected each slash away with his own blade. The man launched a counterattack. With a grunt, Kellen spun away from it and threw a shoulder into the man, upsetting his balance. Stumbling backwards, the man started to fall. Before hitting the ground, he placed a hand down and cartwheeled through the air. He landed in a fighting stance facing Kellen...and grinned.

Incensed, Kellen rushed his opponent, somersaulting under a slash. For an instant, he had the advantage by being behind his adversary. He lunged at the man, who rolled forward to get away from Kellen's strike. As his attack dissolved into another slash, the man was on his feet, parrying Kellen's blade. Breaking contact, Kellen stepped sideways and circled his adversary like a wild beast hunting its prey. *Clang...clang...clang*, they continued.

For several minutes their battle raged, with neither man gaining an advantage over the other. Kellen pushed the action, aggressively attacking his opponent. Their frenzy of sword strikes and parries went back and forth. Then, with an abrupt lunge, followed by a low sweeping kick, Kellen knocked his adversary to the ground.

As the man tried to roll to get to his feet, Kellen stepped on the handle of his sword, pinning it to the ground. He touched his own sword to the man's throat...and smiled. "I beat you, Hapco!" He hopped and jumped away from the man. "I won!" he boomed. "Woo hoo!"

Hapco sat up and humphed. "I guess you did, Kellen. Congratulations." He stood up and dusted himself off. Picking up his sword, he held it passively in front of him; Kellen did the same. Hapco bowed slightly, saying, "Well done, Kellen. That is enough. I yield to you...for now." He motioned at a wall. "Get some water."

Kellen guffawed. *"For now*, Hapco? Really?" he shook his head and slapped his thigh. "All right, we'll rest a little before continuing. I think I could go all day." His whole life had led him to this one moment. Since he was ten, he had trained every day in the ways of the warrior.

At first he had trained his body, performing a rigorous regimen of kicks, punches, and other routines. After mastering those techniques, he next practiced with the spear until earning the privilege of training with the katana. It was an elegant weapon, which he had embraced with every fiber of his being. Today, he demonstrated his proficiency with it. "I think this is the beginning of a new chapter in my life, Hapco. Wouldn't you agree?"

Slowly nodding his head, Hapco concurred. "Yes, Kellen. Today is definitely the beginning of a new part of your life." *If only you knew what this really means, you might not be so happy. Now your future is truly uncertain.*

After draining the last drops from a waterskin, Kellen apologized, "Sorry, Hapco. I just finished our water. I'll walk down to Koa Springs and refill it. I'll be back in a few minutes."

"No. I will go instead. I need a little time to think about your next lesson, and," he pointed southward, "the walk will help clear my mind. When I get back, you had better be ready for another round of sparring."

"You got it, Hapco. I'll be ready for you again." He winked. "I promise." Kellen moved to the edge of the training area, along the crest of a flattened hillock. He gazed across Salvation's landscape. *Beautiful*, he thought. Groves of trees and fields of wheat and barley were scattered all over the countryside. Everything was blossoming as it always did year after year.

Sitting down, he watched his friend descend the hill towards the spring. Kellen lay back on the ground, looking up at the sky. A broad smile crossed his face as he thought about his morning sparring session with his good friend and teacher.

Kellen gazed up at the cerulean sky, a blanket of bent grass beneath him. With his katana and scabbard beside him, he inhaled deeply, enjoying the crisp aroma of cherry blossoms and magnolias. At eighteen years of age, he had grown into a fine-looking young man. He wore black tattered pants and a grayish short-sleeved shirt. His black leather boots extended halfway to his knees, and a black belt adorned his waist. The clothes fit loosely on his body, allowing him the ability to move without restriction. Standing slightly less than six feet tall, he was a few inches taller than Hapco. His hair was sandy brown and cut short. The solid muscles in his arms and chest had been forged by countless repetitions of sword strike after sword strike. Thick legs were the direct result of thousands of precise kicks and lunges. He was an impressively built warrior.

During his midmorning training breaks, he liked to stare into the heavens and daydream about the mysteries of his life. *Why don't I remember my family? Why did we have to leave New Caporesso without them?* He put a blade of grass between his lips. *What happened ten years ago that was so terrible that it made me forget my past, and who I was? Why can't I picture my mother, brother, and sister?* Closing his eyes, he tried to recall their faces. *Nothing. They're gone.* He tried calling their names. *I'm sorry; I don't remember them anymore.* Annoyed, he snorted. *Sometimes, I feel like I can't really remember my own name either.* Opening his eyes, he sighed heavily. *Why have I forgotten all about you?* His family was like the remnants of a fading dream on the edge of his consciousness, shrouded in the mists of his mind. Trying to focus harder only made the visions evaporate faster. Eventually he would not even dream about them. They would just fade from his thoughts, conscious or otherwise.

He had been only eight years old when he and his father, accompanied by Hapco and his adopted children, Kyra and Yen, left the country of New Caporesso. It was not by choice, but rather some unfortunate circumstances made it necessary for them to flee. *What circumstances?* There was something about the clash of swords and the smell of death, but it was unclear in his mind. His father had told him their lives depended on their flight. *But that doesn't make any sense. Who'd want to hurt us?* They left empty handed, with just the clothes on their backs. There had been no time for goodbyes. Their westerly journey led them through the Western Wilderness. Emerging from its darkness, they found the thriving village of Salvation. *It was our salvation too. Without it, we would have died.*

Kellen's thoughts drifted to his stoic father. Ketrik was a simple man, one who kept the knowledge of their family to himself. *Why won't he tell me who I am?* He had taught Kellen many things about New Caporesso and Salvation's history, but nothing about their own family.

Ketrik was also the town blacksmith. He worked diligently at his craft, forging tools for farming, cooper's and miller's tools, and spears for hunting, whatever customers requested. Ketrik produced the most utilitarian of tools for the villagers, but his greatest talent was making weapons for war. The swords and other battle implements he created were ingenious works of art.

I wonder what it is like to kill a man, he pondered. *What could drive men to resolve their differences by trying to end each other's life? Why would anyone desecrate those beautiful weapons by spilling blood with them?* Kellen could not comprehend the usefulness of violence. *Why does Father create such things? We have no need of them here in Salvation.*

When Ketrik first began as an apprentice to the blacksmith, some of the villagers would hassle him over his smithy work. They refused to pay him, citing some imagined imperfection in the work. Ketrik always stayed calm, never giving in to anger. Instead, he simply stared at the men, speaking softly to them. No threats, no yelling, no violence, but by the end of the conversation, the villagers always paid in full. Kellen did not think it was what his father said; it was his penetrating stare. It was like he was glaring into their souls and deciding if he should send them to meet the Boatman or give them a reprieve for their mistake. It was not a mistake people repeated.

The villagers realized quickly that Ketrik's simple appearance belied his true nature. They discerned the difference between Ketrik's unwillingness to engage in fisticuffs and his ability to do so. The people still talked about the night when three bullies jumped him. They had tried to *teach* Ketrik a lesson about showing them respect, but received a beating so soundly that they were unable to work in the fields for a month. After that, the villagers learned not to push this quiet, reserved man. Eventually, the entire village treated him with great respect, as though he demanded it without uttering a word.

For a common man, he's earned the kind of admiration normally reserved for the village elders. I wonder what there is in him that makes him stand out. Kellen closed his eyes, engulfing his senses with the sounds and fragrances of the cool spring day.

It smelled fresh and alive, not like the foul stench etched into his memory from New Caporesso. Even today, the thought of it made him nauseous. There was nothing specific about it anymore, but somehow, the reek had upset him. *That doesn't make any sense. What could have been so vile that it still makes me sick?* Shaking his head, he erased the images from his head.

He was still daydreaming when Hapco returned. Those thoughts would have to wait. Only his future was important at the moment.

Hapco grinned at Kellen. "Ready to continue, my friend? You bested me in our morning session. Your father will be proud to hear about your conquest," he chuckled. "Care to try again...or are you too tired?"

Try again? Too tired? Kellen had been waiting for this day since he was ten, the day when he would be Hapco's equal in battle. Today was that day; Kellen knew it. He finally understood what it meant to be *one* with his sword. Everything seemed to slow down as he fought. There was no longer any randomness in his attacks or parries, each move had a purpose. The wild, flailing student he had been was now replaced by a calculating warrior.

He spit out the strand of grass and anxiously got to his feet. Picking up his sword, teacher and student walked back to the stone walled training arena. Upon reaching its center, they turned, faced each other, and bowed.

Kellen cleared his mind again. With a determined look, he took a guarded step forward. He began the day as a martial arts student, but would end it as a master warrior. *I'm about to realize my greatest dream*, he thought. *I'm ready to embrace my future, whatever it may be, with open arms*, and attacked Hapco.

Chapter 2

Two combatants stood in the training courtyard in the center of Castle Trosho. This citadel was located inside the walled city of Cenkin and was also the capital of New Caporesso.

Each of the warriors was armed and ready for battle. Had they glanced skyward, they would have seen the bluest and clearest sky of their lives. However, they did not look up. Nothing existed except the opponent across the open space. As they moved towards each other, fine sand absorbed their footfalls.

The clash of weapons echoed off the stone walls. Two warriors battled each other with a primal intensity. As one combatant attacked, the other deflected the strikes. Then the defender went on the offensive, slashing and lunging with expert precision. They moved as fluid and matched as schooling fish, anticipating each movement. On and on they battled.

One warrior gained an advantage over the other, and they both stepped back to appraise the situation. Intently they stared at each other while collecting their thoughts before the next engagement.

Prince Col was twenty-three years old and the epitome of a soldier. He stood over six feet tall and had the physique of a skillfully trained martial artist. His muscles were apparent even though they were hidden beneath his uniform. He dressed daily in black leather pants and a black woven shirt. One of his shoulders carried the insignia of the legendary Tu'nide cavalry battalion; the other showed his rank of captain. Black leather boots and a belt completed the ensemble.

He held his broadsword in a two-handed, high, defensive posture. The thirty-six-inch-long sword had the familiar willow-leaf shape and a moderate curve that extended through the handle, canting it in the opposing direction. The blade was wider at the tip, giving it more weight at its point of impact to inflict gashing wounds upon an enemy. It was an excellent weapon for slashing and thrusting techniques.

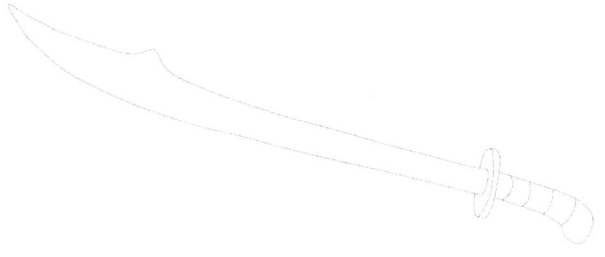

He surveyed the situation around him and realized he was losing the battle. There was a wall near his back. *If she pushes me against the wall, I'll lose my way of escape. If she gets me into a corner, I'm finished. I won't have any room to maneuver, and she'll beat me. I can't allow that to happen.*

Col needed a larger area to attack from and sidestep away from her double weapons. Her attacks consumed more space than he originally estimated. Col had accepted her challenge without considering her a worthy opponent. It was the first time they had fought in over six months, and she was greatly improved. So much so that he could not win today. He thought he would overwhelm her with his superior strength and brutal attacks, but he was wrong. Her defenses were impenetrable. Col stared into her eyes and grimaced. He had underestimated an opponent in the combat arena; it would never happen again.

Princess Vitoria stared right back at her brother. At twenty-one years of age, she was a stunning beauty with soft, exquisite facial features. Her round face and almond eyes were perfectly shaped, and the green of her irises was captivating. When she smiled, her eyes beamed with joy. Full lips and dainty dimples greeted everyone she met, making them feel welcomed immediately. To the cook's dismay, she would crinkle her tiny nose when she did not appreciate the evening meal. Sleek black hair pulled into a high ponytail bounced behind her as she moved.

An athletic build made her seem even more beautiful. Firm arms and sturdy legs supported her. She wore crimson shorts with half a skirt hanging behind her. As she fought, her skirt danced, mimicking her swords' movements like a silk scarf caught in the wind. The short-sleeved, ivory-colored blouse hung loosely from her frame, revealing perfect musculature. The dark boots she wore extended almost to her knees. Her toned, bare thighs were exposed to the bottom fringe of her shorts. It was a warrior's outfit, but it made her look the more feminine for it.

She wielded a twenty-four-inch sword in each hand. Strong, slender fingers held her swords tightly. Her right hand held a falcata; the forward-weighted belly of the inward curving blade delivered a deep, gruesome wound when it met its mark. It was capable of removing limbs or crushing bone if she desired. In her left, she grasped a wakizashi. She brandished it with a reverse grip, using the blade for backhand cuts and stabbing motions. It also doubled as a blocking weapon, used to deflect an attacker's strike.

The weapons were custom-made, and both had a round rod curved on a three-inch radius, attached where the spine of each blade met the handle, pointed in the same direction as the tip. They looked like hooks, and she used them to flip and spin both weapons from standard to reverse grips. These quillions could also be used to catch and trap an opponent's weapon. Her swords were an extension of who she was, flowing with her as she moved.

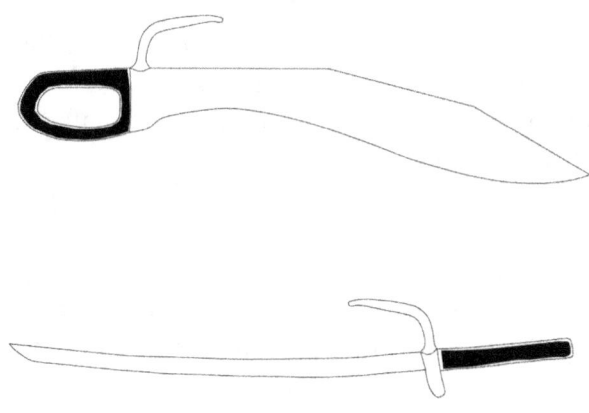

Vitoria's opponent had underestimated her, just as she anticipated. *He's trying to escape the wall. If I can push him there, I'll win in short order. He won't be able to move away from me.* She successfully blocked his path and reversed her grip on the wakizashi. With both blades facing him, she attacked in a blur of motion, alternating strikes as she pressed the assault.

The fire in Vitoria's eyes was frightening. Her style, with a sword in each hand, was effective. She used it to successfully turn away his attacks. Once she felt the advantage shift to her favor, she went on the offensive. The rhythmically alternating movements of her blades resembled a figure eight in the air, her blades humming like the wings of a dragonfly. In a matter of seconds she was pressing him to his limits.

Col frantically tried to deflect each blow as she delivered it. By this point in the engagement, both knew the end was inevitable. He was going to miss a strike and take a slash to the arm, or worse. She would not stop, and he would not yield. Her barrage continued; he would not be able to compete much longer.

Her final attack knocked the sword from his hand, leaving him defenseless. They stood facing the other. She was poised for the final blow, and he, awaiting complete defeat. Neither one moved. It was the sound of hands clapping that brought them back to reality.

Guan, King of New Caporesso and Supreme General of the New Caporesso Army, was clapping his hands in approval of what he witnessed. He was the greatest warrior in the land. No one came close to matching him on the field of battle. Forged in the fires of war for over twenty years, he had claimed victim after helpless victim.

In year 265 of the Second Age, he was the ruler over all of New Caporesso, governing the magnificent land with an iron fist. Guan relished the power he held and did not tolerate dissent. Insurgents and uprisings were crushed quickly. The proletarians were subject to his laws and their voices unheard. He was a brutally hard man, and no one dared to openly stand against him.

He was still clapping, having just observed two combatants, brother and sister, who could have killed each other. Guan's adopted children were excellent warriors, a result of his superior training methods. He had given each of the siblings the perfect weapons and skills to fight each other.

Usually Col disarmed his sister with a brief series of attacks. But today, Col's overconfidence proved to be another worthless trait. He was totally surprised by his sister's improvement.

Guan ogled his stepdaughter. "I see you have been practicing harder than normal, Princess Vitoria. It seems to have paid off. Your skills are greatly improved, Daughter." His eyes lingered below her neckline. "Almost to the point where you may one day beat me in combat," he paused, "but not yet." Disappointed, he looked at Col. "Train harder, my son. It is inexcusable that she disarmed you." Stoking resentment between the siblings, he smirked. "Enough practice for now. Time for your combat studies," he waved a hand, dismissing them both.

Those words were like ice to Col. *One day beat him in single combat? Vitoria?* Guan had never spoken those words to him. *I'm the better warrior. I'm stronger and more intense. How can I not be better?* Just when Col started to get angry, he realized Guan liked to make statements intended to create a rift between him and his sister. This was one of those times. He glanced at his sister.

Vitoria felt herself warmed by Guan's special approval, but she didn't trust it. *One day beat him in single combat!* Guan had never spoken such words of praise to her before. She was practicing more with her weapons. Maybe she had surpassed her brother in the practice arena, but she also knew Guan liked to say things that would create discord between the two of them. *Perhaps this is one of those times.* She faked a scowl at Col.

When their eyes met, they each knew what the other was thinking. *Guan is trying to agitate us...again.* They bowed slightly to each other, signifying the end of the match. Another day of sparring was over. Now it was time to get cleaned up and study combat strategies. The training of a warrior was never complete. Day after day it was the same: each would train for hours with weapons and then study scrolls for hours, trying to interpret and understand the methodology of the techniques and other tactics. They both enjoyed the meticulous work.

Chapter 3

For the second time in as many attempts, Kellen bested Hapco with swords. Taking a break, they sat atop the stone walls that outlined a typical training area on the outskirts of Salvation. The randomly shaped stones had been stacked waist high around the small field, creating an eight-sided boundary for combat practice. The ring was roughly twenty feet between facing walls. What grass still remained in the enclosed area was trampled and sparse. Random tufts grew wildly along the perimeter. At least a dozen such arenas had been built up around Salvation.

Hapco sat cross-legged on the uneven wall, looking east towards Salvation. He said, "I have one more lesson to teach you, Kellen."

"Just one more, Hapco? I thought you said the lessons would go on forever," commented Kellen.

"Hmm. I do have one more lesson to teach you...today." He nodded. "Back to the history of government in New Caporesso; do you remember the different systems from the three kingdoms of old Caporesso?"

Kellen adjusted his seat on the rocks, throwing his legs over one side of the wall towards Hapco. "I thought your questions were gonna be tough today, Hapco. This is easy. The Northern Kingdom had an unstable monarchy. The Central—"

Hapco interrupted, "Explain an unstable monarchy."

"In the Northern Kingdom, power was passed down through heredity from king to king. The king ruled over the people but also maintained a small group of men who made *suggestions* during his reign. He then acted based on his knowledge and that of his advisers." Picking up a stick, he swatted at a gnat, knocking it to the ground. "So the king ruled in conjunction with these men, never disbanding them or refusing to heed their counsel.

"And as long as the king and the royal family were strong," Kellen coughed, "and the advisers advised the king with the interests of the people in mind, the king ruled without incident. But when kings became corrupt, or mistreating their citizens became policy, or the advisers craved more power and wealth for themselves, rebellions occurred. Then the king and his family were," he searched for a word, "*removed* from power, and a new monarch was put in place."

Clearing his throat, he continued. "The new king was crowned based on military strength of arms, being either the most powerful man, or from the strongest family in the northern region. This new family became the new bloodline of the kings. At least until they were overthrown." He looked at Hapco. "Each time we talk about their governments, you always end the lesson saying, '*as best could be recalled in the history scrolls*' or '*for as accurate as the old history records about the creation of Caporesso can be.*' Why?" he inquired.

Hapco shifted his seat to face Kellen. "As you know, the original records were destroyed—"

"Yes…but why?"

"The continual wars between the Northern Kingdom and the Central and Southern Kingdoms led to the destruction of a great many artifacts from each kingdom's ancestors. Chiefly among them were the history chronicles." He shook his head. "Out of spite for the others, the conquering kingdom would destroy the recorded annals from each kingdom. As a result, the only knowledge we have is what was remembered, retold, and rewritten. But each time this was done, a piece of the story was omitted or forgotten. After several retellings, no one was sure how accurate the *new* chronicles really were."

"There was so much violence in old Caporesso. Wasn't New Caporesso supposed to be a better place?" asked Kellen.

"It was a better place, if only for a short time, Kellen. Who knows what has become of it now. Unless they changed the way they recognize dates, it should be the year two hundred sixty-five of the Second Age." He exhaled wistfully, smiling to himself. "For now, answer my questions…and finish the lesson."

"All right, Hapco. The Northern Kingdom was an unstable monarchy." With the stick he traced a simple pattern on the rocks next to him. "The Southern Kingdom was a brutal dictatorship. It was a region where only the strong rose to positions of power; weakness was not tolerated. The ruling person called himself king, emperor, or supreme general, depending on his ambition." Kellen clenched his hand into a ball, "These men ruled with absolute power until the time of their death," then relaxed it, "either during combat or from assassination. Then other men struggled and fought to become the new ruler. Their battles were vicious; often times killing many innocent people to achieve the power they sought.

"The history scrolls here in Salvation concerning Caporesso end four hundred years ago, at the time when these people," he pointed at the village, "left their homeland and came here. I've learned what I could from them, and that, combined with the newer history you and my father have taught me, suggests that no man ruled in the Southern Kingdom's capital city, Sokin, for more than twenty years before dying and leaving the region in upheaval." Kellen tapped the side of his head, "In fact, the only instance of rule passing from father to son that I recall from my studies was from the first to the second ruler, when Brika'cong was murdered by his son, Brika'compa." He shook his head. "It seems to me, living like that would be hard on the people, never having any stability in their government or leaders."

"Well said, Kellen." Hapco nodded his approval. "That region was in a constant state of turmoil, always adjusting to new leaders. It was either at war with the other kingdoms or at war with itself, trying to install a new leader. As you said, it was difficult being a citizen from that realm."

Kellen raised his eyebrows, waiting for Hapco to continue; he did not. "Then…the Central Kingdom was an absolute monarchy. The crown was passed down through the royal family. As far as the chronicles from Caporesso show, the bloodline was never cut. Even if the ruler was a nephew or a cousin, a male heir from the Trosho family line always ruled over the Central Kingdom in the great city of Cenkin."

"That *is* true," added Hapco. "At the end of Caporesso and the birth of New Caporesso, a man named King Hogeland ruled over the Central Kingdom. His ancestry could be traced back thousands of years to the founders of the land. Hogeland was a direct descendant of Trosho, and he ruled as an honorable man. At the end, he did what was best for his people and voted for the first man who governed over New Caporesso."

"I know we were from Cenkin...but I don't remember anything about it." His head drooped. "I can't remember my home. I can't remember what I did as a child...I've forgotten everything."

Hapco opened his mouth to speak, but did not. He uncorked the waterskin. *I do not know what to say to him. I cannot tell him the truth.* He shook his head. "I will talk to—"

"Why did Hogeland relinquish power?" interrupted Kellen.

After taking a drink, he returned the stopper. Wiping his lip on his sleeve, he asked, "What do you mean, Kellen?"

"I mean, why would a king give up his power to a lesser man? Why not defend his kingdom to stay in power." He scratched his head. "I mean, if I were ever a *king* of something, I'd never yield that authority without a fight. I'd—"

"Who says the new king was a *lesser* man? At the time," he sighed, "there was *a* man considered by many to be the best man to lead the unified country." Hapco pointed at him. "Understand, Kellen, up until that point in history, each kingdom was an autonomous entity, trying to increase its holdings in Caporesso through war and conquest."

"I know, Hapco."

"Generation after generation of people was sacrificed to the gods of war. At least once every half century, the kingdoms went to war with one another. When this happened, no one was safe. Innocent people living on the frontiers of each kingdom were butchered by marauding war parties... or worse." He threw his arms down in disgust. "For thousands of years, Caporesso was a barbaric land. Killing was a way of life. Every day most people lived with the reality that it might be their last. The rulers from each kingdom wanted more and more for their dominions." Sadly, Hapco shook his head. "Their quest for *more* was never-ending. Unfortunately, that is our pathetic history. It is nothing we should be proud of, but nonetheless, it is our history and should not be forgotten.

"But when *he* came along," Hapco raised a finger, "*he*...and his friends...had new ideas and ideals that were greater than any one person. They tried to create a country where a man was a man, treated equally by everyone. Not because he was a mighty warrior or clever, but because he was a man. They tried to unify the country and build a world where peace and prosperity were more desirable than death and destruction."

"It sounds like they had noble intentions." Shrugging his shoulders, Kellen asked, "Who wouldn't desire such a place?"

"For fourteen years, it worked." Hapco looked like his thoughts had transported him to another time. "The country prospered under *his* rule, but...the frailty of man was exposed." He exhaled. "They did not see the end coming until it was too late, and it all ended in two hundred fifty-five of the Second Age." Hapco shook his head. "Too late."

They both sat in silence for several moments. A gust of wind blew Hapco's grey-streaked hair into his face. He closed his eyes and patiently waited for the breeze to dissipate.

Interrupting his thoughts, Kellen asked. "What created the conflict between the three kingdoms in the first place, Hapco? I mean, why couldn't the kingdoms get along?"

Hapco chortled, "Perhaps the gods enjoy watching us suffer. Maybe it is just the curse of men." He shrugged, "Do you know what men crave more than power?"

Kellen shook his head.

"Women." He grinned. "No one knows what really happened between the kingdoms. But legend tells us that Caporesso was founded by three brothers, La'may, Trosho, and Brika'cong. They divided the land and lived in their own regions at peace with each other. La'may went north and settled in the Mestoline Mountains with his followers." He waved a hand northward. "They built their first homes in the foothills of the mountain range. Trosho's group preferred the open spaces of the prairies and hills in the central region. Brika'cong went south to the Southern Forest, where he and his people established their community on the edge of the woods. Each brother built a magnificent kingdom for his people.

"They supposedly lived in peace for over twenty years. Then after all that time, the only thing that could come between them, came between them." He caught a fly, and then released it. "An indescribably attractive young woman named Lau'damay appeared. No one knows which kingdom she called home, just one day, she appeared in all her beautiful splendor."

"Maybe she was a gift from the gods," remarked Kellen.

"Or a curse," replied Hapco. "Trosho was the first of the brothers to meet her, and he immediately fell in love with her. After a short time, he sent word to his brothers, telling them he was going to marry this woman. He invited them to their wedding."

"That sounds like the beginning of a happy story, Hapco. How could it have ended so tragically?" asked Kellen.

Hapco slowly nodded his head. "It did end tragically though. The end was so horrible, that the people of Caporesso were never able to escape its consequences. It seemed the entire country was meant to suffer for the evil deeds committed by those three brothers."

"What happened? I mean, what do they think happened?"

"The minstrels used to describe Lau'damay's beauty." Hapco thought about the songs, "Her face was smooth...and round. She had two different colored eyes; one was grey and the other green. I have never seen eyes like that, but can only imagine their intensity. Her figure was, as the minstrels sung, *perfectly perfect in every way*. She was said to have been the most beautiful woman in the entire land. Hmm," he pointed at Kellen. "I think I remember a poem about her...it goes like this:

> An exotic beauty with skin so fair,
> all others failed to compare.
> She was destined to live, forever cursed by that beauty.
> Her eyes were like endless pools of light,
> drowning men's hearts.
> An exotic beauty with skin so fair,
> all others failed to compare.
> With pitch black hair, like a shimmering curtain of night,
> Never finding happiness, she fell into despair at the evil
> things her beauty brought.
> An exotic beauty with skin so fair,
> all others failed to compare.
> She was destined to live, forever cursed by that beauty.

"At least, I think it went something like that. So...when La'may met Lau'damay, he was humbled by her beauty, and he was jealous of his brother." Hapco waved a finger, "But, he bore no ill will against him. However," he sighed heavily, "when Brika'cong met her, his heart filled with lust, and his head filled with plans of betrayal. He saw her and desired her for his own.

"On the day Lau'damay and Trosho were to marry, Brika'cong and his men attacked. They massacred many people from the Central Kingdom, sacking the city of Cenkin. Trosho and Lau'damay escaped with help from La'may. Together, they fled to the Northern Kingdom. While the two brothers were there, La'may fell in love with Lau'damay. They spent one night together. When Trosho learned of La'may's treachery, he gave Lau'damay a choice; leave with him, or die with La'may.

"She chose to leave with Trosho to avoid further violence. La'may felt humiliated and vowed to kill them both. The timing of the next part of the story is unclear, but Trosho and Lau'damay travelled west and built a mighty castle. They named it Castle Lau'damay. It was constructed in her honor, and men loyal to Trosho defended it. It was an impenetrable fortress. After several years of uneasy happiness, she died of unknown causes. "Meanwhile, with Brika'cong in Cenkin, he placed his son, Brika'compa, in control of Sokin in the south. After a year or so, Brika'compa murdered his father and claimed the throne of the Central Kingdom for himself as well. At that time, La'may and Trosho had the opportunity to join forces and rid the world of Brika'compa and his malevolent ways, but they could not forgive each other. As a result, neither brother could overthrow their nephew, nor could Brika'compa vanquish his uncles' armies.

"And so the conflict that began with three brothers over a woman still raged in Caporesso for thousands of years. Countless Caporessoean men were claimed by the cogs of war. *That* war controlled the lives of people in Caporesso until New Caporesso was born. Then for a short time, peace reigned, but you know how that story ended. Deceit and war returned to New Caporesso, asking for payment to honor the gods who punished those three brothers for their betrayal. It seems their descendants will never escape the yoke of its burden. I guess the entire country is meant to suffer for their ancient affronts." Hapco's shoulders sank as he finished speaking. He took another drink from the waterskin and offered it to Kellen.

Kellen shook his head and jumped from the wall. He tried to lighten the mood. "Your stories have dampened my spirits, Hapco. How about one more duel before returning to father?" He picked up his sword and waited for Hapco's reply.

Hapco took another gulp of water. Grabbing his sword, he motioned for Kellen to take the center of the arena. "After you, my friend. One more round before we return to the smithy to tell your father what you have learned today."

Kellen's eyes twinkled. *I'm gonna beat him again, I know it...*

Chapter 4

Vitoria defeated Col in a duel! Queen Mervekka's excitement almost overwhelmed her. From an upper balcony above the courtyard she watched from the shadows. She was proud of her children, but Guan had forbidden her from watching them train. He was their stepfather and did not grant her access to their sparring sessions, trying to hide their skills. So she secretly watched them from afar.

After everyone exited the courtyard below, Mervekka walked forward and rested her hands on the marble railing. The whitish stone, mixed with vibrant reds and greens, was warm from the sun's heat. She knelt on the rough stone promenade and leaned her head against the rail. *Oh thank you, gods. After a decade, you have finally answered my prayers.* Giving a raw sigh, she dabbed at her dry eyes.

Mervekka was in her early forties but still had the fair skin of someone twenty years younger. She was an exotic beauty like her daughter Vitoria. Her long black hair and black eyes were captivating. For the last ten years, she hid herself beneath a black-hooded cloak, concealing both her beauty and sorrow under the shade of her cowl.

She was the queen of New Caporesso, although the title had almost no meaning. In fact, New Caporesso meant little anymore. The ideal that was once New Caporesso had vanished. Guan crushed it years ago, leaving the citizens with his distorted notion of government. The dream symbolized in New Caporesso nearly a quarter century ago had been replaced with an abomination of Guan's creation.

Guan only became stepfather to Col and Vitoria after Mervekka's first husband died. He insisted she marry him for the sake of the people. To keep her children safe, there was little she could do but acquiesce to his demands. Their marriage was nothing more than a farce, enacted in order to adopt her children. For what purpose, she had yet to discover.

They were not a couple, and there was no love between them. At first, they only shared bedchambers when Guan commanded it, but now those encounters were over. In Guan's warped mind, she was at fault for not producing an heir, consequently his interest in her waned until he found other forms of amusement. Not that she minded. She was glad to be rid of him and his defilement.

The tribulations she endured at his hands were innumerable. The cloak she wore hid more than just her identity; it veiled her grief and other scars. He stole her soul many years ago, and now she existed as a shadow of her former self. Over the years, her desire to rid the world of Guan diminished until it nearly flickered out.

Today it was rekindled in the incarnation of Col and Vitoria's fighting spirit. Fighting side by side, they could resist Guan, their combined abilities enough to defeat him. *No, he is too strong. They will need support, but where can they find it? It may not exist.* Her mind raced with many fears and questions. She had waited for this day for so long, she dared not even dream about it. Now it was here, and there was much her children needed to learn. She wiped a single tear. *Tonight, I will explain everything to them about their past. Tonight, they will discover the truth about who they are.*

Chapter 5

After a lengthy duel, Kellen emerged victorious for the third time. With his practice finished for the day, he and Hapco headed for home. An easterly breeze blew, cooling Kellen's neck. The rush of the wind drowned out the other sounds of nature, bringing a sense of peace upon him.

Breaking the stillness, Kellen asked, "What really happened in New Caporesso, Hapco? Why were we forced to leave?"

Hapco continued walking, but did not look at Kellen. "We cannot discuss that now."

"Why not, Hapco? Tell—"

"Kellen, stop it."

Frustrated, he threw his arms up in the air. "Why? Why won't you tell me?"

"Your father will decide when the time is right. He and I both agreed that is how it would be."

Looking over at Hapco, he said, "I'm not the little boy who arrived here in Salvation ten years ago. I've grown up, and so have Kyra and Yen. We're adults now, ready to know the truth about our past lives." His eyes found the path again. "I thought that once I became a warrior, you would share my past with me. Will you—"

"I can tell you nothing without your father around, so do not ask anything further." Hapco's stride remained steady.

"Come on, Hapco. I mean, I've figured some things out, like whom you and my father were in New Caporesso. And—"

"And who were we, Kellen?" Hapco abruptly stopped.

Kellen walked a few steps more before stopping. He cocked his head and smirked. "I don't know exactly who you were, but I have a good idea. Father was someone in the army and so were you, of that I'm sure."

"Hmm…" Hapco scratched his chin. "Why do you think that?"

"The training each of you possesses is beyond what the native villagers know. I'm not sure which of you was a higher rank…you both show each other the same amount of respect. But your combat knowledge is extensive. Look, we were only here in Salvation for a few months before you took over as the master at arms of the armory." He inquisitively held out his arms. "How else could you have been a better warrior than all of the villagers from Salvation, unless you were already a well trained soldier from New Caporesso?"

"I do not have an answer to that, Kellen," he said flatly.

"And when my father was attacked by those men, he almost killed them defending himself."

The corners of Hapco's mouth turned up, and he nodded. "Yes," he crossed his arms. "They did get what they deserved, did they not?"

"I'm not questioning if he did the right thing. All I'm saying is that no ordinary man could have fought off three men so decisively. He must have been trained as a warrior in New Caporesso. I'm not sure where, but it's someplace different from you, of that I'm sure. You each have a different style all your own. And I don't know who trained him, but he was definitely trained. My guess is that the two of you are expert warriors and soldiers. Right?" Kellen looked intently at Hapco.

Without a word, Hapco shrugged his shoulders, flashed a smile, and started walking towards the smithy again.

Kellen rolled his head and followed after Hapco. "Come on, am I close? Hapco? Why can't you tell me? Why did you adopt Kyra and Yen? If you won't tell me, at least tell them." He grabbed Hapco's arm, stopping him. "We're not children anymore. When will you and my father tell us what happened in New Caporesso? When will you tell us who we really are?" His eyes pleaded with Hapco.

Ignoring Kellen's question, Hapco folded his arms, and asked, "Tell me what you *do* remember about leaving New Caporesso, Kellen."

Pausing, Kellen's face relaxed. "Ah...I remember it was ten years ago this spring, that me, you, and father left from Cenkin. We walked and slept on the open prairie. I can't remember how long, but it seemed like forever. We spent one night in Castle Lau'damay, and found Kyra and Yen there." He grinned. "They were both dirty and crying, I think."

Hapco humphed, "I will let you tell her she was crying like a baby, Kellen. Even though I am her father," he shook his head, "I will not do it."

Chuckling, Kellen agreed. "You're right, we better not remind her." He nodded. "We took them with us and went to a village, I think. After leaving, we travelled through the Western Wilderness to escape New Caporesso." Holding out his arms, he asked, "Why did we need to leave New Caporesso? Was someone chasing us? Were we in trouble for something? Why was our situation so dire that we would travel through the wilderness?" Frustrated, he sighed. "Since being here, you and my father taught me that that wilderness was on the edge of the explored lands of New Caporesso. No one dared venture into it for fear of becoming lost forever. But the two of you trusted to a legend that could have been a lie." He took a breath. "We left all that we knew, and headed for an unknown land on an uncharted course." All at once, his emotions erupted. "We could have died in there!"

He realized he was breathing faster and his heart was pounding. It took a moment, but Kellen calmed himself. "There was no way you knew this place existed," he held an arm out, towards Salvation. "You both trusted our lives to some story about a group of people who left Caporesso over four hundred years ago. We followed five hundred pilgrims into the wild...and got lucky." He shook his head. "You told me before, some historians thought they perished on the journey, while others suggested they found paradise, a virgin land devoid of war and persecution, but no one truly knew their fate. The gods blessed us by guiding us on our journey through the wilderness; there is no other logical explanation." Pausing, he waited for Hapco's response. There was none. "You risked everyone's life entering the wilderness and trying to find this place." He slowly shook his head. "Was it out of madness that we left New

Caporesso?" Sounding exasperated, he implored, "Hapco, help me figure this out."

Hapco put a hand on Kellen's shoulder. "No matter what I would like to tell you now, your father and I agreed that we would explain everything to the three of you at the same time. All right?" He raised his eyebrows, searching Kellen's face for a response.

Kellen sighed reluctantly and nodded his head.

Removing his hand, he said, "I will talk to Ketrik as soon as we return home, Kellen. You have my word." He nodded. "You are right: you are old enough to know the truth. Trust me, when the time is right, everything will be explained." *I cannot guarantee you will like what you hear, but you will finally know the truth about your family.*

They continued walking back to the village. As they neared the smithy, excitement replaced Kellen's earlier frustration. He was smiling from ear to ear. He walked with a newfound confidence. In beating Hapco in their duels, he had passed Hapco's test to becoming a master warrior. No longer was it necessary for him to call Hapco *master* or *teacher*. They walked together through the village side by side, passing row after row of grey, weathered wooden homes. Each dwelling looked alike, with the exception of one. Its chimney was taller than all the others, climbing into the sky. Clouds of smoke billowed from the blackened stones. They headed straight for the smithy where Ketrik was hard at work.

"Afternoon, Ketrik!" boomed Hapco as they entered.

Their footsteps resounded inside the wooden structure, causing layers of ash to dance as they walked across the wooden floor.

"Hello, Father! How is that new spade for Ackley coming along?" inquired Kellen, moving beside Hapco.

Ketrik greeted them with his usual emotionless nod. The three men stood there looking at each other. After a few awkward moments, Kellen began to smile. Hapco could not contain himself any longer and smirked as well.

Instantly, Ketrik understood what it meant. He set down his tools and crossed the room in five strong strides. "Congratulations, Kellen!" he lifted him off the floor in a mighty bear hug. "I knew you could do it. I told you it would just take time and practice." He held the sides of Kellen's head and laughed. "Tell me all about it," prodded Ketrik.

Kellen pulled away. "I beat Hapco three times today!" As he spoke, his legs mimicked his words. "The first time, I surprised him with an attack, sweeping his leg and knocking him to the ground. The second time, I aggressively pushed my advantage and disarmed him with a lunge, followed by a spinning hook kick. And the third time..." he looked at Hapco.

"The third time," continued Hapco, "he outlasted me in a thirty minute long duel. By the end, my arms were so tired, I could barely lift my sword." With a glimmer in his eyes, he looked at Ketrik.

"Can you believe it, Father? I finally beat Hapco!" he was beaming with pride.

Ketrik congratulated his son again, "You should be proud of your accomplishments, Kellen. I knew it was only a matter of time before you could best Hapco on a field of combat. Today you did what I knew you could already do, all you needed was time to realize it yourself." Then he turned to Hapco and said, "You should also be proud. You have taught him well, my friend. It was your tutelage that transformed him into a warrior." Ketrik bowed his head at Hapco. "Thank you for the knowledge you have bestowed upon my son."

For once, Hapco remained silent. He nodded his acceptance, for he was just as proud as Ketrik was. Every teacher's goal was to have his students exceed him in their abilities and achievements. Hapco's pride was not injured, nor was he jealous. He knew Ketrik's true intentions, and this was the first step in making that plan a reality.

Chapter 6

Col had been in command of the Tu'nide for nearly three years. His record as a warrior was exemplary. Troopers under his command had never been defeated in battle, but more importantly, casualties suffered by his battalion were always minimal. He was their fearless leader, at the head of every attack. His skill with a sword was only paralleled by Guan's...until today.

He and Sed'la walked through stone halls of Castle Trosho. They passed girls hard at work. Some scrubbed the floors, others cleaned ancient tapestries framed on the walls, and still others went about their daily duties

"I can't believe she beat you, Col," joked Sed'la.

They descended a small stair and entered the mezzanine level, overlooking the throne room. The ancient stone railing was intricately carved with relief images showing the history of Caporesso. The eastern side showed an interpretation of the formation of the three kingdoms, from thousands of years ago. The northern rail depicted Brika'cong's betrayal and the first Wars of the Kingdoms.

The southern railing illustrated the construction of Sokin's gigantic tree wall and Cenkin's stone and mortar fortifications. Images of Norkin and Nurdug's dwellings carved into the side of the Mestoline Mountains were etched into the stone as well. The defensive ramparts coincided with the recognition of the beginning of the Second Age of Caporesso. In the middle of the railing was chiseled: 1 SA.

The western railing was conspicuously bereft any markings. In 1 SA, King Monhag, the king of the Central Kingdom at the time, decided that the last panel should be reserved for an epic moment in the country's history. To date, no event was deemed worthy of being forever remembered as a stone sculpture. Carvings to commemorate the founding of New Caporesso had been planned but turned out to not be necessary.

Silently, Col and Sed'la walked alongside the western railing.

They passed two chambermaids. The girls giggled as they went about their duties, their words inaudible. Col did not need to hear what they said to know what they were saying.

Sed'la smacked him on the arm, laughing. "Well, I guess just about everyone in Trosho has heard about you and Vee. You—"

Abruptly, Col stopped and turned on him. He was nose to nose with Sed'la. "I suggest you leave it alone. Now is not the best time to torment me. You better—"

"Sorry, sorry." Yielding, he raised his hands. "I didn't mean anything." He grinned. "I'm just having a little fun...and *it is* fun." Sed'la laughed again.

Scowling, Col shook his head. "You don't know when to stop, do you?" he started walking again. "Come on, Sed'la...keep up."

"Ha ha ha," with a laugh, Sed'la joined him. "Don't worry about it, Col. I'm sure no one in the Tu'nide has heard about it." He put a hand over his mouth, trying to conceal his laughter.

They descended the uniquely cantilevered spiral staircase and entered the grand foyer. They walked to the center of the room. Sed'la continued, but Col stopped, looking at the giant tapestry hanging on the northern wall. It was a detailed map depicting the land formations and villages of Olde Caporesso.

Realizing Col was not keeping pace, Sed'la backed up and stood next to him. Staying silent for a moment, he clapped his hands. "All right then, Col. Let's get going." He headed for the entryway.

Col bade Sed'la, "Hold a moment." Motioning at the map, he asked, "Do you ever look at it anymore?"

Shaking his head, Sed'la admitted, "Not really. I'm normally in too much of a hurry."

"Hmm…me too." He continued surveying the map in silence.

Cooks and maids passed unnoticed by Col. Several guards walked across the foyer, saluting them. Sed'la acknowledged the soldiers, while Col studied the map.

"Do you ever wonder at the marvel of the country?" He folded his arms in front of him. "Do you ever think about its creation, thousands of years ago?"

"Col…Vee outdueled you today…once. Let it go." He paused. "It's not like your gonna lose control of the Tu'nide. You know it would take an act of the gods to have you replaced. We've survived over twenty engagements together and have lost only a handful of men. Your skill as a commander is becoming legendary." He shook his head. "One loss in a sparring match is inconsequential. Don't let it bother you so much."

He did not hear Sed'la's words. "It's funny, and surprising, that it took the three kingdoms so long to construct their defenses." He cupped his chin.

Sed'la's head fell. "What…Col? What are you talking about?" he asked.

He pointed at the map. "The walled structures and mountain cities, Sed'la. Look at Norkin and Nurdug in the Mestoline Mountains. Why didn't the Northern Kingdom build their cities into the mountain range sooner? How many of their people's lives would have been spared? My father told me that his people lived inside the tiered limestone mountains. He said the cities were engineering marvels and protected the populace by keeping them above the fray." Sadly, he shook his head. "I've never even seen my father's home city of Norkin. How sad is that?"

"Col…" He was at a loss for words.

"And look at Sokin in the Southern Kingdom," he said, motioning at the bottom of the map. "It sits on the edge of the eternal Southern Forest. Those people used the timber from the woods to build a colossal wall of thousand-year-old timbers to protect themselves. I can still remember my father's lessons. He used to say, *'The Southern Forest is a glorious display of the gods' creation. It is comprised of massive, reddish brown, thick-barked tress, some over twenty feet in diameter and two hundred feet tall. The tower-like woodlands stretches for thousands of acres in each direction. Many of the people's homes, shops, and stores supporting the city are built within the canopy of the gigantic trees.*

A plethora of bridges connects the structures, zigzagging from tree to tree. Spiral stairways ascend into the tress, providing access to the lofty abodes.' I used to act like I hated those geography lessons, but I realize now how important they were." He kept staring at the tapestry.

Looking at his friend, Sed'la realized Col was not studying the map. He was looking past it, mesmerized. "Col, I'm sure your father would have been proud of both of you today. He would have congratulated his little girl for beating you. He would have picked her up and given her a big hug for beating the Tu'nide's senior officer." Sed'la put a hand on Col's shoulder, grabbing his attention. "He also would have given you some words of advice, like *'No one is invincible,'* or, *'Learn from today, make yourself better because of it.'* I know he would've said something like that, Col."

Sighing heavily, he nodded. "Thank you, Sed'la. And you're right, it's not that Vee beat me, it's that my father isn't here to see it. Now she can be accepted into the Tu'nide." He shook his head. "I don't know if he wanted that for her, but it is possible."

The sound of horses passing the doorway disturbed them. Dust from the riders rose like an eerie fog, filling the entrance. The sunlight was dulled by the cloud.

"It's time to return to the Preparatory Building, Col. The men are awaiting your orders. Come on." He tugged on Col's arm.

Without a word, Col nodded. Both men crossed the etched marble floor and exited Trosho. Stepping over the threshold, they were swallowed by the illuminated dust cloud.

Chapter 7

Yen and Kyra practiced foot boxing on the eastern edge of Salvation, overlooking the village. Stepbrother and stepsister were both masters of Drador's martial art, Maeda Jiu Do. The arena they trained inside was a dusty patch of field where the grass had been worn away by hours of combat practice. It was surrounded by an eight-sided irregular stone wall. From their location, they could see the smithy where Ketrik was hard at work making iron obey his every whim.

Today was a free sparring session, and their weapons leaned against a wall. Facing each other, they extended their right hands, making a fist. With their left, they covered the right, signifying the victory of good over evil.

"Kyung ye," they grunted and bowed. Starting their match, they circled each other like lions stalking their quarry. After training with each other for years, there would be no easy victory. Each contest was always a heated exchange between the adopted siblings.

Kyra slid in with a front leg kick that dissolved into a spinning hook kick, followed by alternating high and low punches. She missed Yen, but got close enough to trip him, sending him to the ground.

"You can't do that here, Kyra," Yen admonished. "What would Hapco say?" He did a kip-up and landed on his feet, ready to fight again.

She shrugged her shoulders, looking at the ground. When Yen looked down too, she launched herself at him again. This time, she found her mark. *Smack!* Her open hand slapped him on the face, and she kicked his calf with a sharp kick.

"Ouch!" he yelled. "Kyra, I thought there were no leg kicks this time. Come on, will ya?" he limped backward, resetting his stance.

"Ha ha ha," she laughed. "I never agreed to that." Kyra was a graceful fighter. Even though she was smaller in stature than Yen, her size did not diminish her abilities. What she lacked in strength, she made up for in speed and agility, like a jaguar from the Eastern Wood. She was a beautiful woman, the most beautiful in the village. Mesmerizingly grey eyes sparkled when she smiled, entrancing anyone she encountered. Pouty lips and a strong chin garnered as much attention as her sultry eyes. She kept her wavy, chestnut hair cut to shoulder length.

Her slender fingers possessed the strength of men twice her size. Steely muscles were evident in her arms and legs. She wore black patchwork shorts that stopped above her knees and a white sleeveless shirt. Both were generously cut to allow her the freedom of movement to leap from attack to attack. Sometimes, her blouse almost revealed too much. A black belt was cinched at her tiny waist, and her black boots stopped mid calf. Her appearance and twenty years of age belied her experience as a complete warrior.

With another assault, she threw herself at her stepbrother. Ten years ago, she and Yen were orphans near the western villages in New Caporesso. Both sets of their parents had died tragically, leaving them alone in the wild. After finding each other, they were found by Ketrik and Hapco. Hapco adopted them, and raised them as his own children in Salvation. After Hapco took his position at the armory, he began instructing his children in the ways of the warrior. Now, they were both experts.

Yen avoided her attack, ducking under a flying side kick. As she landed, he jumped at her, sending a kick into her midsection. She staggered backwards with a groan. He started another attack, but stopped before getting inside her range. She sensed his approach and lunged at him with a powerful jump back kick, but missed.

"I remember that move from last week, Kyra." He laughed. "You'll have to do better than that to beat me today." He bobbled his head, enticing her to continue.

At age twenty-two, Yen was a handsome young man. He was almost six feet tall and was a solid mass of well-toned muscle. His physique had developed through daily practice with and without weapons. Thousands upon thousands of repetitions forged his arms and legs into sturdy limbs to protect and sustain him in combat. He wore dark brown pants, littered with countless patches. His short-sleeved shirt was an unsightly drab grey. Single edge daggers were concealed inside each of his brown leather boots, and a belt held his pants at the waist.

As she launched another assault, he intercepted her fist, blocking it sideways. Next he hit her in the middle of her chest with an open palm strike.

She cried out like an injured child and pulled her arms to her bosom.

Yen started giggling and stepped away from her. "I'm sorry Kyra," he hooted. "That was just a reaction," he struggled to talk and laugh at the same time, "not intentional, all right?" His laughter continued until it bordered on hilarity.

Her face was red. One part was embarrassment and the other anger. As he continued laughing, her embarrassment vanished, replaced by fury. "Ahh!" she screamed, attacking him. Three low kicks found his legs, while palm strike after palm strike struck his face and abdomen.

His laughter ended after her second kick to his leg. Now he was engaged fully in the contest. She continued her assault and he defended himself. Their arms and legs looked like intertwined snakes jostling for position in a deadly duel, staying in contact as they moved.

He backed away, placing distance between them. Before she could close the gap, Yen initiated his own attack. He used his strength to try to deliver crushing straight and roundhouse kicks. His hand motions were swift and lethal. One strike would dissolve into the next without any hesitation. After years of practice, he had become a master of the rare fighting art from Drador. Yen threw a left-right punch combination followed by a roundhouse kick and then a spinning heel kick.

Kyra blocked the punches and stepped to the side to avoid the first kick, and then ducked under the final one. Then Kyra commenced an attack of her own. It appeared to be a frenzied array of fists and feet flying through the air, but to the experienced observer, it was artistry in motion.

A herd of feral horses gathered to watch the exhibition. Normally, they frolicked in the grassy hills surrounding the town. The elegant animals had once been royal horses to the kings and queens of Castle Lau'damay. But when the ruling hierarchy collapsed and the castle was abandoned centuries ago, the noble steeds were set free. A handful of them wandered through the Western Wilderness, leaving Caporesso forever. Now Niseans, rounceys, coursers, and destriers prospered in the fields around Salvation. Even though the spectators did not appreciate what they were witnessing, it was an extraordinary display of martial arts.

Back and forth they went. Kyra attacked with a left-foot jump front kick that dissolved into a right-foot roundhouse kick, followed by a punch combination that ended with a reverse sidekick. Yen blocked everything she threw at him.

He stepped away from the front kick and blocked the roundhouse. He met the punches with forearm blocks of his own and met her reverse side kick with a spinning heel kick. He faked a low kick and jumped into a high, punching strike. He hit his mark, "Ooh no! Sorry!" he chortled. "Accident." He waved a hand at her, trying to catch his breath as he spoke.

Kyra was momentarily knocked off balance. She regained her composure and wiped her nose with the back of her fist. Looking at her hand, she wiped the blood on her shorts. "Ooh, you're in for it now!" With that, she launched another brutal assault. Yen did his best to avoid and counter her strikes. Their grace and skill were a beautiful spectacle.

Their legs met in a mutual strike and returned. Open hands slapped off of each other in a series of strikes and parries. Yen threw a punch, but left his arm exposed for a split second. Kyra leapt closer, grabbing it. As she did, she rotated her hips and tossed him over her side. He landed in a heap. Twisting his arm, she placed her knee on his throat.

Yen looked up at her from his defenseless position and gagged for air, "Ahh...all right, let's call it a draw."

She chuckled at the notion and released her hold on him. She concentrated on slowing her breathing. *How long have we been training?* It seemed like hours, but neither one would yield on this day. Both of them were soaked in sweat and panting heavily. Offering him a hand, she helped him to his feet. They would have continued sparring, but they looked down at Salvation. To their surprise, they saw Hapco and Kellen walking to the smithy side by side.

Kyra looked at Kellen and thought something about him was different. He was still as handsome as ever, but somehow, he was changed since last she saw him.

Yen noticed something new about Kellen almost immediately. *Walking side by side?* Still huffing from their match, Yen remarked, "Hey...I think Kellen beat—"

Before Yen finished his sentence, Kyra exclaimed, "Kellen won! He beat Father with swords today."

They gathered up their weapons and raced to the smithy. This was an important day for everyone, though none of them realized the true significance of it.

Chapter 8

Vitoria soaked her body in a warm bath, the aroma of lavender salts filled the room. With the weathered shutters closed, candelabras provided just enough illumination. Shafts of sunlight pierced the steam rising off the water. The heat soothed her muscles. The stone walls were covered with patches of moss, but the tile floor was cleaned daily.

She moaned as her youthful attendant poured more hot water into the tub. "Oh…that feels good, Gail."

"Imma glad you like'n it, Princess Vee." She said in her broken Dradorian accent.

Even though her name was Vitoria, only Guan used it. To the rest of her family and friends, she was known as Vee. It was a nickname her younger brother had given her a long time ago.

Gail set down the bucket and moved to Vee's side. She wore the traditional, form-fitting garment of an unmarried woman from Drador, with a short-sleeved dress that stopped at her knees. The earthy colors enriched its appearance and enhanced her figure. Her thong sandals tied above her ankles. The Dradorian style differed from that of Cenkin by exposing more of their tanned flesh. Cenkin women were more prudish than those from other parts of New Caporesso.

But not Vee, she had an inner confidence that women lacked in Cenkin. She was a bold young woman who pushed boundaries anytime she could, wearing what she liked rather than what was expected of her. There were those in Cenkin who felt her shorts were too short to be worn in public, but that only encouraged her to continue her ways.

"Youa seem more happy today. Did sumpin' good happen in dat training yard?" she asked, scrubbing Vee's back.

With her eyes closed, she mewled, "Hmm...yes, Gail." She paused. "Lower. Ah...that's the spot."

Removing the sponge from the water, Gail wrung it out. She poured an aloe on it and cleaned Vee's arm. "Well? Tell me wot it was, mum."

Beaming with pride, Vee said, "I defeated Col in our duel today. We—"

"Oh dats very good, my lady. I knew if youa kept practicin', you'd beat'em." She walked to the other side and washed Vee's other arm. "But, ifa I may ask ma'am, why do you practice? I mean, no other ladies do. So why you?"

Vee glided to the other end of the tub and reclined on a submerged lounge. Her black hair fell beneath the water's surface. "I've trained for so long, I almost forget why I started. At first I didn't want to train. I hated it."

"Hated it, mum?" Gail shook her head. "I finda dat hard to believe."

"It's true. About six months after father died, mother married Guan. He insisted I begin training like Col." She chortled, "I was a stubborn child. I—"

"Excuse mum...wot mean *stubborn*?"

"It means...well it means...hmm. I guess it means I didn't do what I was told to do."

Gail added more water. "Oh...I see."

"Sometimes, I'd stand in the courtyard and do my exercises so slowly that my teachers got angry with me. They'd tell me I was a despicable little girl and call me Princess Bratty."

"Sounds like'm they not nice to you, mum." She giggled. "I'd like'a to see'um train wit you now." She made an awful face and punched in the air with both hands. "You'd beat'em up real quick, mum."

Vee laughed at Gail's display. Lifting her leg from the water, she scrubbed it, removing the last remnants of her battle with Col. "I was a difficult student at first," she said. Water dripped from her heel as she cleaned it. She let it fall into the water, splashing Gail.

Gail squealed as water speckled her dress and face. "Ah! Sometimes I think you'em never grow up, mum." She pulled at her dress, shaking the material to help it dry. Looking back at Vee, she asked, "Wot changed you?"

"My mother. Seven years ago, she came to me and told me I needed to give up my childish ways and train to become a warrior. She explained, *'The world is evil and treacherous. No one can be completely trusted in matters of loyalty and fealty. You cannot even trust Col to always stand by your side in your defense. Men's minds are easily tainted and corrupted. They can betray even their best friends if the promise of reward is large enough,'* she said."

"Dat seems like'm a lot to tella fourteen year old girl."

"It was, Gail. I asked her why she talked about fealty, love, and betrayal." She raised her hands out of the water and shrugged, saying, "I didn't understand what it all meant. And she said, *'To protect you from Guan. He manipulates people to his will. He can turn friends against each other and make them do horrible things. Now he pits you and Col against one another, knowing when to praise one of you just to infuriate the other. A day will come when you will have to choose between Col and Guan.'*"

"No..." she said, surprised. "She didn't say dat to you, did she?"

Nodding her head, she said, "Yes, Gail. She did."

Scratching her head, she asked, "Wot did it all mean, mum?"

Vee smirked, "I'm still not sure. Even after all this time, I haven't figured out everything mother talked about. We haven't talked about it since, but she did tell me that once I beat Col in a duel, she'd explain everything." She swished her hands in front of her. "Gail? My robe please." Standing up, water dripped from her body as she waited.

Gail helped Vee put on the robe, the end of it falling into the water. She stepped from the tub and wrapped the garment tightly around herself, allowing it to dry her body. Moving to a vanity, she sat on the padded bench, where she dried her hair with a towel.

"Her story frightened me enough that it convinced me to train. At first, it was very difficult, but after a short time, I found that I enjoyed it. After a year or so, I realized I was getting good, and *that* encouraged me to practice even harder. I went from hating it to sometimes training for eight hours a day. I've completely embraced the way of the warrior, but..." her voice trailed off.

"But what, mum."

Vee turned in her seat, facing Gail. "I don't know if my father would be proud of me or not, Gail. I don't know if he would've wanted me to become a warrior." She shook her head and said, "I just don't know."

"Well, mum," she put her hands on Vee's shoulders. "I know he woulda been very proud of you. He'd be mad crazy not to be. Trust me, mum."

"Thank you." She grabbed Gail's hand and squeezed it.

Smiling at Vee, Gail said, "You'd better hurry up, mum, or you gonna be late for supper a'gin." She walked to the windows and opened the warped shutters, letting the afternoon light fill the room. "So I guess'em supper is gonna be special tonight, mum. You gonna learn more truth. Right?" She set a brush next to Vee on the vanity in front of her.

Looking in the mirror, she brushed her silken hair. With a glimmer in her eye, she replied, "I hope so, Gail. I truly hope so."

Chapter 9

The fire in the pit was dwindling, untended. The tools Ketrik had been making today would have to wait until tomorrow. More important matters were at hand.

"This calls for a celebration!" exclaimed Hapco.

"Right you are, Hapco," agreed Ketrik. "Long before we journeyed here, the good citizens of Salvation honored their master warriors with celebrations when they bested the master at arms." He pointed at Hapco. "Since they put you in charge, no one has beaten the master until now!"

"I still promote students to master warrior status," countered Hapco. "And the few I have promoted are excellent soldiers." He shrugged his shoulders, "They just are not as good as Kellen."

"Not even Yen or Kyra have beaten you. His party should be the biggest one ever thrown in Salvation." Ketrik's excitement had not faded.

"Only you have beaten Hapco since we arrived, right, Father?" Kellen asked respectfully.

Ketrik and Hapco looked at each other but said nothing.

Kellen continued, "I have heard some of the others talk about your training sessions with awe. They say watching the two of you was like watching the legends from the ancient scrolls come to life. It is something they will never forget," he looked at each of them, "so they say."

"They exaggerate, Kellen," responded his father.

Hapco quickly agreed, "Yes, Kellen, we fought well, but it was hardly legendary. They are too kind." With a grin, he jerked his head towards Ketrik. "Besides, he could barely keep up. I always took it easy on the Norkinean."

Ketrik guffawed at the facetious comment. "Who says you were the only one taking it easy?" His smile broadened. Before Hapco could retort, Ketrik changed subjects, "Come, Hapco, we must begin making preparations for a ceremony in honor of Kellen." He headed out of the smithy.

Hapco nodded at Kellen, "You did well today. Your abilities are even greater than what you demonstrated." He put his hand over his chest. "When you find true confidence in yourself, you will become the greatest warrior in Salvation. Combat will push you, and take you to levels you never imagined possible. Embrace what you are, and you will be successful in battle."

"Thank you, Hapco," he bowed. Kellen thought Hapco's comment was odd. *Combat and battle, where will I find that? Certainly not here in Salvation.* "Your words honor me. I don't know what to say."

"Then say nothing," Hapco replied. He turned, following Ketrik's exit out the door. Stepping into the sunlight, he saw Ketrik already talking to two young men. *He still stands regally. Head high...chest out...eyes front. And no one has seen through his façade yet. Thankfully, tonight should be the last night of it.*

Ketrik was telling Eromo and Wesne about Kellen's dueling accomplishment, "That is correct, Wesne. He beat Hapco with swords today. We must hold a party in his honor. Will you assist in planning it?"

Wesne glanced at Eromo, then said, "We'd be honored, Ketrik." Wide eyed, he looked at Hapco as he approached. "No one has ever beaten you." Wesne was tall compared to the other residents in Salvation. His lanky limbs made his movements appear awkward, but holding a two-handed battle axe, he found his rhythm. His preferred weapon had a large blade with a ferocious spike on the backside. Wesne's brown pants and maroon shirt were neatly mended, a testament to his meticulous ways. "This is amazing!"

"No doubt," joined Eromo, "simply amazing. I knew Kellen was close to doing so, but hearing those words is remarkable." Eromo was built the same way as Kellen, strongly athletic with sinewy muscles. He had a knack for antagonizing Kellen, but it was all in good fun. "We'll arrange for it to be at the main pavilion."

"Even if a wedding reception were taking place, the pavilion would be ours," laughed Wesne. "This moment in Kellen's life is more important than a simple wedding." He nodded his head. "I think everyone would agree. Let's go, Eromo."

Taking their leave, the two men went in search of others, to share the good news and arrange a party.

As they left, Kyra and Yen arrived. They inquired of their father, already knowing the answer.

"What happened?" Kyra asked anxiously.

Hapco professed. "Kellen defeated me in a duel today."

Kyra's face lit up. "I knew it. Didn't I tell you, Yen? I told you he beat Father." She slapped his arm.

"Yes, Kyra, you told me," he sighed. "You told me the whole way over here. You must be clairvoyant or something," he said sarcastically.

The four of them walked inside the smithy.

Kyra crossed the floor and greeted Kellen. She threw her arms around his neck, "Congratulations, Kellen. I knew you could do it," and kissed him on the mouth. As her lips found his, she realized her mistake and backed away from him. Her face turned bright red.

Yen made a funny face. "I'll try to control my emotions a little better, Kellen," he chortled. "But in all seriousness, well done." He slapped him on the shoulder. "You defeated Hapco sooner than I thought you would, but I knew you'd do it eventually. Out of the three of us, I knew you'd beat him first."

Kellen's face flushed with embarrassment after Kyra's kiss. *That was almost as amazing as I thought it would be.* Wiping his lips, he shook his head, "Thank you for your words, Yen, but it was only one day's session." He was uncomfortable with the praise from his friends.

"Do not discount your actions from today, Kellen," admonished Hapco. "You improve with each session. Few soldiers can say that. Confidence." Hapco pointed a finger at his heart and then touched the side of his head. "Remember what I said, confidence in yourself and your abilities is all you need to be a successful warrior in battle and in life. Understand?"

Kellen nodded his comprehension. Hapco was right, and Kellen knew it. His abilities were impressive, but he did not trust in himself. He was always afraid of injuring an opponent, and as a result, he held back. The technique was there; he just needed his heart and mind to catch up with the rest of his body.

Kyra regained her composure, "When do I get a shot at you myself?" she asked, not making eye contact with Kellen. "You beat Father; now I want a chance at revenge, to restore our family honor."

Yen pushed her aside. "Who says you're first? As the elder sibling in the family, that right should be mine." He folded his arms across his chest and stretched his neck. "I demand satisfaction in the name of the family!" He laughed.

Ketrik snapped, "Enough jokes about honor and revenge!" He instantly spoiled their joyous mood. His words took them aback. No one dared say a word.

He grinned, explaining, "Besides, I get the first sparring session against the new master warrior." Ketrik barely finished his sentence before breaking into raucous laughter. And just like that, they were all laughing and praising Kellen again.

Chapter 10

Eromo and Alecia walked towards the impressive pavilion, west of Salvation. It sprawled north and south between Koa Springs and Refuge Creek. The structure was massive, as far as pavilions went. It could fit thousands of people comfortably, though it would take hours to greet everyone. Sturdy oak posts supported the wood-shingled roof.

"I'm kinda surprised everyone could put something like this together so quickly. Aren't you, Alecia?" asked Eromo.

"Not really, Brother," she replied. "Everyone understands the significance of Kellen's accomplishment. It's never happened before. I mean, no student has ever beaten Hapco before, just Ketrik." Alecia carried a bowl of fresh salad into the pavilion. Like Kyra, Alecia was very attractive. Long, naturally curly red hair and deep-set blue eyes set her apart from other women in Salvation. Her strong cheekbones and slender chin had caught the eye of many men.

She sat the salad bowl on one of many twenty-foot long pine tables in the center of the pavilion. Each was lined with bowls and plates of food for the smorgasbord.

Their friends Esra and Hasru approached.

Esra placed a platter of salted pork on the table. Its smoky aroma filled the air. "Aah. That smells delicious, don't you think, Alecia?"

"Hmm, it does. Your mother worked fast to prepare it." She hugged both young men, and stood on her tiptoes to tussle Esra's hair. "You're still getting taller each week I think. You grow like a weed."

He pushed her arms away, and straightened his hair. "How many times do I have to tell you, Alecia? Don't touch my hair. All right?"

Alecia made a pouty face. "Are you mad at me now, Esra?" Dramatically, she put a hand on her brow. "I don't think I can go—"

"Fine, Alecia," he sighed heavily. "I'm not mad at you, but don't do that."

She frowned, saying, "I won't," and then winked at him. "Besides, look at the feast prepared as a tribute to Kellen," she held her hands over the table before them. "It's been a long time coming. His abilities have been making progress in leaps and bounds over the past year. He finally understands everything about his movements," she said, her ponytail bouncing as she spoke.

Eromo added, "He no longer punches or kicks with conscious effort. Energy just flows through his body. He finally understands what Hapco has been telling all of us."

Hasru said to Eromo, joining the conversation, "I know, but Kellen is the only one who can do what Hapco has instructed us to do. Hapco's words sound simple, but I think they're impossible to interpret." He shook his head and reached for a turkey drumstick.

Alecia smacked his hand, saying, "You wait until we've given thanks. And you know, if you keep eating the way you do, you'll be too big to fight." She put a hand on his extended belly, and mouthed the word, *Wow*.

Knocking her hand away, he rubbed his stomach. "Hey! Quit teasing me; I'm just naturally this way." He humphed, "What does it matter anyway? I don't think I'll ever be able to do what Hapco wants, no matter how big or small I am. His words don't make sense to me the way they do to Kellen."

"Yeah, but at least you'll be in good company, Hasru," commented Esra. "None of us can do what he teaches. Yen and Kyra are close, but they have not reached that level either."

"And he's their father!" exclaimed Alecia. "They get extra instruction from him at the end of the day, and they still have trouble. Maybe Kellen really is extraordinary."

"He is not that special, Alecia," Hapco surprised them from behind. They turned, greeting him with respectful bows. "His abilities are not magical or mysterious." He studied their faces. "Do any of you know why he succeeded in beating me?" he asked.

For a moment, they were all silent. Then Alecia replied, "It's Ketrik."

Everyone turned to look at her.

"What?" She shrugged. "We participate in the same lessons as Kellen. His father teaches him things that we are not privileged to learn, almost like another martial art. Ketrik has made the difference in his training." She felt Hapco's gaze linger and his expression turn more serious. She waved her hands in front of her. "No, Hapco. I don't mean it like that. You're a great teacher, and I'm honored to have learned from you. I just mean that the extra instruction Kellen gets has made him that much better than we are."

Hapco's expression did not change.

Alecia's red face betrayed her embarrassment. "All right," she clapped her hands in front of her, "I'm gonna stop talking now."

Hapco maintained his dour expression a moment longer, and then his infectious smile reappeared. He chuckled, "I know, Alecia. You are exactly right. It *is* Ketrik who makes Kellen better. I have taught you all everything I can about Maeda Jiu Do," he looked at their faces, "including Kellen. Ketrik's additional instruction has made him a better warrior. His individual style has enhanced Kellen's abilities." Hapco thought to himself, *The additional tutelage of a man from the north has advanced Kellen's swordsmanship beyond every man born in Salvation.*

Their contemplative silence continued, and then Eromo observed, "Look at everybody congratulating Kellen." Their eyes found him at the center of the pavilion.

Men took turns shaking his hand and offering words of encouragement on this momentous occasion. They joked that he would be their next training partner, or that he should tell them the secret to defeating Hapco.

Standing beside Kellen, Ketrik nodded his head in acceptance of comments offered to him. He looked around for Hapco. "Hapco," he shouted and waved, "you should be here too. Come back," he called. "Your students will understand. They can release you for now."

Hapco looked at the group around him and casually said, "My king calls me." He started walking away.

Eromo grabbed his arm. "Your king? What does that mean?" he asked.

"Uh…nothing." Hapco was flustered a moment, "Just a joke between us. It's nothing more than that, and certainly nothing worth repeating. All right?" Turning, he puffed his cheeks and exhaled. He walked over to where Kellen and Ketrik were standing. "What have I missed?" he inquired.

"Only compliments and congratulatory comments from the village, Hapco," answered Ketrik. "And I am afraid I accepted them by mistake. You are the teacher everyone wishes to speak with. This is your time as well as Kellen's." He leaned closer to Hapco's ear. "In any event, I need a break from the crowd. You stay and greet the well-wishers."

Hapco nodded. "As you wish." Turning, he shook hands with the men standing nearby. Graciously, he accepted the praise but was not boastful over the accolades. He quietly allowed Kellen to enjoy the evening for himself.

Ketrik moved away from the crowd and stood alone. He watched as friends joked and carried on together. The sounds of children playing and chasing each other in the areas around the shelter filled the air. Young girls painted the faces of the younger girls, making them giggle with glee. Women cooked more food on the open fire pits around the pavilion and prepared additional salads from heaps of fresh vegetables and fruits. The tables were full of wonderful dishes, all with savory aromas tempting the taste buds.

He rested a hand on one of the many hand-hewn posts used to support the pavilion's roof trusses. Watching the young men and women mingling and flirting with each other made him think, *To be young again.*

The band played an odd assortment of musical instruments. Their melodious tunes filled the air, making Ketrik wistful for a time long ago. He raised his mug and thought, *I wish all of you were here to see Kellen and what he has become.* Taking a drink of ale, the sweet tone of Kyra's voice calling returned him to reality.

"Ketrik? It's time for supper. Let's go. You should sit with Kellen today." She took his arm and walked with him to the dais where Kellen was already sitting.

He stopped and looked in her eyes. "Today is not for me, Kyra. Collect Yen and your friends. All of you should sit with him. You help with his training more than you know. Each of you is partially responsible for today, each of you in your own way." He motioned at the table. "Go on, fill your plate and enjoy this wonderful meal."

Kyra nodded her acceptance and went to gather her friends. Taking their places around Kellen, they laughed and joked about his success.

The meal was served, and the villagers enjoyed its nourishment. Bowls and plates of food were passed around the tables several times. They ate and drank for hours. The men enjoyed the ale especially. Everyone had their fill of roasted salt pork and tenderloins. Bowls of salads were filled, emptied, and refilled. The villagers knew how to celebrate.

A special day melted into night as the celebration drew to its conclusion. Guests, weary from too much food and too many pints, offered their final congratulations to Kellen before heading out into the darkness. It was at this time that the village elders approached Ketrik and Hapco. Their minds were clear, as well as their intentions.

Orazio approached Ketrik, "Today has been a glorious day in the growth of your son, Ketrik. He began the day as a boy and ends it as a man. We must speak with you about this development."

From the moment they first arrived in Salvation, their lives were set to meet at this junction. The elders were interested in Ketrik's past and in everyone's future. Until today, they had respected Ketrik's request to let his history remain unspoken, but now was the time when they would press Ketrik and Hapco for answers. Who was Ketrik? Who was Hapco? Why had their families fled New Caporesso? How had they arrived in Salvation?

It was time for these questions to be answered. Ketrik and Hapco both knew it, but were still reluctant to do so. Why did the elders need to reopen the old wounds from long ago? The last ten years in the village had been wonderful. Their children had grown into respectable adults. They were excellent warriors and knew right from wrong. The time in Salvation allowed Ketrik's son to grow up, free from being hunted and pursued. Why did anyone want to disturb that peace?

Hapco put a clay pipe between his teeth, lighting it. He puffed at it, the smoke rising into the air. Looking at Ketrik, Hapco nodded.

Silently, they agreed.

Kellen, Yen, and Kyra were also anxious to hear the answers to everyone's questions. In fact, they had many to ask themselves. Especially Kellen, for he was the youngest when they escaped New Caporesso, and his memory had faded the most. He sat down next to Kyra before Ketrik began his story. Bumping shoulders, they looked at each other and smiled awkwardly. Tonight Kellen would discover who he was.

Ketrik sighed, "All right, Hapco and I will explain everything tonight. But understand… tomorrow, you may not like what you have heard."

"Why are you here?" one elder asked.

"How did you find us?" inquired another.

"Are you criminals?" asked a third.

Ketrik held up his hands, silencing them. With everyone's attention focused on him, he proceeded to tell them their story, starting at the beginning, in a time before the land was called New Caporesso. He described life as it was centuries ago. Terror, murder, and death were a way of life in the Northern Kingdom, in the land of Caporesso. Ketrik continued with his story, telling them everything he knew.

Chapter 11

Col and Mervekka sat in the unfastidious lower kitchen. The haphazard stone and mortar walls oozed slime. The scent of the meal being prepared masked the dank odor of the room. There was a scratching at the door, and it opened.

Mervekka looked up from the table as Vee arrived. She was late. "Looking at that old map in the foyer again my dear?"

"Yes, Mother. Am I that predictable?" she asked with a shrug.

Her mother smiled. "That is all right; the quest for knowledge is a good thing. Maybe your map study will prove itself useful one day," she pointed at the servant's entrance, "but tonight, you almost missed fresh cabbage soup."

"Who cares about your studies?" blurted Col, clearly disheartened. "What good will they do you? It's just useless knowledge." He waved a hand in the air. "I'm not sure why you even learned to fight."

Without recognizing his true concern, Vee asked, "What's bothering you, Brother? Are you mad I beat you?"

Looking away from her, he replied, "Vee, I would hope you understand that I'm above something as petty as jealously. As a warrior in the Tu'nide, there's no place for it. We function as an integral unit, no man better than any other. We act as one." Glancing at her, he said, "Now that you're almost a soldier—"

"Col," Vee interrupted, "you talk about soldiering like I could be one. I'm not allowed to be a *combat* soldier...am I?" She looked at her mother for an answer. "I thought women were forbidden from actually fighting in the army."

Mervekka responded, "A woman has never been accepted as a soldier on a battlefield, but they are not forbidden. Very few people know, but all requirements to becoming a soldier are superceded if a warrior defeats the commander of the Tu'nide in a duel. If that happens, the person is immediately eligible to become a soldier, fit for combat. Before today, no woman has ever accomplished it." She looked approvingly at her daughter. "You fought well this morning, Vee. I watched you and Col as you trained in the courtyard." She beamed, nodding. "You looked like a graceful warrioress with your swords."

Surprised, Vee asked her mother. "You were there? I didn't see you."

"Your stepfather does not allow me in the courtyard while you train," she replied. "You know he tries to control me and the way I interact with you. Just like forcing us to eat down here, he tries to hide your development. He does not want me to know you have become a warrior." Sighing heavily, she added, "Guan's true power is controlling the truth." Clearing her throat, she declared, "Vee, winning your duel today is an important event in your life. You bested the ranking officer in the Tu'nide, and with that comes a gift; the opportunity to join the Tu'nide."

Hearing the welcomed news, her face lit up, "I can join the Tu'nide? Really?" She glanced from Col to her mother. "That's fantastic...it's what I've wanted since I began training...it's—"

"It's dangerous, Vee." Col added. "I'm not sure you understand the true meaning of being a soldier: men die; they make sacrifices. Most people don't understand what that means. To most, those are just words; there's no reality behind them. But my men know the truth. We ride into battle together, knowing that everyone will not return."

"I thought your unit had the fewest casualties in the army?" she asked.

"We do, Vee, but men, my friends, still die. They risk their lives defending our country...and each other. In fact, once we lose sight of the walls, our only concern is for each other. Orders take care of themselves, but survival is a group task." He leaned forward, examining her. "Are you prepared to have four hundred men rely on you completely? To ride tall in your saddle when arrows and spears are flying around your head? To stand your ground when a line of screaming bandits charges your position, brandishing the most fearsome weapons you've ever seen? Are you ready to risk everything to protect your comrades?"

Mervekka interrupted before Vee could answer, "Col, what is wrong? Your words go deeper than the result of today." She studied him. "Something else is bothering you."

With a troubled expression, he looked at his mother. "I miss Father. Today is an important day for Vee...and he isn't here to see her." He turned to Vee. "We don't know if he wanted you to become a warrior or not. Guan encouraged this, but for what purpose? His actions ruined our family. He—"

A sound at the doorway interrupted them. Servants entered the kitchen, bringing dinner to the bowed table.

Abby, the eldest lady in waiting and Mervekka's oldest friend, set the spit-roasted wild goral on the table. "My lady, here it is!" she boasted. "A caravan from Nurdug arrived today with a dozen of these animals. I insisted that Cook obtain several for you. Hopefully, the ones in the pen will make babies," she giggled. "But I thought a special dinner for a special night was in order." She looked at Vee.

Vee graciously bowed her head. "Thank you, Abby. It smells delicious...I can't wait to try some. What does it taste like?"

"Umm...It can be gamey at times, but Cook took extra time to make it just right. He used his *secret* ingredient on this." She inhaled deeply. "Can't you smell it?"

Sniffing at the roast, Vee lied, "Yes, Abby, I can smell everything he did."

"No sense waiting for it to get cold." Abby sliced the animal, placing pinkish slabs of juicy meat on each of their plates.

Other servants brought potatoes and a variety of fresh arugulas, fiddlehead ferns, lettuces, and beets to compliment the meal. The cool kitchen made the girls serving food shiver, their bare feet numb. Their thin dresses dragged on the damp floor, tearing at the hems.

With a mouthful of food, Mervekka said, "Hmm...Abby, this is wonderful. I can't remember the last time I ate this."

"You don't? Why it was at your wedding reception, my lady." Abby smiled warmly.

Mervekka choked. A flood of emotions almost overwhelmed her. She wiped her mouth and dabbed her eyes. Setting down her napkin, she said, "That will be all for now, Abby."

"Yes, my lady." Abby bowed and shooed the other girls out of the kitchen.

Mervekka and her children were alone. She took a drink of wine and set her cup down. "Col...Vitoria, I need to talk to you...about Guan...and the day your father and brother died."

They looked up from their plates.

Vee set her fork down. "You haven't called me Vitoria for years, Mother; this must be important." She picked up a radish and crunched it.

"What about that day, Mother? We've heard the stories and know the history. What else do you want to talk about?" Col asked, not sure where the conversation was headed.

She reached out and grabbed his hand, squeezing it. "I had to wait until the time when you both could handle yourselves in combat. As I watched Vee fighting, I realized today is that day. You are ready to learn the *truth* about the day your father died. You are ready to take action in the name of those who cannot."

Col looked intently at her. "What are you talking about, Mother? I thought we knew the truth."

Mervekka forced a smile, "Col, it is time to tell you about our family's path, not the fantasy yarn as told by Guan. But to tell it, I need to start at the beginning." She took a deep breath, "Nearly twenty-five years ago, New Caporesso was born. But decades before that, it was just a land called Caporesso. Life was not precious; death was everywhere. Marauding soldiers roamed freely in each of the three kingdoms." She continued, telling them everything she knew.

Chapter 12

Ketrik began his story, "The forgotten history of Caporesso is filled with warfare and devastation. The Northern, Central, and Sothern Kingdoms were sworn enemies, and at least once a generation, they went to war. The insults that led to the kingdoms declaring war on each other were mostly forgotten. Everyone assumed there were reasons for continuing the conflicts, but no one ever mentioned them.

"Fighting became their way of life, and as the centuries passed, the sole purpose of each kingdom became the domination of the others. Thousands of men were lost in the bloody struggles until one kingdom emerged victorious, even if only for a short while. The vanquished were victimized by the conquerors, suffering indescribable atrocities. Villages were razed to the ground. Libraries and schools were burned to spite the defeated foes.

"Because of this ruthless behavior, the written history of ancient Caporesso is by and large, gone, lost to the fires of destruction. Scholars from each kingdom worked to rebuild the archives, but to no avail. Over time, the written words were forgotten until only half-remembered stories remained.

"The original chronicles of the three families who established the kingdoms no longer exist. The names of Trosho, La'may, and Brika'cong have been forgotten, except as names of castles. No longer are those men spoken of with reverence as the founding fathers of that magnificent land. And Lau'damay is only known as an abandoned citadel on the road to the west, and not the rare beauty that she was." Regretfully, he shook his head. "Only a handful of men even remember who they were."

Mervekka described how the Second Age of Caporesso came about. "After centuries of inescapable bloodshed, each kingdom built defensive structures to protect its cities' inhabitants from the horrors of war. This is when Cenkin's monstrous wall of stone and mortar was built. And Sokin erected its interlocking, gargantuan wall of timbers around that mighty city in the Southern Kingdom. The Northern Kingdom carved the cities of Norkin and Nurdug directly into the Mestoline Mountains. It took years of toilsome labor to turn those cities into shielded fortresses, out of reach from outside attack. The completion of these fortifications signaled the beginning of the Second Age of Caporesso.

"The history of the Second Age was recorded and maintained in private libraries in each kingdom. They proved that history was truly in the eye of the beholder. No two accounts of an event were written the same way. This fact reflected the attitudes of the kingdoms. When a kingdom recorded a favorable episode in its history, the other two kingdoms wrote of it as a wicked occurrence." She sighed, "Such was the way of things in Caporesso.

"Unfortunately, the kingdoms continued waging war. It was an endless cycle that repeated itself for many generations. Fathers and sons knew too much death. Mothers and daughters lived with constant fear and loss. The citizens of the kingdoms did as their rulers bid, marching to war when commanded or defending their lands as duty demanded.

"In the east," continued Ketrik, "the residents of Drador used stone and timber to build a double wall around their city, turning it into a mighty fortress. Manned bastions guard the community, raising the alarm when danger approaches. Due to its small size, the entire population acts as a militia. Men and women train regularly, becoming gifted warriors. Over time, they created their own martial art called Maeda Jiu Do. It is an aggressive style that combined simple aspects of hand techniques, foot boxing, and grappling into an efficient fighting system that could be employed by anyone, regardless of size and strength. A novice of that art is still a formidable foe.

"The western villages of Werlo and Dreglo never built permanent fortifications for protection. Instead they rely on the marshy conditions surrounding them. They use these natural barriers expertly, ambushing would be attackers in the bogs, cutting them down with barrage after barrage of deadly arrows. Survivors have described such attacks, that each volley blots out the sun. Many armies marched to conquer these peaceful villagers, only to be defeated in the unforgiving quagmires." Ketrik continued his narration.

Mervekka filled her goblet with more wine. "Since the completion of the city defenses over two and a half centuries ago, no kingdom has been conquered. Yet war and death still existed. Unfortunately, that was the way of things in Caporesso." She paused and took a drink. Setting the cup down, she advised Col and Vee, "Get comfortable, the rest of the story will take a few hours to tell," and continued with her tale.

Chapter 13

In the Northern Kingdom, the rain fell with a steady rhythm, seemingly washing away the filth of the old traditions of Caporesso. With it came the fresh smell of a cool autumn afternoon. The year was 230 SA and the land was changing. *It* was tired, tired of the old ways. Tired of war and destruction. Death had roamed freely for too long.

Two men slowly rode northwest. One was shackled to his saddle horn, the other free. As the bound man looked at the mountain-city of Nurdug, a myriad of thoughts raced through his mind. With his chains rattling, he spoke to his captor, "Pak, I have ridden this course hundreds of times, and never once did I look at the mountains the way I see them now." Shaking his head, he admitted, "I never appreciated their beauty, always taking them for granted." He pondered their splendor. "They are breathtaking, are they not?"

Pak ignored him, maintaining their course.

The Mestoline Mountains were a spectacle to behold. The man gawked at the imposing cliffs with a childlike wonder. From the foothills, they rose vertically hundreds of feet. Above the impassable sheer face, the evergreen-forested mountains climbed towards the heavens. Beyond the alpine timberline, they reached ever higher, their peaks disappearing into the clouds. The limestone and granite rampart stretched from the Western Wilderness to the Eastern Wood. The rocky face acted like a barricade, keeping the citizens of Caporesso from escaping northward.

Fall showers spawned impetuous waterfalls from the rocky crags, some plummeting hundreds of feet. In the sporadic forest below the mountains, a myriad of red, yellow, and orange rain-soaked leaves still clung to their branches, refusing to perish as the season demanded. The trees blazed with color, a contrast to the dreary hues of a rainy day. Terikk inhaled deeply, taking in the precious air.

He looked at Pak. "Do you not see the beauty of the mountains, Pak?"

Again, there was no response.

Undiscouraged, Terikk continued, "Nurdug is an engineering phenomenon. Look how the grand facades and buttresses of the city are exposed. Do you see the craftsmanship of our people here?" he asked.

The rain slackened. Pak said nothing.

"Do you remember the stories? The stories about miners, and sculptors, and masons building Nurdug and," holding his saddle horn, he pointed westward with both hands, "Norkin." He nodded his head at Nurdug. "Look at the mountain-city. Almost two and a half centuries ago, our ancestors abandoned their homes in the foothills, seeking refuge *inside* the mountains themselves.

"Those skilled men whittled the rock, forcing it to obey their designs. First, they tunneled into the mountain, and then began climbing in the darkness. There they found a lacework of tunnels already forged by the gods." His horse splashed through a puddle. "The miners reinforced what was there and created more. Then they carved and mined the stone, building our homes and shops. Tunnels on the inside and walkways on the stone face connect everything, Pak. Have you ever wondered at how it was all built? Of who imagined it for the first time?"

A gust of wind blew the rain into their faces, stinging at their eyes. His silent companion remained quiet, deep in thought. On the often-travelled road, they moved closer to Nurdug.

"They say it took several decades, but once completed, the cities of Norkin and Nurdug became unassailable. The only access is by first entering the mountain. Look," he pointed at a slab of stone, "I can see the closest gate." Shaking his head, he admitted, "I know it works, but not *how* it works. Somehow, that stone will be lifted, and we will enter. It is simply amazing." He sighed, saying, "I wish I had more time to explore our great kingdom. I know when we enter the gate, I will ascend the Central Ramp and be taken to King Jor'kul in Palace La'may. There he will pass judgment over me, and my life will be forfeit." Looking at the man beside him, he asked, "Pak, have you nothing—"

"What would you have me say, Captain Terikk?" he barked. "Why are you talking about the mountains? Of course I know the stories...I know our people made homes inside the hollow mountains. Why are you telling me about them?"

Terikk answered solemnly, "Maybe...because it is the last time I will ever see them."

"I know, Captain," he dropped his head. "But, sir, what would you have me do?" Pak turned his head, looking at Terikk. "Why didn't you flee when I told you to go? Why didn't you listen then? Now, I can't think of a way for you to escape."

"Pak, *flee* is not something I could have done. I swore an oath to defend the Northern Kingdom from all enemies, some from other lands...some from within. I am not ashamed of my actions, and I will not fly like a common criminal. I will face King Jor'kul and abide his decision. But..." he tried lifting a hand but his chains prevented it, "some say he is a new kind of king, one worthy of the title. Perhaps there is a chance he will listen to me; perhaps he will listen to reason."

They approached the white gate. Black cloaked guards greeted them, confirming their identities. With a shout, unseen men activated the mechanism that lifted the slab. It took several minutes to open. Pak and Terikk guided their horses inside the tunnel as it closed behind them.

Crossing the threshold, Terikk looked left and right. For the first time, he spied the counterweights and thick ropes used to work the gate. They were rising back into position, sealing the opening. Pulleys creaked and moaned against the strain. As the door was sealed, several men struggled to replace support timbers under the weights, taking the load off of the ropes.

"Terikk," Pak interrupted his study, "we must go."

They moved deeper into the tunnel, passing rusted iron sconces on their left and right. The coal fires illuminated the damp passageway. Each hoof fall resounded off the walls.

The tunnel was empty for a hundred feet. Unarmed soldiers met them at the first juncture, their weapons stowed. They wore no chain mail inside the mountain. The chamber was brightly lit, leaving no shadows beneath the thirty-foot high ceiling.

A man stepped forward, holding up a hand. "Where are you headed?" he inquired.

Pak replied, "Taking this man to be judged by King Jor'kul for disobeying orders."

He smirked, "Heard about this one. To the left there, trooper. Up you go." He motioned at a narrow passageway.

Pak and Terikk's eyes searched for the path. Finding it, they saw more torches climbing upward. The ramp began its long ascent inside the mountain.

Following the winding trail, Pak said, "Well, sir, I hope you're right. You had the chance to run, but didn't. You saved my life, and I'm forever indebted to you. Unfortunately, I'm repaying that debt by marching you to meet your executioner."

Calmly, Terikk replied, "Who knows, Pak. Maybe the executioner is a better judge of character than General Kelt."

Pak laughed heartily at the remark, the sound echoing inside the hollow limestone mountain.

Chapter 14

Terikk stood before King Jor'kul in the Great Hall of Palace La'may. It was located in Norkin's middle level. Terikk's hands and ankles were shackled, but he held his head high.

Two-story windows in one wall granted the sun access, but the dismal light of day did little to brighten the grey hall. Hundreds of torches and several giant fireplaces provided additional illumination. The large room had an atrium sloping away from the windows, its peak forty feet above their heads. Hand hewn stone columns with timber trusses supported the ceiling. Birds nested in the rafters, their songs providing constant diversion.

Two palace guards stood behind Terikk. They wore brown, long-sleeved leather gambesons bearing the emblem of the realm, a snarling bear. Double wrapped belts held their bastard swords, while their shields were slung across their backs. Black wool pants and knee-high boots completed the uniforms. Other guards were stationed around the oversized room.

Handmaidens busily swept the uneven stone floor and tended the fires. Advisers to the king sat at a long table, watching the proceedings with great interest.

Terikk listened to an account of his actions being presented to the king. For disobeying orders, he was at risk of losing his life, but he was not afraid.

"What do you have to add?" Jor'kul boomed, pointing at him.

With no fear, Terikk eyed Jor'kul. "Sire, General Kelt ordered us to attack the villages along the western shore of the Grimm Creek. His command was to kill everyone there, including the women and children," his voice cracked.

The advisers looked at one another, shaking their heads in disgust. They murmured amongst themselves.

"We attacked the first village," Terikk continued, "destroying everything, burning it all to the ground. The dead were left to rot where they fell. But, before our assault, most of the women and children fled to another village to the north. Those who stayed behind were cut down like beasts," again, his voice betrayed him. "General Kelt ordered us to follow the refugees and finish what we started. He wanted us to murder everyone."

"Murder?" Jor'kul repeated. "Watch yourself, trooper. It is not murder to kill during battle." He stared at Terikk, trying to interpret his body language. "Where is the honor in disobeying orders?" Jor'kul admonished.

With a stone face, he answered, "Sire, it *is* murder when we are killing unarmed peasants." His eyes did not waver. "Soldiers wear a uniform and are trained to fight. The villagers hardly know how to lift a sword, let alone mount a defense. Most are too old or too young to protect themselves." His shackles rattled as he talked. "Where is the honor in butchering them? Kelt ordered us to slaughter the children like animals." Yelling at Jor'kul, he demanded, "Tell me, where is the honor in that?"

The advisers' whispers grew louder, their discontent mounting.

The guards stepped forward, knocking Terikk to the floor. "Don't take that tone with your king, soldier!" barked one of them.

Jor'kul paused for a moment, searching for a rebuttal. "Our enemies do the same thing. How many families have perished at their hands? How many lives have been lost to their war parties?" In a disgusted tone, he asked, "Why should we be any different?"

Terikk looked up from his knees. "Sire, just because they do it does not make it right." He shook his head, "As soldiers we follow orders without hesitation. We do unspeakable things and then say, 'We were just following orders.' That is how we absolve ourselves from the atrocities we commit. I say, 'I killed that little girl because my king ordered me to do it,'" he paused, turning his head. His emotions sprang upon him for a moment. Clearing his throat, he continued, "And that is how I justify my behavior." Exhaling, he locked eyes with Jor'kul. "We cannot continue the indiscriminate killing, sire." He shook his head again. "If we do, it will never end."

"What makes you think you can question our institution of warfare, trooper? It is the oldest custom we still posses from our ancestors. You—"

"I only question," he interrupted, "how we can kill citizens from the other kingdoms and not expect the same in return? Why do we terrorize innocent people, killing without restraint?" He tried pointing outside. "Our people will never be safe outside these halls. As long as we continue butchering *their* peasants, *our* people will always be in danger too. Is that any way for your people to live? Yes, they are safe here inside Norkin and Nurdug, but what kind of life is it for them to never feel the grass beneath their feet? Or walk through the woods below, or gaze upon the Mestoline Mountains in their magnificence, sire?"

Jor'kul answered plainly, "It is the life we have lived with for almost two and a half centuries. Do you really think you can change the way of our world?" He mocked Terikk, "Is that *your* destiny, trooper?"

"I do not know what fate has in store for me, sire, but I have had enough of the blood. I cannot kill for killing's sake anymore. If that means my death…so be it. But I will no longer kill for you, or my ancestors. They may have started this barbaric tradition, and they may have had a reason, but where is that reason now? Why do we fight the other people of Caporesso? Can you answer me, sire?"

Jor'kul gave no reply.

"What makes them so different from us? Is it only because of where they are born?" Terikk shook his head. "That logic is old, sire, old and warped. How can we make this world better, if all we care about is death? There has to be something greater than sending a family to meet the Boatman, sire. There has to be something else."

Angrily, Jor'kul responded, "You want to forget the past. You want to cut ties with the old ways…for what?" With his arms outstretched, he asked, "What lies ahead that could be worth ignoring who we are?"

"Peace, sire," he replied. "Peace and the chance to live as men in this world without the fear of being killed because of where we come from." He shook his head somberly. "Why is that such a terrible thing to consider, sire?"

The advisers were silent. A few of them smiled.

"What kind of peace could we have?" Jor'kul asked incredulously.

"Any kind, sire. The way things are now, we kill *them*, and then *they* kill us. What have any of the kingdoms gained by continuing the old ways?" He paused, holding out his empty hands. "Nothing. Our so called victory is killing peasants and destroying their homes. We gain no land, we gain no wealth, and we gain no power. All we do is destroy lives. And they do the same, but at the end of the battle, the only real gains we can claim are overcrowded cemeteries."

Jor'kul glanced at his advisers and sighed heavily, "We act as we have always acted. We do not know anything else, but violence and loss. War has been our way of life...our religion for so long, how can we change?" he asked simply.

"I do not have the answers, sire, but I do know where to start...stop the killing. We cannot prevent the other kingdoms and their marauders from slaughtering our people, but we can control what our soldiers do. We can cease initiating hostilities against the other kingdoms. We can let their people live without intervening in their lives. Our army should still patrol our region, safeguarding the people, but our days of riding off to war on some unnamed battlefield should be over, sire." He glanced at the advisers. "And who knows, maybe the other kings will see the wisdom of your ways and follow the Northern Kingdom into a new age in Caporesso. An age of peace."

Jor'kul waved a hand at the guards. They released Terikk, allowing him to stand up. The king sat down on his ordinary throne, lowering his head. He placed a hardened hand on his brow and shook his head. Slowly, he looked up at the man in front of him. "What is your name, soldier?"

"Terikk, sire."

"Terikk, you speak with the wisdom of a much older man." Jor'kul looked at the other soldier beside him. "Who are you, trooper?"

Nervously, he replied, "Pak, Your Majesty." His voice cracked.

"Are there any inaccuracies in the account concerning the action around Grimm Creek, Pak?" he asked directly.

"Sire, no inaccuracies, only omissions from the report, sire," he professed. "Captain Terikk's story is correct. General Kelt ordered us to destroy the second village, and Terikk refused to do so. Then the general ordered us to arrest Terikk. He assigned four men to escort Terikk back to Norkin for punishment. We departed immediately, and have had no contact with General Kelt since we left. The report ends there, but not the account, sire.

"We were away from General Kelt for over a week when we encountered a cavalry squad from Drador. Outnumbered twenty to four, we released Terikk from his bonds. He organized our defenses as we prepared for battle. Terikk ordered us to move inside a thick copse of trees, figuring the troopers would have to dismount to pursue us." He glanced at Terikk. "They did, and we fought on foot against our dismounted enemy.

"The battle lasted no more than five minutes. Terikk fought like a warrior from an epic legend. I think he was possessed by Thro'ce himself. By the end, the soldiers from Drador were all dead. My comrades, Paro, Joll, and Chen were also killed in the battle. I was wounded and at Terikk's mercy. He could have killed me and fled, but he didn't. He tended my wounds, and then built a pyre for the dead." Pak looked at the man beside him. "Captain Terikk returned to Norkin with me in tow, to face you and your judgment. I know I'm nothing, and have no voice here, but, sire, don't punish this man. His action at the village was the only honorable course to follow," he finished and stood at attention.

"A trooper tries to give me advice?" Jor'kul waved his hand in Pak's direction. "Be silent and stand at ease, trooper." He turned back to Terikk, surprised the man still showed no fear.

One of the advisers stood up and asked, "Terikk, why did you fight against the Dradorians?"

"Not fighting would have resulted in my death," he answered.

"Then why didn't you kill Pak and flee?" asked a second man.

Terikk answered with confidence, "Sir, I doubt you would understand my reasons. I did nothing wrong near Grimm Creek, and I have no reason to run away." He looked at Pak, "Besides, where is the honor in killing a wounded friend?" Facing the advisers again, he said, "My conscience is at ease with my decisions. I have no reason to hide."

Jor'kul asked, "Are you afraid for your life, Terikk?"

"No, sire. I acted the way any honorable man would have. I have done nothing wrong in the eyes of the gods. If I were placed in the same situation again, I would refuse the order again," he answered with resolve, his eyes fixed on Jor'kul.

He stared back at Terikk. "You talk like a man who fears nothing."

"I am not afraid of death. It will find me at the time of its choosing. But I will face it with a sword in my hand, a shield at my side, and dirt beneath my feet. It will not take me in old age, nor will it be at the hands of an executioner," he responded defiantly.

Jor'kul nodded his head and chuckled. He looked at one of the guards, "Laknor, take this man to the jailer. I need some time to discuss matters with my advisers. I will send for him when I am ready."

Laknor nodded, motioning for Terikk to walk ahead of him. Together, they exited the hall, walking onto a barren terrace overlooking the countryside. Terikk approached the railing, taking in the sight. From it, he had a commanding view of the surround. The roads were waterlogged, and the leaves on the trees below drooped with water droplets clinging to them.

The rain had stopped falling, but the sky was still grey. An elaborate system of terra cotta gutters and downspouts ran full, removing the runoff from the city. Spouts shaped like lotus flowers had been chiseled into the stone, discharging the water like hundreds of fountains to the ground below.

Terikk rested his hands on the railing, his chains banging it. Directly in front of him, he saw three rainbows reaching for southern lands. Their bright colors lifted Terikk's heart. Continuing to watch them, their colors muted and blended into a shade of pink. Turning west, he saw the setting sun beginning to peak through the clouds. Its radiance lit up the western sky, diminishing the brilliance of the rainbows. Terikk gave a thin-lipped smirk, sighing. *Hopefully the sun is not setting on my life as well.*

Chapter 15

The Central Kingdom stretched from the fortress-city of Drador in the east to the marsh protected villages of Werlo and Dreglo in the west, running from the plains north of Sokin in the Southern Kingdom to the foothills of the Mestoline Mountains in the north. This made the Central Kingdom the largest region in Caporesso. The enduring land was characterized by rolling hills in the west and fertile plains to the east.

Located in the heart of the region was Cenkin, the second largest city in Caporesso. A quarried stone and mortar wall shielded it. The giant rocks had been cut from the ground and moved into position around the city, taking decades to complete. Hundreds of masons worked on the structure, beginning with its deep foundation and ending with its guardian gargoyles atop the parapet wall. Their expert skill and craftsmanship were evident in every step of the construction. With mortar joints so thin, the rampart appeared seamless, making the already imposing fortification look like a massive slab of impenetrable rock. It snaked its way around the city, including large parcels of land for farming and tending herds. As the city engineers had laid it out, Cenkin was self reliant, appearing to be siege proof.

The inhabitants of Cenkin lived within the protection of the silent sentinel. Many thousands of timber and brick dwellings lined the streets of Cenkin, making it a thriving metropolis. Behind the mighty wall lay Castle Trosho, the keep where generation after generation of Trosho's descendants lived. It dominated the landscape, its towers and spires visible from beyond the wall. Since the rampart's completion nearly two and a half centuries ago, no enemy had set foot inside the ancient castle.

From a hilltop west of Cenkin, King Hogeland had a commanding view of the city. Had he looked, he would have seen the western paddock, where the vertically grown crops provided a greater yield of food while consuming less land. In its southern portion, herds of buffalo and deer grazed without concern.

But he was not looking at the city. He knelt between two graves covered with fresh dirt. Distraught, he buried his face in his hands.

"Come, my king," a man said, placing a sympathetic hand on the king's shoulder. "King Hogeland, it's almost time for you to be presented to the people. Your coronation is set to begin shortly, sire."

Hogeland pushed him away, ignoring his words. "Why, Quinz? Why did the southerners attack and murder my father…and my sons?" Tears ran down his face. "Why did they kill the rightful king of the Central Kingdom and *my boys*?" He held his head. "They were only at the Stone Pine Forest, nowhere near southern lands. We have not sought war with the south for decades. Why would they attack us unprovoked? For over twenty years, my father never marched to the north or south seeking conflict. We only protect what is ours, guarding our own villages against usurpers and bandits. Why did Guan invade our lands?"

"Sire, I don't know why they attacked. Men from the south are wicked, relishing the pain they create. Since Guan seized control of the Southern Kingdom, it is as though a tyrant from antiquity roams the land once more." He tried to console Hogeland again. "But we must go, sire." Quinz touched the grieving man's shoulder again. "Your father and your father's fathers honored the traditions of the Central Kingdom as they were crowned. You must let the people see you, sire. You must be strong for them."

"I thought *this* day was going to be a glorious day. In the year two hundred and thirty five of the Second Age, I am king of the Central Kingdom." He choked on his words, "But I did not know the cost would be so dear. My father. And my little boys, Kelil…Laort!" Clutching his chest, he gasped for air. "The line of kings will end with me, and it feels like my heart has been rent from my body. It seems Trosho's curse has been handed down to me." He tearfully recited an old poem.

A noble man, and father of Caporesso was he.
His family's fate is a sorrowful tale.
His brothers' lust for Lau'damay tore them apart.
A noble man, and father of Caporesso was he.
First Brika'cong sacked a city for her;
then La'may did lie with her,
Plunging Caporesso forever into civil war.
A noble man, and father of Caporesso was he.
His family's fate is a sorrowful tale.

He blabbered, "The people do not deserve a weak man like me, Quinz. They deserve a better man."

"Sire, your sentiments today only proves that you are a man with real emotions. Forgive my impertinence, sire, but Caporesso's history is full of men who cared for nothing but themselves." He knelt beside Hogeland. "Anyone can see that you are capable of love, sire. Love for your sons, and for your people."

A cool spring breeze blew on Hogeland's face. He turned his head, looking at Quinz through bloodshot eyes. "What do you suggest I do?" Pointing at a nearby gravestone, he lamented, "Their mother is already here; she died six years ago giving birth to them. My father has been set on a pyre with coins over his eyes, waiting for the Boatman. How can I leave my boys here? How can I go on without them?"

"My king," Quinz bowed his head, "that is the way of things. The living must make their peace with the dead and move on. But I cannot tell you what to do, sire. I can only offer advice."

"And what would you advise? A full scale war with Sokin?" he scoffed.

"No more wars, sire." He shook his head. "Forgive me again, my king, but the old policies of the Central Kingdom are worn out. They don't work anymore, and your father knew it. That's why he did not ride to war for all those years."

"I never knew he felt that way." Hogeland hung his head. "He and I never spoke about it."

"I know, sire," admitted Quinz. "As his adviser, I counseled him that we should avoid bloody conflicts at all costs."

"And what did he say?" he asked.

"He asked me, 'Why?' and I showed him the Second Age chronicles from the library. Campaign after campaign revealed the same undeniable truth." He held out his empty hands. "We never gained anything. Whatever lands we captured, we eventually lost. The villages we controlled were ultimately surrendered." He paused. "The only consistent element throughout was the loss of soldiers. Men from all the kingdoms were butchered and sacrificed to the gods of war. Your father realized the cost was too high, vowing to never waste lives like that again." Quinz stood up. "Even though he is dead, sire, you can continue his work. You can make the Central Kingdom and Caporesso a better place for everyone."

Hogeland shook his head. "I do not know if I have the strength anymore, Quinz."

"You must find the strength, sire." Quinz pointed at the city. "Your people need you today. You must be strong to resist Guan's invitation for war. That must be his plan, to draw you out from behind the wall. Do not give in to his lust for blood, my king; it will only lead to destruction. Think of your people. Think of your warriors. You have the power to lead them to death, or grant them—"

"Enough, Quinz!" angrily, Hogeland interrupted. He took several deep breaths, realizing what he had known for many years. "Now I understand what my father started. I was raised to abhor violence and bloodshed. My values parallel Cenkin's policy for the last twenty years. I know the traditions we adhere to were created in a time when war and destruction were our way of life. But now, there is a chance to establish peaceful doctrines that will end the violence once and for all, keeping the people of Cenkin safe." Wiping his eyes, he resolutely declared, "My father began it, and I will finish it." With a glance at the graves, he admitted, "Having lost my boys, I understand the grief the common people have felt for centuries. I hope to never force this emotion upon anyone while I am king." He sat motionless for several more minutes. Finding his strength, he stood. "Quinz, we have the power to bring peace to the people of the Central Kingdom." Teary eyed, he looked at his sons graves again. "For them, I will build a more peaceful world."

"We must go, sire." He held out an arm, directing Hogeland. "Your people need you."

Hogeland regarded Quinz, asking, "Do you think my sons will mind if I leave them in this cold place, alone on this hill?"

"No, sire," he sadly shook his head, "I think they will understand," and a tear fell from his eye.

As King Hogeland was presented to his people, he made a bold declaration. "My people...hear me," he raised his hands, silencing the crowd. "Today, I buried my sons. And tonight, my father will embrace the Boatman."

The crowd murmured, the sound of women weeping filled the air.

"I proclaim to you now, we will *not* go to war with the Southern Kingdom. My sons were precious to me," he put a hand over his heart, "but I know your sons and husbands are just as precious to you. And as my subjects," he paused, "you are precious to me! I will not sacrifice *you* seeking vengeance for myself. The death of your loved ones will not return my boys to me. Our ancestors' worn out ideas keep the graveyards full and our city with widows who cannot find consolation.

"I do not know how, but we will forge a new path for ourselves. We will create something new in Caporesso; a kingdom of conscience that no longer seeks violent expansion across its borders. I do not know how long it will take, but we will persevere until we find peace...together!"

The good citizens of Cenkin in the Central Kingdom cheered and celebrated their new king. His promise of life instead of death was a welcomed relief. Peace was a novel idea, worth pursuing. But as it turned out, the patience required to find peace was almost worse than meeting the reaper on a battlefield. Hogeland's idea was noble, but he would need help if he was to succeed in leading his people into a new era.

Chapter 16

The sound of a key turning a lock awoke Terikk. The wooden door creaked open, and a man entered.

"Terikk...Terikk. Are you in here?" the man half whispered.

Coughing, Terikk replied, "Yes...I am here. Who is that?"

"Pak, sir. I've come to get you out. It's finally time to go."

"Go? What do you mean?" he asked.

"Just come with me, sir. You'll see when we get outta here. Come on."

"All right." The sound of Terikk struggling to get up echoed in the tiny cell. With a thud, he fell. "Help me up, Pak," he said with effort.

Moving further into the dark cell, Pak assisted Terikk in getting to his feet. He was unsteady and weak. Pak put Terikk's arm over his shoulder and helped him out.

Stepping into the torch lit hall, Pak saw Terikk clearly for the first time. He gasped, "Ah! Terikk...are you all right?"

Terikk's hair was as long as a horse's tail. His beard looked wild, like a juniper affixed to his face. Leaning against a wall, he rested his head. "I am fine, Pak." He looked at the frayed ends of his shirt and his tattered pants, both black with filth. Inhaling deeply, he asked, "What day is it?"

"It's five days after the vernal equinox, sir—"

"What year," he breathed heavily. "What year is it, Pak?"

"Two hundred and thirty seven, sir," he replied quietly.

Terikk's breathing quieted. For several moments, there was no sound in the dimly lit hallway.

"You were locked in here for six and a half years, sir."

"My gods," he gasped. "Six and a half years...has it really been that long?"

"It has, sir. I'm sorry there was nothing I could do for you. The only solution I ever came up with was helping you escape, but I knew you'd never follow me." Pak chuckled, "You're stubborn that way, sir."

His breathing increased, and he looked at Pak. "Why now? What happened? Why am I free now?"

Pak grinned. "Just come with me, sir. It'll be easier to explain that way. And trust me...this is no escape."

Together, they moved away from the jail. No one observed their movement. They climbed several flights of stairs beneath Palace La'may. Flames flickered and danced against the walls, but again, no one watched them pass. Reaching the top of the final stair, Terikk recognized where they were.

"Pak, are we entering the Great Hall?" he asked.

"Yes, sir, we are. Just keep going. Everything will be explained shortly."

"Last time I was here, things did not go the way I had planned," he chortled.

"Really?" Pak asked sarcastically. He chuckled, "Besides, I didn't think you had a plan last time."

"If I did, it did not work," he joked.

"At least your sense of humor is coming back, sir." The door in front of them opened as they approached. "We're almost there...they'll explain everything, sir."

"I hope this conversation goes better than my last one. It cannot be any worse."

"Oh I don't know, sir. This time, they could kill you," he said with a wink.

Terikk glanced at Pak, grinning. "I do not know what is going on, but I know I have nothing to fear this time. Thank you for helping me."

"It is my pleasure, my kin—I mean, sir."

Entering the hall, Terikk noticed several men near the king's empty throne. Guards were stationed around the room as before, but the servants were nowhere to be seen. The usual commotion of the room was absent, replaced by a strange stillness. Finding his strength, Terikk released Pak and stood on his own, they crossed the floor.

A man from Terikk's memory greeted him. "Terikk, I am pleased to see you again. The last time you were here, things did not end very well. Today will be different, I assure you."

Scrutinizing the old man, Terikk remembered who he was. He pointed a finger at him. "You were here with King Jor'kul when I was here. You were an adviser to him."

The man nodded, "Yes, Terikk, your memory has not failed you. My name is Troonz, and I am glad to see you still remember that day."

"How could I forget it? It was my last day as a free man." He studied the other men with Troonz. "Do I have you to thank for my release?"

Troonz tilted his head, replying, "You have yourself to thank for that."

Terikk shrugged his shoulders and shook his head. "I have no idea what you are talking about, Troonz."

"That day, you talked about ending the violence and bringing peace, two concepts that went against our entire way of life. King Jor'kul arrested you to keep you from causing an uproar." Gesturing at the men behind him, he said, "We thought about what you said. We thought long and hard." He started pacing in front of Terikk. "But understand, changing the kingdom's way of thinking is not something that could have been accomplished overnight. It is something that will take time. Your ideas were radical; Jor'kul thought they were inflammatory and that you were a revolutionist. So against our advice, he kept you locked up." Troonz sighed heavily, "But now...the king is dead."

Nodding his head, Terikk asked, "When did he die?"

"Five nights ago...an illness claimed his life."

"So you are now the new king of the Northern Kingdom," surmised Terikk. "Thank you for releasing me from my—"

"No, Terikk, let me explain." Troonz glanced at the men behind him. "I am not sure if you were aware of this before, but Jor'kul was king because *our* families," he motioned at the advisers. "*We* wanted him there. His family had no real power, but he was someone we could advise and control. We supported him, and he ruled as king for almost fifteen years.

"But after hearing your ideas, we were intrigued. Behind closed doors, you had us asking one another, *'Could peace be better for the people?'* We discussed and debated this topic for many years, never finding an answer." He stopped, and crossed his arms. "As fate would have it though, peace came to us. Throughout our history, most of our wars have been with the Central Kingdom, but we have had no military engagements with them for almost five years. They have not entered our realm since two hundred and thirty five of the Second Age, and our troops have not sought them.

"After two years with no violence, the people began talking about *no wars*, and *no more death*, and *peace*. Now after six and a half years, they thrive like never before in our history, even to the extent that we have expanded beyond our mountains, building new settlements in the foothills our ancestors used to call home." His expression showed his satisfaction. "Peace has come to us, and the people want to hold on to it. The very notion you suggested came to fruition, Terikk.

"But Jor'kul was discontent. He became the warmonger we used to fear from the other lands. He desired war again." Troonz turned, looking out a window. "He organized the army and planned to attack Cenkin, shattering this peace. We advised him against it, but he would not listen to us. He was out of control." Turning back to Terikk, he said. "Luckily," he eyed Laknor, "Jor'kul died from a sudden illness, saving thousands of lives." Troonz stepped closer to Terikk. "Do you understand what I am telling you?"

Terikk silently nodded. "Except...which one of you is king?"

Troonz smiled. "Terikk, we are too old to be kings, too old to run a kingdom. These men and I are meant to be advisers to the king, to give him advice when he needs it. Jor'kul let the power he wielded control his mind. I think you are stronger than that."

"*We* think you are stronger than that," interjected another man.

"We decided unanimously, Terikk. You are to be the next king of the Northern Kingdom. Your ideals and philosophies are unsullied. Our people need you to lead them on this uncharted course. As events have unfolded, an uneasy peace has been granted to us, yet we did nothing to create it." He shrugged his shoulders, shaking his head. "We do not know how to make it permanent. Without you, eventually we will fall back into the old ways. The people need you to maintain the peace." Sighing, he beseeched him, "Will you help us by ruling over the people?"

Terikk snorted, "This morning I was locked in a cell, forgotten for over six years. Now you ask me to be king." He shook his head and exhaled.

"Well, Terikk, what is your answer?"

Thinking about the prospect for a moment, he again found his inner strength. Standing a little straighter, he replied, "Yes, Troonz, I accept your offer, but…I do not know how to be a king."

"We know; neither did Jor'kul. We will assist you any way we can, as long as you are willing to listen to our advice."

Terikk inhaled deeply, letting the air expand in his lungs. "Then, with your help, I will take my place on the throne of the Northern Kingdom. We will guide our people into a new future, devoid of violence and bloodshed. I do not know what that future holds, but together, we will meet it. We will stay true to the principles of peace, and live without war with the other peoples of Caporesso. The journey will be difficult, and we will stumble along the way, but we will persevere. Our ideals will not be compromised. We will prevail in our quest for peace."

The soldiers and advisers clapped and cheered for Terikk.

At Terikk's insistence, they quieted down. With a smirk, he grasped his shaggy beard, saying, "But before I address the people…I need a shave and a haircut."

"Some clean clothes after a bath would be a good idea too," added Pak.

Everyone laughed heartily. Troonz motioned at Laknor. "See to it then."

Laknor started to respond, but Troonz stopped him. "Hold. I almost forgot…" He stepped back, and knelt in front of Terikk, bowing his head.

The other advisers moved closer and knelt down as well. The soldiers in the room did the same. Pak walked around Terikk, kneeling beside Troonz.

Looking at Terikk, they thumped their shoulders, shouting in unison, "Strength of swords, honor in victory!"

Moved, Terikk touched his fist to his shoulder and responded, "Strength and honor."

Chapter 17

Hogeland honored his word to the people. Together, they were forging a new destiny for the citizens of Cenkin and the Central Kingdom. But as with any journey, the path was wrought with obstacles. Four years had passed since Hogeland ascended the throne. In the spring of 239 SA, his country was changing, but the people had not embraced the way to peace; dissension existed. He realized he needed new advisers to help convey his message.

He believed he had found the person necessary to aid him in guiding the people into a new age. Her name was Mervekka, and she was a brilliant young woman. Being from an influential family, she had received special schooling normally reserved for royal young men. This education and impartiality made her well suited for the position. For too long, the kings of the Central Kingdom had been advised by corrupt men, their only real interests being themselves. Mervekka's youthfulness implied an innocence which seemed incorruptible, but perhaps that was only naïveté.

Seeing her for the first time, he stared like an ill-mannered child, momentarily losing the faculty of speech. Mervekka's silken black hair touched her shoulder blades. Her black eyes were exotically captivating and symmetrically set in her round face. Her robust lips and smile were naturally perfect. Delicate cheekbones and her dainty nose were naturally tanned.

Hogeland had to remind himself to breathe.

Her blue cotton dress was modest but still accentuated her petite figure. The long sleeves ended with a loop that encircled her slender middle fingers. The bottom of the dress glided over the floor, making her appear to float like an apparition.

He shook his head, breaking the spell he was under. "Lady Mervekka, thank you for agreeing to meet me in this mundane setting." He waved his hand around the dank kitchen in a lower level of Castle Trosho.

Mervekka curtsied. "I am honored to make your acquaintance, sire, in any setting of your choosing. Although," her eyes surveyed the room. Vines grew up an uneven wall, reaching for the sunlight entering through a small window. "I am curious why you picked this particular place."

He chuckled, "Even though I am king, it is almost impossible to find someplace to have a private meeting that is actually private." Putting a hand to his ear, he remarked, "There are inquisitive people everywhere in Trosho, and I have issues to discuss with you. It is important for you to respond freely, without concern for who you might offend, including me." He pointed around the room. "I thought the servant's kitchen would provide us all the privacy we required." Pulling out a chair, he offered it to her.

Mervekka sat down, and Hogeland moved to the chair opposite her. On the battered table between them were a pewter pitcher and two mugs. He poured water for them both, offering a mug to Mervekka. She took it, setting it on the table.

Hogeland gulped at his water; a dribble ran down his well groomed beard. He said, "Lady Mervekka, as I mentioned, I am not trying to deceive you, but I have questions which require honest answers."

Her brow wrinkled. "I am not sure I know what you mean, sire, but I will try and be honest with you." She was unsure as to what Hogeland was referring. "Have I done something to offend you?"

"No, my dear." He acknowledged, "I am being mysterious." Clearing his throat, he plainly asked, "What do you think of my policy to not seek to expand the borders of the Central Kingdom? Do you agree with my military plan, refusing to engage invading armies? Even as they encamp around Cenkin?"

Caught off guard, Mervekka's expression showed it. "Sire, your policies are the law. We cannot question them." She averted her eyes.

Waving a finger, he reproached her. "Lady Mervekka…that will not do. I asked you to be honest with me. It is your answers that I need." He shook his head, saying, "I will not hold anything you say against you. You are safe here," he held up both hands, trying to encourage her to speak freely, "please."

She grabbed her mug and took a sip. Setting it on the table, she did not let go of the handle. "All right, sire, I will answer you. The people do not understand why we do not defend our own land; even your father did that. For four years, we have not initiated contact with anyone. As far as we know, the Northern Kingdom remains dormant inside their mountain-cities."

Holding his gaze, she continued. "Your citizens do not understand why you prevent the army from protecting the city when an army approaches. Each summer of the last four years, the armies from Sokin have marched to our walls. They bivouac here for weeks, destroying the newly expanded villages around Cenkin. They burn crops, and steal hundreds of heads of livestock, yet you do nothing in response to this threat."

"Lady Mervekka, the crops and livestock that Guan steals are inconsequential. In the western paddock, we grow enough food and the herds are large enough to support us for years if necessary. Rebuilding the outlying villages is also an easy task." He spoke in earnest, "It is easier to rebuild a home than bring a man back to life, so I see no need to defend those dwellings of twigs and clay."

Mervekka nodded her head. "I do see your point, sire; I am merely expressing your subjects' concerns. More importantly, a growing number of people believe you are leading us to destruction. Some feel their senile king will fail them when they need him most." She took another drink of water, hiding behind her mug.

He cocked his head. "Senile? I said be honest, not mean spirited."

Choking, she replied, "Sire, I am sorry, but you asked me—"

Hogeland interjected, "Lady Mervekka, it is all right." He chuckled. "Excuse my interruption. Now tell me…what do *you* think?"

She sat silently for a moment. "You are extending the lifespan of your citizens, sire. Your father began it, and you are continuing it. Instead of men being chewed up in the cogs of war, they are allowed to build lives with their families. With fewer resources reserved for the army, more of everything is distributed to the people, including food." She held out a hand. "Especially food. They live better now than they ever have, at least in recent memory, sire."

"Yes Lady Mervekka, all of that is true." He crossed his arms. "Then why do people think I am failing them?"

She shook her head, shrugging. "I would surmise that they feel unprotected." Finding her confidence, she released the mug. "The people trust the strength of the wall, but each time the southern army has approached during these last four years, your people feel apprehension." She confessed, "I do not understand why, sire, but they do. It might be because of the fact that our army flees from the southern soldiers, making your people believe our army is inferior, and afraid to fight. Everyone in Cenkin has heard of the south's Supreme General Guan. They know he is a barbarian of a man, seeking conquest and our destruction. Seeing the army's flight from him has left your people feeling hopelessly defenseless, sire."

He nodded his head in agreement, "Reasonable concerns, but unwarranted." Shaking his head from side to side, he assured her, "The wall is impenetrable. No man-made machine is powerful enough to breach it. Trust me when I say, we are safe behind it. And besides, with the army quartered away from the city, they train daily, staying vigilant in their preparation to defend the citizens of Cenkin." He leaned forward. "The commanders' orders are to redeploy inside the city, not retreat, at the approach of an invading army." Sitting back quickly, he asked, "Why should I let our warriors die on the fields around Cenkin? As their king, it is my duty and obligation to protect *all* of my citizens, including the soldiers. They are not mindless pawns to be disposed of at my will."

Mervekka's eyes grew wide. "My apologies, sire, I had no idea." She stammered, "I...I...I did not know the army is so well prepared; no one does."

The edges of Hogeland's mouth turned up. "My dear, do the people really believe I am that inept? And *senile*?" He chuckled. "Of course the army is ready to protect us from armies from the north or south. We have our brave soldiers and the wall. Why should I send the army to be destroyed when the wall will protect everyone?"

"You should make the people aware of that," she blurted out.

"I should?" His posture stiffened.

"Sire, no. I meant, I mean…" She was flustered by her impetuous response.

He waved a hand in front of her, cutting her off. "Lady Mervekka, I asked you here for a specific reason." Pausing, he asked, "Have you guessed it yet?" His intense gaze did not intimidate her. "No, of course you have not. Your mind does not work that way…and I mean that as a compliment."

"Sire," she shook her head, her hair swishing behind her, "what are you talking about? My mind does not work like what?" She raised both hands, questioning his comments.

"Lady Mervekka, I need someone I can trust, someone whom I can ask for advice and get a truthful response. I need someone who can see the possibilities I cannot. I need someone to help me explain to the people what it is I am trying to accomplish." He swatted an imaginary fly, saying, "Ah…my advisers still give counsel based on their own interests. They never offer a response without first determining how it benefits them." He sighed, "I thought Quinz was immune, but the temptation has proven too strong." Pounding the table, he declared, "That will not suffice anymore. I need someone who thinks about the people first, not personal gains." Leaning closer to her, he asked, "Do you know of whom I speak?"

Silently, she shook her head.

Hogeland smiled warmly at her. "You are that person, Lady Mervekka." Sitting upright, he admitted, "I knew before we met this evening that you were honest and loyal, but I was not sure if you had the resolve to answer me candidly, or if you would just tell me what you thought I wanted to hear. I have talked to many people about you, my dear. Everyone is of the same opinion: you are brilliant, and have no hidden agendas. Your word is your bond. Some of them say you could be queen one day—"

"But I am not of the royal bloodline, sire." She looked uncomfortable with his words. "I could never rule over the people of the Central Kingdom."

"Maybe the time has come to create a new standard for choosing the ruler of our kingdom. Why does a man's father determine who should be king?" He shrugged. "Better men and women exist, but they have no chance to lead our kingdom because of a tradition that is eons old. Maybe that institution is outdated as well. People still insist that your being a woman makes you less of a person to be taken seriously." Making a sour face, he declared, "To that I say, hah! Rubbish! This is a new time in our history, and it requires fresh ideas.

"Your suggestions will be better because you are a woman. You are not tainted with the evil thoughts that run rampant in men's minds. People say you do not think of yourself first, the way men do. And that you think of the people of Cenkin as your children. That is something I need now, more than ever." His excitement was obvious. "I need a person to help me guide the people into this new era, an age without us racing to war." He pointed at himself. "This is the time when we must look to ourselves to make our society better. What I have done so far is only temporary and will fail if the people cannot see what I envision for them. I need your help making them understand my ultimate goal. Can you do that? Will you help me do that?" he implored her.

"And what is your ultimate goal, sire?" she asked softly.

"To build a kingdom where everyone lives without the fear of death in the service of the king, in a place where everyone has enough to eat. Where children laugh and play without knowing the heartache of losing their father in some useless battle on some unnamed battlefield. I want our people to prosper through farming and trade." Hogeland spoke with conviction, "I want the army to become something the people acknowledge and respect and honor, not a means to satisfy the societal bloodlust we have lived with for centuries. We must escape our past and create a new destiny for the people. Our dreams can become realities—"

Mervekka interrupted, "A destiny of peace for all of us. We must establish a mindset where your people look to the future with hope and not trepidation. Cenkin can become a society where families grow, and live happily together. A kingdom where your citizens are considered equal— strength will not determine who is better or who has higher station. The people will be heard, their wants and desires paramount in your decisions. They will have a voice in how they are governed." She longingly spoke her last dream, "Death will become something that only claims the old and the sick. No longer will our sons be cut down to feed the fires of war." Standing up, she smiled at Hogeland and excitedly answered his question, "Yes, my king, I will help you forge this new path for the people." Her eyes sparkled with energy. "I am honored to be at your service." Bowing her head, she waited for his response.

Hogeland stood up and walked over to her. "Lift your head, child," he touched her chin with a rough hand. "I want what is best for my people, but I am not sure how to make them understand. Together, we will lead the people of the Central Kingdom into a new age, an age of reason and peace."

He extended his hand to Mervekka. She looked at it for a moment, and then embraced it. They shook hands, a gesture not condoned between men and women. Looking at her, he said, "I guess if we are going to give the people brand new ideas to live by, we should dispense with the useless protocols we still follow."

Mervekka looked tenderly at the older man. "Yes, sire." She leaned forward and hugged him.

At first he stiffened, resisting her hold. But as her embrace continued, Hogeland relaxed, hugging her in return.

Straightening herself, Mervekka stepped back. She looked at Hogeland. "Thank you for this opportunity to do something for the people. I know we can bring greatness to the citizens of the Central Kingdom, we can steer them to a bright future."

"Lady Mervekka, I believe we can do much together as well. Tomorrow, I will arrange for you to have a meeting with General Aacrel. We need his support in order to find success. Get some rest tonight; you will be busy tomorrow. He is a hard man, but a sincere one. He will listen to what you have to say, but I do not know how he will react."

She nodded. "Yes, my king. I will meet with him and persuade him to join us." She bowed. "I take my leave, King Hogeland. May pleasant dreams find you tonight."

"And you, Lady Mervekka." He nodded his head.

Turning, Mervekka exited the kitchen. Walking through the corridors of Trosho, she headed for her home. As she went, she could not help but think about the myriad of possibilities ahead of her. *Will the people believe what I say? Will King Hogeland trust my suggestions? Will General Aacrel listen to me and join us on our quest to create the kingdom's new identity?* These and many other questions would need to be answered in the coming days and weeks. She would worry about Aacrel in the morning, but tonight, visions of hope for the citizens of the Central Kingdom would be hers.

Chapter 18

It was not an exceptionally warm spring day, but sweat poured from his body. Aacrel performed an old hyeong from memory. The pattern had been the last one he learned while in Drador; it was still his favorite. He glided effortlessly from one position to the next, like a waterspout upon the Lho'mon, his transitions graceful, the movements powerful.

He slid backwards into a fighting stance and launched a front kick at an imaginary foe. Stepping forward, he speared an attacker's throat with two fingers. Dropping to the ground, he threw a turning kick followed by a punch. The kick designed to crush an adversary's knee, the strike used to finish the fight. His green tunic followed his every move, never hindering him.

Getting back to his feet, more imagined opponents attacked. He continued with the sequence of kicks, blocks, and strikes, each one perfect in its purest form. Every kick terminated with a slight pause, emphasizing his control over the motion. Aacrel relished the time he spent practicing forms. It helped him clear his mind and focus his thoughts...usually.

While many soldiers questioned the practicality of the patterns, Aacrel knew their true worth. The series of moves was not important; it was the mastery of one's self. Men strove to perform the hyeongs flawlessly, but even the slightest deviation, a kick too low, or a strike overextended, meant more training. Perfection required a dedication and patience few men possessed.

"Yah!" Aacrel's back kick hung in the air, a punctuation of the movement. He lowered his foot and continued the pattern. *Who does she think she is? I do not like being summoned to meetings, especially concerning politics.* Distracted, he stumbled and stopped.

A man snickered behind him, saying, "She is not even here and you lost your focus, General."

Slowly turning his head, Aacrel saw Lieutenant Subto approaching. "What did you say, Lieutenant?" he barked.

Subto snapped to attention, "Sorry, sir. Poor timing of a bad joke. I have no excuse, sir."

Aacrel guffawed, "Got you, Subto," he winked, pointing at him. "Your analysis was correct; thinking about her distracted me. But I was not thinking about her like that, Subto."

"Oh...of course not, General," he said, simpering. A breeze blew Subto's cape around him. He also wore the same tunic as Aacrel, bearing an image of a golden lion on the chest. The tunic stopped above the tops of his boots. At his waist, he carried a blue handled katana and wakizashi, both worn on his left side.

He scoffed at Subto's jest. General Aacrel was an exceptional man, being born the son of a Cenkinian soldier and a Dradorian wench. Raised solely by his mother, he had a difficult childhood. Incessantly bullied by the other boys of Drador, he suffered greatly at their hands. To teach him how to protect himself, his mother sent him to a combat college to be trained in the way of Maeda Jiu Do. Thousands of punches forged his solid arms, countless kicks strengthened his legs, and hours of grappling hardened his body. In time, he became Drador's most gifted warrior.

His extensive training turned his body into a perfect fighting machine. When Aacrel fought, it looked like a choreographed dance. His moves flowed from one into the next; there were no stops or discontinuities. It was as if he was precognitive and knew his opponents' next step before they did.

Aacrel's mother died in 233 SA, leaving the teen without guidance. His teacher suggested he travel to Cenkin and join the army. Without dithering, he left his home and journeyed to Cenkin and enlisted. A hearty laugh and boisterous spirit paved his path to becoming an accepted member of society in Cenkin. Demonstrations of his combat skills quickly earned the respect of the men he served beside. By 239 SA, Aacrel was a general in the Central Kingdom Army, and Hogeland's chief military adviser and confidant.

"When are you gonna meet with her, sir?" asked Subto.

He wiped his brow and neck. "I was just on my way now." Aacrel motioned at a waterskin nearby. "Hand that to me, Subto." Drinking heartily, he satisfied his thirst. Returning the cork, he tossed the sack to Subto. "Thank you." He wiped his mouth. "When I return, I will update you on the...situation."

Aacrel picked up his twin katanas and placed them in his belt, side by side. Each sword was one yard long, with white cord wrapped handles. The blades curved slightly, with a sharpened outer edge. Extending over half the length of the back of his blades were notches, giving the weapons a ferocious, sawlike appearance. They were exquisite pieces of art which could deliver death from Aacrel's capable hands.

Tying his cape around his neck, he headed off to meet Mervekka.

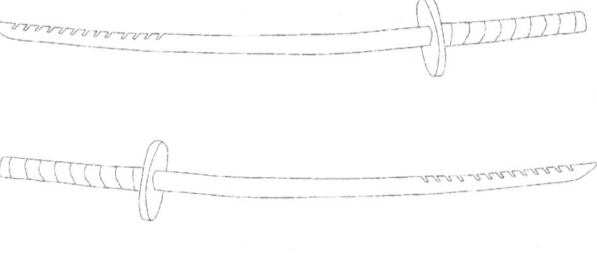

Standing near a livery, Aacrel waited for her. The location was more like a barnyard than a meeting place for the king's advisers. Oddly, the normal commotion of Cenkin was missing. There was no one around. Aacrel was alone except for a few roosting chickens and resting horses. The smell of fresh straw filled the air, and the sounds of flies buzzing was all around.

It seemed strange to meet a lady there, but her note was very clear on the location. The longer she delayed her appearance, the more impatient he became. He glanced up at the cool spring sun and decided it was time to leave, when a hooded figure approached from the west.

"General Aacrel, I am sorry for my delay. King Hogeland was giving me his final instructions." She walked directly up to him and extended her hand to shake his.

He looked at it and crossed his arms.

Awkwardly, she retracted her hand. "Well...my name is Mervekka and King Hogeland has asked me to be an adviser to him." Lowering the cowl of her cloak, she revealed her face. "He—"

His eyes grew wide as he saw her for the first time. Coughing into his hand, he recomposed himself. "I know who you are, Lady Mervekka, and I know of your new position for the king. Why did you call for this meeting, and why pick such a location?" He appeared discontent.

Mervekka smirked at the interruption. "King Hogeland suggested we meet somewhere where no one could overhear our conversation." She motioned to the openness around them. "A place like this, where no one can hide, seemed like a logical spot. As to the nature of this meeting, that will take longer to divulge."

She walked towards a group of barrels beside the livery. Mervekka stopped and turned; Aacrel had not followed. "General, please do keep up. We have much to discuss and are getting off to a rocky start." She motioned for him to follow.

Aacrel reluctantly joined her. *This is a bad idea and will not be productive*, he thought.

She pointed at a barrel. "Care for a seat, General?"

Her taunt irked him, but he kept his emotions under control. Coolly, he said, "Lady Mervekka, you summoned me, and I do not like being summoned...by anyone." He spoke clearly, "What is it you want?"

"General, King Hogeland speaks very highly of you. He says you are a loyal man, loyal to your king and kingdom. He also says you are an honest man who does not hide his true feelings. I have heard other people say those same things about you." She cocked her head to the side. "I am here because King Hogeland wants me to ask you something."

Aacrel nodded his head. She spoke with a confidence he had not witnessed in many woman. "It is nice to know my king holds me in high regard."

"He does, General, more than you know." Mervekka recalled to him the conversation she had with Hogeland. Aacrel listened in silence, only asking sporadic questions to clarify certain points of the narrative. After an hour, she finished. They both stood in silence, looking uneasily at each other.

Mervekka asked him, "Well, General, what do you think? Are you ready to help our king build a new kingdom?"

Aacrel shook his head from side to side. "Lady Mervekka, your story is incredible. I never imagined it could happen." He stepped closer to her and raised a fist in her face.

His movement startled her, and she stepped backwards, bumping into the stone wall. Mervekka was about to raise her hands to defend herself when Aacrel spoke.

"Lady Mervekka, I have dreamed for many years about a different way of life, a way without all the violence and war." He pumped his fist at her. "If you are serious about pursuing a new course for the Central Kingdom, then you have my swords and my word. I will help you unveil this new plan to the people. Together, we will make them see this new path is nothing to be afraid of. I am yours until we are successful...or death finds us."

Mervekka chuckled briefly. "Come now, General, hopefully we can stave off death for a little while. We have much to do." She was relieved to find someone else who shared the same beliefs about peace as she and Hogeland did. However, his response troubled her. "General, when I arrived, you appeared angry at my very presence. Now you are ready to join King Hogeland and myself as we embark on rewriting the philosophies of an entire kingdom. How did I persuade you to join us so easily?"

"Lady Mervekka, I was not angry, merely concealing my reaction to meeting you. As you said, you heard of me before you talked to King Hogeland last night." He cocked his head to one side. "I also know of you. I know what people say about you. They say you are an exotic beauty, too beautiful for words to describe." Hesitating, he added, "And for once, I can say the gossip is accurate. They also say—"

She became uncomfortable at his comment. "General..."

Aacrel held up a hand, "No, my lady. That was not meant to offend you in any way. It is a compliment. I was—"

"General, I know what people say about me, but my looks should not predetermine that I am good for only one thing." Defiantly, she crossed her arms.

He sighed, dropping his shoulders, "I am not very good around women, my lady. Please forgive my awkwardness. I meant to flatter you...not insult you." He bowed deeply.

Mervekka waited a moment, considering her response. "All right, General." She nodded. "I will let it pass." An uneasy silence remained. "Ah...What else do the people say about me?"

Offering a wry grin, he answered, "They also say that were it not for you being a woman, you could be king one day. At first I thought they were just words, but having met you, and listened to you, I see it and believe it now." He nodded his approval. "There is conviction in what you say, a quality absent from many men in this world. Peace is a noble and honorable pursuit.

"For many years, I have studied the combat arts. I have no master here in the Central Kingdom, and know more about fighting and death than any man in this kingdom. Consequently, I have been forced to study the finer points and theories of combat. In doing so, I have discovered a hidden truth." He opened his arms in front of him. "Combat in anger is wrong. Men train to fight, and they should. But at the pinnacle of their training, they should be commanded to fight a friend to the death." He paused, seeing her shocked expression at his hypothetical situation. "Killing a stranger from another land is easy, but killing a friend is impossible. Only then would people see that every time we kill another man, we kill a part of this world."

Surprised by his words, Mervekka asked, "Then why do you still fight? Why are you in a position to lead men in battle?"

"I swore an oath to protect the people of the Central Kingdom, and I am duty bound to follow my king's orders. For the last few years, our orders have been to defend the people from raiders from the north and south, not ride to war. We have had no contact with the north, but the south still invades." He exhaled. "I remain a general because it puts me in control. When victory is ours, I call off the attack. There is no disfiguration or butchery of our fallen foes; we treat the dead with respect. As a general, the men look to me for inspiration and leadership. They see me fight with honor, never giving in to bloodlust or rage." His answers were somber.

Mervekka was even more surprised by his responses, "I have misjudged you, General. I thought you were a bloodthirsty man, intent on seeking glory from your exploits. Please forgive my misconception." She bowed her head slightly.

His raucous laughter shattered the stillness, startling the napping horses. "And forgive me, Lady Mervekka. I was wrong about you. I thought you were just another woman, intent on clouding men's minds with your beauty and honey lies. Nothing could be further from the truth. You are an admirable person with merit in what you say. It is I whom you must forgive." He bowed at his waist, lowering his head below her shoulders.

"General, please, we both made mistakes entering this meeting. I trust we have remedied those issues at its conclusion." Her eyes twinkled.

Aacrel looked into her onyx eyes. This time, he offered his hand to her, "It was wrong of me to deny you my hand when we met. It will not happen again, my friend. Our reputations have preceded us, and in this case, they were accurate. We will be powerful allies in this new kingdom King Hogeland is trying to build."

Mervekka took Aacrel's hand and shook it vigorously. "Yes, General, we will find success because we are unified in the pursuit of creating a better life for the people of the Central Kingdom. For starters, you can simply call me Mervekka."

Aacrel smiled warmly at the beauty before him. "And you may call me Aacrel." He was amazed at what happened in only an hour. His first thought was the meeting was going to be a waste of time. Now he realized it would change the destiny of the Central Kingdom...forever.

The weeks and months ahead would be trying for all of them. Something like this had never been attempted before, and maybe it would spell doom for Hogeland, Mervekka, and Aacrel. Then again, just maybe, the people would embrace these new ideas. Maybe they would accept the notion that peace was better than war, and that life was better than death. Today, it seemed anything was possible.

Chapter 19

Gallows for public torturing or executions were situated near the northern edge of Sokin's timber wall. The gibbet's posts and wooden members were dwarfed by the enormous, red-barked logs in the rampart behind them.

The wall was the result of hundreds of master carpenters' tireless efforts. Using the forest to supply the material, these craftsmen struggled for decades building it. Trees with diameters at least thrice the height of a man were used as the main construction elements. Bundled pilasters anchored the wall intermittently, with iron bolts and bent rods used to lash the structure together. Grotesque wooden gargoyles were positioned along the top of the parapet, silently watching over the impassable barricade. The rampart was as imposing as the men from the south.

Hundreds of emotionless soldiers stood in formation in the main bailey outside Castle Brika'cong. They watched as a brutal punishment was administered. The men did not flinch as the whip found its mark; they did not shudder when the prisoner screamed in anguish. The unblinking soldiers from the Southern Kingdom were hard men, neither feeling pity for their victims, nor remorse for their actions. Instilled since childhood were the notions that weakness was not to be tolerated, that they should be loyal to the ruler of the Southern Kingdom, and that wretches from the other kingdoms were inferior beings. These blindly loyal men would charge off a cliff if their general commanded it.

The grassy yard was filled with soldiers and Sokin's peasants. All able-bodied men served in the army. Those unfit for service or too old did not watch the flogging, hiding themselves out of humiliation. Women came of their own free will, bringing their children. Together, they enjoyed the spectacle of public scourging. Women cheered each time the prisoner cried out. Children teased and mocked the poor man's suffering. His anguish was their entertainment.

With the crack of a whip, Metlok screamed in agony. "Ah!" he shrieked. "Please...make it stop, General," he sobbed, "make it stop!"

The flogger delivered another lash to the suspended victim, cleaving flesh from his body. Blood poured from open wounds.

Captain Metlok's arms were secured to the gallows' crossbeam above his head, his feet dangling over the ground. According to the list of enumerated crimes, he was being disciplined for inciting a rebellion against Supreme General Guan. Most likely he would not survive the punishment.

Guan sneered, "You tell me, Metlok, which is worse?" He motioned for the flogger to stop.

Metlok's shirtless torso was bloody. He wailed, "Please...General... forgive me!" Open gashes on his front and back were exposed. His raw wounds looked fresher than a newly butchered calf. Over forty lashes had ripped his body to shreds. Swinging like a pendulum, he blabbered, "I'll never disagree with you again, sir." Metlok struggled to breathe, each raggedy breath more labored than the previous one.

Approaching Metlok, Guan grabbed a handful of his hair. He yanked back on the tuft and asked, "Which is worse?" His lip twitched. "Disagreeing with me in public or enduring your punishment?" He flung Metlok's head forward, spitting on him. "When I give an order, you obey it." He slapped Metlok across the face. "There is nothing for you to think about, or question," he snarled. "Godsdammit! You follow my orders without hesitation." Moving away from Metlok, Guan motioned for the flogger to strike the defenseless man again.

Instantly, the whip snapped through the air. Metlok howled, "Ah! Gods, help me...gods, help me!"

Grunting, the flogger paused, adjusting his grip on the weapon.

Pleading for mercy, Metlok rasped, "Mog…Kill me, Mog…end my suffering." His body hung limply from the ropes, swaying to and fro. Metlok looked at the man peeling flesh from his bones, seeking empathy.

Mog's eyes were compassionless, but he stopped and looked at Guan.

Metlok's glassy-eyed gaze turned to Guan. "I only asked…why we keep…sending troops to the other kingdoms?" he wheezed. "I wasn't leading a revolt against you. I didn't question your authority…or your ability to make decisions." Exhaustion and dehydration were taking hold of him. "General…or supreme general, or my king…or glorious dictator… whatever you want us to call you…I've never questioned your ability to lead this kingdom…until now." He found a moment of strength. "You are a plague to this land. You won't rest until you have destroyed us all, and all of Caporesso." A weak smile crossed his face.

Enraged, Guan screamed, "You miserable bastard!" He snatched the whip from Mog and shoved him off the gallows. Mercilessly, he scourged Metlok. After several minutes of incessant beating, Metlok appeared to take his last breath, his head falling backwards. Guan refused to stop. Incensed beyond words, he continued flogging Metlok until the man's arm ripped from his body. Metlok's lifeless body thudded to the blood-soaked ground. Only then did he stop.

Guan dropped the whip. With his black tunic's sleeve, he wiped the sweat from his forehead. Coldly, he shouted, "Apparently this demonstration is over." From the gallows platform, he addressed the crowd. "I hope you wenches have enjoyed the spectacle!"

The southern women hollered and hooted their approval.

Relishing their bloodlust, Guan chortled evilly. He shouted orders at the soldiers, "Return to the garrisons and continue preparing for the journey. With this diversion over we can get back to planning our assault against Cenkin." Looking at the faces watching him, he cautioned, "Hopefully there will be no further distractions to deal with." He nodded at his captains to execute his orders.

Captain Moto shouted, "All right, you maggots, you heard the general. Back to the garrisons." He pointed at the soldiers, his mail shirt jingling under his black tunic. "Move it!"

"Get moving, you leicans, or you'll end up like Metlok." barked Captain Druvl. "Understand?" He drew his broadsword from his double wrapped belt, waving it threateningly

The men sprang into action, heading to their predetermined destinations. The preparations for the invasion were almost complete. Securing supplies for the journey was the only remaining task. By morning, everything would be ready.

Slowly, the women and children retired from the area, laughing as they went their different ways. Children lingered, pretending to whip their friends with sticks.

In silence, Moto watched Guan withdraw from the courtyard. "He's impressive, Druvl, isn't he?"

Druvl nodded in agreement, "Yes he is. He's definitely the most feared man in Sokin. No rival will dare challenge his leadership for many years, probably decades. At the first hint of dissension, another man will be killed."

"In fact, Guan may kill someone just to set an example, even without real cause," admitted Moto. "He might send a message before someone gets the idea to question his power."

"It certainly would prevent anyone from even thinking about it," acknowledged Druvl. "Metlok's punishment was brutal, and it was administered without dithering,"

They turned and walked towards the ready room where the final arrangements for tomorrow's expedition were taking place.

"And to think, Metlok was his most trusted friend and adviser. I guess one's position should never be taken for granted," Moto remarked.

The two men crossed the bailey, walking away from Brika'cong. Soldiers moved along different paths. Dozens returned to the wall, taking the next watch. Some carried saddles to the livery. Others carried crates filled with supplies to a corral. Sokin was alive with activity, the anticipation of the next day almost palpable.

"Metlok and Guan had been friends since childhood, and he served under Guan's command for almost five years." Druvl shook his head. "I think the man is truly heartless," he said. "It's glorious, isn't it? I'm surprised it took him seven years before supplanting Markan as ruler in the winter of two hundred and thirty four of the Second Age. Now no one would dare oppose him."

"I know *I'll* never voice a disagreement with him, in private or otherwise. My opinions will safely remain my own." Moto stopped when they neared the wooden door of the ready room.

The single-story stone and timber building was twenty feet wide by forty feet long. Shaker shingles covered the roof. The Sokin soldiers used it to prepare battle plans and discuss travel routes. Today was no different. The sound of men talking and laughing escaped the building from the window openings. Iron shutters adorned the space outside the windows, and spindly vines climbed chaotically up the walls.

Moto and Druvl eavesdropped on the soldiers inside.

"We are the greatest warriors in all of Caporesso," a proud soldier boasted. "There is no other region like the south. Those cowards from the north hide inside their mountain halls. They have no honor or aptitude for greatness." He laughed, "They spend their time in darkness, with sheep and goats." A raucous chorus of laughs followed. "I'd wager one warrior from Sokin could crush ten so-called soldiers from Norkin. They are a pathetic lot."

Another spoke with contempt. "The whelps from the Central Kingdom are no better. They are physically weak and dimwitted. They're simple proletarians, waiting to be conquered. Soon we will oblige them, and it won't matter if they hide behind their wall. We'll smash it down and march into that wretched city." He chuckled. "I will enjoy tossing prisoners from the top of the wall." Applause and more laughter followed.

"We are the only ones with a vision of the future," began a third soldier. "One country united under the banner of the Southern Kingdom will be celebrated throughout the land. It's Guan's destiny to rule over a unified country. And with our new war machines, we will make it so in no time at all!" he boomed.

A fourth man spoke, "No longer will their wall thwart our efforts. We have marched to Cenkin without victory for the last time!" They all cheered. "No longer will we encamp around that city and remain idle. I've endured four campaigns over the last four years, and never killed anyone. They just hide behind that wall like women!" he yelled. "Our catapults will persuade them to fight us. They will indeed!"

"Our enemy this time won't be livestock and crops. No disrespect to Guan," advised a fifth soldier, "it's not his fault they hide, but I'm tired of destroying everything around Cenkin. I enjoy the spoils that we steal from them, but there is no honor in herding sheep and buffalo home to Sokin. There is no glory in transporting their grains and vegetables back either. Ah...how I long for the chance to fight a man from Cenkin."

"You'd have a better chance of finding a whore in a cloister for Hestia than a man in Cenkin!" shouted the first man.

Even Moto and Druvl laughed at the remark. They moved from the window and entered the building. The group of fifty men stood at attention. Moto waved a hand, "As you were. Is everything ready for tomorrow, Sinq?" he inquired, removing his ceremonial cape.

A soldier took their capes, hanging them on hooks. Only Guan wore the garment daily. He liked the way it enhanced his fearsome aura.

"Yes, sir," the man answered. "The last of the supplies are stored, and the catapults are ready to travel." He pointed to the far side of the building. The large double door was open to corral beyond. Moto could see the dozen catapults they had constructed over the last several years. With these weapons in their possession, they would batter down the walls of Cenkin and gain access to the city. *At last!*

Sinq walked with Druvl and Moto towards the squadron of catapults. Druvl said, "Cenkin's walls will be no match for those. It doesn't matter if we attack from the north, south, east, or west. Either they will pound the walls to dust or turn those gigantic doors into splinters."

Moto shook his head in agreement, "The once *impenetrable* walled city of Cenkin will be breached," he derided. "I'll bet they..."

A man from inside the compound shouted a command.

Chapter 20

A soldier from the ready room barked an order, "Detachment... attention!" Everyone turned around to see Guan cross the threshold. They saluted him and shouted in unison, "Strength of swords, honor in victory!"

With a wave of his hand, Guan acknowledged them. "Continue," was all he said. His gaze searched the room for someone. *Where are they?* When he saw Moto and Druvl in the corral, he motioned for them to join him.

Together, the three men exited the building and walked across the dusty yard. Hours of training on the grounds had reduced the grass to sand, watered with the blood of warriors from Sokin. He was proud of his soldiers and their abilities.

Guan was in his mid twenties and wore the scars of a battle-hardened man. He was over six feet tall and carried extra muscle on his large frame. He was not overweight, no, far from it. Guan's size was the epitome of a powerful one-man war machine. His intimidating presence spawned fear in the hearts of their enemies.

The black uniform he wore was similar to that of the army. He wore a mid-arm length riveted chain mail shirt under a tunic. The shiny mail stopped mid-thigh while the tunic finished below his knee. On the tunic was the image of a hooded serpent, its venomous fangs barred. Leather boots and a cape completed his uniform. Red feathered skull epaulets adorned his cape, adding to his menacing appearance. The mail gauntlets he normally wore were tucked into his double wrapped belt.

His impressive broadsword hung easily from his waist. Its two-tone blade looked like the union of the familiar willow-leaf-shaped sword and a cleaver. The intimidating blade was much wider than its contemporaries, the width beginning at the crossguard and extending through the tip of the weapon. The slight curve of the blade continued through the handle, tilting it in the opposite direction. The sword was forty-eight inches long with a fourteen-inch handle. The cord-wrapped handle had a single-edged dagger hidden inside it. On top of the blade were seven rings, which made an eerie clanging noise when Guan wielded the weapon in battle.

Brute strength was his most vicious tactic. With his frenetic energy, few opponents could withstand a barrage from his sword for very long. His agility was impressive for a man of his size. Devastating leg kicks and powerful hand techniques assisted him in overcoming his foes. The gods seemed to have forged him for the single purpose of destroying life.

"The years without war have been slowly destroying our way of life," he lectured Moto and Druvl. "The crops we grow sustain us, but do not provide us with anything in abundance. We flourish based on the materiel we plunder form the other kingdoms. My proletarians relished the multitude of grains from the Central Kingdom. The gangs of elk from the north were a staple of their diet for decades. The herds of okapi from the east were a delicacy I thoroughly enjoyed. We have struggled to find replacements for the luxuries we have lost."

He stopped and turned, looking at Moto and Druvl. "We have the opportunity to replenish what has long been amiss. Our new war machines, our catapults, will finally lay waste to that wall around Cenkin. My warriors will crush their pathetic excuse for an army in a day, and we will be victorious.

The spoils of war will be ours again." Grimacing, he boasted. "Hogeland's days are numbered as king of the Central Kingdom." He grinned wickedly. "After I murdered his father and sons, I thought for sure he would march out and meet us." Shaking his head, he admitted, "I underestimated the cowardice at work in his heart. But now, five years later, he cannot escape me." Thinking about the proposition of Hogeland's death made him grin broadly. "I am anxious to see his head mounted on a Sokin spear."

Moto took the opportunity to speak, "Allow me and my men to storm the breach first, General. I promise to present his head to you as you desire." He bowed deeply, awaiting a reply.

Before Guan could respond, Druvl interjected, "But, sire, you know my men and I long to be your instrument of war. Release us upon those cowards and I will reward you with a mighty gift." He bowed as well.

Guan chuckled, "My captains. You both serve me well and will be rewarded." Looking at each of their faces, he assured them, "On the day we break through the wall, you may enter the city together. See that your rivalry in combat never manifests itself away from the battlefield. Consider yourselves as brothers, sworn to fight side by side. Do not let jealousy undermine your camaraderie. In battle, you only have each other to look to for help. Do you understand?" he asked them.

Druvl answered first, "Sire, Moto and I only wish to serve at your pleasure. There never has been, nor will be any animosity between us."

"That is the truth, General," Moto agreed. "We're loyal to you, the army, and each other. Nothing can destroy those bonds."

"Good." Guan nodded with approval. He started walking towards Castle Brika'cong again. "I wanted to ascertain your opinions concerning Metlok's replacement. I thought Tyr would make a fine captain. What are your thoughts?"

Both men looked at each other, trying to keep stride with Guan. "He would make a fine captain, sire," replied Moto.

"I can think of none better," answered Druvl.

Guan nodded in silence. *Just as I thought, they would have agreed with anyone I nominated. No matter, that is at should be. No dissent from anyone... over anything.* "Very well, bring him to the castle this evening, and I will promote him to the position." He sneered, "Tomorrow, we begin our journey to Cenkin for the last time. It should be noted that this spring, of two hundred and forty of the Second Age, will be Cenkin's last under King

Hogeland. Soon, it will be mine. Remember this time so that you will cherish our future more dearly," he boomed.

Moto and Druvl sneered at the thought of conquering Cenkin. They joined Guan in his laughter. The three men laughed loudly for several minutes. When it subsided, Moto and Druvl silently saluted Guan and took their leave. They knew tomorrow would be the start of a new future for all of Caporesso.

Chapter 21

Fourteen months had passed quickly since Mervekka invited Aacrel to join her and Hogeland on their mission to build a better way of life for the citizens of the Central Kingdom. In 240 SA, the fresh air of late spring blew gently. Remnants of its coolness washed over the land. The hills looked alive as the mantle of grass danced like waves upon the shores of the Lho'mon.

They were slowly making progress. The people had listened to Hogeland's words and not rebelled against him. Mervekka had explained that changing the identity of the kingdom would take time. New policies were needed. New ways of using the army were also necessary. Patience was required to embrace the peaceful doctrine.

Aacrel's soldiers continued to patrol the outlying lands and protect the frontier settlements. They maintained their daily regimen of training and riding sorties. Day after day was the same. The patrols normally reported no contact with the north, and only sporadic activity from the south, but today was different. Just after midday, scouts returned to Aacrel's headquarters just north of the Lho'mon River with troubling news.

"General Aacrel!" Subto frantically saluted.

Aacrel looked up from the table where he was seated. "Yes, Subto, what is it?"

"General, I observed riders from the north!" he pointed. "A cavalry force over a thousand strong, sir. Heading this way! We've evacuated the people from the villages, and they are moving towards Cenkin. They should be here by tomorrow night." He was out of breath.

The report was disconcerting; the Northern Kingdom had been quiet for so long that some people in Cenkin believed their days of war were over. A force of one thousand men was nothing to ignore. That many men could only mean one thing, "Subto, are the northmen attacking as they approach?"

"No, sir, they're just riding at a walk. It's like they're pushing us ahead of them. They're in no hurry to engage anyone, sir."

Aacrel thought for a moment. *Could it possibly mean something else?* Standing up, he walked over to Subto. "Good work. Continue escorting the people back to Cenkin. How long has the caravan been on the move?"

"Two days, sir," his breathing returned to normal. "There aren't enough horses for everyone to ride."

Aacrel nodded. "Ride back to the caravan and give the men this order, 'Do not engage the enemy.' If they wanted to attack at speed and obliterate your convoy, they would have done so already. That is not their purpose. I must draft a report and send it to Cenkin to advise the king. I will follow you soon and join you on the road."

"Yes, sir." Subto saluted and exited the tent.

Aacrel returned to his desk and wrote a report for Hogeland. As he finished it, another messenger burst into his tent.

"General, General!" the man was very dusty, unlike Subto. Aacrel did not recognize him. "Trooper Smitkel reporting, sir," he stood at attention.

"At ease, trooper. Give your report."

"An army is approaching Cenkin, sir. It's at least ten thousand strong and headed—"

"Trooper, I have already received a report of an invading army. It was reported as only one thousand men." Aacrel looked skeptical. "Are your numbers accurate?"

"Yes, sir. They are moving slowly but should be at the walls within a week," he was breathing hard from the ride.

"A week? Subto's report said they would arrive by tomorrow night. Why the discrepancy in the speed of this cavalry force?"

Smitkel looked confused. "Cavalry, sir? They have some, but the main body is infantry."

"Subto reported a force of one thousand cavalry from the north." Aacrel crossed his arms. "How can you—"

"They're from the south, sir," Smitkel interrupted. "The army I'm reporting is coming from Sokin. We've seen General Guan's banner flying at the head of the column. They are coming to attack. They have strange new weapons in their midst. Several large machines and we have no idea what their purpose is."

Aacrel stood up and leaned on the table. *An army from the north and south at the same time?* Cenkin would be surrounded by their enemies. "Return to your unit. Evacuate as many people as you can, Smitkel. Get everyone out before Guan catches them. Move everyone to Cenkin as fast as you can."

"Sir, the surviving villagers have already entered Cenkin. They saw the army coming and fled. The southerners are destroying the villages as they advance," he made a quizzical face, "but they are not going after the people yet. I don't understand why." He coughed. "From our southern outpost, we saw flames climbing into the sky and rode to investigate. It took me a while to find your camp here, sir. Our scouts are patrolling and keeping an eye on the advancing army. We're too outnumbered to attack, but are monitoring their activity sir."

"Good work, Smitkel. Return to your outfit with this order, 'Avoid contact with the advancing army at all costs.' If Guan is there, he means to attack Cenkin." He tapped his temple. "And try to find out what those new weapons are for. Return to your unit. Go."

Smitkel saluted. "Yes, sir."

Could this really be happening? The Northern Kingdom and the Southern Kingdom were bringing war to Cenkin at the same time. Two armies from two kingdoms, on the fields around a city had not happened for eons.

The southern army was advancing more slowly. He thought about a plan of defense. Aacrel decided to ride north and determine the intentions of the northern cavalry. There would still be time to return to Cenkin and see to the defenses of the city.

"Orderly, come here." Aacrel added information to his report. *I will return to Cenkin in two days to prepare for the advancing southern army. Safeguard as much of the herds as possible. For now, I must see what the northern cavalry holds in store for us.* He folded the paper and handed it to the orderly. "Take that to King Hogeland immediately."

The man saluted and departed. Aacrel sat for a moment, thinking about possibly defending the city from two enemies at the same time. *I cannot believe any man from the north would join forces with a man like Guan. The north has been idle for so long; I wonder what they are planning. A cavalry force of one thousand men will never breach our wall, and they know that. I cannot believe they are coming to support Guan.* He shook his head. *What are they doing?*

The only way to discern their purpose was to ride north and find Subto's men. He walked out of his tent and called to the men around him. "Soldiers, strike the camp. We are riding north to investigate an advancing cavalry regiment. Only take what we need, leave the rest. We will not return to this position for some time." Facing north, he added, "Time is of the essence; we must ride within the hour."

Chapter 22

Terikk and Pak rode at the head of the column as they moved through the Central Kingdom. It was a beautiful land with lush fields of grass and scattered groves of blossoming trees all around them. The spring winds brought the fresh smell of wild hyacinths and ling heather. Terikk closed his eyes, remembering the aromas. It had been years since he last rode this far south. He was surprised at how much he had missed the landscape.

The column stopped to rest their horses. "My king, I would estimate we are about two days away from Cenkin. Would you agree, sire?" Pak asked.

Since Terikk's ascension to the throne of the Northern Kingdom, he had worked towards this day. It took three years, but finally in 240 SA, he convinced the people that it was necessary to try and form an alliance with the other kingdoms in order to maintain peace. Without a treaty in place, the possibility of hostilities with marauding soldiers still existed. Meeting face to face with the other kings, and discussing alternatives to war was the only way to ensure their new way of life. They would start in Cenkin.

"Yes I do. We have not encountered any villages for the last several days, so I would say we are within reach of Cenkin. By tomorrow night at the latest, we should be there." Terikk did not know what would happen after they arrived. He knew a thousand men on horses looked like an invading force and not an emissary on a mission of peace.

"Sire, what do you think is going to happen when we arrive at Cenkin? I mean, do you think anyone will really believe we want peace?"

"I do not know," he sighed. "If we meet someone dedicated to war, I fear he will not believe us." He shifted his weight in his saddle, looking around the countryside. "But if we encounter a reasonable man, a good man, who hears what we say and can ignore the past, then maybe. Maybe he will listen."

Pak was silent for a moment and then asked, "Do you think they know we're here, sire. I mean riding south, towards Cenkin." He pointed ahead of them and said, "The villagers are fleeing to Cenkin, and probably have arrived. Undoubtedly they will have informed them of our existence." Shaking his head, he said. "But we still haven't observed any troop movement. Surely they would engage us and determine our intentions if they were near. Right, sire?"

"They know we are here, Pak. Make no mistake, they know we are here." Terikk scanned from side to side, looking for signs of soldiers from Cenkin.

"Then why haven't they appeared, sire?"

"I would conclude that they do not know what we are doing. They are confused by our actions, or should I say, lack of them." He glanced at Pak. "History recounts how our raiders would overwhelm their villages at full speed. Killing everyone and burning everything." Terikk waved his hand in a circle. "This is the largest cavalry unit ever organized from the north, yet our horses are walking south. We have not attacked anyone, and have not razed any villages. We caught them off guard, and they do not understand our intentions." As his gaze turned to the east, something caught his eye. There was movement on the crest of a hill, about three hundred yards southeast of their location. Terikk nodded his head, "Over there, Pak, are the men from Cenkin. They are watching us from a distance. We will continue due south and let them come to us when they are ready."

As both men were looking southeast, riders emerged from a grove of white pines less than two hundred feet from their position. An alarm rang out from among the men of the Tu'nide. "Riders southwest! Riders southwest!" The men quickly mounted their horses, getting into formation.

Terikk and Pak turned to see twenty men on horses emerging onto the road ahead. The small grove had hidden the riders until they wanted to be seen. One of the men was positioned further ahead than the others.

He must be in charge. "Pak, ride forward with me. We must meet these men." He glanced over his shoulder. "Voleg, keep our men here. Deploy them in ranks," he waved his hand along the ridge they occupied, "but do not advance."

"Yes, sire. But what if they turn out to be hostile in nature, sire?" inquired Voleg.

Terikk tilted his head, "Pray to the gods that they are not hostile. Stay here and prepare the men. Do not move without a signal from me. That is my order."

Turning around, he regarded Pak. Leaning closer, Pak quietly asked, "But what if they *are* hostile in nature, my king?"

He chuckled and touched his bastard sword hanging from his horse, "Just keep smiling, Pak. No one gets angry when you smile." Terikk coaxed his horse forward, riding towards the waiting group of men.

Chapter 23

"Are you sure this is a good idea, General Aacrel? I mean we're kinda exposed and outnumbered." Subto pointed at the long line of northern cavalry, not more than two hundred feet away.

"We will be fine, Subto." Aacrel glanced at him, simpering. "Just don't make any sudden movements towards your sword." He observed two northmen riding to meet them. "All right, Subto, nice and easy. It is time to meet these invaders."

Aacrel spurred Din, his faithful bay courser, forward. They rode until they were within a perch of the unknown men from the north. Holding up a hand, Aacrel addressed them, "I am General Aacrel, commander of the Central Kingdom Army. You are trespassing on these lands, and your presence is not welcomed or solicited. You have disturbed our citizens, forcing them to abandon their homes and seek shelter inside Cenkin." Motioning at the line of northmen, he said, "You must know this force will never breach our walls." Aacrel pointed north. "Turn your men around and head home."

The man across the way responded. "General Aacrel, I am honored to make your acquaintance." Bowing his head, he said, "Your reputation precedes you, sir. They say you are a reasonable man." He spoke with confidence.

"I know what I am about, friend." Aacrel did not appreciate the flattery. "Who are you?"

"I am Terikk, king of the Northern Kingdom. Pardon our presence in your land, but we have not come for war. The fact that we have not destroyed the villages we passed should indicate the truth of my words." He looked at the man beside Aacrel. "We could have attacked and slaughtered your people, but did not. We are not here to send men to the graveyards, or set them alight on pyres," he stated. "The Boatman does not need more mangled men; we have sent enough to him already. What we desire is peace between our two great kingdoms." Terikk met Aacrel's gaze. "Will you hear our proposal?"

Subto almost fell off his horse.

Aacrel was shocked at the words he heard. "I too have heard of you, King Terikk. People say you possess many qualities, but telling deceitful lies was never mentioned as one of them, *my liege*," he mocked. "Why would you start today?"

Terikk shook his head. "General Aacrel, I am not deceiving you." His horse whinnied and fidgeted. "We are here to try to negotiate peace between our people. We have not engaged in open war for many years, but the threat still looms. There are those from Norkin and Nurdug who seek an agreement with the Central Kingdom, stating that neither kingdom will go to war with the other." He paused. "A mutual, unofficial armistice has existed for years. We want to make it more," Terikk tilted his head, "permanent."

Pak's smile never wavered.

Aacrel understood how a declaration affirming peace would be pragmatic. For all practical purposes, the north and central regions were already at peace. "You know, King Terikk," Din nickered and moved around restlessly, "had you have come here two years ago, with your same message and purpose, I probably would have sent you away." Aacrel chuckled to himself and shook his head. "Circumstances are different now...better for both of us I think." He steadied his horse and looked at Terikk. "You will find people in Cenkin willing to listen to your ideas, people searching for peace, and I...am one of them."

Pak's smile vanished when his mouth fell open. The shock of Aacrel's words was almost too much for him.

Terikk looked at Pak, slapping him on the arm; his smile returned.

"King Hogeland and Lady Mervekka are two others who desire peace for our people," continued Aacrel. "If we can secure it by establishing an agreement with you, then so be it."

Terikk opened his mouth. "I told you they would be reasonable, Pak," he joked.

"Uh…" Pak was speechless. He had expected yelling and cursing in their immediate direction. He had feared they would be chased out of the region. Actually finding a man willing to discuss peace had been furthest from his mind. "Yes, sire, you said they would be." He sighed, "I'm glad you were right."

"General Aacrel, we rode—"

"King Terikk," Aacrel interrupted, "we are both commanders who know each other's reputation. Can we dispense with our titles when speaking? I am Aacrel," he extended his hand.

Terikk nudged his horse closer, moving alongside Aacrel. He grasped Aacrel's forearm. "And I am Terikk." They shook heartily. "I believe I have found a *good* man from the Central Kingdom."

"You have, Terikk. And I believe you are an honest man from the north. Together, I hope we can create something for our people that has never existed before…" Aacrel's voice trailed off. The thought was so strange that he dare not utter the word aloud.

"Peace, Aacrel…peace." Terikk released his arm. "I cannot say it will be easy. The history between our kingdoms is one of violence and destruction. We are embarking upon a journey that has no guide. Mistakes will be made, but hopefully they will not undermine our true intentions." His horse moved nervously. "I was going to explain the presence of our cavalry," he motioned over his shoulder.

Aacrel raised an eyebrow. "Yes, go ahead."

"We know your walls cannot be breached. Our army is incapable of smashing down the gates, and we reasoned a cavalry force would appear less imposing. But in case we were not received hospitably, we wanted the mobility of being able to ride away for our own protection. Yet, we wanted a force large enough that it would not invite sorties from your army. Our force of one thousand men seemed like a reasonable solution."

Aacrel nodded his head. "It worked. Our soldiers observed your column days ago, but were outnumbered and would not engage you. As a result, there have been no casualties for either side. Well done, Terikk."

"Thank you...Now to our terms of peace, can we set up camps here," he pointed around them, "and hold discussions until we arrive at an acceptable solution?"

Aacrel shook his head. "Other events are unfolding as we speak, so I must decline your invitation. I wish to do as you suggest, but at this time cannot. An army from the south led by General Guan is advancing towards Cenkin. Reports are that he brings new war machines to our city. I am afraid I must return and prepare for the defense of the city." He looked south for a moment, then back at Terikk, "Perhaps you should return to Norkin for now. When our fight with Guan is resolved, I will send word to you that we can meet here again and hold those discussions."

Terikk sat silently for a moment, thinking. "Just when our two societies are about to discuss terms for peace, Guan appears. He will ruin everything." He hung his head, sighing, "What do you think his machines do?"

"We have no idea. My guess is that he believes they can destroy the wall, but for now, it is only a guess."

"The walls or the gates." His horse danced around. "Our people respect you as warriors, but if Guan's army breaches the wall, your city will fall," Terikk warned.

"I know, I know. We may be forced to march out and fight, like the days of old. One army facing another terrible army." He looked skyward and shook his fist, "Will the gods of war let us find peace, or do they set their wills against us on purpose? Agh!" he shouted. "I must return to Cenkin and formulate a battle plan. May the gods bless you with a safe journey home, Terikk." Din blustered. "Until we meet again, be safe." Aacrel walked his horse backwards a few steps and was turning around when Terikk called to him.

"Aacrel, a few more minutes of your time will not affect your defense of the city." Terikk held out a hand, beckoning Aacrel to wait a little longer. "Give me a few more minutes."

"All right, what else is on your mind?" Aacrel asked.

Terikk motioned for Pak to move away so he could not hear their words. Aacrel saw the dismissal and sent Subto back to join their own troops.

"I talked about peace between our kingdoms." Terikk spoke with certitude. "We want peace, and it seems as though your people do as well. However, it appears Guan does not. I do not mean this as an insult to your people, but if Guan succeeds in destroying Cenkin, any chance of ending hostilities dies along with it." He sounded hopeful, "Let us negotiate an alliance—now.

"Our Tu'nide can accompany you to Cenkin and aid you in your battle against Guan." He motioned at the line of men behind him, "One thousand men on horseback could provide you with a tactical advantage. My men plus your army and cavalry might be enough to shift the tide of the battle to your favor." His horse nickered. "There would be a chance that we could eliminate the advantage of his new weapons by attacking them at speed and destroying them...If Guan will not allow us to establish permanent peace between our people, then let us form a temporary alliance to keep your people safe. What say you, Aacrel?"

"I know your horsemen are the most skilled in the land. Your Tu'nide would save many Cenkinian lives." He shrugged his shoulders. "But what do you seek to gain?" Aacrel asked. "You have offered to risk your men's lives to defend Cenkin. What do you want in return for this...alliance?" He sounded skeptical.

"If you are destroyed, our dreams die along with yours," he said bluntly. "If you are conquered, Guan will let his army heal their wounds, and ultimately march north to continue his conquest. His quest for power will either destroy all of us, or unite us in purpose." He looked at the ground and shook his head. "What do I want in return?" Terikk looked into Aacrel's eyes, "An end to war. And if the only way to achieve that is to assist you in the defense of Cenkin, then so be it. Will you accept our aid?"

Aacrel did not need to think very long before answering, "Terikk, I would be honored to fight at your side. Maybe together in battle we can conjure the design for solidarity. Maybe shedding blood together will create the bonds of friendship our two nations have never shared."

Calling to Pak, Terikk instructed him to send four riders to Norkin. They were to inform his advisers of their intention to form a temporary pact with the Central Kingdom. Then together, they would fight Guan and the southern army. After the battle, Terikk and Aacrel would begin the peace process. Pak left to issue Terikk's orders.

Terikk and Aacrel smiled in spite of what lay ahead. Even though they were going to battle side by side, they believed the first building blocks of peace had been laid. Their meeting was a good one.

Aacrel extended his hand to Terikk again. "Strength of swords..."

Terikk firmly grasped his new friend's arm. "Honor in victory."

Together Terikk's Tu'nide and Aacrel's detachment rode for Cenkin. They moved at a trot, hoping to reach the city by midday of the next day. Aacrel simpered to himself. *King Hogeland and Lady Mervekka will be very surprised by what I am bringing back with me.*

Chapter 24

The night of their third day together, Terikk was invited to a stately dinner with King Hogeland in Castle Trosho. The luxurious dining hall could have held at least two hundred guests, but this evening, only four people were invited. Two-story stained glass windows lined three walls of the peninsula-like room, allowing the remaining daylight to illuminate the space.

Terikk was given the opportunity to survey the grand room. Asymmetrical rocks from the Lho'mon were used in the thirty-foot-high walls. Oak columns and scissor trusses supported the vaulted ceiling. Portraits of the line of kings hung on the walls. Larger than life marble statues of heroes from Cenkin's past lined the walls, the most impressive figures being those of Thro'ce and Leshliac. Elegant candelabras, eight feet tall, were interspersed with the statues, adding brilliance to the room.

He was impressed at the opulence displayed before him. Norkin and Nurdug were more elemental in their décor. He spoke to Aacrel, "Was this room and its lavish decorations meant to impress and humble your guests?"

"When it was built many centuries ago," Aacrel replied, "yes, that was its purpose. Today, this room sees few visitors." He shook his head, "We have not received an emissary from another kingdom for many generations. You are the first outsider to see this room in a long time." He sighed, "In a very long time."

"The statues of Leshliac and Thro'ce are some of the most impressive stone sculptures I have ever seen. The detail in the faces, their anguish is almost palpable." He reached up to touch Lesliac's sword, but stopped.

"There used to be an old poem about their battle, but I forget it now," admitted Aacrel.

Terikk continued admiring the statues in silence. After a moment, he asked, "What kind of madness could bring two brothers to fight to the death?"

Aacrel shook his head, but did not offer a reply.

Doors at the far end of the room opened and several servants entered carrying many platters of food. All at once, the smoky aroma of a freshly roasted okapi filled the room. The okapi was followed by something that looked like buffalo ribs. Bowls of watercress, radishes, and artichokes accompanied the meal. Terikk and Aacrel left the stone heroes and walked to the table.

"Ah…it all smells wonderful," Terikk commented. "I have not eaten like this in a long time." He sniffed again, "Umm, I cannot remember the last time I tasted fresh okapi."

"Nor I, my friend," admitted Aacrel. "This type of meal is reserved for the king and his cabinet. Today is a special day for all of us here in Cenkin." He put a hand on a high-back chair at the table. "We will continue the conversation that we started with King Hogeland from yesterday. But for now," he held his arms out over the food, "we will be well fed."

A new commotion at the far end of the room drew their attention. King Hogeland entered and headed straight for them. He nodded at Terikk, "Pardon my lateness, gentlemen. I was looking for the adviser I told you about last night, Terikk." He stepped to the side, revealing a young woman behind him.

She moved closer to Terikk and curtsied. He gasped, almost paralyzed.

"I would like to introduce Lady Mervekka." Hogeland motioned between the two of them. "Mervekka, this is King Terikk of the northern realm. He comes to us with a proposition that I believe you will be interested in hearing."

"It is an honor to make your acquaintance, King Terikk." She bowed her head slightly. "Aacrel has briefed me as to your purpose, and I am interested in speaking with you at great length." Her lips tightened at the corners as she looked Terikk over.

Terikk barely heard a word she said. She was so breathtakingly beautiful that he had difficulty forming words, "I...umm...ah...I am..." Sensing everyone looking at him, he managed to say, "It is I who am honored, Lady Mervekka." He glanced at Aacrel, seeking assistance from his new friend.

Aacrel sensed Terikk's quandary and intervened, "I do not mean to be presumptuous, sire, but the food smells delicious, and Terikk and I have not eaten much today." He asked Hogeland, "May we sit and enjoy this glorious feast?"

Hogeland laughed, "Of course, of course. You are right, Aacrel. Let us sit and eat while the meal is still hot. We can talk over supper." He motioned for everyone to sit down. He sat at the head of the long table, a wall of westerly windows at his back. The waning rays of daylight entered through the well placed windows, bathing the room in light. Mervekka sat to Hogeland's right and Aacrel at his left. Terikk took the seat next to Aacrel.

Terikk watched as the servants helped pass the platters from person to person. At least ten young women served them. The blonds and brunettes wore conservative short-sleeved dresses, revealing little, while accentuating their curves. The vertical lines of the outfits made the girls appear taller and more slender than the women of the north. They blushed as Terikk watched them work.

Each dinner guest filled their plates with meat and vegetables, and began eating. For several minutes, the only sound was that of knives and forks scraping over pewter plates; the silence became awkward.

Aacrel chuckled, "I think everyone is just a little too tense right now. At the moment, we all appear to be on the same side. Let us talk amongst ourselves as friends." He looked at one of the servers, "More ale and wine," and smiled. "Come now, Mervekka, talk with Terikk."

Surprised, they both looked up from their plates. Aacrel looked at Terikk, raising an eyebrow.

Terikk looked intensely at his new friend. He stole a glance at Mervekka, then addressed Hogeland, "King Hogeland, is there—"

"King Terikk," he interrupted, "there is no need for our titles any longer. As long as you do not mind, may we dispense with them?"

Nodding, Terikk continued, "All right, Hogeland. Is there any news of Guan and his approaching army?"

Nodding his head, Hogeland crunched a watercress. "Yes, Terikk, there is some. My scouts estimate that his army will be here no earlier than four days from now. We have time to discuss defenses and prepare a battle plan," he said, sounding supremely confident. "We do not need to discuss that tonight over supper."

A dozen servers returned with jugs of wine and pitchers of ale. They filled the men's mugs with a type of ale. Mervekka accepted a tall goblet of a greenish yellow liquid that Terikk was not familiar with.

Hogeland picked up his mug and gulped the beverage. "Aww. That doppelbock is from a good barrel. Would you agree, Terikk?"

Terikk grasped his mug and drank from it. "Hmm, Hogeland, this is good. I have never tasted anything like it before. It is very…malty," he licked his lips and smelled the air, "with a chocolaty aroma of some kind. We do not produce anything like this in the north," he took another drink. "Yes, this is very good indeed, very filling. Do you care for the…" he looked at Mervekka and then at his mug. He chuckled, "What was it you called this, Hogeland?"

"Doppelbock," he replied.

He looked at Mervekka again, holding her eyes with his, and asked, "Do you like the doppelbock, Mervekka?" She smiled sweetly at him, and he almost choked on his beer. Her face was flawless, her features exotic. He knew she was the most beautiful woman he had ever seen. Surely she was with Aacrel, so there was no use pursuing the matter any further. Tonight, he would simply enjoy gazing upon this rare beauty.

"I do not care for ale as much as my king and Aacrel do." Both men chortled at her comment and continued eating. "At this time of year, I like a nice sauvignon blanc. Its flavor reminds me of fresh melon and vanilla." She asked inquisitively, "What types of wine do you produce in the north, Terikk?" Picking up her goblet, she sipped from it.

"I do not enjoy wine that often, but we make crimsons and alabasters." He was still looking at her perfect face. "They typically are sweeter than those you produce. I would guess that is due to our colder climate."

Mervekka carefully set her goblet on the table. Covering her mouth, she cleared her throat. "How do you know what our wine tastes like?" she asked directly.

Stumbling with his reply, Terikk said, "We have...I mean we took...I mean..."

Aacrel laughed, "Enough, Mervekka. You know how he tasted our wine. It is the same way we collected fine bottles from the north and south. Each kingdom stole them from the others." He laughed again, trying to ease the tension. "But that happened years ago," he exaggerated his words with a wave of his hand. "I believe none of us were even alive the last time such a thing occurred." Holding up his mug, he boomed, "Lucky for us, they stole a lot of it!"

Hogeland chuckled.

Everyone continued eating, only making small talk for the rest of the meal. After they finished, servants brought small glasses of a dessert wine.

Hogeland raised his glass, "Here is to a new future between our two kingdoms. May it be one filled with peace and prosperity."

"Here, here," was the reply.

Terikk sipped his wine and turned to look at Aacrel; he guffawed. Aacrel laughed as well.

"What is so funny?" demanded Mervekka.

"This wine is from the north, specifically from the city of Nurdug," replied Terikk. "It must have been...misplaced...many years ago." He grinned at her and took another sip of the delicious icewine.

The four new friends sat around the table for several more hours. The wine and ale worked its magic, just as Aacrel had hoped. Each of them was more at ease with the others. Old stories were told for the first time. Terikk learned about Aacrel and Hogeland. They all learned about Terikk. They could have laughed and talked all night, but too much wine made Mervekka grow weary.

Standing up, she addressed them, "King Hogeland, it is time for me to retire for the evening. I trust we will talk about more serious matters in the morning." She bowed her head, and then looked at Terikk. "Gentlemen," she said flatly.

Terikk and Aacrel struggled to their feet, bowing as she walked away. When she was gone, they dropped back into their chairs. After the doors closed behind her, Terikk asked, "Did I make a fool of myself all evening?"

Aacrel laughed and turned to him. "Not all of it."

Terikk smacked Aacrel's arm and laughed to himself.

"No, Terikk, you did fine. It is not the wine that made the evening difficult for you. It was Mervekka herself. She has that affect on most men; do not feel ashamed. But she was right," Aacrel cocked his head to the side, "enough for tonight. We need some rest for what we will face over the next few days. We will talk more about her later, but for now, do not worry about what transpired over supper." He stood up and called a servant to assist Hogeland from his seat.

"He is right," slurred Hogeland. "Mervekka's beauty touches every man's heart and weakens every knee. You handled yourself better than I expected." Two servants approached and helped Hogeland to his feet. He wobbled in place, "Gentlemen…" he stumbled, "I must find my bed before…" the servants steadied him, "I cannot." Holding his arms, they assisted him out of the hall.

The servants cleared away the desserts and drinks, leaving Terikk and Aacrel alone.

"Aacrel—"

He raised a hand, stopping Terikk in mid sentence. "Nothing more tonight, Terikk. I need sleep…so do you. We will meet again in the morning. Then we will plan to defend this city and continue the peace talks with Hogeland. Tonight was a good night, but tomorrow will be a better day. I feel that the gods have blessed each of us by bringing us together." He scoffed, "But enough prophecy for now, it is time for sleep." Getting up, he called another servant from an anteroom, "Show King Terikk back to his quarters." Aacrel turned and bowed to Terikk, "Goodnight, my friend. May you have pleasant dreams."

"Thank you, Aacrel, and I agree with you, tomorrow will be a good day for all of us." He returned the bow. Turning, he followed the young servant out of the dining hall, watching her hips sway as she led him to his room. They made their way through the castle corridors until arriving at Terikk's chamber.

Stepping to the side, she said, "Good night, King Terikk. May you enjoy pleasant dreams this evening." Shyly, she gazed into his eyes and giggled. Then turning around, she ran away, leaving him alone.

Closing his door, he thought about Mervekka. *Yes, I think my dreams will be good tonight. Very good indeed.*

Chapter 25

Guan rode out of the Stone Pine Forest, away from the main body of his army. The trees hid his soldiers and their catapults. It was late afternoon and the sun was going down in the west. From his position, Cenkin lay northwest, but he rode northeast. Entering the Field of Angl, he stopped in the middle. He remembered fighting there once before, when he was a much younger man, nearly still a boy. Anticipation had gripped him last time, anticipation and excitement. The other young soldiers had been scared, but not him.

He shook his head, realizing he was breathing heavily. The visions of his first battle caused his heart to beat faster. The sensation rushed through his body, making it tingle. He felt so alive during combat. The feeling gave him an advantage over all other soldiers on a battlefield. No one could stand before him and survive.

Captain Tyr rode up behind him. "General Guan, I have word from the catapult unit, sir. They say they will be through the woods by nightfall." He saluted Guan.

"Good news, Tyr. From here, I think we will send them to the eastern gate and smash it to bits. Hmm," he vocalized, thinking about entering

Cenkin for the first time. "I trust the good peasants have returned home to tell their king of our imminent approach."

"Only the ones who survived, sir," Tyr added coldly.

Guan closed his eyes. He tilted his head back and sighed, "Ah, excellent work, Tyr. I see my promotion of you had merit. Moto and Druvl both speak highly of you; make sure their support was not mistakenly given." Glowering at his new captain, he warned, "Do not fail me." Then he gazed at the walled city. "I want the entire army in position here tomorrow morning. I want those miserable cowards to look at this army and shake with fear. I want the anticipation of death ripe within them, so much so that they look forward to their own demise." He closed his eyes again. "Leave me, Tyr. I want to enjoy these visions alone."

"Yes, sir. Hyah!" Tyr saluted and rode away in haste.

Guan was alone once more. With his eyes still closed, he spoke aloud through clenched teeth, "Tomorrow, I will seize my destiny. Tomorrow, I will conquer that which could not be conquered. I will be recognized as the greatest warrior in all of Caporesso." He gripped the reins tightly and shouted for everyone to hear, "Nothing can stop me!"

Chapter 26

From the top of the wall, Terikk and Aacrel saw a lone rider enter the Field of Angl. Another man joined him for a few minutes and then departed, riding into the blackness of the Stone Pine Forest. The man was left unaccompanied again. A gust of wind carried the essence of his words; he was yelling. The two men could not discern what he was saying, but they had an idea.

"That must be Guan, trying to intimidate you, Aacrel." Terikk chuckled to himself. He rested his arm on a stone hawk, its talons outstretched.

Aacrel smirked and looked at Terikk. "He is. Remind me to be afraid tomorrow," he chortled.

Two guards approached them. They saluted to Aacrel, and continued on their patrol.

"Any reports from your scouts?" asked Terikk. He strained his eyes to try to make out the lone figure in the field.

"No word yet," he shook his head. Aacrel took a seat atop the parapet wall, unafraid of the height. He put one hand on the head of a sitting jaguar, and the other on the back of a fierce Talbot. Turning his head, he studied the man in the field.

After several minutes, the rider retired from the Field of Angl, returning to the forest. Both men gazed at the woods, silently listening to the wind.

Aacrel's hair blew into his face, but he refused to brush it away. Turning to Terikk, he asked, "What do you think of Hogeland and Mervekka?"

Terikk eyed Aacrel. He nodded, saying, "I like Hogeland's ideas so far. His words are not unappealing to me." Placing his arms behind his back, he continued. "It sounds like he and I desire the same thing for our kingdoms. Some of the specifics we have discussed are the same, and I am sure we will be able to come to terms concerning the boundaries of the northern and central realms. We already agree that we will need to establish and *enforce* laws for the people to live by; violence will not be tolerated any longer. That will be the toughest part of this alliance, keeping the people from harming each other."

"I know," agreed Aacrel. "We desire peace for the people, but not all of them wish it were so." He slapped the Talbot's backside. "We are going to ask them to forget about the thousands of years of war that have existed between our kingdoms. For some, it will not be easy. The past decade has been devoid the bloody campaigns, but people still remember death and heartache. Each kingdom blames the other for their hardships."

"Then it will be up to us to lead them past that," he said confidently. Terikk used his arms to emphasize his words. "We will have to convince them that living together is better than the old ways. It will not be easy, but it is what we must do to make this work." He touched his chest. "I know in my heart we can come to an accord that allows our people to live in peace, but first we must survive our impending confrontation with Guan."

"Ah," Aacrel waved a hand. "We will survive the battle, of that I am sure. But," Aacrel raised an eyebrow at Terikk, "you did not fully answer my question."

Terikk's brow furrowed, "What do you mean? I told you what I thought about Hogeland."

"Yes, but what of Mervekka? I asked about her, and you ignored me." He wagged a finger in front of Terikk.

Terikk's face lit up. "She seemed," he paused, trying not to smile, "nice."

"Nice? That is all you can say?" Mockingly, "*She seemed nice?* Come now, tell me the truth."

"Ah, Aacrel." He tilted his head skyward briefly. "She is the most beautiful woman I have ever met. Her dazzling eyes, her silken hair, her button nose, her delicate ears, her face, just everything about her is perfect. Then on top of that, she is the most brilliant woman I have ever encountered. Listening to her speak at dinner the other night was a delight. She is a credit to your population. My people will think better of you if only because of her.

"When she asked me a question, I had a difficult time keeping my composure. My tongue felt like it was twice its size," he chuckled at the memory, "making me sound like a fool. Her affect on me was intoxicating. I have never experienced that before, around any other woman. She is an exquisite gem." He nodded his approval of her. "I hope you and she are happy together."

"Well...why not tell me how you really feel about her." Aacrel chortled and slapped the Talbot again. "She is beautiful. I only met her for the first time about thirteen months ago. I felt the same way, overwhelmed. Since then, I now understand her ideas and convictions. Even without my support, I believe she would have won over the people. They would have followed her and Hogeland on their quest for peace. She is a remarkable woman." He waved his hand in the air, addressing Terikk's comment. "But there is no *we*, or us being happy together. She is a close friend, but nothing more." He nudged Terikk, "She is available, my friend."

"Well, I thought that...I mean...I thought you and her were a... so, you are saying you and Mervekka are not a couple?" he stammered.

Aacrel laughed, "No, Terikk, we are not. She has my love and my respect. She has my sword, no matter the numbers, no matter the outcome." He put a hand on Terikk's shoulder, "You, however, are not an enemy. Speak with confidence to her; be yourself."

Terikk shook his head, chuckling, "What kind of men are we, Aacrel? We have only known each other for a few days, yet on the eve of battle, here we sit and joke like we have known each other our entire lives. Your city is about to be attacked by an army of at least ten thousand men, commanded by a ruthless man." Pointing at the forest, he said, "They have new machines for war which we know nothing about." He slapped his thigh. "And here we are, conversing about a beautiful woman. What is wrong with us?"

"We have been in enough engagements to know every battle may be our last." Aacrel chuckled briefly. "It is better to live in the moment instead of planning for a future that may never happen." The wind gusted. "What is wrong with us?" He shook his head. "Nothing, my friend. Through our experiences, we have learned how to judge a man quickly and determine his quality, and I judge yours to be of the highest possible. Our lifetime of experiences made us friends long before we ever met."

Subto came running up the steps to the top of the wall. He continued running until he stood in front of them. Saluting, he tried to speak. "Sorry, sir, it's a…long way…up here…I've never run all the way…up here before. Wow!" He gulped for air. "The scouts have reported back, and the machines appear to hurl large rocks through the air. We've never seen anything like it before. The Southerns operated it without realizing we observed them. With a series of cranks and ropes, they retracted a reinforced basket attached to a big log," he used his arm as a prop, "into a horizontal position. With considerable difficulty, they loaded large rocks into it. Then two men pulled levers, releasing the basket. It flew forward until the log was almost vertical. The boulders continued through the air and landed about four hundred yards away. They left an impression in the ground. At that distance, they will be out of range of our archers.

"We heard them give orders to roll the *catapults* to the eastern gate and get them into position as soon as possible," he shook his head, "I don't know, sir, I don't know if the gates can withstand a bombardment from those machines. They might smash through the doors if we don't stop them first."

Aacrel nodded his head, listening to Subto's report. "Thank you, Subto. Keep this information to yourself. I do not want it to start a panic." Aacrel scratched the side of his face. "Dismissed, Subto, and…I suggest you walk down."

Subto saluted and began his descent. Aacrel paced back and forth. Terikk turned to look over the wall again. In the distance, he could see shapes moving along the tree line.

Terikk walked to the edge of the stairs and called after Subto, "How many men did you estimate in their army, Subto?"

"About ten thousand men, King Terikk. Almost all infantry. They had a small force of cavalry as well, less than one hundred horsemen, sir. We estimated ten thousand men in uniform. Our scouts believe they have around two hundred archers, but mostly regular infantry. Anything else, sir?"

"No, Subto, thank you." Terikk looked at Aacrel.

Aacrel cocked his head. "What does their number matter?"

"Guan is confident, too confident," he grinned slyly. "He has no cavalry or archers to support his troops. The catapults will be susceptible to a blitz attack." Terikk chuckled, "I think I have a plan, Aacrel." Gazing over the wall again, he grinned, "Yes...I have a plan that just might work. How do you feel about drawing swords together tomorrow, side by side?"

Aacrel nodded and extended a hand to Terikk, the two men shook heartily. He did not understand what Terikk meant, but he believed this man to be a solid tactician. Somehow, he would see them through tomorrow. Somehow, he would help them prevail against the warmongers from the south. Aacrel believed without a doubt, that this man from the north would help him protect the people of Cenkin.

Chapter 27

The morning twilight announced the new day. Guards stationed along the walls of Cenkin were in a perfect position to watch the sunrise. Shades of red and orange flooded the horizon. In that moment, the sky and land looked serene. Soon the day would unleash its horrible design upon the city. The good citizens of Cenkin could not have imagined what lay in store for them.

Aacrel and the army from the Central Kingdom moved into position on the Field of Angl during the night. Seven thousand men, armed with swords and spears, occupied the northern and eastern edges of the field, forming a right angle. His soldiers stood ready to defend their city. They had not engaged in a full-scale battle for many years, but old memories were awakened, and the men remembered their purpose; they would protect the city with their lives.

Looking southwest, Aacrel saw the first ranks of the Southern Army emerging out of the Stone Pine Forest. The fan-like canopies of the juvenile trees hid Guan's men during the night. As they left the shelter of the trees, they marched like a well-disciplined group of men. Their straight lines ran east to west. They were an impressive assembly of ten thousand.

Along the left flank of Guan's army were their new war machines. Even though Aacrel knew their intended purpose, he could not believe they would be effective. *How can rocks smash stone walls?* Terikk had talked for hours, convincing him the weapons would be successful. Together, the two men decided on a battle plan for the coming fight. Now Terikk and his Tu'nide were nowhere to be seen. The men from the Central Kingdom stood alone.

Aacrel saw the catapults in their splendor as they were dragged closer to the city. The baskets were in the upright position. Ropes were attached to the massive logs. He could see several pulleys along the length of the units. Burly Clydesdales struggled against the weight of the units. He realized Terikk was correct; these machines *could* open the doors of Cenkin to the horde of soldiers from the south.

As the army moved closer to the city, Aacrel's men grew restless.

Subto hurriedly rode up to Aacrel and saluted, "Sir, the army is in position. Four thousand archers are still inside Cenkin, ready at the parapet." He hastily surveyed the moving army, "How do you know the Southerns will attack us?"

"Guan is an excellent soldier. He cannot ignore us in this position. If he sends those catapults to the wall alone, our men will destroy them." Pointing at Cenkin, he explained, "If he sends his army to the wall with them, we will crush their flank and annihilate them completely." He pulled Din's reins, steadying him. "No, Subto, Guan's only option is to fight us first and then launch his assault on the wall." *Terikk was right; this will work!*

"I hope you're right, sir." Subto looked around, "Where are King Terikk and his cavalry?"

Aacrel continued watching Guan's army in the distance. "They are not here, Subto." He felt the first rays of daylight on his face. "Do you think we can trust him and those men from the north?"

"Do you think we can, sir?" replied Subto.

With a stone face, Aacrel replied, "With every fiber of my being, I trust Terikk. I do not have time to explain why I feel so strongly about him, but I do. He will not fail us today, Subto." He looked at Subto and nodded. "To your post then. Wait for the signal to attack." He pointed at him, "Under no circumstances are the men to advance without my orders; make sure they wait for my command."

Subto saluted. "Yes, sir. I understand your orders, sir. Godsspeed today, General," he rode away to the left flank of their line on the eastern edge of the field.

Aacrel grinned to himself. *Keep coming, Guan. We are waiting for you. Come meet your destiny on the Field of Angl.*

Chapter 28

As the sun was rising, Guan's army advanced north out of the forest. He munched on pine nuts. They were exclusive to the Stone Pines they had slept beneath, but he failed to appreciate their goodness. The scent of fresh pine was wasted on the southern soldiers. Their focus was solely on the eastern gate of the city. They would have the sun at their backs as they invaded the city. Every advantage would belong to them as they assaulted Cenkin.

Guan rode ahead of his men. The glint of sunlight on steel caught his eye to the northeast. Turning to look, he was momentarily blinded by the sunrise. He raised a hand to shield his eyes and spoke aloud, "What is that?" As his eyes adjusted to the light, he realized what he saw. "The Central Kingdom Army is in the open!" he cried out. "So, the fools have chosen to die outside their precious wall. Splendid." This was unexpected. Guan was certain the cowards from Cenkin would hide behind their wall again. The catapults would have to wait. They could not be maneuvered and operated without the army to escort them. "Halt the march!" he yelled. He called to his captains, "Moto, Druvl, Tyr, I need you immediately!"

Orders were barked, halting the march. Guan's captains were summoned to his side. In a matter of minutes, they were found. The three men rode quickly to meet him.

Tyr arrived first. "General Guan, reporting as ordered, sir," he saluted.

Guan yelled at him, "Tyr, what is the meaning of this? Why was I not informed of the advanced position of that army?" He pointed at the mass of men.

Tyr held a hand to his eyes, and looked where Guan was pointing, "Sir, they were not there last night. They must have moved into position in the early hours of the morning. At your command, our scouts were recalled to prepare for battle, sir."

Druvl and Moto rode up to join them. Moto spoke, "We were on the left flank, sir. Accept our apologies." They both bowed their heads. As daylight increased, they saw the army in the distance. Moto asked, "What is going on, sir?"

"Moto, we must change our plan for battle. The wall will have to wait." He pointed at his soldiers. "Realign the men to march onto the Field of Angl. We will attack and crush their pitiful army." His horse fidgeted. "Those curs think they will be remembered in song for their glorious defense of the city. All they are doing is expediting their own demise!" he shouted. "With them dead, our invasion of the city will be that much more unimpeded. Leave the catapults in this position." Waving a hand at the machines, he commanded Moto, "Assign a detachment to guard them. We will return soon and rededicate ourselves to razing the wall. See to the men, captains."

They rode away from Guan and returned to their lieutenants. New orders were given, and within minutes, the entire army adjusted its course. Three lines of over three thousand men each wheeled into formation. When the signal was given, they began a steady march towards the army of the Central Kingdom.

Horns were sounded and drums beaten. Steady on they marched. Nothing would stop these men from the south. They were the chosen people of Caporesso, and they would conquer everyone. They would erase the world's memory of the army in front of them. It would be as though the men from Cenkin had never existed. It was their destiny.

The sun climbed higher into the sky, its light blinding some of the soldiers from the Southern Army. It did not matter. They were superior soldiers and could not be defeated. They marched northeast into the field. Steady, straight, and true, their half-mile long line never wavered or broke apart. They were professional soldiers on a mission to greatness.

Soon they would be there, engaged with the enemy. Swords would be crossed and shields shattered. They would kill many enemies. Only a handful of their friends would fall. All of their training had led to this inevitable moment. Fate was almost upon them. Without a verbal order, their pace quickened. They knew what to do and soon would be unleashed to do it.

As their lines advanced into the Field of Angl, the cowards from Cenkin changed their formation. When the southern men began the march, their line closed a triangle shape against the central men, but now the central army adjusted its lines. The two lines of men which formed a right angle merged together. When they finished the maneuver, the new battle line was straight and longer than the Southerns. The men from the south appeared to be outflanked, but no matter. Men from Cenkin were pathetic excuses for soldiers and would fall before the advancing army from the south. They continued moving northeast, the sunlight increasing in intensity. Charging up the gentle slope, the confidence of the Southern Army was high.

But then they heard the sound of thundering hooves descending on them. It sounded like a stampede of ten thousand horses. Impossible, there were not that many horses in the Central Kingdom. Uncommanded, the army slowed to listen to this strange sound. Their commanders were shocked by what they heard, and even more so by what they saw.

The Southern Army was in the middle of the Field of Angl. To the north and east of them, was the army from the Central Kingdom. The captains of the Southern Army wavered at what they saw to the northwest. The soldiers who saw it first were unnerved. A cavalry force, the largest they had ever seen, was hurtling towards them. The horsemen were riding straight towards their left flank. They would hit the edge of the line and crush it. Instantly, the Southern Army would have riders on their flank and in the rear of their formation. They would be destroyed. The cavalry would ride behind their line and butcher the men before they could turn to fight.

Guan's perfect victory was gone. It was about to be replaced with absolute defeat. There was nothing he could do to stop it. He had been outmaneuvered. Cursing, he lamented, "Godsdammit. This is impossible. This cannot happen!" He seethed with rage.

To his surprise, the advancing cavalry stopped and reformed their lines. Two men rode forward. Guan looked northeast, he saw two more riders moving towards him. *What is happening?* He had never been so panic-stricken before in battle. Guan realized there was nothing he could do to salvage the situation.

Holding up a hand, he shouted, "Halt the march…halt the march!"

His command was echoed throughout the southern army's lines. The men stopped advancing. Staying in formation, they did not know what was going to happen next. They were at the mercy of the wretched central men.

"Tyr, come here," Guan barked, "Ride with me to meet these mysterious men. Somehow, they have stolen victory from us without crossing a single sword. We must see to their demands." He growled, "But even if it means our death, I will not surrender to these cowards," Guan spurred his horse forward.

Silently, Tyr obeyed his general and followed. He hoped someone could save them from this horrible field. The only way he saw anyone leaving it was dead. It seemed the men from Cenkin would not suffer the Southerns to depart. Tyr thought death was the only fate he and his comrades would find today.

Chapter 29

Six riders met between the three hosts of soldiers: two from the northeast, two from the northwest, and Guan and Tyr. Guan scanned the faces of the men across from him. *What is this? A woman in my presence!* He tried to hide the disdain on his face. *How dare they bring a woman to treatise with me?* In his mind, they were fit for only one thing, and there would be none of that today. With considerable effort, he controlled his anger.

The man from the cavalry unit advanced closer to Guan. He saluted and spoke, "I am King Terikk from the Northern Kingdom. I am in command of the Tu'nide, with over a thousand men in the saddle today. We desire to hold a summit with you." He paused as his horse blustered. "Inform your men, they are not to maneuver or break rank. We know we have you at a strategic disadvantage in this position. With cavalry in your flank and rear and infantry to your front, your army does not stand a chance against us. If we fight today, they will be destroyed." He stared fixedly into Guan's eyes. "Order your men to stand down, and we will talk. Otherwise, we will continue the attack."

This man from the north spoke with a confidence Guan was not accustomed to hearing. His horsemen had Guan's army in a defenseless position. There was nothing he could do to save them. Guan turned his head to the side. "Tyr, go tell the men to stand down and stay in formation. Our battle plan has been thwarted." He looked at the line of men behind him. "Bring Moto and Druvl with you when you return."

Terikk continued, "Thank you, General." He watched Guan's adjutant ride away. "There is much we want to discuss. Will you yield the field and listen to what we have to say?"

Yield the field? Guan's blood boiled. *The insolence!* His face flushed with rage. He struggled to stop his hand from drawing his sword. That would not help him achieve his goal of dominance over the country. No, he would have to listen to these feeble men. "Yes, Terikk, I will listen to what you have to say." He looked at the other men with Terikk. "I am Supreme General Guan from the Southern Kingdom. I command the Southern Army and the Southern Kingdom. We will yield the field...today."

The man from the army moved his horse forward. "I am General Aacrel of the Central Kingdom. I command the army you see before you." A steady breeze blew, disturbing his ponytail. "Two months ago, given these same circumstances, we would have destroyed your army. However...things have changed and we would like an opportunity to discuss new ideas with you." His horse neighed and tossed its head, completely unaware of the bloodshed that they had avoided. "May we prepare a table here in the middle of this field? Here, we will talk amongst ourselves about alternatives to war." His expression seemed somber yet hopeful.

Guan had no choice but to comply. He looked at Terikk and then Aacrel, "Prepare a table for our discussions, gentlemen. I am interested to hear what you have to say," he lied. "War is our way of life; our culture and economy are based on it. But I will listen to your arguments." There was nothing else he could do. "Do you suggest an alternative to violence?" he asked sardonically.

The woman on the horse moved forward and addressed him. "General, your reputation as a military leader precedes you. I am honored to finally meet you. My name is Mervekka, and I am the chief adviser to King Hogeland." She sat like a man on a horse. "I speak with his authority and in his name. I know today is a fortuitous day. The circumstances surrounding this encounter are not coincidental; it is the work of the gods." She kept her steed steady. "I am pleased you will join us in our discussions."

This Mervekka gave the impression she believed she was an equal to these other men. The notion amused Guan, and he nodded at her, "Lady Mervekka, I am pleased to meet. Let us sit and talk. I will willingly listen to what you have to say." He was amazed by her beauty. Her face was exquisite, her eyes, enthralling. Her body... This woman caught Guan completely off guard.

She dismounted her horse, and somehow there was an effortless grace present in the motion. Terikk stepped down from his steed, Guan did the same, and Aacrel threw a leg over his horse and jumped down.

Terikk and Aacrel walked towards Guan, stopping in front of him. Each man offered their hand to shake Guan's. He accepted the offer. He would need to be careful talking with these men. They had his army at a disadvantage, but had failed to use it. They did not have the fortitude to do what they should. If the situation had been reversed, he would now be celebrating a victory and the death of thousands.

Mervekka walked over to Guan and extended her hand. It surprised him, but he did not let his expression show it. He took her hand, shaking it gently. Her aroma was enchanting.

She said, "Come, General, let us sit and talk about something new."

"And what is that, Milady?" he asked.

Again, she smiled at him, "Peace. Peace between the Central Kingdom and the Southern and Northern Kingdoms." A light breeze blew her hair across her face. "It has never worked before because no one ever tried. But today, here, between the four of us," she looked from face to face, "we have the opportunity to create something new. We can start the process of unifying the land and building a country where our people can live together in peace. We have the chance to make this country better for all of them." She brushed her hair from her face. "Today, we can lay the foundation for a new country, for a new Caporesso," she spoke with sincerity.

Guan heard her words, and they were appalling. Peace came after death. Only old women desired peace in their lives. However, he was so captivated by her that he was almost speechless. Softly he said, "Yes, Milady." His mind raced, one country, united together, with him in control. He could achieve his goal of ultimate power and accomplish it faster without destroying his army in the process. Maybe their ideas would be of benefit to him.

They sat together, talking freely. The hours passed quickly.

By the time they finished their discussions that day, the basic plan for a peace initiative was set in motion. Additional time was required to refine the plan, but there was plenty of that. Men's lives had been lengthened because of their meeting. Wives and children would be grateful for the safe return of their husbands and fathers.

It was decided that Guan would send his army back to Sokin immediately. He would keep a small unit of Dragoons for security. Terikk would send the Tu'nide home to the north, while only a detachment remained. Aacrel ordered his army to retire from the field.

Five large tents were assembled for King Terikk, Supreme General Guan, General Aacrel, King Hogeland, and Lady Mervekka. They realized it would take time to finalize their plans for a peaceful Caporesso. For the sake of the people, they would stay as long as it took. They would not abandon the field until they agreed upon the proposed articles of peace. Debates and discussions would follow, but they would resolve their differences. They would stay on the Field of Angl until they successfully unified the country.

Chapter 30

In the autumn of 240 SA, six months after they began, New Caporesso was born. This new country was based on the ideal that every life had value. No kingdom was better than any other. The citizens from each kingdom were equal, regardless of size or strength. Terikk, Hogeland, Mervekka, Aacrel, and Guan successfully did what they set out to do. They formed a new country that would protect the people.

Almost every aspect of the new country was addressed. A new government was being established. Each region, including the western and eastern villages, would send representatives to Cenkin. They would all have equal representation. Delegates would discuss and debate issues important to the country. No decisions would be made unless a consensus was reached. Even the location for the capital of New Caporesso had been accepted. Cenkin was centrally located in the land and was the closest distance to each of the other kingdoms.

They convened inside Trosho's throne room for their final meeting. It was as impressive as the dining hall. The same stone used for the wall had been used to construct the great room. Carved stone railings oversaw the proceedings. The cobblestone floor was comprised of different colored rocks, and the fifty foot high atrium was magnificent. Sycamore columns supported the ribbed vaulted ceiling. Beginning at the mezzanine level were giant stained glass windows on all four walls.

Guards from each of the kingdoms stood silently, watching. Though their leaders appeared to get along, the soldiers were skeptical of their counterparts. Warriors from the south wore their black uniforms, proudly displaying the hooded serpent. Soldiers from the north dressed in black pants, their brown gambesons emblazoned with the fierce bear of lore. Men from Cenkin wore black pants, and dark green under tunics bearing the golden lion from their legends. None of the men were armed.

Hogeland and his invited guests stood around a table along the eastern wall. They sampled the fine foods and drink. Regional delicacies were served. Smoked okapi from the east was a favorite, bison ribs from the central region were enjoyed, northern elk killed by Talbots was new for most people, the pheasant stew from the west was delicious, and the southern python jerky was a spicy treat. Servants from each realm tended to the ambassadors. Goblets were filled and more food served. The men and Mervekka talked and laughed like old friends. At least most of them were friends.

Only one aspect of the government was not in place: the king. Mervekka suggested voting to select the king of New Caporesso. "Between King Hogeland, King Terikk, and Supreme General Guan, we cannot choose a king ourselves. We have created a country for the people; it only seems logical that its citizens choose their leader as well."

Hogeland responded to Mervekka's suggestion, wheezing as he spoke "Lady Mervekka, I like the idea of allowing the people to choose their ruler. I have said since we began, bloodlines are no way to select a good man...or woman." He winked at her. "You want *them* to have a hand in how they are governed." Sighing heavily, he waved a boney finger, "But I feel your choice of candidates is inferior."

Guan raised an eyebrow. "What do you mean, Hogeland? Explain yourself...carefully," he warned.

Chuckling, Hogeland replied, "I mean no offense to you, Supreme General Guan." He coughed. "I am the candidate I was referring to, not you." His shoulders slumped. "I am sick, my friends. I do not know if I will survive the winter."

Hearing that for the first time, Mervekka was almost shocked to tears. "No, my king. You cannot mean that." She shook her head.

"My dear...you know I think of you as a daughter," he took her hands. "I wish you a long and happy life, but as for me, mine is nearing its end."

She studied his eyes. *His hardened face looks so frail.*

"My heart was broken many years ago when my sons were stolen from me. It is a wound I have never recovered from." He wheezed again.

No one looked at Guan, but he shifted his weight and crossed his arms.

"It has taken a toll on me, and my energy is not what it was twenty years ago," he chortled. "I am not sure I will be alive long enough to rule over New Caporesso for more than a few months. What would be the point of that?" he inquired. "And besides, one kingdom was problematic enough," he shook his head and chuckled. "I tried to do what was best for my people, and I would like to think I had a small hand in creating New Caporesso."

"Of course you did, sire," interjected Aacrel. "Without you, this never would have happened. You started every—"

"General," he turned to look at Aacrel, "you are my most trusted general. I know the army will be in capable hands once I am gone." He coughed, "But we all know who is chiefly responsible for the birth of New Caporesso." His eyes found Mervekka again. "Only a woman knows how to birth a child." He gazed into Mervekka's compassionate eyes.

"No, my king," was all she could muster, and lowered her head.

"No more tears, my dear. Never again cry because of something out of your control. You must be strong for *your* country. Be strong for New Caporesso. *She* is your child; protect *her* as though *she* were your own." Hogeland wiped the tear from Mervekka's cheek. He looked benevolently at her, releasing her hands.

An awkward silence fell over the room. Even the roosting cardinals were sympathetic to Hogeland's words. He walked over to the table and picked up a goblet full of southern wine.

"So now you all know why I cannot be king." He breathed with difficulty. "The ruler of New Caporesso must be young and full of life. As a substitute," he coughed, "I suggest General Aacrel be nominated in my stead." Hogeland turned and nodded at him. "He is a good man, and a good judge of character. There are none better from our homeland. He would make a fine king." Hacking, he continued, "And I also nominate Lady Mervekka. She is an exquisite person, and the mother of this country. Either candidate would make a fine king or queen of New Caporesso."

Aacrel humbly bowed. "King Hogeland, I am honored by your consideration."

"I too am honored by your words, King Hogeland," Mervekka's surprise showed. She bowed elegantly. "Sire, I would rule as you taught me." Looking at Hogeland, she saw a weakened man. It was the first time she truly noticed his decline. She sighed, and turned to Guan, asking, "Are you offended by the suggestion that I could be elected queen of New Caporesso?"

"Would it matter, Milady?" he answered coldly.

"Of course it would. If you have issue with it, I will withdraw myself from contention. I will do nothing to create strife between us. Our example, our actions will hold this country together. If we bicker and fight, the people will resist a unified nation. If they see harmony between us, they will accept this unification." She looked at Guan, Aacrel, and Terikk. "Whoever is chosen will rule over the land, but the other three must remain as advisers and hold the king accountable for his actions. That is the only way to keep each kingdom truly represented, and prevent the king from giving into the temptation to become a tyrant."

The guards from each kingdom heard her words. They looked at each other and nodded their approval.

Guan studied her. He was amazed at her loyalty to this new country. It meant nothing to him. It was only a convenience, a path to obtaining control over the land, but to Mervekka, it was very important. *Interesting.* "You surprise me again, Milady. Knowing you would not seek election if I opposed it is unexpected. It pleases me to know that you care so much for this new country we have created."

"It means more to me than you could possibly imagine, Guan," she acknowledged. "I would sacrifice anything to keep *her* intact."

"I too would hate to see *it* abandoned before *it* had a chance to establish *itself* as a powerful empire." He looked at each of them. "I have no objections to Milady being nominated as queen."

Hogeland stepped forward, "We have the four names of the candidates for ruler of New Caporesso." He asked, "How should we go about selecting the king or queen?"

A debate followed. Suggestions were made and rejected. Everyone had his and her say in the process. Discussions were heated but never became arguments. The four new friends worked together. Their mission had been to create a better country in which to live. So far, they were successful. Personal gain did not appear to be an issue for any of them.

At least, that was what three of them believed. Guan's ambition remained hidden. He agreed to their proposals while hiding his disdain for them. He would wait until the time was right before attacking. For now, he was content to allow this course be run and discover what the election held.

Chapter 31

In the spring of 241 SA, New Caporesso had its first ruler. The newly elected king of New Caporesso was going to live in Castle Trosho inside Cenkin. As was Cenkin's tradition, he entered the city through the western gate. He was greeted with more pageantry and fanfare than a conquering hero from antiquity. The citizens of Cenkin, and their countless guests, gladly received him with open arms. The promise of peace and prosperity were intoxicating ideas to the people. They all looked forward to abundant harvests and profitable trade with the neighboring kingdoms.

King Terikk rode pass the enormous tent city to the southwest of the city and into Cenkin on his noble steed. The elegant stallion carried him in regal fashion. On either side of him were Aacrel and Guan, Aacrel to the right and Guan on his left. They flanked their new king. Mervekka rode sidesaddle behind them, looking beautiful in her ceremonial dress.

People from Norkin and Nurdug came; men and women from Werlo and Dreglo made the journey; Dradorians and men from Sokin travelled to Cenkin to welcome their new king. They all appeared to be at peace with one another. The crowd cheered and hollered as their new leaders passed.

Terikk was the celebrated king, while Aacrel and Guan were both generals in the New Caporesso Army. Mervekka was Terikk's chief adviser, and her duty was to counsel him on the internal matters of each kingdom. Each of them appeared to have accepted his or her new roles with gracious aplomb.

They rode through the winding streets of Cenkin, heading for Trosho. Citizens from each kingdom and village had travelled to Cenkin to witness the spectacle. For the first time since Trosho, La'may, and Brika'cong went to war, the citizens of Caporesso were united. Some of the people cried with joy; others shouted their approval. New Caporesso had turned out to welcome their new king and his cabinet.

Castle Trosho had been home to the many kings of the Central Kingdom. Now it would be the home of the first king of New Caporesso. As they moved through the streets, a cry rose up from the people. "Long live the king! Long live the king! Hip hip huzzah! Hip hip huzzah!" The mob of people was genuinely happy on this momentous day.

As Terikk entered his new home, he proceeded to the throne room and took a seat at the table. At his request, the guards and most of the servants were away, celebrating the day. Two maidens remained to serve him. A small meal of fruits and meat had been prepared.

Aacrel entered the room and joined Terikk at the table. "Sire, may I sit with you?"

Annoyed, Terikk looked up at his friend, "Aacrel, when we are alone," he shook his head, "do not do that. It is not necessary. In fact, I do not like it. We are friends, and you do not need my permission to sit with me. All right?"

Aacrel chuckled, "As king, I must address you as such. It is your right and my obligation." He grinned devilishly and said, "But I will try not to do it when we are alone."

Nodding his thanks, he asked, "Any news about the delegates from the other regions?" He poured a second mug of ale for Aacrel.

"Thank you," he said, taking the cup. "Every region has chosen the people they want to represent them. I am not sure how many people are coming from each place, but all of them should be here by the summer equinox. I think some should arrive next week." He snatched a strawberry out of a bowl and devoured it.

"That is good to hear." Terikk sighed, "We will probably spend many months deciding how everything is to work together."

Spitting the stem on the floor, Aacrel remarked, "I know, but we all agreed that it was necessary to make this work. This whole idea is new to everyone." He shrugged his shoulders. "It is going to take time."

"Time...I hope everyone remains patient during the process," he shook his head. "Where is Guan?"

"Um...he said he was going to check on his new quarters and meet with his Sokin aide, Donetsk." Aacrel took another drink. "Guan has surprised me. I thought his losing the election would affect him more adversely. I have not noticed any difference in his demeanor. Have you?" He sipped the cool drink.

"I was also concerned there would be issues, but there appear to be none." Terikk raised his class and offered a toast, "My friend, here is to long life and happiness for us both."

"Here here," returned Aacrel. They clanged mugs and drank from their cups. Both men fixed a plate of food. Aacrel inquired, "Is there anyone else you want to ask their whereabouts?"

"And to whom are you referring?" Terikk replied, eating some melon from his plate.

"You know who I mean," he pointed at Terikk. "Mervekka. You have hardly spoken to her these last few days. What is going on between the two of you?"

"I do not know, Aacrel," he set down his mug and pulled his plate closer. He ripped a piece of meat apart and took a bite. "Give me a sword and a conflict," he chewed, "and I am confident in myself. But put me with Mervekka...I just do not understand her. Normal women are hard to deal with, but Mervekka...she is..." he paused.

"Abnormal," Aacrel completed his sentence, then laughed. "Yes, Terikk, tell her that. She would love to hear that from you." He laughed harder.

"That is not what I mean. Sometimes her beauty is...I find myself a babbling fool, unsure of myself. Being around her can be...difficult." Terikk shook his head, his expression sullen.

Aacrel chewed some blueberries and grapes. "Terikk, last night I was with Mervekka." He gulped, realizing his mistake instantly.

Terikk's eyes narrowed, and he glared at his friend. He opened his mouth to yell when Aacrel raised his hands, surrendering.

"No, Terikk, no. Gods no," he exhaled. "Poor word choice. I mean we were in the same room talking about you." He sighed in relief, "You never have to worry about me, my friend. I do love Mervekka, but not like that. Do not question that, or my loyalty," he spoke earnestly. "Yes, we were talking about you. She thinks very highly of you."

"She does?" Terikk tried not to smile. "Really? What did she say?" He gulped his ale.

"I am afraid I cannot tell you." One side of Aacrel's mouth turned up. He looked at his plate, tormenting his friend. "It would not be fair of me to tell you, after we talked in confidence last night."

"What? In confidence?" He smacked the table. "You brought it up! If you did not want me to know about it," he set his mug down roughly, "then why say anything?" Staring at Aacrel, he smirked. "As your king, I command you tell me what was said."

"Sorry, *sire*, but you told me not to treat you like that when we were alone," he started laughing.

Both men sat, eating more of the food before them. Neither spoke. The only sound was Aacrel chuckling to himself from time to time.

After a few minutes, Terikk asked again, "What did she say?"

Aacrel rolled his eyes. "She said you should ask her yourself. She has feelings for you, but I will say no more." He held up a hand. "Go to her, and ask yourself. You will not be disappointed by what you find out." He said emphatically, "Trust me, you will like what you hear."

Terikk beamed with life. "All right, Aacrel, I will go and find her now." He stood up from the table and walked away.

As Terikk was leaving, Aacrel shouted after him, "She is in the main training courtyard." He swallowed his bite of food.

Finishing his meal, he stood up and walked over to the throne atop the dais near the north wall. He looked around to make sure he was alone. Satisfying himself, he sat down on the king's throne. "Oh…feels nice," he commented and adjusted his position in the chair, "but a little too stiff for me." Snickering, he got up. Descending the stairs, he opined, "The best man was elected king of New Caporesso. Long live the king," and walked out of the room.

Chapter 32

Mervekka strolled in the training courtyard. She enjoyed spending time there, it helped her to clear her mind and think. Hogeland was at her side, his arms behind his back. They walked on the grassy pathways around the training area. The sand in the training pit had been raked smooth.

"Lady Mervekka, do not be troubled by his lack of attention. You frighten him," Hogeland stated. "He knows his way around a battlefield, but not his own heart." His cough returned.

"Hogeland," she looked down and said, "it seems strange not calling you king anymore."

"That is quite all right, my dear. I do not mind it at all. I wore that title for a long time. Quite honestly, I am relieved to let someone else carry its burden. A better man could not have been chosen." He looked caringly at her as he said, "Aacrel would have made a fine king, but Terikk is perfect. He has a special quality about him that few men possess."

"I agree," she nodded. "He does have something about him that is hard to explain." She placed her arm through his. "Why do you think he ignores me? He cannot really be frightened, can he?"

"You would be surprised how much power you hold over men. Your beauty makes them feel vulnerable, even the strongest and bravest. You humble them without even saying a word. Just give him time," he assured her. "He will find the words he is looking for."

The sound of approaching footsteps disturbed them. "Who is there?" Mervekka demanded.

"Uh...it is me, Mervekka. I was looking for you...and Aacrel said you might be here...in the courtyard." He slowly entered the area. "Oh, Hogeland, I did not realize you were here as well." Bowing his head, he backed away from them." I can leave you both alone if you would like."

"King Terikk," Hogeland spoke, "this is your castle, and these are your grounds. Understand that," he pointed at him. "I was just telling Lady Mervekka that I was growing tired of walking and am ready to retire." He winked at her, pretending to cough. "It would please my heart if you would keep her company in my absence. Can you do that for me, sire?" he held out Mervekka's hand, offering it to Terikk.

Terikk nodded his head, looking caringly at Mervekka. "Yes, sir, I can do that for you." He walked over to Mervekka and accepted her hand.

Hogeland closed Terikk's hand around Mervekka's and held them together for a moment. "Then I take my leave from both of you." Turning away, he left them alone in the spacious courtyard.

They stood in silence, him holding her hand gently. The moment turned awkward as the stillness continued. He turned his head and coughed. Mervekka simpered uncomfortably, not sure what to say. Terikk had appeared so confident while negotiating the creation of New Caporesso. Nothing flustered him, not even Guan. Now, when only she was present, he seemed lost.

She initiated the conversation, "Today's ceremony was spectacular. It was a good sign that so many travelled from so far to welcome you. Your citizens really outdid themselves."

"Yes they did, and it was a nice ceremony." He struggled to keep the conversation going. "I did not realize how long of a ride it is from the western gate around the city to Trosho. It took longer than I thought. Much longer." There was another pause between them. "You looked radiant in that gown; you still do." He tried to look at her without directly looking at her.

Mervekka smiled and released his hand. "Thank you, I am enjoying wearing it." Looking down at the full-length gown, she grabbed the folds of the dress. She lifted the edges and swiveled her hips. The dress twirled this way and that. The ivory-colored silk shimmered in the sunlight of the courtyard. Its short sleeves and sweetheart neckline preserved her natural modesty. The pleats and ruffles accentuated her petite figure beneath it. Around her neck, she wore a crystal-studded choker.

"You look beautiful in it," he exhaled. "I mean...you look beautiful... out of it too."

"What?" she gasped.

His face flushed. "No...What I meant was...I mean you look lovely every day, even when you are not wearing that particular gown." He put a hand on his forehead and shook his head.

She guffawed loudly. Then covering her mouth with both hands, she continued to giggle. "Hogeland said you could stand alone in the face of many enemies and not be worried, but you waver at the thought of being around me. Is talking to me so difficult, my king?"

His posture stiffened and then softened. "Yes, I admit it. You have that affect on me. You must understand..." He gazed deeply into her eyes. "I have never known a woman like you. I have never been around someone who makes me feel the way you do." Terikk caressed her cheek.

Mervekka closed her eyes; his touch was exhilarating. Reaching up with her hand, she clasped his.

He thought she would remove it from her face, but she did not.

Her eyes opened, and they sparkled. She moved his hand in front of her and held it with both of hers. Turning his palm up, she placed her tiny hand in his. "Your hands are rough, my king. From years of battle I am sure. I hope you find peace as the king of New Caporesso." She looked up into his eyes.

He stared into hers. "I do not believe that Hogeland was tired, do you?"

She smiled and said, "No, I guess not. He thought we should have some time together to talk. What do you think?"

"I think that was a very good idea." He looked down at her hand, then back at her face. Terikk closed his hand around hers and pulled her closer to him. She exhaled. Their faces only inches apart. "Mervekka, I love you. I have for a long time. With what we have gone through, and with our position in New Caporesso, I was afraid to tell you how I felt." He dropped eye contact momentarily. "I thought it might adversely affect our relationship and stall the peace negotiations." Caressing her hands, he asked, "Can you understand that?"

She adjusted her hands so she could hold his. "Terikk, I have loved you for a long time too," her voice cracked. "I thought you did not feel the same way. Especially once the elections started. You became so detached." She frowned. "Our interaction ended and you would only talk to me if Aacrel or Guan were present. I was not sure if I had done something wrong." Leaning forward, she rested her head on his chest.

"How could you ever do anything wrong?" Terikk wrapped an arm around her waist and held her tightly. "This is what I was afraid of." She looked up as he continued, "Us becoming one. It will infuriate Guan. He will think we are already planning to oust him from the government."

Dreamy eyed, Mervekka gazed at him. "Then what should we do? I do not think I can hide my feelings for you any longer, now that I know you feel the same way." She whispered, "What can we do?"

"The only thing to do is talk to Aacrel and Guan. We will explain that *this* just happened. We did not intend to fall in love with each other; we just did." He let his other arm fall around her waist. "There is no ulterior motive behind our actions. The gods have blessed us with finding one another to share the rest of our lives together."

"What is the worst that can happen?" she quipped. "We equally wanted to create New Caporesso. I do not believe Guan will do anything to destroy her in her infancy. He is not evil." She was not sure she believed those words, but what choice did they have? "Let us go and talk to them." She tried to move away from him.

Terikk stopped her, pulling her closer. He leaned forward and gently kissed her.

Her knees buckled at the sensation.

Slowly, he pulled his head back and stared into her eyes.

Beaming, she reached up to kiss him again. Wrapping her arms around his neck, they kissed passionately. Mervekka hoped the moment would never end, but it did.

Backing away from each other, they both smiled. Together, they turned and exited the courtyard, heading in search of Aacrel and Guan. They were going to tell them about their feelings of love. Hopefully, their friends would understand how they felt. If not, the future of New Caporesso might be in jeopardy.

Chapter 33

Evening approached as Mervekka and Terikk found Aacrel and Guan in the throne room. Both men listened as they described their feelings of love. Each man had a different reaction.

"Well it's about time you two!" exclaimed Aacrel. "I am happy for you both." He hugged them.

Returning the hug, Mervekka kissed him on the cheek. "You are not upset?" she asked.

"No, nothing could make me happier. You are perfect together." Aacrel was elated. "You will make a perfect king and queen." He turned and looked at Guan. Sensing his agitation, he asked, "Guan, what do you have to say?" almost afraid to learn the truth.

Guan got up from his chair, and stomped across the uneven stone floor, his steps echoing in the hall. Lingering in the shadows on the far side of the room, he mumbled to himself.

Aacrel commented quietly, "Apparently, Guan does not share my enthusiasm." They left him alone to collect his thoughts.

Guards with long spears were stationed around the room wearing newly designed tabards. They were azure blue, with a combined motif of the emblems of the three kingdoms. The pattern resembled an oval-inspired triangle, with a point towards the top. Uneven pathways connected each symbol as a display of unity. The serpent from the south was in the upper position, with the lion of the Central Kingdom to the left, and the northern bear to the right. Guan had insisted on the design.

Several of the soldiers moved from their locations, giving Guan his space. Servant girls made sure not to disturb him. Other workers swept the floor, but stayed away from him as well.

After what seemed like hours, Guan rejoined them. His stoic face looked stonier than usual. "Forgive my silence. I needed some time to think about what you said."

"Understandable, Guan," Mervekka replied. "What is your initial reaction?"

"Surprise and shock. At first glance, I would say you are aligning the Northern and Central Kingdoms together," he elucidated, "and at the same time, isolating us in the south. Are you planning on combining your armies and marching to Sokin already?" his anger spilled through as he spoke. "Or does that come later?" he shouted, spittle flying from his mouth.

"Guan, that is not our plan." Terikk tried to calm him. "Our feelings for each other have nothing to do with gaining power." He explained. "We are not trying to form secret alliances behind your back." He looked at Mervekka. "I love her. There is nothing more to it than that."

His eye twitched. "But look at it from my point of view." Calmer, Guan put it in plain words, "Whether you admit it or not, your marriage *will* create a union between the Northern and Central Kingdoms. Your two kingdoms will be bound by marriage to serve and protect the other. Where does that leave the Southern Kingdom?" He looked from face to face. "Alone," he answered. Guan was unhappy but gained control over the fury in his voice.

Mervekka spoke again, "No, Guan, not alone. The three kingdoms have already formed a union. In creating New Caporesso, the kingdoms pledged to let peace work. Our marriage would do nothing to change that dynamic. However," she sighed, bowing her head momentarily, "if you feel threatened...if you do not approve of our marriage, we will not pursue it further."

Terikk walked up behind her and placed a hand on her shoulder.

Guan's face showed his surprise, "You would what? You just told me how much you love each other." He stepped closer to her. "Now, if I withhold my blessing, you will forgo your marriage completely? You would sacrifice your happiness for the sake of this country?" he could not believe what he was hearing.

Mervekka looked him in the eye. "Yes, Guan. You are an honorable man, and we would never intentionally do anything to betray your friendship. A *no* from you would end our discussion of marriage." She heard herself say the words, but was not sure her heart could suffer the cold reality of it.

Her words caught Guan off guard. He stopped to think for a moment. "Milady...Terikk," he looked at each of them, "this conversation has taken me by surprise." On its own, his eye danced erratically. "You have come to me in good conscience; I must do the same for you." A plan was conceived as he spoke. He fought the urge to laugh, knowing exactly what to say, "I need some time to think about what you have said and how it impacts New Caporesso and our standing as officials in this new government. Allow me till tomorrow morning to give you my response. It is only fair to you that I take time to reflect on what this means to everyone." *How can they say no? I sound so diplomatic.*

Terikk stepped around Mervekka. "Take as much time as you need, Guan. This is an important decision for all of us." He offered his hand.

Guan accepted Terikk's hand and shook it. They nodded at each other, and then Guan left them alone in the throne room. He hurried to his quarters, where he would think long and hard about this unexpected proposal. Guan smirked to himself as he walked. His plan was developing quickly in his mind, and he knew it would ensure his eventual ascension to the throne of New Caporesso.

Chapter 34

"Well that went better than I expected," an amazed Aacrel exhaled. Terikk agreed, "Yes, I half expected him to draw his sword and come for my head." He touched his throat. "His temper can be so unpredictable."

"I think that is the best possible answer he could have given," continued Aacrel. "It does make sense that he needs some time to think about this development. I am sure your declaration surprised him, and we know he can see things quite differently than we do." He nodded after Guan, "He just needs to think it through and realize there is no hidden agenda at work here."

Silently, the guards returned to their posts.

Mervekka was not listening to Aacrel. "Do you think he is planning something?" she voiced.

Terikk turned. "What do you mean?"

"What if he takes this time to conjure a scheme to do something horrible? He could ask us for riches, or land. We do not really know what he is capable of, do we?" She looked at them both.

Aacrel forced a nervous chuckle. "Mervekka…" He shook his head, not knowing what else to say. Looking at one of the guards, he jerked his head towards the door.

Bowing deeply, the guard understood the meaning. He ushered the servants out of the room. Then the remaining guards filed out of the throne room, leaving the three friends to discuss things privately.

Terikk walked over to her and put his hands on her shoulders. "Do not do that. Do not envision the worst in him; it will only upset you." He kissed her forehead. "Guan and his army came here as the aggressors a year ago, that is true. Now look at what we have accomplished. We have a unified country under one banner, and we could not have done that without him. He has proven himself to be a man of his word. Why should we expect treachery now?"

"I know we all worked hard to create New Caporesso, but something tells me to be cautious of him." Mervekka sounded discouraged, "If we make him angry, I fear he will turn on us and betray everyone, even New Caporesso."

"Mervekka, without Guan's help, we would have failed." Terikk tried to reassure her. "He could have disrupted our plan before it was complete. He was a large part of why we were successful."

"No, Terikk," she shook her head, "it was all of us, working together."

He stared at the beauty in front of him. "No, Mervekka, as Hogeland said, you were the driving force behind us. Our differences would have gotten the better of us, and failure would have followed. It was you… you held us together and kept us going. You were the voice of reason that whole time." He took her hands in his. "It was you who wanted to help the people of Caporesso. Hogeland was right, New Caporesso is your child, and we are her fathers. Without you, we would have let her die and gone to war. Destruction is easier than creation. Any fool can destroy; only a loving mother can give life.

"But through that whole time, Guan never deceived us. He was true to his word and honored ours. Do not think that he goes off to scheme for his own benefit. He has earned our respect and gratitude. Guan is a part of this now. Even he would be troubled by her disintegration." He shook his head, "No, Mervekka, do not think about the bad things that could happen. Trust me." He kissed her forehead again. "It will be all right in the morning. I promise." Terikk hugged her tightly, whispering in her ear.

She kissed him on the cheek. Backing away, she admitted, "I apologize for my rant. It was wrong of me to despair."

"No need for an apology, Mervekka." Terikk added, "Today has been a stressful day for all of us. This is our first day with the king of New Caporesso in his castle." He looked affectionately at her. "And it is the first day that we professed our love for each other. I plan to retire for the evening, and dream about what our future holds, my love." Terikk kissed her hand. "I suggest you do the same."

"You are right, it has been a long day, hmm," she cooed. "I too am off to bed, where my mind will dream of our new life together."

Silence followed.

Turning, they both looked at Aacrel, who was sitting alone. His chin was in his hand. "Boy oh boy, I do not know how much more of the two of you I can take. You are making me sick already." In a mocking tone he added, "*Good night, my love,*" and in a different voice, "*Good night,*" then in his normal voice, "blah! Dealing with this might be more difficult than creating a new country." He waved a hand at them, "Good night to both of you," and headed for his room.

Terikk and Mervekka laughed as Aacrel left the room. Today had indeed been long, and they were both exhausted from it. A good night's rest would rejuvenate them both. They said their goodnights and headed their separate ways, both of them wondering what Guan would say in the morning.

Chapter 35

Mervekka walked through the corridor to her room. Wrought iron sconces held lighted torches, lining the passageway. A golden colored carpet ran beneath her feet, threads of red and black made nonsensical patterns in the material. Random wooden diagonals were interspersed in the smooth stone wall, giving it a third dimension.

She hummed to herself as she moved. *This must be what it feels like to be in love. I feel like I could burst!* She was so lost in thought, that she did not see the cloaked figure standing in the alcove at the end of the hall. Skipping the last few strides, she stopped when she reached her door. A voice from behind called, distracting her.

"Lady Mervekka, wait for me, child. I'm a'comin as fast as I can."

Before turning around, Mervekka knew who it was. She asked, "Abby, where were you?" You are never far from my chambers. How did I arrive here before you?"

"It's the strangest thing, child. A messenger came calling me. He said you wanted to see me in the lower kitchen. So I went there, but then you weren't." Looking confused, she shook her head, "No one was there. I waited for an hour, but figured I should get back here in case you changed your mind." The older woman cleared her throat, "So what *did* you want, my dear?"

"Abby, I never sent for you. There must be some mistake." She dismissed Abby's remarks as trivial and opened the door. Mervekka turned around as she crossed the threshold and stopped Abby. "That is enough for tonight. Since you were on a wild goose chase looking for me, you must be tired," she chuckled. "I release you for the evening. Get some rest, Abby. I can take care of myself tonight."

"Are you sure, my lady? You know it's no trouble at all. It's been a big day for everyone and I know you must be exhausted. I don't mind helping you tonight." She tried to enter the room.

Mervekka stopped her again, "No, Abby, I want to sit for a spell before getting ready for bed. All right?" Her eyes went wide, "I will see you in the morning," she chuckled. "Now go."

"As you wish, child, have it your way. I'll be back, bright and early." She giggled. "Don't stay up too late. Goodnight, my lady." After bowing, she watched Mervekka close the door. Abby turned around and headed back the way she came, never noticing the mysterious figure hidden in shadow at the end of the hall.

Closing her door, Mervekka stopped to let her eyes grow accustomed to the dimly lit room. It was darker than usual. Several candelabrums normally alight were not. She picked up a candlestick from the entranceway and walked towards the unlit candles.

A voice from the other side of the room startled her, "Forgive my intrusion, Milady."

Startled, she dropped her candle, extinguishing its light.

"I have been thinking about you and Terikk, and your proposition of marriage." He breathed steadily. "I wanted to discuss my conditional acceptance with you. I hoped to do so privately, without the threat of being disturbed," the voice sounded ominous.

Her eyes slowly adjusted to the darkness. The only light in the room came from candles on a small nightstand next to her bed. Across the room, she observed the outline of Guan's silhouette. He stood motionless in front of the window, waiting for her to respond. "Of course, Guan, there is no intrusion," she lied. "You merely surprised me, that is all. I did not realize you wished to see me tonight. None of my maidens informed me you were looking for me." Mervekka was more than a little concerned to see him in her chambers. She stepped further into the room, trying to get closer to the nightstand.

"I had hoped to talk with you tonight, so I can give Terikk my answer in the morning." His breathing quickened. "And no one came looking for you because I did not tell anyone I sought you, Milady. None of your servants know I am here." His voice was a menacing whisper, "No one knows I am here. My captains believe I have gone to my quarters for the night." He clasped his hands together in front of him. "Your declaration of love for Terikk took me by surprise, and I needed some time to think about its ramifications."

The candlelight flickered and danced on the stone walls, giving the room an eerie glow. Mervekka tried to respond with confidence, "We told you today, Guan, there is no plot to deceive you. You are an integral part of New Caporesso, and we need you to make everything work. It will fail without you." She inched closer to the nightstand, searching for something.

"Yes, Milady, I know," he hissed. "I realize my significance to New Caporesso, and feel I should be compensated." He paused forebodingly. "If you want my permission to marry Terikk, I need…something…from you in return. In fact, I am entitled to it." Slowly, he advanced towards her.

"I would grant you anything within my power to give, to obtain your approval for my marriage," she gulped. "What do you seek?" her voice was weak, gripped with fear.

"Are you familiar with the right of the first night custom in Sokin, Milady?"

"We are not in Sok—"

He interrupted her, "The chieftain of the kingdom is granted the first," his breathing skipped a beat, "knowledge…of the bride."

Beginning to understand his meaning, she whispered, "No…You cannot want that. Guan?"

"Hush, Milady?" His eyes ran lustfully over her body. "You are a beautiful woman, perhaps the most beautiful woman I have ever seen."

"Guan, do not say that. You cannot mean it. We worked together building New Caporesso; we are friends and nothing more. Terikk and I love ea—"

He rushed her, placing a hand over her mouth. "Shh…Milady. Shh."

She tried to scream but could not. She tried to get away from him but was trapped. Terrified, there was nothing she could do; he was too strong. Frantically, she struggled to reach her nightstand.

"Looking for this?" He held up a short sword. "This was tucked beside your bed, Milady. Luckily I retrieved it before you did." Chuckling darkly, he tossed it towards the window. It clattered to the floor. "Milady, you said you would grant me anything within your power to give." He leaned his face closer to her. "Well...I need you," his nose brushed against hers, and he felt her tremble. "I have never known such an exotic beauty like you before. I have wanted you for a long time, but could not figure a way to sample your...pleasures...until now." He brushed her hair from her face. "I need your embrace tonight."

Mervekka closed her eyes and shook her head from side to side. She wanted to break free from his grasp. Desperately, she tried to escape, but he restrained her. He pressed his body against hers, pinning her against the wall. Tears rolled down her cheeks.

"No tears, Milady, not tonight." He wiped them away. "Tonight you should be happy." Smirking, he softly kissed her forehead.

She recoiled at his touch, his evil face making her sick. He had a wild, animalistic look in his eyes.

Guan's voice quivered with anticipation, "I discovered your weakness today, Milady," he snickered. "Do you know what it is?" He waited for a response; she offered none. "It is *not* your love for Terikk, but rather, your love for New Caporesso. I know you love *her* more than anything in this world; she is even more important to you than Terikk. I wonder what you would sacrifice to protect her." He sniffed her hair.

Her eyes were wide with fear.

"I am going to remove my hand from your mouth, do not cry out. I have seen to it that no one is in the corridor, Milady," he said matter-of-factly. "If you scream, I will..." he shook his fist menacingly in front of her. "Do you understand?" he asked assertively.

She closed her eyes and nodded.

He stepped back from her.

She tried to move away from the wall, but he maintained a hold of her wrist. "Are you out of your mind, Guan? You will never get away with this. I will tell Terikk and Aacrel of your betrayal immediately. You will be charged with treason against New Caporesso and—"

"Milady," he interrupted, "you do not understand." He grinned wickedly. "As far as New Caporesso is concerned, this night will never have happened. Tonight is between you and me. No one else will know of our secret pact."

"What are you talking about? What pact?" She kept twisting her arm, trying to break his grip. "Why do you think I will not tell Terikk about this? Have you gone insane?"

"You will keep this secret because," his voice was a raspy whisper, "I have the power to destroy New Caporesso. But you on the other hand," he leaned his body against hers again, "you alone have the ability to save her."

She stopped struggling. Her fear for herself dissipated. Only concern for New Caporesso remained. She gasped. "You would never do such a thing. Together, we built—"

"If you refuse me, Milady, I will withdraw my support for New Caporesso and it will crumble in my absence. While your government collapses around you, I will return to Sokin and rebuild my army; we will build hundreds of catapults this time." He spoke slowly, his words clear. "The new army I conscript will have over twenty thousand men at my disposal, it will be the largest army ever put afield in Caporesso. When we return to Cenkin, we will not be deceived. My army will annihilate whatever force Terikk and Aacrel put before us. And then I will crush Cenkin; thousands will die."

She opened her mouth to object, but said nothing.

He humphed, "As you said, if the people sense discord amongst us, New Caporesso will fail. So tonight, let us share love's embrace." He exhaled deeply. "For your people, let us share our innermost passions with one another. For one night, we will form a union of our own. And in return, New Caporesso will be spared a horrific fate." He lifted her chin, looking into her fearful eyes. "Reject me and I will ride for Sokin tonight. The fate of your subjects will be sealed in your denial.

"How could you live with yourself," he faked concern, "knowing that you had the power to keep your country alive but did nothing to save her? You alone will be responsible for the failure of New Caporesso, and the deaths of thousands." Still holding her chin, he licked his lips, parched with desire. "For your people, share the night with me and New Caporesso will live on. And in the morning, I will grant you my blessing to marry Terikk."

She shook her head free. "I could never do that, Guan. I could never betray Terikk. I could—"

"I am not concerned with *you* betraying *him*. Are you prepared to betray New Caporesso, Milady?" He loosened his hold of her wrist. "That is the question you must ask yourself. Will you let *her* burn in the morning because you would not negotiate *her* survival tonight? What would you do to save *her*, Milady?"

Mervekka was speechless. She shook her head in silence. Fully understanding the reality of her situation, her head slumped forward. *I have to save New Caporesso. He is right, how could I live with myself if I do nothing to save her.* Reluctantly, she nodded.

"Save your country, Milady. Save them all," a thin smile crossed his lips. "Save New Caporesso by offering yourself to me, and in the morning this will all be just a pleasant memory. This is the price to save New Caporesso and be with Terikk." He asked slowly, "What say you?" and anxiously awaited her reply.

She finally broke free of his grip and walked away from him. She did not run or try to flee. Mervekka resignedly walked to the bed and sat on its edge. Without looking at him directly, she held out her hand, beckoning him to come closer. When he stood before her, she leaned over and blew out the candles, concealing their treachery in darkness.

Chapter 36

Guan finished dressing. "Your country is safe, Milady, and our pact is secured. Tell no one of our time together." He drank from a pitcher of water. "Pain and suffering for New Caporesso will be the consequence if you divulge our secret." A single candle was lit, its dim flame illuminated his face. "I will treasure this night for the rest of my life." He chuckled lewdly, "Your...passion," he exhaled, "was remarkable."

He walked to the door and turned. "Tomorrow will be a special day for you and Terikk. It is the beginning of your new life together, and you have earned my blessing." Securing his belt, he sneered, saying, "Keep the memories from tonight close to your heart, Milady."

She lay motionless on the bed, staring at the ceiling, the white sheets covering her haphazardly. Mervekka was awake but did not respond to his comments.

As he was leaving her chamber, he smirked, "You have saved your country, Milady...and will be a glorious queen." Closing the door, he whispered, "Long live the queen. Long live the queen."

When the door shut, she sat up and pulled the covers to her neck, covering her entire body beneath them. The evil memories from the night would haunt her dreams, but she did what was necessary to protect New Caporesso. She was not willing to watch *her* die when she alone could protect *her*. If it was Mervekka's duty to safeguard her people, then so be it. She would wear that mantle and keep her secret hidden from the world.

After several minutes, Mervekka's body rebelled against her. Shaking uncontrollably, she burst into tears, weeping hysterically. A wave of panic came over her, and she frantically looked around the darkened room. She whimpered, "My gods, what have I done...how can I go on...what will Terikk do? Oh...what will he do?" Her mind raced with images of her tribulation. She wildly shook her head, "No. Guan would have destroyed everything. I had no choice, but to do as he demanded. Terikk would understand...I know he would," she cried.

Exhausted from her ordeal, she lay back on the bed. "Hmm...I need sleep." Her words were slow and distant. "After I rest...I will...I will know what to do then." She closed her eyes and prayed, "Gods, give me the strength to do the right thing for my people...give me the strength to do whatever I must," and fell asleep.

When she awoke, it was still dark outside. She wondered, *Have I slept for five hours or five minutes?* Wiping sleep from her eyes, Mervekka felt a sense of clarity come over her. Slowly, she sat upright, brushing the hair out of her face. "I can never tell Terikk," she whispered into the darkness. "He would declare war on Guan and that would tear New Caporesso apart. The country would be divided and destroyed, all because of Guan's deceitfulness." Her self-pity had turned to determination. "I will never allow that to happen." New Caporesso had special meaning to her before, now *she* meant everything to Mervekka. *She* had to survive so that Mervekka's sacrifice was not in vain.

All her hopes and dreams for herself were gone, stolen by Guan. She would have to live them through this new country. Clenching her fist, she avowed, "Gods hear me. Give me the strength to keep New Caporesso safe. Help me bear my shame in solitude. Forgive me my trespasses and protect the people. Hopefully one day, they will understand what I did for them... and forgive me."

It was still dark when Guan skulked away from Mervekka's chambers. After his footfalls faded into the darkness, the cloaked figure at the end of the hall stepped from his alcove. He walked to Mervekka's door and stopped. He put a hand on the wooden door and whispered, "Forgive me, Lady Mervekka. I could not help you tonight. But one day, when you need me, I will be there for you. If I must offer my life to save you, or that which matters most to you, I will. This I swear."

The only reply was the sound of Mervekka sobbing. Making sure the hallway was empty, the cloaked man retreated from Mervekka's chamber. The muffled sounds of her crying would linger in his thoughts for years to come.

Chapter 37

The red dawn awoke a sleepy New Caporesso. Chickens were tended and eggs gathered. The cattle were milked and fed. The day began like any other since New Caporesso was born. Her citizens did not know of the horror Mervekka endured for their sakes. They were oblivious to the choice she made on their behalf. Had they have known, they would have wept for her.

The morning found Mervekka already awake. Her eyes were puffy and bloodshot from lack of sleep. The images of what she endured tormented her mind. Her head was spinning with the possibilities of what might happen if she told anyone about Guan. Each scenario she conjured seemed worse than the others. She resigned herself to the fact she would remain silent. She would be strong for her people and her king.

Her room looked small this morning, almost tomblike. The twelve foot high ribbed ceiling felt close. As she stared at the stone and timber walls, she thought the spacious room was shrinking around her. The open shutters let in the unwelcomed light of day.

In silence, Mervekka got dressed with Abby's help. Mervekka thought, *She can never know.* Abby applied powder under Mervekka's eyes to help with the swelling.

Leaving her room, Mervekka walked like a specter through the corridor to the majestic staircase. This morning, the black and red threads in the carpet looked different. Their normal benign patterns reminded her of demons mocking her as she passed. The red lines shimmered like a river of blood, making her dizzy.

As she descended to the grand foyer, she heard Aacrel calling her name. "Mervekka, Mervekka?"

She closed her eyes and gathered herself. *This is it. Act like nothing happened.* "I'm here, Aacrel, not so loud."

Aacrel bounded up the steps to meet her. "Someone looks like they did not sleep well last night." He grinned, pointing at her eyes.

She nodded, but did not look at him. "Hmm."

"Mervekka?" he touched her arm.

She recoiled.

Not realizing her reaction, he informed her, "Terikk and Guan have gathered in the throne room. Let's not keep them waiting."

When Guan left her chambers in the night, she knew this dreadful moment was inevitable. She needed to be strong. She was strong, stronger than Guan could have anticipated. Mervekka would keep his secret. Her revenge would be to live in a unified land at peace with its fellow citizens. Guan would be like a nightmarish dream and nothing more.

Aacrel and Mervekka walked to the throne room. She entered first, and saw the guards standing at their posts. Feeling their gazes linger, she almost gasped, *They know! Somehow they know what happened.* She gulped and blinked her eyes. *No, I am imagining it. They do not suspect anything. They are not even looking at me.*

Terikk was seated on the mundane throne located at the top of the dais. Guan stood beside him; he looked like a proud cock in a hen house, waiting to make an announcement. They walked towards Terikk. As Aacrel and Mervekka got closer to the throne, they bowed politely and greeted their host.

"Greetings, King Terikk. Thank you for granting us this audience," Aacrel boomed. Simpering, he looked at Mervekka and chuckled, "I'm sorry, Terikk. It sounds strange to hear myself talk like that, in a place like this. How did we ever end up here?" He held his arms outstretched. "Did we really do this? Did we really change this country into something new and unseen in its history?"

"Yes, Aacrel, we did it." Terikk replied. "The real credit belongs to Hogeland and Mervekka." He stood up.

"Where is Hogeland?" asked Aacrel.

"He sent word that he was not feeling well today," he replied. "He would also like to see you later this morning, Mervekka."

Seeming preoccupied, she asked, "Is it anything serious, my king?"

Terikk shook his head, "No, I think he enjoys sleeping in nowadays. And he deserves the rest after everything he started. His original ideas, combined with your fortitude brought us here." He studied her beautiful face.

Mervekka bowed her head graciously, saying, "Thank you, my king." She did not look directly at anyone. "We all played our parts to make this country a reality." She spoke with no emotion, "Let us enjoy what it has become, and what it will be."

Terikk continued, "You are too gracious, Mervekka. As king, I want to make my first proclamation to all of you," he pointed at his three friends, "the four of us can dispense with all of this high court poetry and frivolity. When we are here together, speak to me as the friends we are, not like someone of great power is seated before you. Here we are equals, with an equal voice to be heard." He looked at each of them, "We are the best of friends."

Mervekka grimaced at the words. *Not all friends.* She looked at the servants preparing the table with a small meal. *They are looking at me; those girls never look at me. They must know.* Again, she closed her eyes. *No, stop it, Mervekka. You are imagining something that is not there.*

A smile slinked across Guan's lips, "My friends, I have wonderful news for you today. I was awake all night considering the possibility of a marriage between Milady and Terikk. My first reaction was to worry about alliances, wars, secret pacts, and dishonoring old friends." He extended his arm like he was pushing something away. "I was thinking as I did many years ago; forgetting all we accomplished in the last year. I am sorry for insulting all of you," he bowed his head. "I humbly ask for your forgiveness.

"When the sun greeted me this morning, I was left with one simple truth; you are the most honorable people in this land, completely above reproach. The North and Central Kingdoms do not seek a special alliance against Sokin. New Caporesso is the allegiance we have all sought." He placed a hand over his heart and leered at Mervekka, "I can see the love in your eyes and hearts. I do not know why I was blind to this truth last night; I simply could not see it." Smiling, he announced, "Today, I wish both Milady and Terikk infinite happiness and love in their new marriage! May the gods look favorably upon your union and bless you with many children!"

Terikk rose from his seat, gazing at Mervekka. He looked at Guan and took his arm in the hearty handshake of two veteran soldiers.

After a brief hug Guan spoke again, "Forgive me for not offering this answer last night, Terikk. I insulted you and your future bride, and I am sorry for that offense." *The other offense, I rather enjoyed.*

With a shake of his head and a wave of his hand, Terikk said, "There is nothing to forgive, Guan. A decision without thought can lead to an undesired consequence. We do not want there to be any apprehension between any of us."

Guan descended the stairs and approached Mervekka. The corners of his mouth turned up wickedly, and he grabbed her hand. "Milady, please accept my sincerest best wishes for your upcoming wedding." He bowed deeply, kissing her hand, "I know you will make a beautiful bride." Straightening himself, he gazed into her eyes, a self-satisfied look upon his face.

Mervekka glared at him. Through tight lips, she said, "Thank you, Guan, for your gracious decision. We are honored to have your approval. We look forward to you serving us as a *trusted* general in the New Caporesso Army."

That was contentious, thought Aacrel. He tried to lighten the moment, "Are children planned in the immediate future? I hope you have at least a dozen," he boomed, "but with that many running around these halls, you may need Guan and me stationed here to keep everything under control!" He guffawed. "We can send reinforcements when you are outnumbered by your horde of little ones!"

Terikk and Guan joined Aacrel in a laugh.

Aacrel shook Terikk's and then Guan's hand in turn. He congratulated Terikk again and asked, "When will this wonderful marriage be held?"

Guan answered quickly, "I insist it should be as soon as possible. I feel horrible about my hesitation last night, and I want the two of you to begin your lives together as soon as possible. Let the wedding be held by the end of the week. No more delays to your happiness. Please, my friends, I insist." He looked from Terikk to Mervekka. *You are still glowing, Milady.*

Aacrel nodded at Terikk. "I agree. You are king. Make this happen as quickly as possible."

"I have nothing to wear for the ceremony," Mervekka stated plainly, staring into the distance.

"Nonsense, the gown you wore yesterday was gorgeous. I am sure it can double as a wedding gown." Terikk looked closely at his future wife, his smile disappearing. "Nothing would please me more than to wed you by the week's end, but if you require more time to make sure this is right, I will gladly grant you the time you seek."

Begrudgingly, she looked at Guan, and then turned to Terikk. She forced herself to look in his eyes. "No, my love," she said, placing a hand on the side of his face. "I have had all the time I need to reach my decision." She fought to hold back a tear. "The sooner we are married, the happier I will be. Now what plans do we need to make?"

And so, Mervekka was to marry Terikk by the end of the week. Plans were made and dresses mended. Cenkin's residents and numerous guests were invited to the ceremony. Everything was set for the first royal wedding in New Caporesso's history. The people were jubilant for the joyous occasion. The celebration would close the last year's worth of new ideas and wonderful accomplishments. The unified country was at peace, and the king was about to marry the perfect woman to serve as queen to her people. All seemed well in New Caporesso.

Chapter 38

Five weeks after the ceremony, Mervekka awoke early. Her heart was racing and she was panting. She frantically looked around the room. *Where am I?* Terikk was lying beside her. *Oh...we are in bed...at home.* Her breathing slowed and she surveyed the room. Her wardrobes were on the far side of the room, her gowns and clothes neatly stored inside them. Terikk's armoires were ajar, just as he always left the doors, his shirts haphazardly hung on hooks. A chaise lounge was at the foot of the bed, her silk robe draped over it.

The grate in the stone-faced fireplace was empty, but there was a small stack of kindling on the raised hearth. The log mantle displayed Terikk's bastard sword, while his shield hung on the chimney above it. Elk and moose antler inspired chandeliers were dark above her head in the vaulted ceiling. Beams of an early summer morning penetrated the shutter cracks, lighting portions of the room.

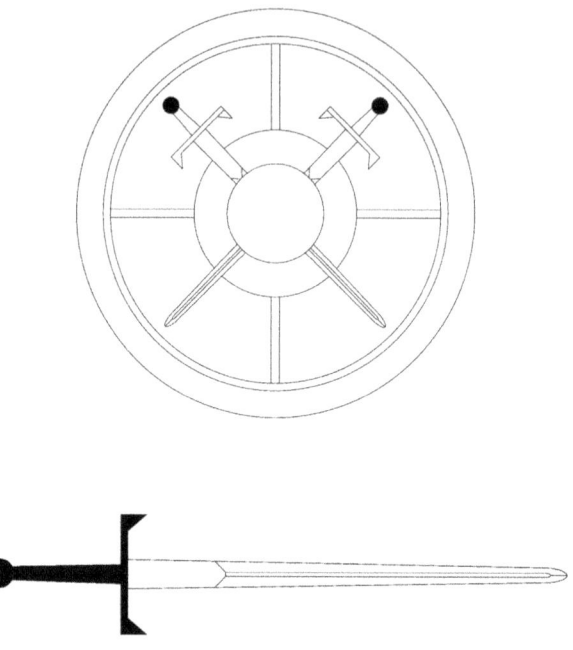

She looked at the wooden reinforced door; both bolts were still in place. *Guan visited my nightmares again.* Her stomach grumbled and she wrapped her arms around it. "Something is wrong, I feel—" Placing a hand over her mouth, she ran from the room.

"Mervekka," a groggy Terikk was roused by her voice, "hmm...what is wrong? Tell me, what is the matter?" She was gone before providing an answer. He tried to follow, but Abby stopped him at the door.

"Sire, the queen needs some time alone. She does not feel well this morning."

He could hear her retching in the distance. "Abby, what is wrong with her?"

She looked gently at Terikk and shook her head, "Nothing is wrong, sire. It's the morning, and she has the sickness, sire."

"What sickness, Abby?" He did not understand.

"The queen is pregnant, sire! Congratulations." Abby laughed. Losing her restraint, she hugged Terikk. Realizing her gaffe, she let go of him and regained her composure, "I'm sorry, sire. I don't know what came over me."

He was dumbfounded, "What do you mean? She is really...I mean already...I mean so soon...Wow!" He put his hand on his forehead. Then he reached for Abby and gave her a big hug. Releasing her, he admitted, "Abby, I am going to need some help with this."

She chuckled, "Of course, sire, of course. That's what I'm here for. You can always count on me."

Chapter 39

The year was 255 SA. New Caporesso had been united for fourteen short years. The citizens completely embraced their new way of life. War was all but forgotten, only a distant memory. The country was one cohesive land, its people unified in peace. Longtime enemies coexisted with their fellow New Caporessoeans. Laws were enacted and enforced as deterents to random violence. The death and bloodshed of the old land was replaced by temperance and prosperity.

The armies from the north, south, and central regions disbanded. Out of them, a new army was created in Cenkin. Its mission was to protect the country from marauders and bandits. At first, the task seemed monumental, but as the months and years passed, their goal became a reality. Fewer and fewer raiders persisted across the country.

The country's population was increasing, former soldiers settled down to raise new families. Dozens of new settlements were established away from the protection of the major cities. The villagers tended their fields and herds without the fear of death. The citizens' lives were simple, their survival certain.

New Caporesso's economy flourished. Trade routes from the cities of Norkin and Nurdug to Sokin and Cenkin thrived. Caravans travelled from city to city, selling and trading goods as they moved. Smaller convoys roamed the land, visiting the upstart communities. Everyone enjoyed the novel items produced in the other regions.

The ideas of Terikk, Aacrel, Mervekka, Hogeland, and Guan had taken hold. The people realized peace was good. Abundant goods and excess food meant there was enough of everything for everyone. The people flourished without war. New Caporesso appeared to be a success.

Sadly, in the winter of 241 SA, Hogeland succumbed to his illness. In his last weeks, he and Mervekka spent many hours together. They talked about the country and its infancy. He insisted that now was the most important time for New Caporesso. He told her that, as the rulers of the land, they could not sit back and idly watch the country develop, they needed to watch over her and provide guidance. He warned her not to grow content with all they had accomplished, imploring her to stay alert, and be on guard against any treachery.

As was his wish, he was buried beside his beloved wife and young sons; even Aacrel wept at the funeral. The city mourned his passing by carving his likeness into four gargoyle sentinels on the parapet walls. They faced in the four directions of the wind, forever guarding Cenkin from the approach of outside danger.

Terikk and Mervekka heeded Hogeland's advice, and governed the country as benevolent rulers. The elected representatives from the various regions kept them abreast of the needs of the people. No decision was made without considering its impact on their subjects. The goal had been to create a better country for the people of New Caporesso in which to live. In that, they succeeded. People were treated as equals. No longer were the strong and savage rewarded for their barbarism.

Good men and women like Terikk and Mervekka were the chosen ones, determined to lead the country into the future. The people loved Terikk so much that they elected him king for two more terms. His two previous six year terms brought stability and growth to the country. During the second year of his third term, there was no reason to expect any great adversity in their future. In 255 SA, the growing pains of the country appeared over. It appeared as though nothing could derail the new nation.

Not only did New Caporesso thrive, but Terikk and Mervekka did so as well. Three children were born during their reign as king and queen. The oldest child, Col, was born nine months after Terikk and Mervekka were married. He was thirteen years old now, and the image of his mother. Vitoria was two years younger than Col, and at age eleven, was a vivacious little girl. Her straight black hair and green eyes suggested that one day she would be a rare beauty. Her parents named her Vitoria, but everyone called her Vee. It was the nickname her baby brother, Shua, had given her. Shua was eight years old and resembled his father.

The royal family had been blessed with many gifts. They helped create New Caporesso, they had three wonderful children, and the citizens of New Caporesso loved them. Everything appeared perfect. Mervekka tried to be happy, but knew in the back of her mind, all was not well. The passion that had once been in her heart for Terikk was diminished, being replaced by melancholy emotion. No matter how she tried, she could not put that one night behind her.

In her heart, she believed Guan would use his carnal knowledge of her to influence her future decision-making ability. He would wait until a time of his choosing, and then threaten to reveal their indiscretion. She would be forced to do as he desired—again. *What have I done? How will I ever make it stop?* Mervekka realized she was his puppet, whom he could control at his whim. Was keeping New Caporesso intact worth the price she was paying? To her, the answer was a definite yes. She would sacrifice anything to save her country.

Chapter 40

Guan was a warrior and a man of action. A battlefield was his cathedral; combat, his creed. Peacetime had reduced him to an obedient dog. Filled with contempt, he obeyed his master, the king of New Caporesso. For fourteen years he bided his time, waiting for the opportunity to strike at the heart of the institution that enslaved him. The time was almost right.

To save his army, he helped form New Caporesso all those years ago. Now he wished he had let them meet their doom on the Field of Angl. It would have been a better fate for him and his men, rather than become like docile sheep. Terikk ordered them to keep the peace, nothing more. There was no conquest, there was no aggression. To Guan, there was no honor in being a servant of the people. He was meant for greater things. He was meant to rule over these pathetic peasants.

Shortly after the formation of New Caporesso, Guan realized his mistake, but it was too late. Events were set in motion that could not be undone. The entire country wanted peace, even his beloved Southern Kingdom. The notion was an abomination he could no longer tolerate.

He paced in his quarters, waiting for the monthly report from Commander Tyr. *He is late.* Guan could not stand lack of punctuality, and would have replaced Tyr from duty, except for the fact he was the best soldier under his command. He was a better tactician than Moto and a better leader than Druvl.

Guan's lodgings were elegantly decorated. He had insisted on a circular room in the southern spire of Trosho, with two-story windows looking north, south, and east. The rounded walls were expertly crafted from precisely chiseled stone. The plank floor creaked as he walked across it, sagging as he went. Animal heads hung on the walls; there were several wolves, a lion, a cougar, and brown and black bears. Brass sconces held torches, and a chandelier constructed from deer and Bontebok antlers held candles, lighting the room.

Along the southern edge of the room, was a large bed with ram horns on the thick posts; there he entertained Cenkin's wenches. In the center of the room were a round table and scoop back chairs. He normally ate his meals alone there. His sword habitually rested on a stand in the middle of the table. Three armoires on the northern wall held his uniforms and other essentials.

Starting along the west wall was a spiral staircase that led to the loft above. It was there that he made his plans, that space was his alone. A desk, chair, and candelabra were the only items on the platform. The room was as he requested, but in his heart, he longed for the timber dwellings of the south.

A knock on his door made him turn his head. "Enter," he knew it was Tyr by the thumping. As the door opened, he admonished the man, "You are late, Commander Tyr." He exaggerated a sigh, "I do not know why I tolerate this unprofessional behavior in one of my soldiers. See that it does not happen again, or I shall be forced to find someone else to do your job, like your predecessor. Do you understand?"

"A thousand pardons, General," Tyr bowed at the waist as he spoke. "The guards were running late today, and I had to wait until they were out of sight before I could approach. Our secrecy is of the utmost importance, sir."

Guan nodded his head. "Yes, Tyr, secrecy is critical. You do understand that very well." He waved a hand. "I should have known there was something beyond your control delaying you. You know better than to disappoint me."

"Yes, sir. As you've said, the Cenkin guards are getting lazier. They make their rounds later and later every day. I expect one day soon, they will not even bother patrolling," he said in a disgusted tone.

"Do you have word from Commanders Moto and Druvl? How goes their training at the Sokin camp?" Guan asked with anticipation.

Tyr pulled out a letter and read it. "To General Guan," he cleared his throat, "The men are ready to bleed and die for you. There is no glory except that which comes from you, General. Give us the order. We are ready to do your bidding. Strength and honor."

A grin crossed Guan's lips. "They sound ready, Tyr, and now the time is right." He folded his arms behind his back and looked out a window, "When I realized the enormity of my mistake all those years ago, it was too late. To my displeasure, Sokin had already accepted Mervekka's drivel, seemingly changing their beliefs overnight." He huffed, "I guess that whore's beauty tainted the minds of our people. I had to wait until the people from Sokin remembered who they are." Making a fist, he explained. "I had to wait until they craved retribution for the destruction of their way of life. I needed them to yearn for war once more." He turned to face Tyr. "And that time is now.

"Take this down: 'To Commander Moto. The time has come to assemble the army. March them to the established rendezvous point. Send word when you arrive. Avoid contact no matter what. Maintain advanced scouts to make sure the way is clear. Dispose of anyone who can report your activity, without exception. I am counting on you, Commander. Make haste and stay hidden.' Sign my name, and give the message to Donetsk. He awaits your arrival at the stables."

"Yes, sir," nodded Tyr.

"Our hour of glory is almost here. Soon Moto and Druvl will move into position, and the time for action will be at hand. The New Caporesso Army is fat and lazy, a direct result of Terikk and Aacrel. They have failed to maintain a well disciplined army." He spoke with contempt, "Both men are incompetent fools." He scoffed, "I have even warned them, telling them to stay vigilant and ready for war, for none of us can know the future." He slammed his fist into his open hand. "Yet they ignore me, and let the men fall into complacency and disarray. That disorganized rabble could not even hold back a flock of sheep!" his anger and excitement showed through.

Tyr replied in a somber tone, "Yes, sir."

Guan sensed something wrong. Turning, he looked at Tyr. "What is it, Commander? You do not seem yourself tonight."

Looking at the floor and then back at Guan, he admitted, "Sir, you know my loyalty is to you alone, but I can't help but wonder if this is a mistake." He lowered his eyes again. "New Caporesso has been at peace for fourteen years, and things are good. The country is flourishing. Is peace such a terrible thing to endure, sir?" Tyr was not sure how Guan would respond.

"Commander Tyr..." Guan realized he was having second thoughts about the mission. *Insolent fool!* He would have punished him, but Tyr was an integral part of the plan to overthrow Terikk. *No, I must convince my commander that we are doing this for the people of New Caporesso.* "Tyr, you are one of the best soldiers under my command, perhaps the best. The men respect you. I know that your intentions are venerable and that you do not seek to undermine me." Guan regarded the wavering soldier in front of him.

"No, sir, I would never say or do anything to question your authority. I am here to serve you." He raised his hands. "I only ask...are we are doing the right thing, sir?"

Guan considered his response for a moment. "Tyr, are the weak fit to lead us?" he asked defiantly.

"No, sir,"

"Why not?"

"Because they can't make the right decisions to protect us. They lack the vision to lead us to greatness," responded Tyr.

"And what should we do to the weak?"

"Remove them from power, sir. They will only drag us down and destroy us," Tyr answered with forced enthusiasm.

"That is right." Guan paused, "Remember the old ways, Tyr. Remember what your parents taught you. Remember what your teachers taught you. Mercy is for the weak. We are better because we are strong. The other kingdoms are inferior to us. We should rule over all of New Caporesso, we, the people of the Southern Kingdom. As it is, New Caporesso is destroying the essence of who we are." He shook his head in disgust. "Will you help me save our way of life? Will you help me save our people, Tyr?

He replied, "Sir…"

"Terikk and Aacrel have led us astray; they have failed New Caporesso. They allowed it to become a land full of lazy dogs. You know this to be true, the army is all but disbanded, and Cenkin is defenseless against attack," he moved closer to Tyr, putting a hand on his shoulder. "What should we do, Tyr? Should we sit by and let them lead all of us to destruction?" He searched Tyr's face for an answer.

"No, sir, we can't allow that. We must act on behalf of the citizens of New Caporesso. Only we can save them from themselves." He nodded his acceptance.

"Yes, Tyr. We must save them. Terikk has already betrayed them. If we do nothing, then we will not have protected them either. The only way to keep them safe is to seize control of the government." He backed away from Tyr. "We must create new policies to keep the churls safe. A well-trained army must be maintained. The one in place now is useless, and must be destroyed in order to rid this country of its filth."

Tyr's eyes appeared to fill with hope as he listened to Guan's propaganda. "Sir, forgive me for questioning your intentions. You've helped me see that this is the only way to protect the people of New Caporesso. We must preemptively strike against those who would let them fall into despair."

"Understand, Tyr, I do not want to do this, but it is the only way to safeguard the proles." He nodded. "I am glad you realize why we must. Only we can protect New Caporesso. It is up to us, and it will start here, in Cenkin. Do you understand?"

"Yes, General, I understand completely, sir. Strength of swords, honor in victory," he saluted.

Guan studied Tyr for a moment. Satisfied the man had accepted his reasons for rebellion, he dismissed him. Tyr turned, and walked out of the room with the message for Moto in hand. Guan knew that in the dead of the night, a rider would be sent from the city. The messenger's path would lead him southeast to the site where Moto and Druvl were training an army. He sneered to himself. This army's single purpose was to rid New Caporesso of its worthless soldiers.

Once destroyed, Guan would lay claim to the throne of New Caporesso. With no one to stand in his way, his ascension to power would finally fulfill his destiny to rule over the worthless people of New Caporesso. Only three obstacles remained in his way, Terikk, Aacrel, and Mervekka. He would dispose of Terikk and Aacrel at the same time. His eyes widened, *I will have Tyr kill them and prove his worth again.*

He walked over to his window and looked outside, pondering. Mervekka was different; he was not sure he wanted her dead. He had not forgotten their night together. Sometimes, when he closed his eyes, he could still see the terror in her eyes and smell her fear. The memories drove him wild. The fact that Col was born roughly nine months after their encounter only encouraged him. The possibility existed that he was the boy's father.

Contemplating Mervekka's future, he placed his hands on the cold sill in front of him. Stone faced, he peered outside. The Field of Angl beckoned to him in the distance. He started to laugh. *That field bested me fourteen years ago. Soon, my army will be here at the gates of Cenkin again, but this time with a different outcome. There will be no surprises this time. This time, I will crush the pathetic army before me and claim the throne of New Caporesso for myself. This time, I will have my glory and immortality!* The sounds of his wicked laughter filled the room.

Chapter 41

Tyr walked away from Guan's quarters deep in thought. He was loyal to Guan and had been for almost two decades. Like all men from the south, the willingness to obey his general's orders without hesitation had been indoctrinated into him since birth, he could not deny it. However, a part of him speculated that Guan's actions were being driven by his lust for power. Was he really trying to protect the people of New Caporesso as he said he was? At times, he talked about them with so much disdain that Tyr doubted if Guan cared anything for them at all.

The last fourteen years in New Caporesso had been good. Terikk proved himself to be a good king and a faithful servant of the people. He acted on their behalf, not his own. Power and wealth were not his goals. He truly wanted his people to have a better world to live in than the previous one, where they merely existed. Tyr knew Terikk would never intentionally do anything to place the people of New Caporesso in danger. Why did Guan imply he was doing just that? It made no sense to him.

He scratched his head as he walked. *Which oath is more important? The one I swore to Guan or the one to Terikk and New Caporesso? The one to Guan is old, almost twenty years old, maybe it is no longer valid. My oath to Terikk and New Caporesso was to protect them from all enemies. What should I do?*

Times had changed, and Tyr was no longer Guan's minion, to be ordered to kill at his whim. He was now a freethinking man, a follower of Terikk and Mervekka's teachings. They were trying to make the world a better place, and Guan was about to destroy them for it.

The upcoming weeks would hold many questions for Tyr. He believed his actions would determine the ultimate success or failure of Guan's coup. He feared the fate of New Caporesso rested in his hands. Would he try to save it, or aid in its destruction? Tyr felt the weight of the world on his shoulders. How would he respond to his dilemma? Only time would tell.

Emerging from Trosho's mighty entrance, he touched a hand to his pocket. The written orders from Guan were there. He did not pull them out to peruse them again; there was no need. There was nothing he could do to change them. Tyr headed off to the nearby stables in search of the scout Guan had selected to ride to the Sokin camp.

Donetsk was one of the best scouts in the land. Tyr knew he would carry the message safely and arrive undetected at Moto and Druvl's camp within three weeks. The army would reach Cenkin within another month. After that, the New Caporesso Army would be destroyed. Then, the model that was New Caporesso would be gone forever.

Tyr did not know what he could do to save New Caporesso and its king and queen. Perhaps there was nothing he could do, except follow destiny's course and make a stand when the time came.

Chapter 42

Fifty-two nights later, Tyr returned to Guan's billet. His expression was somber as he handed a letter to Guan.

"Do not look so troubled, Commander," Guan studied Tyr as he took the note. He quickly read it. "Everything is ready, Tyr. Commanders Moto and Druvl have arrived. Their scouts report no one has reported their position. The few who witnessed their movement were quickly dispatched before informing anyone of their existence. Excellent." He moved to the window, eagerly looking southeast towards the Stone Pine Forest. There was nothing to see. No movement and no indication that an army of over ten thousand men was waiting to descend upon Cenkin in the morning.

He turned to Tyr. "Write this down. 'To Commanders Moto and Druvl: well done. Proceed to the eastern encampment. Attack in force and with speed. Silence is pivotal. Annihilate the camp before they can bring their archers to bear. Kill everyone, no prisoners, no quarter given. Raise the black flag!'" he exclaimed. "'After the destruction of the first camp, split your forces, sending half around the walls to the north and the other to the south. Destroy both camps simultaneously.

"'Continue to the western gate. By then it will not matter if the alarm has been sounded; kill anyone still in position there. The gate will be opened from the inside, and someone will be awaiting your arrival. Godsspeed, *Generals*. Success and glory are yours for the taking, claim it and it shall be yours!'" Guan raised his fist as his excitement overflowed. Clearing his throat, he continued, "'Commence the attack on the eastern encampment before first light. Stealth and speed are the keys to our victory. Do not fail me.'"

Tyr scribbled everything Guan spoke. He signed Guan's initials and folded the letter. Standing up, he placed it in his pocket, waiting to be dismissed.

Guan approached him. "Tomorrow will be a glorious day. The gods favor us, and our success is guaranteed." He slapped his adjutant on the shoulders. "I have a special assignment for you. Select ten men, take them, and kill Terikk, Aacrel, and anyone else with them. Tomorrow morning, they are walking to Getty's Grove to the west. They plan to discuss Cenkin's new trade policies. I have declined to go with them, citing other duties which require my attention. When they are away from the city, kill them. Destroy the bodies. I want no remains ever found, but bring me their weapons. They will be my trophies from this conquest. Do you understand?"

Stone-faced and with no emotion, Tyr answered, "Yes, General, I understand. They will be killed and their bodies burned. Consider it done, sir." Saluting, he said, "Strength of swords, honor in victory." He waited for Guan's dismissal and then exited the room. The door closed behind him, and he walked down the hallway towards the staircase. After descending one flight, he stopped and leaned against the wall. His knees were shaking.

The time is here, and I must decide what to do. Guan's plan is perfect. New Caporesso will be destroyed in the morning. All of the dreams and ideas that comprised it will be dashed to bits. There is no hope for any of them. If I try to help Terikk, Guan will kill me. If I do not help him, I sacrifice my soul. What choice do I have?

He continued to the stables, giving the written orders to Donetsk. Tyr watched as the young man rode away with haste. He would return to Moto and Druvl. They would review the orders and make their final preparations for the assault on Cenkin. Tomorrow, New Caporesso would cease to exist. The soldiers defending it would meet a bloody death, butchered at the hands of Guan's army. Tomorrow, the Boatman would welcome many new souls. There was nothing Tyr could do to hold back the tides of war. The only path before him was to follow his orders and pray for forgiveness.

Chapter 43

Guan anxiously awaited first light. From his perch on the western wall, he had watched the shapes of Terikk, Shua, and Aacrel leave the city an hour earlier. There was nothing he could do about it. He would have to rely on Tyr to dispose of them. Guan's charge was to collect Mervekka, Col, and Princess Vitoria. He needed to capture them before they could escape. Mervekka's participation was necessary to legitimize his coup.

He walked towards the southeast corner of the wall. Because of Terikk's poor leadership, the night watch had been abandoned, leaving Guan alone atop the wall. As he passed Hogeland's southern gargoyle, he spat on its bald head. Reaching the southeast corner, he surveyed the surround. The sun was still below the horizon, only the wind moved over the land. He stood silently, watching for what seemed like an eternity, and then he saw what he was searching for. Emerging from the Stone Pine Forest tree line was a long line of soldiers. They were followed by more and more soldiers. It was a beautiful sight to behold.

Closer and closer they came. Silently, the giant wave of soldiers raced towards their foe. Guan's eyes fluttered, and he could not help but grin. All his years of planning were about to be rewarded. Finally, his dream of becoming the absolute ruler of New Caporesso would be realized. Every minute of his life had led him to this moment in time. His destiny was about to be fulfilled.

A cool spring morning greeted the new day as night's darkness was melting away. The pitter-patter of water dripping from pine trees was everywhere. Squirrels chittered and ate pine nuts from the branches, while birds announced the coming sun. The grass around the forest was damp from the morning dew.

The day's calm was broken by the footsteps of soldiers as their boots kicked the droplets of water away. Soon, the ground was trampled and dirty. Evil had been unleashed. General Moto and General Druvl surveyed their target.

"They are still asleep, Moto. Not even sentries or pickets are posted!" Druvl whispered.

"Yes, Druvl. General Guan's reports were correct. These worthless soldiers are ill prepared for war." He smirked at his friend, "Let's go say good morning to them." Moto motioned for the first brigade of soldiers to advance. Quickly, the other units followed at the quick step. Within a matter of minutes, all four brigades of southern men were moving towards their unsuspecting victims. Silently, death approached the sleeping men from New Caporesso.

Chapter 44

Screaming children shattered the quiet morning. Col and Vee chased each other in the training courtyard inside Castle Trosho. The space was open to the sky, allowing it to be filled with the day's natural light. The training area consisted of a twenty-five foot square area of fine sand. Combatants practiced their weapon techniques in this central area. A fifteen-foot wide grassy area encircled the pit and was used for empty hand and ground fighting training.

The outer area was decorated with small trees and boulders. These appeared to beautify the scene but were also used in training. Fighting on and around objects was a necessary skill for a soldier. The training space was bathed in a drab, grey twilight, with the sun just breaking above the eastern horizon. Within the hour, its light would fill the courtyard.

Today, however, the combat obstacles were convenient hiding places. Vee squealed as her brother chased her around the bushes. Col shrieked as he jumped from rock to rock. Their morning playtime in the area was the best time of the day. Sometimes they played for hours on end.

Mervekka watched from the promenade. She liked to sneak in and watch her children play together. Their interaction always amazed her. When they were alone, they could play for hours and never argue. There was something about being on their own that made them more agreeable to each other. Mervekka loved being a mother, and the simple joy of watching them was almost enough to erase the memories from that horrific night. *How could I have ever been disappointed in him, thinking he was Guan's?* She shook her head. *No, he is so gentle with his sister, there is no evil in him. I was wrong to ever think that could be true.*

Shua left with Terikk and Aacrel to explore Getty's Grove. They departed Cenkin before dawn and walked the two miles, reaching the edge of the trees before sunrise. Shua had already been playing in the woods for an hour as the sun broached the horizon. Fallen ironwood and garland crab trees made perfect citadels. Intertwined junipers were sturdy ramparts, protecting Shua's keep.

He pretended he was a soldier, fighting a sinister enemy. Running from tree to rock, he ducked behind them for protection from his enemies' arrows. He always found a good stick to carry for his sword. Sometimes, his wooden enemies wounded him in battle, but he always emerged victorious. He was invincible in the woods. His father and Aacrel watched him play with a boyish delight.

Shua had tried to rouse Col and Vee to join them, but they would not budge from their beds. He tried several times, only to be rejected. Sleep was more important to them. Now, he was playing by himself and having a grand time. It was their loss they were missing all the fun. Today was perfect.

Terikk and Aacrel stood away from Shua talking about affairs of the country and other issues. Aacrel admitted, "I am not sure what is going on. The kingdoms report that their trade outposts are enjoying great profits. We know the deposits are being made into the kingdom's banks, but the Cenkin treasury is reporting a loss. It is as though the money is being siphoned off and used someplace else. How can this be possible?"

"How long has the treasury been low on coin from the trade taxes?" Terikk placed a hand on his chin.

"It appears to have started about twelve months ago."

"That coincides with the time a new officer of the treasury was appointed. Right?" Terikk scratched his head. "He was selected by Guan, was he not?"

"Yes to both questions, but," Aacrel shook his head, "I cannot believe Guan has anything to do with these discrepancies. Can you?"

"Perhaps we still see in our old friend much that is gone." He sighed, "He is not the same man he was when we formed New Caporesso. He has distanced himself from us, putting up barriers." Terikk shook his head. "He receives reports from his aides, but fails to provide us with the information." Rubbing the back of his neck, he said, "We need to talk to Guan about his actions over these last few years. He will not accept our line of questioning without at least a verbal fight. I fear we may have let him go unchecked for too long. If he brings conflict to the city, our men will not able to repel him." Terikk admitted, "Our army is no longer comprised of prime soldiers ready for battle. He warned us to stay vigil and ready for war. Perhaps he was warning us of his intentions."

Aacrel let out a long sigh, "It is true about our army, but do you really think he would, or could attack us? We decided together that peace was in the best interest of the country. War only brings destruction. Peace has brought prosperity for everyone."

"But he is a true soldier, Aacrel. And what is a soldier without a war?" Terikk raised his hands. "Nothing. We must speak with him directly when we return." He called to his son, "Shua! Come along, it's time to return home."

"Aah, Poppa, I was storming Castle Lau'damay. I breached the walls this time!"

Terikk chuckled. "Another time, Son. Now, we must go."

Shua, his father, and Aacrel began the walk back to Cenkin and Castle Trosho.

Chapter 45

Moto's men butchered the first camp of sleeping soldiers. There was practically no fight. Most of them peacefully slept through their own deaths. Those pitiful men were not fit to wear a soldier's uniform. They received a just penalty for their lack of watchfulness. Moto and Druvl were both disgusted with the army's defense of Cenkin.

"The alarm has not been raised yet, Druvl. We killed over five hundred men, and no one mounted any resistance. They are a disgrace to the soldiers who wore those uniforms with honor. Death by the sword of a Southern is better than they deserved." He spit on the ground, "The swine!"

Druvl wiped off his sword. "Better for us that they don't fight well today. Guan will be pleased by our success and the absence of our own casualties. But the fight is not over, Moto; three more encampments await our early morning call!" he laughed.

"Then let's see to the remainder of the day. I'll take the first and second brigades to the northern camp. You take the third and fourth south. Speed is the key," he slammed his fist into his hand. "Move at a steady pace, and hopefully we will engage both camps at the same time. Make sure everyone is incapacitated, and then continue west. If we ambush both camps successfully, the alarm still may not be sounded."

"After that, it won't matter if it is or not." Druvl grinned, "It'll be too late for them to stop us. Once inside the walls, they will have no choice but to surrender or perish," he chuckled. Extending a hand to Moto, he said, "No quarter to the enemy. Good luck, General Moto."

Moto accepted his friend's hand and shook it. "Raise the black flag. And good luck to you, General Druvl." Both men nodded at each other and turned to lead their men to their next engagement. The sea of southern men was about to become an unstoppable tidal wave, crashing upon the fragile shores of Cenkin and New Caporesso. It seemed nothing could withstand the onslaught of death.

Druvl ordered his men to advance quietly southward. Five thousand men made their way around the wall with no resistance. As they reached the southern face of the wall, they paused. Druvl observed the defending soldiers still asleep. *We still have the element of surprise!* He ordered them forward at the quickstep.

Within fifty feet of their quarry, the distant sound of battle reached their ears. *The alarm!* Moto was engaging the northern encampment. *We must hurry.* "Attack, attack, attack! For glory and Guan!" Brandishing his sword above his head, he implored his men forward.

The groggy men from the southern camp grabbed their weapons and rushed to their posts, but it was too late. Druvl and his men attacked with speed, cutting through the defending soldiers like a swarm of fire ants taking down their helpless victim. The New Caporessoean men were acting on old instincts but could not muster a unified defense. Within twenty minutes of the first clash of weapons, the men from the outpost were either dead or mortally wounded.

Another victory for Druvl and his men. Now on to the western gate, where they would destroy the final encampment. Druvl cried out, "To the western gate. No quarter to anyone!"

His soldiers cheered in unison. Men shouted, "Raise the black flag!" over and over again. Quickly, they reformed their lines and headed west. Not even the gods themselves could hold back this surge of men.

Chapter 46

The first rays of the new day gave an orange glow to the training courtyard. Mervekka was still enjoying her children when something caught her eye. *Wait! What is that?* On the courtyard level, she noticed a cloaked shape standing near a stone column. *Oh no!* She recognized the figure of the man in the shadows. It was Guan. She ran from her position, descending the flight of stairs in several giant bounds.

Charging onto the training level, she ran towards Col and Vee, her dress frantically chasing after her. They were startled to see her.

"Momma, what are you doing here?" asked Vee, giggling.

"Run to me!" she screeched, but they were paralyzed by her fear, unable to move. Mervekka's heart was pounding.

In a blur of motion, Guan ambushed Col, grabbing him from behind. "Be silent or die right now!" he rasped into the youngster's ear.

The boy shrieked and tried to look over his shoulder. He was horrified to see Guan towering over him.

Screaming, Vee charged at Guan, hitting him on the arm.

Guan backhanded her, knocking her headlong into the sandpit. She lay in a heap, unaware of anything for several minutes.

It felt like something was holding her back, preventing Mervekka from reaching her children. She screamed, "Guards, help me! Protect my children!"

Men wearing black uniforms stepped closer to Guan, but they did not restrain him. Disbelievingly, Mervekka saw the hooded serpent on the chest of their tunics. They were wearing Sokin's old uniform! *They are Guan's Dragoons. He has betrayed me again!* Standing beside Vee, there was nothing she could do.

Guan nodded at his men and they surrounded her. One of them hit her in the midsection with his spear, knocking her to the ground. Sand splashed onto her face.

"Surrender immediately, Milady," he demanded, "or your children die now."

Realizing she had no other choice, she acquiesced, "I surrender. Just spare my children," she pleaded. Cradling her daughter, she held her tight. There was no way for Mervekka to protect them, they were all at Guan's mercy.

He released Col, and the terrified boy ran to his mother, huddling behind her.

"Milady, how are you today?" Guan asked in a carefree tone. "Is this not just the perfect morning?" He breathed deeply, enjoying the crisp air. Causally, he paced back and forth in front of her. "You should know that my army is sacking Cenkin as we speak, and no one is coming to save you. My generals Moto and Druvl have returned with my army and have engaged yours. Your men do not stand a chance against them and will be destroyed." An evil smile tried to form on his face. "I have also sent a squad to…collect your husband, son, and Aacrel. Maybe they will survive the encounter, maybe they will not. But rest assured, I will soon be in control of Cenkin and New Caporesso."

He stopped walking and glared at her. The corner of his eye spasmed. "How does it feel to know that all of your friends from our peace summit will be out of the way by the end of the day?" Smacking his chest and exhaling fully, he confessed, "I find it rather refreshing and a cause for celebration." A tingle ran down his spine. "Tonight I will commemorate my glorious victory and successful coup d'état!"

Mervekka could not breathe; her head was spinning. She tried to speak, but made no audible sounds. Helplessly, she watched Guan.

Stepping closer, he continued, "You again have a choice before you, Milady, like that night so many years ago. Stand with me. Recognize me as the new king, and you and your children will live." His eye danced erratically. "The secret that we share will also remain hidden. No one needs to know about Col." He licked his lips. "Stand with me and the hostilities end today."

His words sounded far away, like he was talking into a jar. Mervekka tried to clear her head. Dazed, she repeated Guan's words, slurring, "I have a choice before me?"

He smirked, "Defy me and everyone will learn of our affair. The people will hear how we conspired to overthrow Terikk and seize control of New Caporesso by force." He clapped his hands together. "I will tell the proles that on the eve of your engagement, we colluded to conceive a child who would be the heir to the throne of New Caporesso; Col.

"Our plan was to bide our time and gather support for our great cause. Once our army was strong enough, we struck with all of our strength in one mighty blow." Pointing a gnarled finger at her, he declared, "When my army controls the city, the people have no choice but to accept me as their new king." He chortled sinisterly. "Yes, Milady, the people will believe me," he bluffed, "and they will embrace me as the new ruler of New Caporesso."

She regained her composure enough to question his plan, "Who will believe your lies, Guan? I will deny your accusations and the people will arrest you. You will be convicted of murdering the king and plotting a rebellion against the government, which is punishable by death." She tried to sound confident.

"Believe me?" Guan inquired. *I must convince her to do my bidding, or I will be at risk. I need her or the people will not follow me.* "The whole city will believe me. After I explain what has happened, I will simply let you speak to them." He shrugged his shoulders. "Your emotion will betray you, confirming to the peasants that I speak the truth. They will curse you, and demand you be tried for treason." Mocking her, he said, "And as you know, that crime is punishable by death."

Vee groaned, trying to wake up, while Col hid his face behind his mother's dress.

"How perfect, the lady who gave these people peace and justice will be sentenced to death by her own system." He chortled, "I will enjoy that series of events immensely. You could have told Terikk and the people of my sins the morning after they were committed. They all would have believed you then." Sighing, he said, "But to wait fourteen years to announce the offense makes it sound fabricated. Those miserable churls will believe my story, that you were a willing participant in all of this. And if you speak against me now, it will appear as though you are trying to double-cross me and seek power for yourself."

Her brow furrowed as she listened to his discourse and her face went white.

Ah, I see she believes my words. "Yes, to come out now against me would only be an admission of your own guilt to the entire country. You have no choice but to do as I say, or you will certainly die by the hands of your people.

"But you interrupted me before I could finish describing what happens to you if you defy me." Guan chuckled, "How foolish. If you defy me, I will make you watch as I torture your children!" He eyed Vee's unmoving body. "How much pain do you think Princess Vitoria can withstand?" Looking at Col, he threatened, "How long before Col cries out, wishing for death?" Slowly nodding his head, he assured her, "Trust me, it will be horrible.

"And you," he pointed at her, "will watch it all, knowing you could have prevented it." His eye winked as he snarled at her, "Ultimately, they will die, but you Milady, you will live for many years as my...prisoner. The memories of your children dying in front of your eyes will drive you completely mad, but you will live on." Guan guffawed. "That is the other choice before you, Milady."

He sounded sure of himself. The more Mervekka thought about his words, she realized he was right. *You bastard!* Again, he outmaneuvered her and was in a position of control over her. She had to save her children and keep them alive. To do that meant recognizing him as king.

Reluctantly, Mervekka bowed her head and said, "Guan, you have my support." She held back her tears. "I will announce you as the king of New Caporesso. In return, my children must remain unharmed and our secret untold." She spoke determinedly, "If you deny me this, I will call whatever loyal men I can find to my side, and we will fight you in the streets! We will fight you to the bitter end, until none of us remain! Spare my children and I will do as you wish."

Guan said contemptuously, "As you wish, Milady. No harm will come to Col or Princess Vitoria." Nodding at her, he ordered the guards to escort them to the queen's chambers for the time being. He would call upon her when he was ready.

Mervekka carried Vee while Col clung to his mother's dress as they walked through the corridors of Trosho. Uncontrolled tears rolled down her cheeks. *Ah! I never said goodbye this morning. I may never get the chance to say goodbye to my son.* The thought staggered her step. Regaining her balance, she continued towards her room.

A second thought came to her; New Caporesso was dying too. Guan was killing *her*, and *she* would never be the same. Everything Mervekka and her friends had worked so hard to build was being destroyed. The trustworthy government, the peace between the kingdoms, the prosperity of the people, it was all about to end. Guan would never allow things to continue as they had before, no, he would rule as a tyrant.

Arriving at her room, the guards opened the door. Mervekka entered and laid Vee on the bed. Col ran and hid on the far side of the room. Before she could turn around, the guards had locked them inside.

After several minutes, Vee awoke and looked at her mother. "What happened, Momma?"

Col jumped up on the bed. With tears in his eyes, he asked, "Where's Poppa? Where's Shua?"

A wave of emotion overtook Mervekka, and she could not answer. All she could do was hug her children. She hoped to make them feel safe with her, but realized none of them would ever be safe again.

Chapter 47

Late in the morning, Moto and Druvl met at the western gate of Cenkin. Bodies lay haphazardly on the ground. Blood and limbs were everywhere. The day was still young, but the men had been in three engagements. The final battle at the western gate went just like the previous ones. Bloodstained tents were ripped to shreds. Their men overwhelmed the soldiers at Cenkin's final outpost. Now the southern men controlled all four gates of the city.

Both men were dirty and had blood on their black uniforms. Moto bore a fresh cut on his face, and trickles of dried blood were on Druvl's arms. The four brigades involved had similar injuries, mostly superficial.

Druvl greeted his friend with a hug. "Good to see you again, Moto! Was the battle as easy for you and your men as it was for us?"

Moto smacked Druvl's back. "Probably easier! Only a handful of my men were injured, and no one was killed. I've never been in such a one-sided battle like this before. Our men were so superior in every way that there was almost no honor in fighting." He shook his head in disgust. "The men here were despicable soldiers."

"It's not that I doubted Guan's reports concerning their vigilance," Druvl admitted, "but I found it hard to believe that an army could be as unprepared for war as he described. But he was absolutely correct." He coughed. "Did you leave any survivors in the north?"

"No, Druvl, when we moved west from the outpost, everyone was dead or dying. We left a battalion of five hundred men to occupy the position and control access out of Cenkin. Any survivors to the south?"

"Dead to the last man, Moto," he looked pleased with himself. "We too left a battalion to patrol the outpost and keep anyone from escaping." Turning, he looked at the gate behind them. "Now, let's see to this western gate, it's supposed to be open for us already."

As they moved towards it, the doors creaked and moaned. Slowly, it opened outward, and a captain under Guan's control greeted them. "Good morning, Generals. General Guan bids you welcome to his city. I am Captain Festo, and he sent me to escort you to Castle Trosho where he is waiting for you. He wants you to follow me." Festo spoke with Guan's authority. "Send two of your brigades around the outside of the wall to the north gate. Bring the other two with us through the streets of Cenkin. General Guan does not expect much resistance inside the walls, but he wants your men to display a show of force." He nodded at them. "See to your men's orders, then follow me."

Moto ordered the first and third brigades to march to the north gate. The other two filed into formation. They followed Moto and Druvl to Trosho with Festo as their guide. The citizens of Cenkin hid inside their homes, hoping to stay out of the way of the conquering army.

The southern men walked through the streets, arriving at Trosho. They met no resistance along the way. Not one New Caporessoean soldier stood before them in defense of Cenkin. Guan's plan had been perfect, and there was no one left to fight back.

Guan met them at Trosho's wooden portico. More bodies were scattered around the entrance. "Welcome, Generals Moto and Druvl. I trust your battles outside the city were successful." He looked at the blue sky, "You have arrived sooner than I anticipated; excellent. Give your reports, gentlemen," he demanded.

Druvl responded first, "General Guan, the New Caporesso Army is gone, sir. Anyone stationed at an outpost around of the city has been destroyed.

Our injuries are minor, and we are prepared for additional combat as soon as you need us, sir," he saluted Guan.

"Hail, General Guan, thanks to your reports concerning troop strength, our battles were successful," added Moto. "The soldiers we encountered are either dead or will be soon, sir. We caught them completely off guard." He shook his head. "They were unable to mount any kind of defensive measures, and we cut them down where they stood. Like General Druvl, sir, our casualties are minimal. Minor wounds and only a handful of men dead."

"You have done well, Generals. I see my trust in the two of you is well deserved." He nodded at both men, "With no army left to fight with; the city is now secure. The castle is also under my control. The remaining inhabitants have no fight in them, and those that did are dead." An evil chortle escaped his lips. "And my Dragoons have the royal family locked away.

"Festo gave you the start of your new orders." He looked at Moto, "Take the men at the north gate three miles further north. Divide them and move away from the road, keeping them in battle formation." His mouth formed a wicked grin as he spoke, "I will announce to the people that those soldiers still loyal to Terikk may leave the city and head north. When the retreating cowards are in your midst, slaughter them." Guan's eye danced at the thought. "I will make sure they are unarmed, so their defense will be limited. No quarter to the enemy! We will make an example of them."

He turned to face Druvl, "The other two brigades are to search the peasant's homes for deserters. When you find soldiers hiding, kill them and the owners of the home, kill everyone. Then burn those homes to the ground. We will make everyone aware that harboring enemy soldiers is a crime punishable by immediate death." Chuckling, he said, "That will persuade other people to throw the cowards out of their homes. Kill anyone wearing a uniform." He looked at Moto and then Druvl, their expressions blank. "Never give someone the chance to come back and seek vengeance against you." His eye blinked several times. "We must act decisively now to prevent any future uprisings against us. Do you understand?"

"Yes, sir." They responded in unison, then saluted, "Strength and honor, sir."

Guan dismissed them to do their grisly duties. He knew they would perform as ordered. They feared him more than committing atrocities against defenseless people. Soon, he would be crowned king of New Caporesso. His lifelong dream was about to be fulfilled. He turned and entered Trosho. Guan headed for the throne room, there was much he needed to discuss with Mervekka concerning his coronation.

Chapter 48

Terikk and Aacrel observed the approaching soldiers. "Today must be a nice day for a walk, Terikk. Even Tyr and a squad of men are enjoying the beautiful day," Aacrel's tone turned serious, "in attack formation." He turned to Terikk, "Something is wrong."

Speaking to Shua, Terikk said, "Stay behind Aacrel and me."

"Yes, Poppa, is everything all right?" he asked innocently.

There was no reply from Terikk or Aacrel. Both men intently watched the soldiers.

When the two groups were half a perch apart, they both stopped. Terikk inquired, "Commander Tyr, what is the meaning of this?"

Tyr knew his men had been briefed by Guan, and they understood their orders. He replied, "When I joined the New Caporesso Army, I swore an oath." He drew his sword and his men did the same. They quickly moved into a semi-circle around Terikk and Aacrel, advancing closer.

Both men drew their weapons instantly, Terikk's sword and shield at the ready, and Aacrel's double swords clinking together.

Terikk started to speak but was interrupted by Tyr. "My king, I swore an oath to protect you and your family, and to follow orders as an honorable soldier from the land of New Caporesso." He lowered his head and sighed, then looked up at Terikk, "Today I fail in my mission. I pray that the gods and my men will forgive me." With a two hand grip, Tyr raised his sword and struck at the soldier to his left, removing his right arm above the elbow. Turning to his right, he thrust his sword through the side of that soldier, slicing through his spine like a spear through a wild boar. His battle cry rang clear on the prairie.

The melee commenced. Confused by Tyr's actions, his soldiers hesitated.

Terikk and Aacrel did not understand what happened, but they realized the advantage was theirs. They both attacked to the front and away from the center of the soldiers.

"Run, Shua," was all he needed to hear to understand they were in trouble. He sprinted for the woods, never looking back.

Aacrel jumped and slashed at his opponents, killing three of them quickly. Moving effortlessly, he dispatched each attacker with a slash and a thrust. As they fell, he moved to aid Tyr in his battle with two men.

Terikk blocked an attack with his shield, before slicing through the soldier's throat. He spun quickly, smashing his shield into another man's face, knocking him down. He ducked under another thrust, stabbing through his attacker's stomach. Returning to the downed man, he stabbed him through the heart, ensuring he was out of the fight.

In less than sixty seconds, all of Tyr's men were dead. Limbs had been hewn and heads lopped from their bodies. The carnage was quick and deadly. Better them than the leaders of New Caporesso. Terikk and Aacrel emerged unscathed.

Tyr was catching his breath and looked at Terikk and Aacrel. Dropping his sword, he fell to his knees, begging, "Forgive me, my king, General Guan gave orders for me to bring these men here and execute you, General Aacrel, and your son." He lowered his head and looked at his hand; it was shaking. Looking back at Terikk, he continued, "I could not follow his orders. I could not violate my oath as a solider of New Caporesso and destroy you. Please forgive me, sire."

Terikk glanced at Aacrel and exhaled, "Tyr, you just saved our lives. It is not for us to question your loyalty or your methods. Right now, we are confused by what just happened. Explain yourself." He looked at Aacrel and nodded his head towards the fleeing Shua.

Wiping the blood from his swords, Aacrel ran to retrieve the boy.

Tyr repeated his orders. A coup was underway. He told Terikk of the army, under the command of Generals Moto and Druvl, which had come from southern training grounds. They were attacking the New Caporesso Army at that very moment. Tyr did not think anyone could stop the southern men. Guan's plan was perfect; today he was unstoppable.

He described how Guan wanted to capture Mervekka and their children. Tyr knew nothing more than that, he did not know if Terikk's family was going to be executed or harmed in any way. He broke down as he described what was happening in Cenkin. "Forgive me, my king, I've failed you and the people."

Cleaning his sword, Terikk asked, "What can I absolve you from, Tyr? You saved my son's life. You saved us." He acknowledged Aacrel, who returned with Shua. "What else could you have done today?" he asked, sheathing his weapon.

"The queen, sire...your children. I could have done...something...to help them. I could..." his voice cracked.

Terikk was silent, thinking about his family. *What can I do to save them?* His mind returned to the man before him. He shook his head, saying, "No, Tyr, anything you would have tried inside the city walls would have resulted in your death. Guan would have realized where your true loyalty rested and would have killed you. Then he would have sent other men loyal to him to find us." He motioned at Tyr. "Without your help today, I do not know if Aacrel and I would have survived."

"So Guan has incited a revolt against you and is attacking Cenkin?" Aacrel summarized Tyr's story. "What are your orders, Terikk? We must search for your family."

From their location, they could not see the city walls. Terikk spoke to Shua, "Stay here with Commander Tyr. Aacrel and I will return shortly." He nodded at Aacrel and the two men ran up the hill east of them. From its summit, they saw the walls of Cenkin. They looked towards the city. What they saw shocked them.

"Look at the top of the ramparts, Terikk," pointed Aacrel. "The banners of New Caporesso are no longer flying. They have been replaced by Guan's black flag." His face turned ashen.

Terikk's gaze fell to the base of the wall. "The west gate is open, Aacrel. And see the bodies all around it?" He shook his head in disbelief. "Our men are dead." He fell to his knees, dropping his head. "We failed to protect them. We failed to protect the people of New Caporesso." After a silent moment, he looked at Cenkin once more. "My family is defenseless."

Aacrel responded, "Terikk, we have no time to lose. We must return and find them. I will tell Tyr to stay here with Shua and we will go. Wait for—"

"My friend," Terikk interrupted, "have you heard any battle alarms? According to Tyr, the battle began at the east gate before sunrise, and then moved to the north and south entrances. Tyr said the only outpost that sounded the alarm was the northern one, and for only a short time." He sadly shook his head. "I am afraid they are all destroyed. Aacrel, we have no men left to lead. We were so busy enjoying the successful creation of a new country that we allowed the army to decay." He exhaled sharply. "There was no need to worry about an outside enemy conquering us. It rose up from within our own ranks. The people charged us with protecting them from evil, and we failed." Terikk strained to see in the distance.

"It seems we penned our own demise when we began marveling at the good things we accomplished," added Aacrel. "How ironic? Guan came to Cenkin fifteen years ago to conquer it and was merely delayed. He patiently waited until we lowered our guard, and that of an entire country." Ashamed, Aacrel bowed his head.

"Now, he will crown himself king of New Caporesso. The country he wanted to take by force, by fighting each kingdom, is now his in a single day." Terikk stood up. "The other kingdoms will accept him as their new king because they have no choice. The old armies are gone. No one can stand against him and his men."

Aacrel looked at Terikk, "What about your family? We cannot just abandon them?"

"What other choice do I have?" he asked resignedly. "Tyr said Guan's army encircled the city and entered through the west gate. Our soldiers are gone, and Guan is victorious. My family is in Castle Trosho, on the far side of the city. Are we to attack and battle ten thousand men by ourselves, Aacrel?" Forlorn, he looked at Aacrel. "Even if we could get there, what assurance do we have they are not already dead? It would be insane to try and rescue them." He turned his head, wiping a tear from his eye.

"I do not know what to say, Terikk. Command me, and I will follow your orders." He looked at his friend, unable to assist him with his struggle.

"There are no more commands to give. I must leave here and head west." Terikk turned and looked at the distant horizon. "Shua and I must go west, further than anyone is known to have gone for hundreds of years. We must trust to the old legends, and seek refuge in a new land, untouched by war." He lowered his head. "Tyr said Guan was inside the castle looking for Mervekka and my children before the attack. There is no chance we can get to them now." Terikk broke down. "No, we must survive to fight another day. Shua must live, and to do that, I must take him away from here. My only solace today can be found in keeping him alive. I will give him the opportunity to grow up and become a man. The fall of Cenkin is the price I must pay for Shua to live."

"Terikk, you would leave your family?" Aacrel asked softly.

Fighting back tears, he sniffled, "I must make my sacrifice and move on. I will ask the gods for forgiveness later, but now, I must look to Shua's safety and his future." After a final look at Cenkin, he descended the hill and headed for Shua and Tyr.

Aacrel lingered, looking at Cenkin. His expression turned to a snarl and he raised a fist skyward, "Gods, I pray to you for mercy. Spare Terikk's family, keep them safe from harm. Take my life as ransom for theirs. Protect Mervekka and her children until we return to liberate them." He spat with anger as he spoke, "Safeguard them, and take my life as the price for their survival." With a last look, he turned and chased after Terikk.

Chapter 49

Aacrel caught up with Terikk as they returned to Shua. The boy was sitting on the ground, hugging his knees and staring straight ahead.

Terikk looked at Aacrel, "I have no more orders left to give you, my friend. I release you from your duties as a general of New Caporesso. You are free to see to your own safety. If you choose to flee in another direction, I will pray to the gods for them to protect you and grant you safe passage. I hold no ill will against your departure."

Looking surprised and injured, Aacrel remarked, "Terikk, honestly, I have never served under your command. I am here because you are my friend." A gust of wind blew his hair. "I would follow you to the gates of the Netherworld, without hesitation." He grasped the handles of his weapons, "My swords are with you always, never forget that. Our friendship was forged in the fires of war; we are a part of the brotherhood of swords. Tell me you are returning to Cenkin, and I will join you on that suicide mission."

"May I never give such a desperate order," he tried to smile. "And I know that you serve of your own will, but I wanted to make sure you were free to make your own decision without blindly following me." They looked at each other in silence for a moment. "We must leave this country, and you know it. Our only escape is to the west, and we must go now. No time for supplies and horses, we will find what we need along the way. Agreed?"

"Agreed," Aacrel pointed at Tyr, who was sitting in silence, staring at his soldiers' corpses. "What about him? Does he come with us?"

Tyr had been quiet since finishing his explanation of Guan's rebellion. He was sitting on the ground, contemplating a scheme. "Sire, I believe I have a plan for a safe escape."

Terikk looked at him. "You saved us from certain death, Tyr. Today is not the day when I question your judgment. What do you have in mind?"

"Sire, if I flee with you, Guan will send scouts to determine my whereabouts. They will continue searching for me until we are found together. When that happens, they'll kill us all. That means I cannot go with you." He stood up. "But to aid in your escape, these bodies must be destroyed. My orders were to burn your remains so that no one would ever know where you died. We will light a pyre for them, but only my troops will be on it." Tyr paused at his words before continuing. "I will return to Castle Trosho and tell the tale how my men were killed. In the process, we also managed to kill the three of you. Me, as the only survivor, was horrified and driven insane at the loss of my men. I burned everything, until nothing remained but ashes and melted steel. No discernable objects exist." He looked from Terikk to Aacrel, "The only problem with this story is that I cannot return uninjured." Sighing, he stepped closer to Aacrel, "I need some sort of wound from the battle. What would Guan believe?" he lowered his eyes and looked at the ground.

Terikk understood his question and swallowed hard. "Tyr, today you have proven yourself to be a great man from New Caporesso. If more men were like you, perhaps this day would never have happened."

"Guan will suspect betrayal if your wound is not severe enough." Aacrel moved closer to Tyr and put a hand on his shoulder. "I am sorry, Tyr, you deserve a better fate than this, but I cannot give it to you." Aacrel looked solemn.

Terikk could not look at Tyr, "I wish there were something else we could do, but..." He shook his head sadly.

Tyr calmly chuckled, "I understand, King Terikk." He sighed. "I finally make good on a promise I made many years ago. I am honored to serve you and your family in any capacity possible." Tyr stared into Aacrel's eyes, "I think a hand sounds about right. Wouldn't you agree?" His face questioned Aacrel. "Yes, a hand for a king and a general sounds like a fair price."

Aacrel almost choked on his words, "Tyr, I think you are the most selfless man I have ever met. Extend your arm so the monster in me may satisfy your request."

Tyr produced his left arm and looked away.

Aacrel drew one of his swords and took a two handed grip on it. Holding it over the midsection of Tyr's forearm, he yelled, "Fenrir!" and chopped.

Chapter 50

Tyr lay unconscious for almost an hour. In that time, Terikk and Aacrel dressed his wound and poured water for him. They proceeded to drag the bodies of the dead soldiers into a pile. They doused them with oil from Tyr's men's pouches and ignited a flame in them. It burned intensely. They picked up the ownerless heads and threw them into the inferno, the myriad of arms they left on the field.

By the time the bodies were ablaze, Tyr awoke and took in his surroundings, trying to remember what transpired. One look at his left arm and he remembered. The intense pain brought him to his senses. With a whiff of the air, he knew the pyre was burning high. He looked up at Terikk and then Aacrel. In a whisper, he asked, "Was it a clean cut, General Aacrel?" he coughed. "I'm sorry that this is the only service I can offer you. You are good men and deserve a better escort out of this country. Forgive me…and my inadequacies," he coughed again through the pain.

Terikk choked back his emotion. "Tyr, you shame us. You have offered everything you possibly could today to save us, to save my son. I pray to the gods that we may one day return and liberate New Caporesso from the evil that has taken root. On that day, the entire city of Cenkin will learn of the heroic feats performed by you, General Tyr, to defend your king when all others chose to abandon him and his family."

Aacrel wiped away a tear and helped Tyr to his feet. The hobbled man stumbled a moment before regaining his balance. "I think I can be convincing as an angry commander who lost his arm and his men in the same day. Guan will understand my rage and the burning of everything." He coughed, "I take my leave. May the gods speed you on your journey. I hope we meet again in the not too distant future. Until then, I will pray for you." He swayed and looked at Shua, "Good luck, Prince Shua. I hope to see you again when you return to reclaim the land of New Caporesso for you and your people." Tyr saluted the boy. Holding his mangled arm, he stumbled away.

Shua still sat on the ground, rocking back and forth. He heard the commander's words, but did not respond. The shock of the day finally consumed him, and he was unable to speak. He stared at the fire, watching it devour the remains of the soldiers. The black and orange flames climbed into the sky, laughing at him. Shua imagined he saw the men's souls fleeing their bodies and reaching for the heavens. Then with cries of anguish, they were sucked back into the Netherworld to join the other anonymous soldiers of yore.

The sizzle of flesh melting from bone singed his nose. The soldiers' bodies were disintegrating before Shua's eyes. The charcoal and coppery smells were nauseating. He was in a trance and could not look away from the horror of it. *Is this what death looks like? Will my life end the same way?* The stench made him vomit.

Terikk ran over to Shua and tried to comfort him. As his father held him, Shua remained silent, staring blankly at the fire as its flames reached upward. He was mesmerized by the horrible spectacle he was witnessing. The sight of dissolving flesh and pungent odors would never leave his mind, haunting him forever.

Aacrel watched as Tyr staggered towards Cenkin. Hopefully, he would tell his lie convincingly enough that his life would be spared.

After several minutes, Terikk joined Aacrel, watching the brave Tyr move closer to Cenkin. The two friends knew they might never know his fate. That was the deal they made, it was not fair, but an act of self-preservation.

As the fire burned out of control, the three refugees from New Caporesso turned west, and without looking back, started their journey in search of a new land to call home. How far west would they go? They would continue until they found somewhere to hide from the atrocities that were taking placing in their homeland. Hopefully, New Caporesso would be able to forgive them for leaving her behind. Not today, but maybe someday.

Chapter 51

By late afternoon, the bloodstained fields around Cenkin were littered with the remains of the New Caporesso Army. Hundreds of men were killed in the first moments of the attacks, and thousands more were mortally wounded. Those who surrendered were massacred. The wounded were butchered where they lay. Guan's army gave no quarter. Their victory at Cenkin was absolute.

Guan was in the throne room, sipping a fine Shiraz and eating fresh fruit. Servants mopped up blood from the cobblestone floor. The bodies of the royal guards had been removed hours ago, but their blood trails remained. He ogled the young women as they scrubbed.

Throwing his head back, he drained his goblet.

He underhandedly offered an armistice to end the hostilities inside the city. Those still loyal to Terikk were given an opportunity to throw down their weapons and travel to Norkin. Safe passage was granted to them. He spoke aloud, "Those fools!"

The wenches toiling to clean the floor looked at him.

Glaring at the women, his eye blinked several times. With a wave of his hand, he dismissed them back to their chore. *Every man who declared himself loyal Terikk was slaughtered at the hands of Moto and his men.*

After the loyal soldiers exited the city, Druvl and his men searched home after home, eradicating any soldiers seeking refuge inside the proletarians' homes. Hundreds of gutless troops were killed, along with the people who took them in. Following Guan's explicit orders, women and children were butchered and their homes burned as examples of what happens to people who defy Guan's orders.

Only one report remained to be given. *Where is that incompetent Tyr?* It was important to know the final outcome of Terikk's life. *How did he die?* Guan was sure he had begged for his miserable life, like the wretched cur he was. As he was thinking about Tyr, four men carrying a litter entered the throne room.

Lying prostrate on it was Tyr. Guan looked him over and saw the blood soaked bandage on his arm. He realized there was no hand beneath the wraps. Guan rose from his chair and boomed, "What is going on here? Why do you bring this broken soldier to me like this?"

The field surgeon responded, "General, sir, Commander Tyr said you would want to hear his report immediately. He said I could finish tending his wounds after that, sir."

Tyr tried to rise up on his good arm and acknowledge Guan. "General, sir," he coughed and gagged for air. "I'm late for my report, sir, I have no excuse. I've failed you, sir," he was in obvious pain, "my men are gone, all dead and burned," he fell back onto the stretcher, coughing.

Guan was confused at the scene before him. Should he be angry with this man? "What of Terikk and his party…what happened to them?" he demanded.

Tyr tried to sit up again, but was unable. "Sir, they're dead. King Terikk, General Aacrel, and Prince Shua are all dead. My men and I were able to kill them, but in the battle I was wounded, and my men perished. Please forgive my failure today."

Guan stood there amazed, almost unable to speak. "Failure? You were disfigured for the glory of the service. Who did this to you?"

"It was Aacrel, sir. I'd just killed Terikk when two of my men stabbed Aacrel from opposite sides. He cut them down quickly." Rasping, he continued his tale, "As I was withdrawing my sword from Terikk's chest to attack, Aacrel blocked my slash and chopped off my arm, sir."

He nodded slowly, still amazed, "And the boy? What of him?"

"Sir, it took the last of my men to finish Aacrel." He coughed. "Four of them against Aacrel, and he mortally wounded them all. As the last of my men lay dying, Aacrel finally succumbed to his wounds. He fell at the king's feet, dead. The boy ran off a short distance," he coughed again, "but I gathered up my strength and went after him. After catching him, I dragged him back to the site of the battle.

"I made him clean and dress my wound, sir. I was so angry at Terikk for the death of my men," he spoke through his tears, "my honorable men... that in a fit of rage, I made the boy build a pyre for the bodies. We burned all of them, even my own men." There was anger in his voice. "As the last of the bodies were set ablaze, I told the boy to stand in front of the fire, and pay homage to his father." Tyr laughed, "The stupid whelp did as I commanded!

"He stood before me, staring at the fire. He started to recite some ancient drivel about forgiveness, but I wasn't listening. I picked up my sword and ran it through his gut, disemboweling him." Tyr almost giggled, "Then I pushed him onto the roaring fire! He cried and screamed before passing out.

"I sat with the fire until the remains of my soldiers were gone. Nothing is left except worthless arms and melted metal. My anger led me to destroy all evidence that they ever existed." Realizing what he did, his face showed his shock. "Sir, I even destroyed Terikk and Aacrel's weapons. I'm sorry I failed to bring you your trophies, sir." Tyr lay back, staring up at the ceiling. His pain was severe, but he was able to focus on his fabricated story.

Guan was shocked. Never before had he heard of such a heroic tale of battle and sacrifice. "Commander Tyr, you need not ask for my forgiveness anymore. It is not necessary. You performed your duty well today, both as a soldier and as man from Sokin." He declared, "Your actions today are a great testament to that." Looking compassionately at Tyr, he said, "My personal surgeons will see to your wounds. They will tend to you, and hopefully you will survive to lead my men in battle once more. I am pleased to have such a capable and worthy soldier in my service." Guan touched his right fist to his shoulder, "I salute you, *General* Tyr!" he nodded ever so slightly,

"You earned that rank today for your actions on the fields west of Cenkin. Thanks to you, Terikk, Aacrel, and Shua are gone. They will never return to cause havoc in this land again. You have freed the people from an uncertain future. You are a hero of New Caporesso! Ah-ooh! Ah-ooh! Ah-ooh!"

The other soldiers cheered with Guan. Tyr tried to smile, but the pain was too much. He laid his head back, and passed out. As he faded off to sleep, he thought of his success. *The lie is told and believed. I did what I could for them. Long live King Terikk! Long live General Aacrel! Long live Prince Shua! Hopefully, they will return one day to save our people.*

Guan watched in awe as Tyr was carried away. The loyalty he displayed was incredible. The history texts would have to include a passage about him, and his noble deeds from this remarkable day.

That made Guan think about Terikk, Mervekka, Hogeland, and Aacrel. How would history remember them? The feeble dream that began in the minds of those four was almost over. Such a fragile thing was not meant to last. Their vision of a new land at peace with itself was all but dead. Would anyone remember what they had done? What would their legacy be? For now, they would only be remembered for their monumental failure.

Chapter 52

Terikk and Aacrel set out on their journey towards the western border of New Caporesso. Shua remained quiet, following in a daze. He had never witnessed death before, and was not prepared for its viciousness. The games he played with Col were nothing like this. He would never look at fighting the same way again.

They moved at a slow jog to gain as much distance from Cenkin as possible. Entering Getty's Grove again, they slowed their pace. Shua looked at the shrubs and broken branches which had been Castle Lau'damay only a few hours earlier. Somehow it all looked different now. His eyes were opened to something he should never have seen. His mind raced, trying to understand what had happened. Leaving the shelter of the grove, they continued jogging southwest.

The trio moved at a steady pace, with Terikk and Aacrel speaking softly between themselves. After travelling for several hours, they slowed to a walk.

Shua spoke with no emotion in his voice, "What about Mother? Aren't we going to get Col and Vee?"

Terikk stopped, and turned to face his son, "Shua, we cannot go back. General Guan has sent his army to destroy us. If we go back, he will surely kill all of us, including you." He knelt down and put a hand on his son's shoulder, "We must go west to the borders of New Caporesso, and then keep going. We will cross through the Western Wilderness and seek the Unknown City."

In his mind, Shua said, *Teachers talked about it like it didn't really exist.* But he meagerly repeated, "Unknown City."

Terikk glanced at Aacrel, "Legends are born from partial truths, Shua. People did set out from Cenkin hundreds of years ago. They sought refuge in a distant land." He sighed, "There was never any evidence that they returned, so they must have kept going. They found what they were searching for and stayed. That is the hope we must carry with us. It will not be an easy journey, but we must persevere.

"Leaving our family is the sacrifice we must make. The decision to do so is mine alone. I know you would never abandon your mother and brother and sister. You would go to them, no matter what the cost." Terikk stood up and looked in Shua's eyes, "But as your father, I must make this choice, and lead us on a path into the unknown."

After a pause, Terikk continued, "All that is important now is that you are alive. I cannot risk your life for that of our family. I know it sounds horrible, but they may already be dead. If we return, we will surely be killed, and for what? So we can lie beside each other in the grave or be burned together in one illustrious pyre?" Shaking his head, he assured Shua. "No, my son. We must live, and you must grow strong. Hopefully one day, we will return and take back this land, but for now, we must flee." Letting out a long sigh, he conceded, "Guan wins today." He tousled the boy's hair and smiled.

Shua tried to muster a smile of his own, but could not. A tear rolled down his cheek and he began to cry. "Momma...mom," he stammered, sobbing.

Terikk fought back his own tears and hugged his son tightly. "It's all right now, it's all right. You do not need to be afraid. You are safe with me; you will always be safe with me."

Aacrel placed a hand on his friend's shoulder, "Terikk, we must keep going. They may send riders. Tyr may have failed in his mission. We do not know." He looked at the openness around them. "If we get caught out here, we will not stand a chance. Please, we must keep moving towards the Paro River."

Understanding his friend was right, Terikk exhaled, "Yes, I know." He lifted Shua's chin, "We have to keep going, Son. You must be strong for your mother. Be strong for Col and Vee. We will remember them always, but now, we must go."

Continuing on their way, they walked until dark, and then lay on the ground to rest. To conceal their position, they did not build a fire. The only food they had was in a small sack Shua had prepared to eat while he played in Getty's Grove. After the light meal, it did not take long for the weary travelers to succumb to sleep's grasp. Under the starry sky, they slept fitfully throughout the night.

Ghastly visions of the pyre plagued Shua's sleep. He did not know it then, but they would be with him for many years to come.

Chapter 53

"Bring me Mervekka at once!" shouted Guan. It was time for her to introduce him as the new king. He waited impatiently while his guards retrieved her.

When she arrived, streaks under her eyes revealed she had been crying. *Useless woman.* The guards led her to the foot of the dais. She tried to shrug off their hands. The cold men looked at Guan, waiting for his command. He lifted a hand and they released her.

She surveyed the room. The royal guards in blue tabards that she had seen for fourteen years were nowhere to be found. They had been replaced by men wearing the ugly black tunics of the Southern Kingdom. Splatters of blood were everywhere.

Her face was puffy, and her dress was torn at the side. In spite of her appearance, she tried to act dignified, "You summoned me, General Guan?"

"Yes, Milady. It is time to talk about your announcement that I am the new king of New Caporesso." He descended the stairs to stand in front of her. "I thought it best to remind you what will happen if you deceive me." Grabbing her chin, he lifted it up. "You will do as I say, or your children will pay the price for your disobedience." He released her face and walked behind her, "I hope to avoid more bloodshed and death, but that choice is entirely yours." Stepping closer, he whispered into her ear, "I hope together, we can find an acceptable arrangement."

The hair on the back of her neck stood up. She straightened her back, but did not turn, "Little of what you suggest will be agreeable to me, Guan. You rebelled against New Caporesso." She turned, yelling, "You killed hundreds of our soldiers!"

Guan instantly lost his temper and slapped her across the face, knocking her down. His eye quivered as his blood boiled. Glaring at her from above, he rebuked her, "You forget yourself, Milady, for we are no longer friends, if ever we were. The coup is over, and I won. Your army is annihilated. Their casualties were not in the hundreds, but in the thousands!" he bragged. "My plan was perfect. I began the day with ten thousand men afield. There are still over ninety nine hundred men ready to make war for me. You should treat me with more respect, you whore!" he shouted.

With deep breaths, he calmed down and returned to his throne. He sat down and threw his leg over the arm. "Milady, please understand, my army is in control of the city. The people will be forced to accept me as their new ruler or die. I only hope the latter will not be necessary. Do you want more death on your conscience?" he asked.

Defeated, she bowed her head, "What must I do to assist you and end the violence, Guan?" Mervekka looked at the ground in front of her. The bloodstains from earlier in the day were faded, but still apparent. She shuddered at the thought of them.

"The people still trust and believe in you, Milady. Confirm to them that a coup has occurred, and that I have emerged victorious. The revolution is over, the war is over, the old king is dead, and I am the new king of New Caporesso," he let her absorb the meaning of his words.

Mervekka's head shot upward, "What do you mean? Where...whe..." Her eyes desperately searched the room. "Where are Terikk and Shua?" She sobbed, "Where is my family?"

Guan smiled wickedly, "They met with Fate this morning, and he was in a foul mood. The gods did not favor them, and they did not survive the battle. Both are dead, and so is Aacrel." He leaned forward in his seat, sneering broadly, "I was told that Shua died screaming like a helpless girl," he taunted her.

She screamed and charged up the stairs. The guards grabbed and restrained her. She could not move. Mervekka cried hysterically, "My son... my baby boy...how could you...you murderer... my family!" Collapsing in a heap, she was overwhelmed by emotion.

"Shh, shh. This is not helping, Milady. Try and calm yourself," he mocked her. "It was not I who killed them. My *orders* were to capture them alive, but *renegade* soldiers ignored my commands. You must believe me, Milady, I did *not* want their deaths." Studying her face, he searched for her acceptance. "I still require your assistance." He waved a hand at her, "Can you hear me, Milady? Will you help me, or must your other children suffer as well? What is your choice, Milady?"

For several minutes, the only sound in the room was that of Mervekka crying. Eventually it subsided, and she lifted her head. Her eyes were bloodshot, and her silky hair was a tangled mess. She brushed it out of her face and stood up. "No further demonstration of your power is necessary, Guan. I will do as you demand," she whimpered. "Spare my children, and I will announce your succession to the throne of New Caporesso."

Guan leered at her, "See, was that so difficult, Milady?" and descended the stairs again.

He is finally close enough. Mervekka threw herself at him. Her knees and elbows found their marks, sending Guan sprawling on the stairs.

The guards closed in on her and pummeled her with the shafts of their spears, knocking her senseless. One hit her in the head while the other slammed into the middle of her back. She staggered forward and stopped momentarily. As she hung in midair, another guard smashed his spear into her unprotected face. She crumpled to the floor, and everything went black.

Her attack lasted only a few seconds, but Guan's face was bloodied and his insides hurt like never before. The guards helped him to his feet and he angrily pushed them away. Enraged, he kicked at Mervekka's lifeless body over and over. Finally he stopped and shouted, "Take her to her room! Lock her inside until I summon her again. Bring Princess Vitoria to my quarters at once!"

The guards picked up Mervekka's limp body and dragged her to her room. They laid her on the bed and left her alone, locking her in.

Hours later, she regained consciousness. Her head throbbed as she tried to remember what happened. Pain gripped her entire body, but she forced herself to stand. She stumbled to the bureau and poured water into a basin. Breathing irregularly, her hands shook as she dabbed a rag into the bowl. Raising it to her face, she looked in the mirror. "Ahh!" she gasped.

Her face was swollen, and her lips cut. There was a trickle of blood still flowing from behind her ear. The guards did their job well. Staring at the mirror, she wiped the dried blood from her face and neck. Purple and blue marks already showed on her face.

As she studied her reflection, she had a sudden realization. "Col...Vee, where are you?" There was no reply. She called again, "Col, Vee, where are you?" Frantically, she screamed for them, "Col...Vee! Answer me!" There was still no reply. Mervekka screamed and sobbed until exhaustion claimed her. Crawling back to her bed, she collapsed atop it, drifting off to sleep. Her dreams were filled with nightmarish spectacles of her family's fate.

Chapter 54

The bright rays of the morning sun awoke Mervekka from her restless slumber. She was relieved to be finished with sleep, too many nightmares this past night. Sitting on the edge of the bed, she tried to stand. Her face and body ached from the beating she endured. Her first attempt failed, but with a concerted effort, she managed to get to her feet. She heard an argument from outside the door.

A woman was yelling at someone. "You will let me in that room. My station is to tend to the queen, and that is just what I plan on doing." It sounded like Abby. "The only way you're gonna stop me is to kill me, now stand aside and open that door!" she ordered.

There was thumping and scratching at the door. Mervekka heard the woman moan. Then she heard a man's voice. "Stop it, you fools! If you touch her again...I swear I'll kill you...then you won't need to worry about his orders." It sounded like he was in pain. She thought she heard the speaker fall into something. "Now open the door and let her in. Now!" he demanded.

The door was unlocked and Abby entered. Her lip was bleeding, but she appeared to be all right. The man who helped Abby stayed in the hall.

A guard slammed the door shut behind her. They heard the sound of a bolt being placed into the door.

Mervekka looked at Abby, "Oh, Abby, are you all right? You're bleeding. Who did this to you?"

"It's nothing, my lady." Abby tried to smile, "I'm all right...I...fell," she looked away from Mervekka. "Don't fret about me, I'll be fine, it's you I'm concerned with." Taking Mervekka's hand, Abby studied her face. "Look at you. Your beautiful face is bruised. What in the gods' names happened?" She sat down on the bed, trying to pull Mervekka beside her.

She resisted and pushed Abby's hands away. "What are you doing here? Who let you in?"

Abby's expression softened, "I know what happened yesterday, my lady, and I'm sorry. Words don't exist to express how sorry I am. I wish I could've taken your family's place yesterday." A tear ran down her cheek. "I would've gladly traded my life for Shua's." Lifting a kerchief, she wiped her eyes. Then she took Mervekka's hand again and looked in her eyes, "I'm sorry for everything, but you have to keep living. You mustn't fight against Guan anymore, if you do, he'll butcher your children. You have to think of them; you're all they have now." She implored, "You must be strong for Col and Vee, my lady."

Mervekka shook her hand free, "What are you talking about, Abby? How dare you tell me what to do?" she snipped.

Abby grabbed Mervekka's wrist, and this time she held on, "Have I ever told you what to do, my lady? I love you, and want to see you live to be an old woman. But if you keep fighting Guan, he'll kill Col and Vee. Is that what you want? That will destroy you." Shaking her head, she pleaded, "I'm not telling you what to do, but you must listen to me, for your children's sake, I beg you."

Falling back onto the bed, Mervekka stared blankly at the ceiling. "I'm sorry, Abby. I know you are only trying to help."

"My lady, you must do as Guan demands. You have to recognize him as the new king. My heart aches for Terikk and Shua, but you must think of your children who are still alive. You must look to their safety, and their future. "Guan is already trying to influence them against you. Col slept in his room last night, but," she lowered her eyes, "Vee was with him."

Mervekka's eyes went wide with fear, and she bolted upright. "What do you mean, *with him?*" Her mind raced with horrible images.

"They spent some time together last night, talking about the events of the day. He explained them one way, making it sound like he was protecting the people. His version of events sounds like he is the hero in this tragedy." Shrugging, she said, "I don't know if Vee believed what he said or not. I haven't been able to talk to her today. I was lucky to get in to see you."

Mervekka sat silently for several minutes, staring into the distance, "It cannot happen again, not to my precious Vee," she shook her head. "He cannot defile my family again," her dry eyes could not produce anymore tears.

"I don't understand, my lady. Again?" inquired Abby.

"Oh nothing, Abby," Mervekka replied, wiping her face. "I'm just babbling."

"My lady, protect Col and Vee. Nothing else matters anymore. Do whatever it takes to keep them safe, even if that means bowing to Guan," she pleaded in earnest.

Realizing Abby was correct, she nodded her head, "I understand what you mean." Mervekka took Abby's hand and squeezed it. "Col and Vee are all I have now. Nothing matters to me anymore, not even New Caporesso." She sighed, "Help me get cleaned up. I need to be ready for Guan's coronation later today." Looking in the mirror, she studied the bruises around her eyes, "Do you think we can cover these up with something?"

Abby smiled somberly, "I think we can take care of that, my lady."

Chapter 55

Hours later, Guan arrived at Mervekka's room. The guards opened the door and he entered. He was surprised to see Abby inside.

"How did you get in here?" he asked.

"I knocked and was granted access, General Guan," she answered timorously.

He looked from her, to Mervekka, to the guards, "No matter. Leave us," he commanded.

Abby bowed and exited the room. At the threshold, she stopped and looked at Mervekka. Both women smiled weakly. Contented, Abby exited the room.

Guan looked at Mervekka; he was surprised to see her looking so... regal. "Milady, you look lovely today, considering what transpired yesterday."

"Yesterday was difficult for me to suffer. But today is another day, and I am ready to face it. Why have you come here?" she inquired, already knowing the answer.

"Why have I come, Milady? Surely you know why." Her tone surprised him. "I came to discern your answer. Will you recognize me as the king of New Caporesso, or must I take other actions?"

She looked him directly in the eye, "Yes, Guan, I will introduce you as king. But first, return my children to me. I have no power over you, I know that, but I still have influence over the people. Leave my children unharmed, and the citizens of Cenkin will be your subjects. However, if you injure Col or Vee in any way, I will cry out to the people and beseech them to fight for me." Her hands were defiantly on her hips. "Yes, Guan, your army will crush them, but they will fight nevertheless. They will fight, and your men will bleed.

"That war will not be decided in a day." She shook her head, "No, that guerilla war will last for months and months. The other cities may even take up our cause and join the fight. Your country will be consumed in civil war. You will win, but your casualties will be severe and the country will never be the same. The wealth and prosperity you have inherited will be gone forever." Crossing her arms in front of her, she asked, "Is that what you want for the people? Bloodshed and devastation and poverty?" Her strength returned. To survive what she had to do next, she would need every ounce of it.

He nodded his head, impressed with her resolve "Yes, Milady. You could do those things and lead this country to the brink of war. Would you do that to your people though," he touched a finger to his lip, "bring them to the edge of the abyss, I wonder?" he was testing her.

"If I lose Col and Vee, I will have nothing to live for. Do you really believe I would not do it?" her response was firm.

Guan chuckled, "Perhaps you are stronger than I gave you credit for, Milady." He turned and looked at the open door, "Guards! Find Milady's children and return them at once." He turned back to face her. "You see, Milady, we can be agreeable."

Mervekka shook her head. "No, Guan, not agreeable, this is merely a coerced alliance."

"Fine, Milady, call it what you will. Your children are being returned, and they will be safe here, inside this castle. They will remain safe as long as you continue to show your support for me as king. If I discover any underhanded activity," he pointed at her, "any kind at all, they will be executed for your treason. Do you understand me, Milady?" He made a fist at her.

Through tight lips, she replied, "Perfectly, Guan."

"Then...the people await your announcement, Milady."

And so Mervekka announced to the citizens of Cenkin that Guan was now their new king. She confirmed the fact that Guan was responsible for the coup that took place the day before. Terikk, Aacrel, and Shua were all killed in the fighting. The details of their deaths were not immediately clear. The New Caporesso Army had been completely destroyed by the vanquishing army. There was no alternative but to recognize Guan as king.

The people booed and called for Terikk. They chanted for revolution and civil war. Rather than stoking their incendiary ideas, Mervekka calmed the people. She convinced them more bloodshed would only tear the country apart and lead to many more deaths. War was not the answer.

Guan stepped forward for the people to see. He was met with jeers and whistles, but Mervekka intervened on his behalf.

"Good citizens of Cenkin, hear me," she held her arms up to silence the people. She appealed to them, "Hear me. This man is now the king of New Caporesso. Do not dishonor him this way. Regardless of his nihilistic motives, he is in control of the city." She paused, collecting her thoughts. "King Guan will lead us into a new future where the values of New Caporesso are still honored. We will not fall into the old ways of treachery and violence. *Together*, we will rule over you as king and queen. Together, we will find common ground to lead you to greater prosperity. *Together*, we will make New Caporesso a better place to live."

The citizens cheered loudly, chanting Mervekka and Guan's names. Smiling broadly, she raised her arms above her head. The people went wild with celebration.

Seething with rage, Guan moved to stand beside Mervekka. His face trembled as he tried to control his emotion. His desire to rip her heart from her chest was only subdued with great effort. He grabbed her hand and squeezed it.

Mervekka winced in pain but continued smiling. She kept looking at the people, but remarked to Guan, "Together, we will lead the people into a new future. It will be one that honors Terikk and Aacrel's ideals."

Guan squeezed her hand harder, but her smile never faltered. "For now, you have won the people, Milady," he whispered. "Do not try that again," he threatened. "For now you will be seen as a part of the government, but if you do something like that again, I will serve your children to you as hors d'oeuvres. Do you understand my intentions, Milady?"

Yanking her hand away from his clutch, she answered, "Yes, Guan, I understand them perfectly well." She looked at the people. The country was under Guan's control, but Mervekka had bought some time for her and her children. Guan could not harm them now, or the people would revolt against him. For now, Mervekka and her children were safe. She prayed silently, *May the gods grant me the strength to plan a future where Terikk, Shua, and Aacrel will have their vengeance from the afterlife.*

Chapter 56

For seven weeks, Terikk, Shua, and Aacrel slowly travelled west southwest. Believing they were safe from Guan, they crossed the narrow Paro River. After a night on its western bank, they turned north and walked for several more weeks. When they were within sight of Castle Lau'damay, they forded the Lho'mon River and approached the ruins from the south.

The castle had been abandoned thousands of years ago. Now, vines and weeds were the landlords of this once majestic structure. It lay as a monument to the strength of nature. No army ever breached its sturdy walls, but over time, the ramparts stoic weight became its own enemy. Without men to maintain the structural integrity of the mortar joints, they crumbled and turned to dust. Then one by one, the massive stones fell. With no defenders to sound the alarm, deer meandered through the citadel as their mood directed them. Fallen timbers and haphazard boulders littered the ground.

Terikk and Aacrel entered the castle grounds ready for battle. Of course they did not expect an ambush, but years of experience kept them cautious. A thorough search of the lower corridors proved they were safe inside the broken walls. They lit a fire in an old throne room. It was the first fire they built since their journey began.

Under normal circumstances, Terikk knew they were within a thirty-day ride of the western border. However, with Shua walking with them, everything was taking longer. Castle Lau'damay was a four week trek from Cenkin, but it had taken them almost two months to walk that far. He could not find fault with Shua though, he was doing his best to keep up and not complain.

Two villages were on the road to the Western Wilderness, Werlo and Dreglo. Werlo was the northernmost of the two. They would have to enter and inquire about supplies for their journey through the forest. Food, water, and horses were essential. Terikk and Aacrel talked about their upcoming expedition.

Terikk put the last of their Bontebok meat over the fire. "Aacrel, we need food for at least ninety days."

"Ninety?" Shaking his head, Aacrel exhaled, "Do you really think it will take us that long to pass through the wilderness?"

"I am not sure," he admitted, "but we cannot rely on foraging for food in the forest." Shrugging, he said, "I have no idea how long it will take us to travel through, but any longer than that and we may be digging our own graves."

Aacrel snickered, "You are a bundle of joy tonight." They sat in silence for several minutes. Turning the meat, Aacrel asked, "Should we enter each village together or separate and then meet on the western side of them?"

"I fear doing so together will raise questions about our identity. Three strangers from the east travelling westward might be memorable for some of them. It is possible that Cenkin scouts could hear of us. But separate, it will be more difficult to acquire supplies." He rotated the skewers holding the meat. "The villagers will question why one person or two need so much food. That also might leave an impression in their minds."

Again, silence followed. "All well and good, Terikk, but you failed to answer the question. What do you want to do?"

"First of all, we need to change our names to hide our identities. Patrols from Cenkin may become a very real problem as we continue west. It will take some time for Shua to remember our new names, so we should change them now." He called his son, "Come here, Shua, I need to talk to you."

Shua walked over by the fire. Looking at it, he stepped back.

"From now on, you need to call General Aacrel, Uncle...Hapco. His new name is Hapco. All right? Just Uncle or Uncle Hapco. And you cannot mention that he was a general. Likewise, you must forget that I was ever king. My new name will be...Ketrik. Do you understand?"

He silently nodded his head. "Is this to hide who we are?" he asked evenly. "How long will we hide?" Shua inquired.

"Yes, my son, we must hide our identities," he tried to reassure Shua, "but, I do not know for how long."

"Can you play pretend with us for a little while, Shua?" asked Hapco.

These few sentences were the first ones Shua had uttered since witnessing the pyre of Tyr's soldiers. "Yes, Uncle. I can play," he tried to wink at Hapco. "But, I want a new name too. Why can't I have a new name too?" he asked naively.

Terikk replied, "All right, Shua." He thought for a moment. "How does Kellen sound?"

Shua mouthed the new name silently, and nodded his head. "I like it, Poppa. I'm Kellen now." He furrowed his brow. "You're, Ketrik, and he's, Uncle Hapco."

Ketrik looked at the food over the fire, "Your meal is ready...Kellen. Come sit and have some supper." He prepared a plate of food for Kellen, and then one for himself.

Hapco did the same. It was good to have a hot meal. The shelter of the castle allowed them to build a fire without the fear of prying eyes spotting the light from a distance. They ate in silence, listening to the crackle of the fire. Its glow danced on the walls, providing a mesmerizing dance to accompany their meals.

After the meal, Kellen moved further away from the fire and lay on the ground. Images of what it could do plagued his mind. He fell asleep almost instantly.

Ketrik and Hapco sat solemnly by the fire. Hapco tried to smile, "Do you remember the first meal we ate together in Trosho's dining hall those many years ago?"

Thinking about it for a moment, Ketrik nodded. "Of course I do. It was a very impressive room." He sighed. "I think the only other time we ate in there was on my wedding day. I always thought I would have more time to..." His voice trailed off.

"I was thinking of the statues of Thro'ce and Leshliac," he reminisced. "There was an old poem about them. I had forgotten it until now."

Listen to me, and remember the old wars;
Two men met near Castle Lau'damay.
Thro'ce and Leshliac fought upon Lho'mon's shores,
The land's two greatest warriors' epic foray.
With sword and shield, they battled their host.
Fighting round Lau'damay for thirteen days,
Each night with wine, their enemy they did toast,
Singing songs of old, over fires ablaze.
Then at last, Thro'ce's spear pierced his enemy's breast,
And Leshliac fell, but not before
His sword rent Thro'ce's heart from his chest.
Their heroic battle done, this, their final war,
These two brothers did fight for honor and glory, so
You would forever remember their
names in the land of Caporesso.

"Tragic story," admitted Terikk, staring blankly at the fire.

"It seems fitting to recall their story. It describes the history of Caporesso, brother against brother and kingdom against kingdom," he sighed, "Now I think it tells the story of New Caporesso's short history as well. And as you said, *tragic*."

The two men sat in silence. Not knowing what else to say, they laid back and drifted off to sleep.

Chapter 57

A sudden noise roused Ketrik and Hapco. *Crunch.* How long had they been asleep? *Crack.* Someone or something was coming. *An animal?* It got closer and closer and then stopped. Another crack came from the other side of them.

Hapco thought, *What is going on? No one knows we are here; how could there be an assault?*

Ketrik and Hapco had searched most of the rooms in the lower section of the castle, and there was no sign of anyone. Neither man stirred, but they were both fully awake. Each man held their weapons in hand and was ready to defend the castle as though it was their own keep.

Kellen slowly awoke, but knew enough to stay silent. His father would tell him to move when necessary. Hapco looked to the right and Ketrik kept an eye on the left side of the room. The entrances were small enough that each man could defend against multiple attackers. The narrow corridors eliminated any advantage a larger group of assailants would have against them. They only had to wait for the assault.

Illuminated by the waning fire, they saw the skinny leg of someone entering slowly at the right side of the room. Then the next leg entered, followed by the rest of the body. Hidden beneath a cloak, it appeared extremely small for a soldier.

The doorway to the left was filled with the shape of a giant creature! But as the shadow became less distorted, they realized it too was a small person. In the flickering light, the intruders did not appear to have any weapons.

Ketrik tapped Hapco's foot and both men sprang to their feet, shouting, "Kee-ahh!" They advanced in their predetermined directions.

The invaders standing in the doorways froze and screamed. One of them started to cry.

What kind of attack is this? Ketrik yelled commands at the person closest to him. "Lay down your weapons! Hands over your head!"

Likewise, Hapco barked at the intruder. "Stop crying! Throw down your weapons!" He pointed at the unknown person. "Yield or I'll cut you down where you stand!"

Hapco's target fell to its knees, "Please, mister, we're looking for food and smelled yours. Don't kill us. We're hungry, that's all. We only wanted to scare you away and take your food. That's all. Honest. We're just hungry." She continued crying.

Surprised by what he heard, Ketrik looked closely at the person in front of him. It was a boy. "Who are you? What are you doing here? Speak now or I'll silence you forever," he raised his sword menacingly in front of him.

The boy lowered his hood and revealed a dirt-smudged face. He appeared to be less than fifteen years old. He dropped his cloak to the ground and made his way over to the girl in front of Hapco. He knelt down and held her close to him. "It's all right, Kyra. You were right; we shouldn't have bothered them. I made a mistake. Now we're gonna die, but at least we'll die together. Stop crying, Kyra, we'll finally be together in Valhalla with our families?"

"Yen, you're a fool," she sobbed. "I don't wanna die! I don't wanna die," the girl continued crying.

Ketrik and Hapco stepped back from them. Hapco lowered his sword and knelt down to speak to the children, "Stop your crying, no one is going to die." He motioned for Ketrik to lower his sword. "Who are you? Why did you attack us?"

Timidly, the boy answered, "I'm Yen, and this is Kyra. We're orphans from the village of Werlo. It's about three weeks to the west. The people banished us for stealing food. Now we have no way to get any. We don't got no weapons to hunt with either. We were hoping to scare away whoever was camped here and take their food. That's all." He hugged the girl closer, "Are you gonna kill us, mister?"

Hapco stood up as Ketrik spoke to the children. "How old are you? What happened to your parents?"

"I'm twelve, and Kyra is ten. My parents died last winter of the pox. Kyra's family died in early spring when they fell through the ice over the Shau'may and drowned." Petting Kyra's head, he rocked her. "We've been together ever since. We'd steal food from the butcher to eat. After a few months of tolerating us, they finally banished us with the penalty of death if we returned."

Ketrik nodded his head, understanding their circumstances. "My name is Ketrik, this is Hapco, and the boy is Kellen." He pointed at each of them. "We are travelers passing through this land. You look like you haven't eaten much in weeks." Nodding at Hapco, he said, "Fix them what remaining food we have. They need something to eat or they will not leave us alone." He studied the two malnourished children, "After you eat, we will talk about what to do with you. If we leave you here, only certain death awaits you. But our destination may not be for you. Eat now, and we will discuss it later."

Hapco looked over the two children. Yen's muscles were lean, and he was of average height. The long black hair on his head needed cut and washed. His appearance was rough, and his clothes were torn. Kyra was built like someone in constant motion, the start of an athletic build. Her hair was matted from lack of care, and shorter than Yen's. Both of them were filthy, with dirt caked on their faces.

As the boy and girl greedily ate their meals, Ketrik and Hapco discussed their future.

"My friend, I know you want to bring them with us." Hapco pointed at the two children sitting by the fire. "You think it is the decent thing to do."

"It is the decent thing to do, Hapco." He nodded at Yen and Kyra, "What would you have me do? Leave them to die here in the wild?"

"Ketrik, five mouths will be harder to feed where we are going." Abruptly, he stopped talking, deep in thought. "But...I think I have an idea. If we take them with us, then we *are* a group of five: you with your son, and me with my *adopted* children. As such, we no longer resemble fugitives from Cenkin.

"We should be able to gather more stores for the journey since we have more children to feed. Our passage will go unnoticed and unremembered." He slapped his thigh. "This is the perfect cover to escape New Caporesso and begin again in the wilderness. Instead of the fear of being hunted, we can worry about our destination, rather than our trail. What do you think?"

"And I thought it would be difficult to convince you to bring them along," Ketrik chortled. "Sounds like you have it all planned out," he smiled at his old friend. "Just when I think I know everything about you, you surprise me with an idea like this. If you are not careful, you may begin to care for these children."

"I will adopt them only to maintain the ruse." He shook his head, "But no attachments will grow between me and them or them to me." Turning to the boy and girl, he added, "It is only to aid our escape that I suggest this."

The children ate their fill and quickly fell asleep. With their bellies full for the first time in weeks, they slept soundly by the fire next to Kellen. As far as Yen and Kyra were concerned, tonight was a good night.

Chapter 58

Kyra and Yen went with the three refugees from Cenkin. They walked for almost three weeks, heading towards the western villages. When they were within a few hours walk of them, they camped for the night. Not wanting to attract any attention from the villagers, they did not build a fire. The wild game they had killed and cooked was eaten cold. The children were each filled with excitement as they went to sleep. Tomorrow would be the first time in over two months that Kellen would see civilization.

Ketrik and Hapco hoped they would be able to gather supplies for their journey. Without them, their quest would be doomed before it even began.

With dawn breaking, Ketrik and Hapco awoke the children and described their plan to them. The two men decided not to elaborate on why they were leaving New Caporesso. It was not important for them to know. They were coming along for their own benefit. By doing so, they would be cared for and able to survive. Both Kyra and Yen agreed to the plan.

"Do we have to call you Father?" Yen asked Hapco. "I already had one."

"It will raise alarm if you do not. I am afraid I must insist you call me Father, or Poppa." Hapco thought about Yen's question. "You know, we will visit Dreglo later today. You do not need to call me anything there, just stay silent. There is nothing wrong with that. How does that sound?"

Yen looked at Kyra and then nodded for the both of them.

Hapco walked over to his friend and spoke softly, "*Terikk*, I guess that is the last time I will call you by that name for a long time. Be safe."

Ketrik replied, "Yes, Hapco, use this time without me to forget *Terikk*. I will try to forget Aacrel and only remember Hapco." He placed a hand on his friend's shoulder, "From now on, those men will only exist in the history scrolls of New Caporesso."

"I wonder what they will say?" pondered Hapco aloud.

Each of them collected their belongings and left the campsite. Hapco and his two new children turned southwest, heading for Dreglo. Ketrik and Kellen began walking towards Werlo.

Looking back, Ketrik shouted to Hapco, "We will meet you this evening on the western side of the villages. Be careful navigating your way through the marshes, they can be treacherous. Gather your supplies and then walk for six hours past the village. Then turn north. We will do the same and turn south. Eventually, we will find each other again. Goodbye, my friend. Take care of your family."

Hapco said, "Thank you for your concern, Ketrik. Look to your family as well. Godsspeed till we meet this evening."

With that, the two groups made their ways to the respective villages. The villagers were cautious of the new strangers, but provided the requested supplies. These travelers were ordinary, just small families heading *northward*, in search of wives. Nothing about them raised any suspicions.

The towns' folk gathered supplies and offered fresh horses to the weary travelers. Everything was graciously accepted. Once the supplies were packed, and they had a hot breakfast, the travelers passed through the villages and continued west as planned. They turned north or south at the directed time. Within three hours of their turns, they rejoined each other's company and crossed the Shau'may River, continuing westward.

Almost two weeks later, they camped on the edge of the Western Wilderness. They gazed intently into the uncharted forest, where no man dared travel. Without sunlight to keep a bearing, it was easy to get lost forever. Once inside, everything would look the same. The dense foliage would make their passing dangerous and slow.

Only one group of people had ever ventured that far and deliberately continued. Wild stories of their journey persisted throughout the land. Some said they found paradise on the other side. Others said they all died of starvation in the forest. Maybe the truth was somewhere in between.

For Ketrik and Hapco, the truth did not matter; they had no choice but to continue on this predestined path. Legends or no, they had to stay the course and discover their own fate. They were a wretched group of survivors, with no future but to seek it in an untamed wilderness.

In the morning, their journey through the woods would begin. It was time now for a good night's sleep, maybe their last one for a long, long time.

Chapter 59

Ketrik raised his pint to his lips and swallowed the last gulps of warm ale. He looked at everyone listening to him. They sat with their mouths agape and eyes wide. No one said a word. Each person just sat, staring at Ketrik. The story he told them was unbelievable. Turning, he looked at his trusted friend. For ten years they had lived in Salvation, and not once did Hapco let slip their true identities.

Hapco lowered his pipe, saying, "Maybe you scared everyone to death, Ketrik." He snapped his fingers to get their attention. "They are all petrified and frozen." Glancing at Kellen, he asked, "Any questions?" There was no response. "Are there no questions?" he asked again.

Addressing the village elders, Ketrik acknowledged, "You asked to learn of our past, our history, and why we came here. Now you know. I know it sounds incredible, but it is the truth. Ask me any questions you have about the story, and I will try to answer them." He cleared his throat, "Let me suggest that it will be easier if everyone continues to call us by the names you are familiar with. To be honest, I am more used to Ketrik than Terikk." He sighed, "I have tried to forget about the evil times of Terikk's life."

The old men just stared, unable to fathom the fabulous story they had heard.

"What happened to my mother and Col and Vee?" It was Kellen who found the strength to speak.

Ketrik looked compassionately at him, "I do not know, Son. Tyr gave us some information, but he was not sure of anything. Please forgive me for leaving them, but it was the only way to save you. Had we gone after them, we would all have died in Cenkin." He stepped towards Kellen and tried to hug him.

Kellen pushed his father's hands away. "Get away from me, old man! How could you have abandoned them at a time when they needed you most?" He ran from the pavilion, back towards the village.

Kyra rushed after him. As she followed into the blackness, she looked over her shoulder and called back, "I'm sorry, Ketrik. He's not making sense right now. I'll bring him back."

Hapco put a hand on Ketrik's shoulder, reassuring him, "He does not know what he is saying. He cannot possibly understand the decision you made."

Ketrik hung his head and replied, "I have gone over this night for months and months. How to tell him and not hurt him?" He put his hands over his face, letting them slide down. "I thought this was it, the way to tell him and leave it open for us to discuss anything else. Now he thinks I deserted our family." Shaking his head, he asked, "Can you blame him, Hapco? Maybe he is right. Maybe I left them to their own fate while we escaped ours. What do you think?"

"Leave me out of this," Hapco rolled his eyes, exhaling deeply. "That day, I agreed with you and your course of action. Leaving New Caporesso was the only way to save him. I supported your decision then and I still support it today. No one can convince me otherwise. Even if Salvation rises up in arms against us, I will stand at your side and fight with you once more."

Sounding tired and worn out, Ketrik asked, "If we fight and die today, how is that different from all those years ago?"

"The difference is that Kellen grew up. He is a man now. We might have found your family, that is true, but we certainly would have died inside Trosho." He emphasized his words, "All of us, Kellen too." He waved a hand in the direction that Kellen ran. "He is a gifted warrior. His journey to adulthood is complete." Hapco pointed at his friend, "You made a decision and he lived, plain and simple. You gave him the opportunity to have a chance to do something about the past. From the grave, he could have done little."

There was an uneasy silence between the old friends.

Yen found the strength to speak, "Ketrik, I have only known you for ten years and knew nothing about your past until today. Your story is almost unbelievable, but I know it is true down to the last detail." He shook his head slowly. "Kellen was wrong to speak to you as he did. You saved his life, and it was a life worth saving.

"Kyra will find him and talk to him. She'll calm him down, and he'll be back," Yen looked serious. "Allow me to selfishly thank you and Hapco for deciding to save Kellen's life and leave New Caporesso. Had you not, Kyra and I would have died, so I thank you for saving our lives too. We are obviously not worthy of your choice, but I thank you anyway." His words caught in his throat, "I would offer myself to the gods, for the safe return of Col and Vee if I could. Kyra and I will always be indebted to you for your actions on that tragic day."

Hapco opened his mouth to speak but stopped.

Ketrik turned to face Hapco, "You have raised him well. His words give me strength." Looking at Yen, he said, "Thank you, but know this, I would never allow you to sacrifice yourself for my family. Your life is also precious, and I value it. You are the son of my friend, so you are also like a son to me." Putting a hand on Yen's shoulder, he pulled the young man closer, hugging him.

"They are not idle words, Ketrik." Yen stepped away from him and looked him in the eye, "I mean, my king." He knelt before Ketrik and bowed his head.

Hapco had never felt as proud of anyone, as he was of Yen at that very moment. Hapco knelt beside Yen and said, "My king, you have my loyalty forever. I swore this oath to you many years ago. I reaffirm it today. My son is a good man and worthy to be of service to you."

Ketrik contained his emotions, "Get up, my friends. You have my loyalty as well. I am no better than you, nor should I be treated any different than you." He nodded his appreciation. "Those days are long forgotten. Today we are all equals, who must advise each other in the days to come. What shall we do together?" Ketrik looked at the elders, who had remained silent while the three men conversed amongst themselves. "What would you have us do? Do you wish us to leave Salvation?"

The elders had sat long enough. Their most senior representative, Orazio, stood up and addressed them. "Your story is remarkable. Your survival against the extermination squad is incredible. Your journey through the Western Wilderness is impressive. We suspected you were wanted men, but never had any idea how serious this was.

"You have remained hidden amongst us for ten years." He clasped his hands in front of him. "We asked you to obey our laws, and you did. We asked you to protect the village from potential invaders, and you trained to do so. You have been model citizens." Shaking his head, he said, "No, Ketrik, you are not our enemy; you are our brothers. Your children have grown into fine young men and a beautiful woman." Turning from Hapco to Ketrik, he praised them, "You should both be proud of how you raised them. Even though you were without women to nurture them, you gave them everything they needed to become respectable adults." Orazio nodded his approval.

The two men nodded in reply.

Before Orazio could continue, Yen interrupted. He looked at Hapco, "I remember the day you found Kyra and me at Lau'damay. It was several weeks after the coup, although I didn't know that at the time. There is something I should have said to you that day, but I didn't realize the significance of it then."

"What is it?" asked a proud Hapco.

He looked at the ground momentarily, "Now I'm embarrassed I waited this long." He smiled nervously. "You could have left us to die, but you didn't. You took us as your children and shared everything you possessed, including your combat knowledge. I understand that that is a precious gift, and you gave it freely to us." Bowing his head, he professed, "What you gave me, I can never repay you. Thank you for saving us...Father."

Father and son embraced each other.

Hapco released Yen and shook his hand. "When your sister returns, she will wonder what she has missed."

Chapter 60

Col and Vee sat like statues as their mother told the amazing tale. Hours passed without notice. When Mervekka finished, they knew the truth about the day their father died, not just the fabricated story Guan propagated. It was almost too much to comprehend.

Mervekka looked at the shock on their faces, "Now you understand why I taught you everything I could about the formation of New Caporesso and its initial government. Now you know how we allowed it to fall from grace." She thought about Terikk and Aacrel, "We bear the shame for our lack of action. Guan is in power because of our failure to protect the people."

To Col, it felt like he had been hit in the head. "He can't possibly be my father. Father was my father, right?"

"My son, I have cried to sleep countless nights, contemplating that same question," Mervekka looked compassionately at him. "Guan convinced me to give myself to him. He preyed upon my maternal instinct for New Caporesso, knowing I would do anything to protect her." Shaking her head, she admitted, "I never told your father. Had he have known, he would have killed Guan. War with the Southern Kingdom would have ensued, and New Caporesso would have died before beginning to live." She looked away, "I kept silent for the people. Creating a unified country was more important to me than my honor.

"The timing of Guan's *pact*, and my wedding night were very close. When I realized I was going to have a baby, I thought about ending the life of my unborn child." She stepped towards Col, "But when the time came, I just could not do it. How could I have governed over the people of New Caporesso justly if I had been able to kill my own child?

"I decided that no matter who your father truly was, you needed the chance to live. That was the choice I made, that for better or worse, you had to be carried to full term." Smiling at Col, she caressed his cheek, "After you were born, I would lie awake at night looking at your tiny face. You were so fragile and perfect. I realized it was not your fault, and that for once, the truth did not matter. Terikk loved you unconditionally.

"In telling you the truth about Guan, you now know what he is capable of," she continued, "but Terikk is your father. That is what I believe, and there is nothing anyone can say to me to convince me otherwise. I believe Terikk's blood and mine course through your veins, just like your sister's." Her face hardened. "Guan is scum, and your father was a great man. I loved him with all my heart." Mervekka sat quietly, thinking about Terikk.

Col thought to himself, *Father is my father. I'm nothing like Guan; I can't be his son.* He would think about it later. For now, he had other questions, "How do you know what happened outside the walls? Who told you about the approach of Moto and Druvl?"

"After the coup, Guan held a banquet to honor those wretched men who served him during the battle. Moto and Druvl both described their actions from that day. For several weeks, I heard other witnesses recount their tales the same way. But since then, Guan worked to rewrite the history. He began describing your father's kingship as weak and corrupt. Guan has tried to make it seem as though he saved the people by rebelling against the *Fool King*."

Col's head was spinning. He got up and walked around the table. "What about father and Shua?" Putting his hands on the back of a chair, he uttered, "Are you sure they're dead?"

"Tyr recounted his exploits only once in my presence," Mervekka replied. With anger in her voice, she said, "He would not look me in the eye." Shaking her head, she admitted, "I have never heard him, or anyone talk about their deaths again. Tyr had difficulty telling the story," she snorted, "pretending to feel anguish over the execution of my family."

Vee's tears flowed. Col went to her and sat down. He wrapped his arms around her, trying to comfort her. "It's all right, Vee."

Looking at her mother, Vee faintly called out, "Shua?"

"There is nothing we can do for them." Col whispered in her ear. "But now we know the truth." Col's grief was turning to anger. He looked at his mother, "You kept this knowledge from us for a reason." Raising an eyebrow, he inferred, "Since you finally revealed it, I take it you have some plan."

"Col, I used to think we would raise an army and retaliate against Guan for destroying New Caporesso and our family. I imagined that together, you and Vee would march into Cenkin and kill Guan. That was what I believed many years ago." Looking away, she put her hand on her forehead. "Now I realize how naïve that notion was. Guan was so thorough exterminating former soldiers and anyone who could oppose him that I do not know if anyone survived.

"Even if they did, I doubt they would be willing to risk their lives in pursuit of a revolution." She put her hands on her hips. "Guan is too strong, his army too well prepared. Rebellion is not a viable option anymore. The old armies are disbanded and destroyed. There is no *new* generation of warriors in New Caporesso. Guan ordered an end to the traditional training of soldiers in the villages and cities. Only soldiers under his command receive combat instruction, and all of those men are from Sokin." Sadly, she shook her head. "There is no one left to help us; we are alone.

"And we must be careful. If we do anything to make Guan think we are scheming against him," she swallowed, "he will kill us all." Pointing at them, she said, "I struck a deal ten years ago to keep both of you alive, and I will not do anything that jeopardizes that now. Somehow, you must survive."

Col looked at his mother, and shrugged his shoulders, "If we don't seek retribution, then why are you telling us all of this?"

"To protect you. I learned long ago that there are two kinds of power. One involves strength of hand," she clenched her fist, "and the other is fear. Through fear, Guan controls people's minds," she touched the side of her head. "He manipulates the truth to suit his will, painting the picture he wants people to see. As I told you, after the coup, he threatened to kill you. The people might have supported me against him then, but I was afraid of the consequences if I attempted to lead a revolt." Admitting her failure, she said, "I allowed the opportunity to resist him, pass. By the time I realized that was what I should have done, it was too late. His plan was perfect, and he executed it flawlessly."

Mervekka looked from Col to Vee, "I can trace the demise of New Caporesso to a single night. I have been ashamed of what happened ever since." She looked away from them, "It was the ultimate betrayal against your father. My real shame is that by keeping silent, I allowed Guan to perpetuate his lies until the time when he murdered your father and brother." Her voice cracked, but she shed no tears, "It is all my fault."

Vee went to her mother and hugged her, "It's not your fault. You couldn't have changed anything or saved anyone. If you had told father about Guan's liaison, they would have fought. Maybe Father would have been killed then, maybe not. In any event, I doubt Shua or I would have been born." She held her mother's face in her hands, "No, Mother, what happened to you was, and still is horrible. But none of it was your fault. You *didn't* allow anything to happen. Guan is solely responsible for his evil deeds, and everything that has transpired."

It pained Col to see his mother so vulnerable. "We have to do something about him. We can't continue to let him get away with what he's done. Vee?" he glanced at his sister. "He murdered our family and destroyed a country. We must do something."

She looked at Col, "You're right. We must, but what? We need support from people outside these walls. Where can we find it? I'm not even allowed outside!" Vee was exacerbated.

They sat in silence for several minutes, thinking about their options. An idea came to Vee, "Col, you should leave the city and head to Norkin. Father was born there. Perhaps he still has hidden allies who are willing to support us in our cause to take back New Caporesso for the people." She glanced at her mother. "We must remove Guan from power, but to do that, we need soldiers. Finding supporters should be easy, but finding those willing to openly oppose Guan will be another story."

Mervekka forced a tight lipped smile. "Vee, Guan will never allow Col to leave the city unaccompanied. He is always escorted by at least a detachment from the Tu'nide. To even ask for permission might lead to repercussions. No, Guan likes to keep both of you under his complete control. That idea will never work."

"Then Col is right, why are you telling us this now?" Vee was frustrated. "If nothing can be done to save our country and avenge our family, why say anything? Our fates appear fixed, and there seems to be nothing we can do to change them."

They sat quietly again, not sure what else to say. Their minds raced with ideas of revenge, war, and the loss of their family.

Col finally broke the silence. "I have an idea to get me and Vee out of the city *with* Guan's approval. We—"

His mother interrupted, "Col, I told you, he will never allow you, especially together, to leave."

Grinning from ear to ear, Col said, "I heard what you said, Mother, but...I have a plan."

Chapter 61

Kyra caught up with Kellen at the small home he shared with his father. It was attached to the back of the smithy. He was pacing around, trying to clear his head.

She made her presence known and entered the main room of the one bedroom home. Walking into the living area, she looked at the decorations on the walls. Gifts from the villagers were hung on hooks and nails, but they were bereft a personal touch.

"Kellen, what do you think you're doing?" she asked.

"Leave me alone, Kyra. This doesn't concern you. Just leave me alone." He stomped back and forth across the plank floor.

"Doesn't concern me?" she wrinkled her brow and pointed at herself. "How can you say that, Kellen? Ketrik and Hapco saved my life. I owe them everything," she acknowledged. "What are you going to do?" she asked again.

Kellen looked into her eyes; they were mesmerizing. He shook his head to stop himself from staring. "I don't know, but I don't need you watching me. Now go!" He pointed out the door.

Defiantly, she crossed her arms, and her hair bounced as she did so. "No, Kellen, I'm not going anywhere. You need to talk to someone," she nodded, "so here I am."

Her hair falls perfectly at her shoulders. Inhaling, he studied her mouth. *I love her smile; it's perfect.* He shook his head again. "No, Kyra, I want to be alone." Turning his back to her, he walked further into the house, stopping in the tiny kitchen, "Why did he desert them in their hour of darkness?"

Following him, she tried to comfort him, "He didn't abandon them, Kellen. He did what he thought was the right, and that meant saving you," she walked up behind him and put a hand on his shoulder. "You would all be dead if he had gone back for your family. Is that what you want?" Her tone turned confrontational, "Would your life have been better if you were all dead, and buried together?"

Without thinking, he spun around, knocking her hand off his shoulder and smacking her across the face. A surprised look crossed his face. "Kyra..."

Slowly, she straightened her head and brushed the hair out of her face. Kyra stood there boldly, anger boiling in her eyes. "Is that the best you can do? Am I supposed to crumble and wilt?" She took a step towards him, challenging him, "You should know me better than that," she snarled.

Kellen looked dumbstruck and stepped away from her, saying, "Kyra, I'm sorry." He raised his open hands and backed away. "I didn't mean that. It just happened. It was an inexcusable mistake and I'm sorry." Her glare was like nothing he had ever seen. She went from calm to rage in an instant. The fury behind her eyes was almost palpable. Moving further away, he prepared to defend himself.

Kyra took several deep breaths, and a sense of calm came over her, "I am not your enemy, Kellen. Don't ever do that again."

"I won't. I was wrong and I'm sorry. I could never hurt you...not you..." he was at a loss for words, "I...lo—" he turned his head and lowered his hands. Looking back at her, he asked, "Why do you defend my father's actions? He left them to die alone."

Her posture relaxed. "What would you have done? Would you have taken your young son on a suicide mission? A mission with no chance of success? There was no way to save all of you. He was given the impossible choice of leaving behind his family to save you, or giving up everything to die together." Holding up her hands, she asked, "What was the right choice?

"Can you tell me now, what is the right answer? I mean..." she shook her head, waving a hand at him. "Who can make that choice? Your father made the toughest decision of his life to save you. But instead of thanking him, you practically call him a coward!" she was getting louder. "By leaving them, he allowed you to live. You learned to fight. You've made friends who would fight to the death for you...friends who love you. I know it sounds horrible, Kellen, but I say he made the right choice."

Kellen sheepishly looked at the ground and then at Kyra. "You're right," he said. "Again. How do you do that?" he chuckled. "Ah...my father's words took me by surprise. I had no idea about any of it. I was overwhelmed and I guess my reaction with him was wrong too."

"No guessing necessary," she responded bluntly. "You were a total ass."

"Right," he snorted. "Why don't you tell me how you really feel," he forced a laugh. "I must find him and apologize. Then we need to talk... about everything."

"All right, they are probably still at the pavilion," she said.

He nodded in agreement, but said nothing.

The momentary silence quickly turned awkward, "Um, Let's go find them," she suggested.

Kellen grabbed Kyra's hand and looked into her eyes, "You are a good friend, Kyra. Thank you for coming after me and helping me understand." Still holding her hand, he looked quizzically at her, "Fight to the death? Hopefully it won't come to that."

"No, probably not tonight," she chuckled nervously.

He had not released her hand, and she had not pulled away. The two friends tried to exit Kellen's home together, bumping shoulders as they went. They glanced at each other, smiling uncomfortably. Releasing hands, they looked into each other's eyes.

Kellen thought, *She is so beautiful, I think I...* and moved to let her out the door. Side by side, they walked back to the pavilion.

Chapter 62

"Hear me out, Mother."

She looked at him, nodding her compliance.

"As captain of the Tu'nide in the New Caporesso Army, I lead patrols away from the city. As of late, we ride to investigate news of rebel activity. For the last year, all reports have proved false, but they still need to be verified." He shifted in his chair. "New information from the west has arrived, detailing the possibility of rebel forces massing around Werlo and Dreglo. Now I am in the process of organizing a reconnaissance patrol."

"Well, I see how that gives you an excuse to leave the city, but how does that help Vee?" asked Mervekka.

Col continued, "You already explained the directive allowing a person to become a soldier after they best the senior officer of the Tu'nide. Once done, that warrior is entitled to accompany them on their next expedition. Surviving a mission in the saddle is the final test one must pass in order to be embraced as a trooper. This rule was established to prevent favoritism and unworthy promotions." He looked at his sister, "Don't you see, Guan has to let you ride with us; tradition demands it."

Mervekka nodded her head, liking the idea, but she still had reservations. "Will he really consider her a warrior and a soldier?"

"Yes, Mother," replied Col, "he has been pushing her in that direction for a long time. Now that she has beaten me, he must let her ride with us. I imagine he is already planning on assigning her to the next mission."

"That gets the two of you outside these walls, but you will not be alone." Mervekka pointed out a snag in their plan, "The Tu'nide will keep watch over you. You will not be able to recruit anyone to our side without being observed." She shook her head. "They will report your activity to Guan."

"Mother," his smile grew bigger, "my men are the most loyal soldiers in all of New Caporesso, but their loyalties are first to me. Remember, these are the only soldiers not from Sokin. They would stand with me against any enemy if my cause was worthy." Col looked away, reflecting, "For years, I've heard rumors suggesting Guan was more involved in the deaths of father, Shua, and Aacrel. I always dismissed them as vicious lies, attacks on his character, but now I know they're true." He sighed, "Somehow I always knew they were true; I just didn't want to believe them.

"You say our family was charged with keeping the citizens of New Caporesso safe." He walked around the table. "So far we've failed, but here's an opportunity for us to amend the past. With help from the people, we can overthrow Guan and remove him from power. We can restore the ideal on which New Caporesso was founded." Resolutely, he said, "To honor Shua and Father's memory, we must follow this course to whatever end. Mother, it's not enough for us just to survive any longer. Our time to fight back is at hand." He clenched his fist, "Everything you've taught us since their death, has prepared us for today, Mother. You have to see that Vee and I are ready to take up swords against Guan, and do whatever's necessary for the good of the country."

Vee added, "It's time for us to be accountable to New Caporesso. It's time for our family to fight for the people once more."

Mervekka thought about their words for a moment. Acquiescing, she nodded her head and asked, "How do you know your men will assist you, Col?"

"What could be more honorable than reestablishing the government of New Caporesso and at the same time avenging our family's murder?" He became animated. "When I confirm Guan's criminal part in this tragedy, my men will support us and our noble cause. There is a bond between us that is stronger than anything he can muster with the whip and rod," he sounded sure of himself.

Vee was excited at the idea, "Once outside the city, we can search for supporters who'd fight with us. The people will join us and help restore order to New Caporesso," the idea of vanquishing Guan filled her with energy.

"The common people will not join you, Vee," Mervekka shook her head, "too much time has passed since Terikk's death. Those once loyal will have forgotten him and everything he represented. They will not be willing to bleed for him again, even in his memory. I believe raising an army is impossible." She hesitated, "But...both of you leaving Cenkin is good. Maybe this time, the reports of rebel activity will be accurate. If they plan to resist Guan, they must have training of some kind." Turning to face Col, she said, "Search for them and find them. Meet with their leaders and convince them we seek the same thing they do: to rid this country of Guan and his wicked ways. Determine if they will support a new revolution to restore the government and return the country to the people. Or find out if they have lost the will to fight for freedom and justice. Ask if they will come to the defense of their queen when she calls them."

Col nodded at his mother and then looked at Vee. "So, we are agreed then?" he asked. "I will ask Guan to permit Vee to ride with the Tu'nide to discern the truth of these reports about rebels in the west. From there, we will devise a plan as we proceed."

"That sounds as good a plan as any, Col," responded Mervekka. "Go talk to Guan tonight. Tomorrow, tell us of his response. May the gods' bless us and allow this to happen."

As Col left his mother and Vee, the queen smiled. A feeling of hope returned to her. The feeling filled her with a warmth that had been absent for years. *We will find support. We will rid this country of Guan. Terikk and Shua will finally have their vengeance.* Mervekka allowed herself the simple pleasure of smiling at that thought. She looked at Vee and they hugged.

When they released each other, Mervekka spoke softly to her daughter, "Vee, I am very proud of you. Your diligent training has brought us to this day. You are almost a warrior in the Tu'nide, your father would have been very proud of you."

Parting ways for the evening, Mervekka watched her daughter. She knew Vee was beautiful, but tonight, there was something more. Vee walked with more purpose in her step, carrying herself with more poise and confidence. The girlish qualities about her had transformed themselves into those of a determined woman. Yes, her victory over Col in the courtyard had definitely changed her. Today, Vee became a woman.

Chapter 63

Ketrik was seated behind a table, with Hapco and Yen in front of him. He rose to his feet as Kellen and Kyra approached, "Well, Kellen, friends or not?"

"Father, I'm sorry for the way I reacted." He lowered his head, admitting his mistake. "I was shocked by your story and couldn't control my emotions. Years of mystery built up inside of me came crashing down in a single moment." Shaking his head, he confessed, "It was nothing like I envisioned. It was better, and worse, all at the same time. My head was spinning and I needed some air. I couldn't think clearly and blurted out the first thing that came into my mind. Forgive my impetuousness."

Hapco puffed on his pipe and chuckled. "I see Kyra talked some sense into you."

Kellen looked at Hapco, "She is a good friend to me." Turning, he eyed the beauty standing beside him, "Her voice was all I needed to hear to realize my error." Gazing into her eyes, he was instantly under her spell. "Having her beside me is like..." he stammered, "I mean...she's like...I meant," he chuckled nervously, "ha ha," and cleared his throat, changing the subject. "Never mind," he flashed his teeth. "I'd like some time to talk to my father." He looked at his friends. "You are welcome to stay and join in the conversation, since I feel our futures are tied together by our discussion tonight."

Ketrik looked at the elders and spoke to Orazio, "I trust we can finish this in the morning."

Orazio raised an eyebrow, "Ketrik, you and Hapco have always been treasured members of our society. Though you may not see it, your service to Salvation has been invaluable. When you arrived here ten years ago, we asked you to contribute to community life, and if need be, defend the town from usupers from New Caporesso. Through your instruction, you have trained our soldiers to be mighty warriors. Their skills have advanced years beyond what we could teach them, and the two of you made that possible." He nodded at both men, "We will finish our conversation in the morning. Ketrik, we take our leave now." Retiring from the pavilion, Orazio stopped in front of Kellen, "Welcome back, son. Listen to your father; he loves you very much," and patted his shoulder as he passed.

The pavilion was empty except for the five travelers from New Caporesso. They moved to the center of the covered area, sitting near a fire pit. The fire crackled as its fuel was consumed. Thick smoke escaped up the chimney, its pleasant aroma filling the area. Hapco threw two more birch logs on the fire and it sprang back to life. They burned intensely for several minutes before dissipating. Heat radiated from the pit, warming the cool spring air.

"Kellen, I did what I thought was right, but I will never know if it truly was. Hopefully, you can forgive me."

"Father, I know the choice was impossible. You acted as you did and we're alive because of it. For all we know, they were already dead when Tyr explained everything to you and Hapco." Shrugging, he said, "You reacted the only way you possibly could, and there is nothing to forgive." Respectively, he nodded his head. "I remember you telling me our family's memory was your burden to carry. Now I understand what you meant."

The two stepped together and embraced, smacking each other's back. Separating, Ketrik looked at his son, "From now on, Kellen, we will make our decisions together. I am no longer the king of New Caporesso. We will discuss and decide our path for the future." He looked at the other three. "We will all decide what course to follow."

"Why aren't you still king of New Caporesso?" asked Yen.

Hapco looked at Yen, and then Ketrik, adding, "I believe he is correct. Why are you not, still the legal king of New Caporesso?" He folded his arms and put a hand to his chin.

Ketrik stepped away from them, raising and then lowering his arms. "Who would recognize me as king? We have no idea what happened to New Caporesso in our absence. I would assume Guan seized complete power and disbanded New Caporesso. I would speculate the land is as it was before we established New Caporesso, constant conflict."

"Right, it could be. But we do not know that for sure, do we?" asked Hapco.

"I suppose not," he folded his arms in front of him, "what is your point?"

Yen stood up as he was interrupting, "Why don't we go back and investigate? Let's find out what really happened. It is the only way to really learn the fate of your family." He looked at Kellen, seeking agreement.

Kyra stepped forward and added, "The five of us could return and travel from village to village in search of news about New Caporesso and the fate of the Royal Family."

Ketrik scoffed, "And then what? Storm Cenkin's walls, the five of us? We would need an army of twenty thousand men, but seem to have none at our disposal." Looking agitated, he brushed the side of his head. "The night air has gone to your heads." Motioning at Hapco, he said, "Please explain to them."

Hapco grinned wide. "But, my king, I am somewhat sorry to agree, but they are correct. Maybe not storming the walls of Cenkin, but we taught them to be warriors for freedom and justice. As we left New Caporesso, it was dying." He gestured at Ketrik, "We know what Guan was capable of. Should we think he did anything, other than become a tyrant over an entire country?"

"If so," Kyra pondered aloud, "is there a land in more need of someone to lead it out of the darkness it has fallen into? I realize the path will be difficult, no doubt. But it's a start to finding the truth about New Caporesso. Did it only live for fourteen years?" Raising her hands, she asked, "Is it now some perverted concept that has its origins from both of you?" She nodded at Yen, "He's right; we *do* need to find out what happened to your family."

Ketrik frowned and looked at Hapco. He turned to Kellen, "And what about you? Is the vote four to one that we go back?"

Kellen looked at their faces, "Before tonight, I dreamt of the day when we could return to New Caporesso and look for my family. Even though the circumstances of our history have changed from what I imagined them to be, I still want to find out what happened." He sighed, "Maybe we'll only find their graves, but at least then we'll know their fates."

"But at what cost, Kellen?" asked Ketrik incredulously. "What if our return results in the death of one of our own party? How will that outcome justify our return?" He looked at each of them. "We have become a family, the five of us. I would not risk your lives for anything, or anyone in this world. Returning to New Caporesso will only put your lives in danger, and I could not bear to lose any one of you." Turning back to Kellen, he asked, "What about you?"

"I could not stand to lose any of them either, Father," he looked directly at Kyra. "But a part of me will never be whole until I find out what happened to them." He turned to address his father, "What if they are still alive? You only surmise they died in the coup. We survived, didn't we? Maybe they did too." His eyes pleaded with his father.

After several minutes in deep thought, Ketrik yielded, "All right, all right," he threw his hands up in the air, "we will prepare for the return journey. In a week, at most two, we will travel through the Western Wilderness and head for New Caporesso. Once across the Shau'may River, we will visit the villages where we found Yen and Kyra. From there, we will turn northeast to Norkin. I may still have friends there. They should be able to tell us what has happened in our absence." Ketrik paused, looking at them, "I guess we are all in agreement on this course?"

They looked at Ketrik and nodded in reply.

"Good," he remarked. "This is the course Hapco and I agreed upon many years ago. But," he glanced at Hapco, "we decided to allow the three of you to arrive at the same conclusion on your own." Scowling at Hapco, he added, "Even though he prompted you a little, the decision was still your own."

Hapco raised his arms innocently, "Hey, it's me."

Shaking his head, Ketrik said, "It is late. Tomorrow, we will begin planning for the return journey. Understand," he raised a hand, "once in New Caporesso, we may never leave that land again. Death may find us there." He pointed at each of them, "Make no mistake about it, returning to New Caporesso in search of our family may mean the destruction of *this* one."

Ketrik was right and they knew it. This group of five refugees had become their own ragtag family. After ten years of life together, the bonds of friendship and love were as great for them as any other family. The loss of any one of them would be devastating to them all. The risk was high, but it was a risk they were all willing to take.

Chapter 64

Standing beside the dining table in the throne room were three young servants. The short-sleeved vibrant dresses they wore were knee length, exposing their skinny legs. They stood ready to serve Guan as his mood dictated. Two pheasant carcasses were still on the table along with half eaten plates of potatoes and other vegetables.

At a wave of his hand, the girls collected the remnants of his dinner. He watched them attentively as they carried his plates and goblets away. A knowing grin slinked across his face as one of them bent down to pick up a fallen cup. Blushing, the girl hurried to the kitchen.

A guard approached, "Sire, Captain Col respectively requests an audience with you this evening. What should I tell him, sire?"

Sipping his wine, Guan nodded, "Did he say what he wants, Belosh?"

"No, sire. He did not. Should I send him away, sire?" he asked.

With a shake of his head, Guan said, "No, no. Grant him admittance. He has probably come to apologize for his embarrassing performance in the courtyard today," he chuckled. Standing up, Guan moved to his throne and awaited Col.

Entering the room, Col moved to stand before Guan. He saluted. "Strength of swords, honor in victory."

Nodding, Guan greeted Col, "What brings you here at this hour, Captain?"

"Thank you for seeing me, sire," he cleared his throat. "After the day's events and supper with my sister, I request permission to discuss her status as a warrior."

Taking a jab at Col, Guan taunted, "I was shocked when she beat you today. I never thought she would be better than you." He exaggerated a sigh, "You had so much potential, but I guess she works harder than you now." Guan paused, smirking, "Perhaps she is more naturally gifted than you ever were."

Col bowed his head, absorbing the affronts. "Yes, my king," he looked up, "she is naturally gifted. There's no other explanation for her abilities. The things she does can't be taught," Col returned the jab, "by anyone."

Guan's expression turned sour. "What is it you want, Captain?"

"I've received orders to take the Tu'nide to Werlo and Dreglo to investigate reports of rebel activity in the area. We are to leave by the end of the week. And in light of Vee's progress in the courtyard, I ask permission to let her ride with us." He let the sentence hang. "This is the only way to complete her training."

"You want her to ride on this expedition?" Standing up, Guan paced along the edge of the dais. He planned on ordering Col to take Vitoria on the mission, but he expected Col to protest the decision. This was unanticipated.

"Yes, sire, you know my sister is ready for the trials of the journey." He nodded. "She is ready to become the first woman accepted into the ranks of the Tu'nide, and I know she will prove herself worthy."

Guan stopped and looked at Col, "I concur; Princess Vitoria is ready to join the Tu'nide. In fact, one day soon, I believe she will lead them in battle," he humphed. "Yes, Col, you have my permission to take her on the expedition. Make your plans and return with them for my perusal." Pointing at Col, he added, "She must be allowed to fight, for this will not be some sham of a mission, but keep her unscathed. If she returns permanently scarred or worse, you will receive the same." Guan folded his arms and glowered at Col. "Do you understand me, Captain?"

With self-assuredness, Col answered him, "I understand your orders, my king. She will return the same way she leaves: perfect."

"Ah…" Guan caught his breath at the word, losing his composure for a split second.

Col saw the flinch, but did not acknowledge it.

Both men were using Vee as a sparring device to gather information about the other.

"Yes, Captain, be sure that she does." Guan waved a hand at Col. "You are dismissed. Return when your plan is in place and the men are ready to ride. I mean, the men and Princess Vitoria." His expression was blank, but Col had already seen what Guan was hiding.

Col spoke and then bowed, "Thank you, sire. I'll report back within the week with our plans." Col turned and left the throne room. A portion of his plan was already in place. He and Vee were allowed to leave Cenkin.

Guan scowled as Col left. He was continuing to undermine the feelings of trust and loyalty between brother and sister. The thought of her replacing him as leader of the Tu'nide would be enough to keep them bickering. Sibling rivalry was a wonderful thing when he controlled it.

Vitoria's training was almost complete. Guan was pleased with the way everything was progressing. Soon, she would be the warrior goddess he envisioned her to be. Soon, she would be ready to take her place at his side.

Movement to Guan's left grabbed his attention. Turning, he saw a man wearing black pants and a black gambeson approaching. "Donetsk, how long were you there?" he demanded.

Bowing, he replied, "Not long, mighty king." Donetsk was small for a man from the south, small and frail. Yet somehow, he had found a job that he was good at—spying. His success stemmed from the fact that he appeared harmless and insignificant. His ratlike face contributed to that impression. Squinty eyes and a tuft of hair on his chin were his only distinguishable features, making him forgettable.

"You should have made your presence known at once, I do not like unknown ears listening to my conversations," Guan admonished.

"It is my job to be unnoticed, mighty king. You chose wisely when you sent me to infiltrate the western rebels and learn their secrets," he flattered. "I come and go as I please, and have learned their troop strength and locations, as you commanded." He bowed his head humbly.

Guan nodded his head. "Yes, Donetsk, I know you have done well." He motioned for him to approach the throne.

Ascending the dais silently, Donetsk quickly climbed to the top step and leaned close to Guan.

"Give your report," he commanded.

"Mighty king, the rebels are there, just as you suspected," he grinned. "And they've been busy this last year. Instead of meeting the army patrols in open battle, they remain hidden, training daily and improving their skills as soldiers. There are at least three thousand men and women in their ranks, with more and more arriving every day. And they are not just from Werlo and Dreglo." He made a circular motion on his chest. "I have also seen the old crests from Norkin, Nurdug, and Drador in their midst. Their numbers are growing and may soon become a real threat to the stability of *your* New Caporesso, mighty king." Tracing a hump with his hand, he continued, "They have concentrated their forces on the heavily wooded inselberg between Werlo and Dreglo. They are working to fortify their position atop Monadnock."

Guan listened intently, absorbing the information. "I leave those miserable proles enough food to eat," he scowled, "and this is how they honor me? I have been too lenient with them for too long. Well no more," he spat. "Since there has been no violence, I cannot unleash the army unprovoked. I need a reason to send them west to deal with those insurgents." He tapped the side of his head. "And I think you can give it to me. The peasants have observed my authority but do not entirely support me." His mouth spasmed, trying to form a grin. "But if the Tu'nide were destroyed by a band of rebels…then the whole country would demand that I send the army to eradicate this world of their existence."

Donetsk's nose twitched as he smirked, "And if the Tu'nide were ambushed in the marshes, that would certainly assist the rebels in destroying them, would it not, mighty king?"

Raising an eyebrow, Guan replied, "It would indeed. Your aptitude for strategy grows as does your skill as a spy," glaring at Donetsk, his tone changed. "Make sure it is never put to use against me. Do you understand?"

"Yes, mighty king," he bowed his head again. "What are your orders?"

"The Tu'nide leave within the week; Princess Vitoria rides with them for the first time. She *must* survive the battle. That is paramount to your task at hand. Understand? As for the rest of them…kill them all. Including Col." He nodded once. "When Princess Vitoria returns, the sole survivor of an ambush, her brother dead, and the Tu'nide destroyed, the last ties to Terikk and *his* New Caporesso will be severed. The country will demand I put down the rebels forever, and I will gladly do so. We will be at war again."

"And Princess Vitoria and Queen Mervekka, mighty king. What happens to them?" Donetsk asked.

A corner of Guan's mouth curled upward. "I believe I will find a new queen to bear me an heir, Donetsk."

Grinning, Donetsk put his hand to his shoulder, declaring, "Mighty king, as the gods are my witnesses, the princess will be returned uninjured as you demand. The rebels will spare her life and keep her safe." An idea occurred to him. "Mighty king, an alternate course has come to me. What if the rebels kidnapped the princess before the battle, thus keeping her out of harm's way? Then the Tu'nide would rush headlong into our trap to rescue her and be mercilessly cut down. After the engagement, the princess will be released and escorted back to Cenkin." Pausing, he let Guan consider the option. "Does this plan sound feasible, oh mighty king," again, he bowed his head.

Nodding slowly, Guan replied, "As I said, your capacity for strategic planning grows. Your plan is deviously simple, yet eloquent. Those chivalrous bastards will charge blindly into your ambush to free her. Hmm. Make it happen and be rewarded for your service." Dismissing Donetsk, he added, "Now return to your friends and prepare them for their task. The Tu'nide should reach their final destination in no more than sixty days; be ready for them."

"Yes, great king. We will be ready for the unsuspecting Tu'nide. This will be their final ride," he chuckled. Standing as tall as he could, he bowed to Guan. Receiving his dismissal, he stealthily exited Trosho and headed west.

Watching him leave, Guan was alone. He spoke aloud, "With Col gone…and the Tu'nide destroyed…I will have what I have wanted all along." He chortled. "Milady's services will no longer be required. Soon Princess Vitoria will take her place beside me, both on the throne and in my bed." Laughing loudly, he stood up, confessing, "Terikk's soul would cry out from the Netherworld if he knew his daughter will soon be my wife."

Descending the stairs, he headed for his quarters; the echoes of his laughter filled the empty throne room.

Tyr entered the throne room unnoticed. As he did, he observed Donetsk conversing with Guan. He could not hear what they were saying and moved as close as he dare, hiding behind a thick sycamore column. In silence, he listened to them. After a few minutes, Donetsk bowed and scurried out of the room.

Remaining hidden, Tyr listened as Guan conversed with himself. His plan sounded devious. The Tu'nide would never expect an ambush from the rebels they were searching for. Heavy hearted, Tyr wondered how he could prevent more horror from befalling Mervekka's family. *Hopefully a plan will present itself to me; otherwise, I don't think she'll be able to handle the death of another child.*

Chapter 65

At daybreak, Ketrik strolled along the outskirts of Salvation. Sighing, he surveyed the surrounding landscape. Nothing ever seemed to change.

Seven wild destriers pranced nearby. Ketrik spoke soothingly to them, "These people are good people. They have lived here peacefully for hundreds of years, and instead of destroying the countryside, they honor it; they honor you," he shushed the horses, reaching out to the closest one. "They farm enough land to feed everyone without depleting the soil. They use enough countryside to graze their herds without turning the grass to dust.

"These people take what they need to survive, but do not gorge themselves on the land's resources." Clicking his tongue against his teeth, he stepped slowly towards the horse. "They live in harmony with everything here," he spoke in hushed tones. "Both they and this land flourish because of their temperance. They have not forced you into a life of servitude, still allowing you to roam freely, just like your ancient ancestors." A stallion skittered closer to Ketrik before bolting away.

He looked at the thick forest bordering the grasslands. They were less than a day's walk away to the east. He knew the forest also surrounded the northern and southern tips of the village. Their portion of green land in the shallow canyon must have have been carved out by the gods. He was envious of a community so at peace with itself and nature. Clapping his hands loudly, he scattered the regal horses.

Smiling, Ketrik walked to Zorca'pizo, the meeting hall of the elders. Inside, he found Orazio and the others waiting for him. They continued the conversation they had begun the previous night. It was a painstaking task.

Orazio was seated behind an elegant wooden table. The other elders sat to either side of him. Their heavy oak chairs were scribed with intricate arabesque carvings. The motif resembled that of the ancient rulers from Lau'damay. The chairs were said to be almost as old as Salvation itself.

Listening to the elders, Ketrik paced like a caged animal, unable to sit on the chair they provided for him. Last night he thought they would offer supplies freely. Today, their offer came with conditions.

After several hours of discussion, nothing was settled. Ketrik grew disheartened by the lack of concessions. "Orazio, taking your people with us is a terrible mistake. With a large group, we will look like a caravan and draw suspicious eyes. If things have returned to the way they were, a war party will observe us and investigate our convoy. If that happens, we will be drawn into a battle which we are unprepared to fight." He shook his head. "And the fact that such a trail through the wilderness even exists is surprising. How it was it created?"

"Yes, we were shocked when they informed us of its existence. My sons, Durian and Webb, asked to be allowed to travel with some friends to explore the Kel'nito Forest. I saw no objections and granted them permission. They said they would be gone for no more than seven months, which did not sound unreasonable. After that time, they returned and informed us they created a path through the Western Wilderness to the edge of New Caporesso. Durian said they made it to see if it could be done. It turned out they were successful." He put a hand to his head. "We told them to never tell anyone of the path."

"Why did you want to keep it secret?" inquired Ketrik.

"To keep everyone safe," Orazio lowered his hand. "There are some residents who desire a different way of life. They long for adventure and uncertainty. The peaceful life we enjoy is not enough for some of them anymore. Some of our children say they have no opportunity to do something greater. They know nothing of the world beyond the wilderness, and they want to understand what it's like to feel alive." He exhaled. "It seems like each new generation is more removed from the founders of Salvation, and they have forgotten everything about the old ways."

"Will the savagery of war make them feel alive, Orazio?" Ketrik clasped his hands behind his back. "That kind of war serves no purpose, other than to fuel its own desire to consume life." He paced as he spoke, "Before our land became New Caporesso, people used to talk about the noble war, and why it should be fought." Sighing, he said, "I realized each side of the conflict believed *their* cause to be noble. Whose cause was nobler? The only result of that kind of war is death and destruction on a giant scale. Husbands never went home to their wives. Children never saw their fathers again." Stopping, he pointed at Orazio, "That is what war is. It does not make you feel alive, it destroys everything it touches."

"I hear your words, Ketrik, but my sons will not. They desire to leave Salvation and head to New Caporesso. Durian says they can travel with you. They will guide you through the forest, and you can teach them the ways of your people." He thumped the table, indicating his decision was final. "I feel this is the best way for you to repay your debt to Salvation."

"Orazio," Ketrik pleaded, "we would do anything to settle our obligations to you, but this is a mistake. We cannot teach your sons how to act like New Caporessoeans in a few weeks. It takes a lifetime to understand the treachery and underhandedness that exists in some people. I am proof of that. Even I failed to recognize the signs, and it has led me to this point in time. We cannot take your sons with us."

"Not just my sons," he said matter-of-factly. "A total of ten scouts will go with you. Durian and Webb will select those who are to accompany you on the journey," again, he thumped his fist on the table.

Ketrik was dumbfounded by Orazio's demands. "Why would anyone want to leave this peaceful land?" The answer was simple, only someone with no knowledge of violence and hardship would ever conceive of something so foolish. "Orazio, what you ask is absurd."

"I do not ask, Ketrik," countered Orazio. "If we," he pointed at the other elders, "withhold our consent, you will not be supplied for your mission. Without supplies, you will be forced to steal from our stores. If you steal from us, you will become our enemies." He spoke from his position of authority. "I do not think that is a path you wish to follow."

Shaking his head, Ketrik responded, "Of course we do not want that, Orazio. You offered us life when we could not provide it for Kellen, Kyra, and Yen. The things you have given us can never be fully repaid. I will not defy your orders, or try to steal from the village to satisfy my own agenda."

Ketrik sat in the chair, holding his head. For several minutes he sat motionless, thinking. Finally, he relented, "Seeing that I have no other choice, Orazio, we will take your people with us. But understand, not everyone may come home. New Caporesso was in the midst of a rebellion when we escaped. We have no idea what we will find when we return. The entire country could be at war."

"Or the whole country could be at peace," rejoined Orazio.

Ketrik looked up at him, "The man seizing control of the country would never tolerate peace again. The country may not be consumed in a civil war, but it most definitely will not be at peace with itself. Mark my words, Orazio; we will face unknown enemies upon our return. With a group of fifteen riders, we will look like an undermanned caravan, ripe for attack."

"Then the men of New Caporesso will learn how Salvation warriors fight," Orazio proclaimed brazenly.

Shaking his head, Ketrik thought, *Old fool.* "I understand and appreciate the reasons Salvation honors the old traditions of Caporesso. Training for combat is an essential part of every man and woman's development, a primary part of their education. They train as their ancestors did, and I commend Salvation for it. You stay ever watchful over the Western Wilderness, guarding against the possible invasion of men from New Caporesso.

"But, Orazio," he pleaded his case one more time, "this new generation of warriors is disinterested in the preparations necessary to be successful in battle. They have grown content with their surroundings, content and lazy." He shook his head. "Most are not dedicated to the combat arts, lacking the discipline to reach their full potential as warriors. When you talk about your highly trained warriors, you only see the few dedicated ones. You ignore the thousands who only pretend to train. Salvation is not as well protected as you assume.

"And you have had no armed conflict with anyone for over four hundred years. There is a difference between training and fighting." He sighed, "Only a handful of your soldiers are actually combat ready. Leading them to Salvation would only put them in peril. They are not prepared for what we may find in New Caporesso.

"Please, Orazio, allow us to return and investigate for a short time, just the five of us. Before Kellen and I proceed with our mission, we will return and advise you of the situation in New Caporesso." He looked from face to face. "If it appears safe, we will bring some of your people back through with us, if not, they will be safer here. Use reason and hear my words. I want to protect your people, not waste their lives in a futile attempt to settle in a wicked land."

Orazio nodded his head several times. Then he motioned to an aide, "Bring in my sons. It is time for them to join the conversation."

Ketrik hung his head, realizing his words had gone unheard.

Chapter 66

Near midmorning, while Ketrik and Orazio were discussing the expedition to New Caporesso, Hapco found Kellen and Yen milling around the smithy. They were looking for something to do. Kyra was packing clothes and other items.

Hapco called them over, "What are you two doing?"

Yen answered, "Nothing, Hapco. Just waiting...for something," he chortled and looked at Kellen.

"Why not spar a little?" he raised an eyebrow. "Go get your weapons," he nodded in the direction of their homes. He clenched his fist as he said, "You should know how those weapons feel in your hands under the stress of combat. Your senses will be heightened, and you will feel the tingle of energy flowing through you. Embrace it. Embrace the devastation your weapons can inflict. Embrace the horror of it, but control its power."

Without any reservations, each young man went to his home and collected his weapons. Yen returned first with two swords strapped to his back. Both nine-inch, black corded handles extended above his shoulders, one to the right and left of his head. The soft scabbards holding the swords formed a figure X on his back. The katana for his right hand was thirty-six inches long. The back edge of the sword was sharpened for the first nine inches from the tip. The sword for his left hand was a twenty-seven-inch wakizashi. Three-inch-long oval crossguards protected his hands.

Yen's swords could be combined by fitting the handles together. The handle of the wakizashi was thicker, and hollow for a length of six inches. The katana handle could then be inserted into the short sword. When joined, a twelve-inch handle remained to wield the dual bladed weapon. The resulting fifty-seven-inch double sword was impressive. A simple locking mechanism kept the weapon secure.

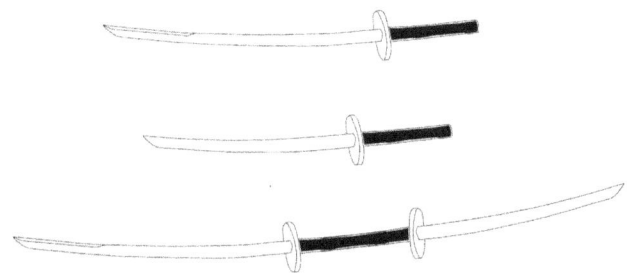

Around Yen's waist hung a leather belt with a tarnished brass buckle. The belt had sheaths for two kukris, which were carried horizontally across his back. The identical weapons were eighteen inches long, with six-inch handles. They were presented for combat with each hand using a reverse grip and the blades turned down.

The kukris had flat bladed handguards to protect Yen's fingers while using them. The guards looked like the massive fangs of an ancient lion, and also served as brutal cutting edges. A single long quillion, or hook, was attached where the blade and handle met. It was on the opposite side of the *fang*, and extended towards the tip of the blade. This *hook* could be used to trap an opponent's weapon or flip the kukri, allowing Yen to transition from a reverse grip to a basic grip in one fluid motion.

The kukri and handguard was a unique looking weapon. The fanglike bladed handguard dissolved into the sinuous kukri edge, terminating with the forward weighted, belly of the blade. As it was configured, the close combat weapon was capable of vicious slashing and chopping motions. Ketrik forged only five sets of the twin kukris for him and his comrades.

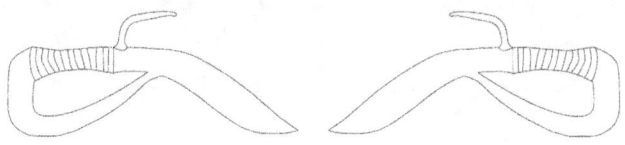

As Kellen arrived, he was similarly armed with a leather belt and horizontal kukris at the small of his back. Across his body, he wore a brown baldric. It ran diagonally from his right shoulder to his left hip. At his hip, the attached frog held the rigid scabbard for his katana. The frog could be opened quickly to allow for the extraction of the scabbard.

His sword was identical to Yen's main weapon except for the color of the handle; it was white cord. The scabbard was also a special weapon. Its end had four, one-inch projections protruding from it. The extensions ended with blunt points, creating a weapon for crushing anything it hit. Armed like that, Kellen held a weapon in each hand. He could also assemble the two pieces together, fitting the entire handle of the sword inside the scabbard. This created a fifty-four-inch weapon with a twenty-seven-inch blade. A small lock held it together.

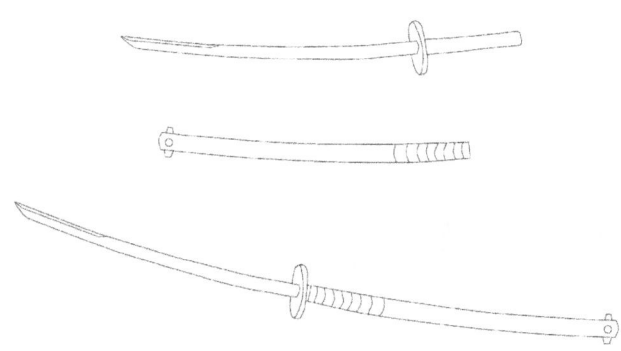

Yen drew his right hand sword and removed the sheaths from his back. Kellen pulled his katana from its scabbard, laying the baldric on the ground. They lightly grasped their weapons with two hands and moved to face each other. Bowing, they stepped into fighting stances. Time seemed to stop as the two combatants stared at each other.

Chapter 67

Just after midmorning, Col and Vee began planning for the upcoming expedition. They collected supplies for the trip and entered the stables to load what they had into wagons.

Col looked at his sister, "Nervous?"

She forced a thin smile, replying, "A little, but not about the mission. It's about leaving mother. She'll be alone here with Guan." She continued loading her gear.

"I know, Vee, I know, but we need to do this for our family and all of New Caporesso. Maybe we can find people willing to fight with us against Guan. He walked over to her and held her hands.

She looked in his eyes, "Your eyes are Father's, not Guan's."

He admitted "I want to believe you, but…" he shook his head, "Guan disgraced Mother and should die. He has created an uncertainty in my life, and no one knows the truth. If he tells the people of his treachery, they will be angry with mother." Stepping away from her, he walked to his horse. He stroked Choa's muzzle, "It's too much to think about right now. We can do nothing about him unless we find support. That is our task at hand and the reason for this expedition. Come, we have much to do."

Leaving the stables, they returned to the Tu'nide Prep Building.

As they entered the building, they were greeted by Col's second in command, Lieutenant Sed'la. "Good morning, Captain." He looked at Vee. "I understand the princess is to accompany us on the expedition."

"Morning, Lieutenant." Col returned Sed'la's salute, "Yes she is, is that a problem?"

"No, sir, we heard a rumor and wanted to know the truth."

"Will her presence create a problem for you, or any of the men, Sed'la?" Col scrutinized him.

Sed'la did not avert his eyes, "No, sir. We have seen the princess train and know she is a skilled warrior. Tu'nide protocol dictates that once a warrior proves *himself* in the training arena, *he* should ride with the unit to gain combat experience."

Col noticed the words Sed'la emphasized. "Do you and the men have a problem with the fact she is a woman?"

He did not answer right away. Sed'la seemed to be choosing his words carefully. "Sir, no woman has ever ridden with the Tu'nide in the history of its existence. And yes, sir, all of the men, including me, are uncomfortable with the idea of her joining us."

"Hey, I'm right here." She pointed at herself.

"Vee," Col interjected, holding up a hand in front of her. "I appreciate your candor, Sed'la, but she won't be a problem, nor will she cause any. Vee is a fine soldier and will serve with distinction in the Tu'nide"

Vee raised her hands. "Seriously, I can hear everything you're both saying about me."

Sed'la looked at her, then back at Col. "Don't misunderstand my concern, we know she's a gifted warrior. But eventually on one of these expeditions, we *will* encounter hostile resistance. Guan's grain requisitions have enraged the people, pushing them to the brink. He demands more and more from them every year. Soon, the majority of what they produce will be sent to Cenkin or Sokin, leaving them with almost nothing for their families. I'm afraid that their discontented grumblings may quickly escalate into violent confrontations." Gesturing at Vee, he asked, "What happens if she gets into trouble, hmm?" He looked at her. "I'll tell you what'll happen; the men will risk their lives to keep her safe. They'll needlessly throw themselves in harm's way to protect her."

"They do that anyway, Sed'la," Col responded. "You know once we take to the saddle, the men watch each other's back. We operate with the sole purpose of keeping our men alive; the orders always sort themselves out in the end. That's how it's been, and nothing will be different this time."

Vee found her voice, "Lieutenant Sed'la, consider me like any other soldier joining the Tu'nide on their first expedition, nothing more or less. I am merely a soldier. I hope to one day be like you and Col, but I need battle experience to make that a reality." Shaking her head, she assured him, "You don't need to worry about me creating distractions for your men. I am a woman and princess of New Caporesso inside these walls," she motioned around her. "However, outside and in the ranks of the Tu'nide, I will be the lowest ranking trooper. Do not treat me with contempt or mock me, but as a soldier trying to become a warrior." Stepping closer, she looked him in the eye. "Can you do that, Lieutenant?"

Sed'la gazed into her eyes, then turned to Col. "Yep, just like you said she'd be, Col." He grinned and turned back to her. "Princess, I know you desire to be treated like an ordinary soldier in the unit. We'll try to do so, but I can't make any promises. The men know who you are and will protect you more than they would each other. I pray we meet little opposition along the way."

Col turned to her. "See, I told you they'd understand."

Vee sneered and bobbled her head.

Sed'la smacked Col on the arm and laughed. He shook his head, saying, "Everybody knows she beat you yesterday. You'll hear it from them once we leave Cenkin." He continued laughing. "It'll be like when we were kids practicing together, and everyone could beat you!"

"Hear what from who?" asked Vee.

A corner of Col's mouth curled up. "The men will have their fun with me, because you, a woman, beat me in combat." He looked at Sed'la and then Vee. "Maybe I should let them train with you for a little. After you beat them, all of them, their opinions of your skill will change. You would humble them, I'm sure of it."

Col got more serious and asked Sed'la, "How are the men situated for the ride? What supplies do we have and what do we still need? How soon can we leave?"

With that, Sed'la and Col turned their attention to the preparations necessary for their expedition. Vee backed away from the men in charge. She exited the building and looked at the afternoon sun. The smell of fresh hyacinths greeted her senses. *I'm a princess of New Caporesso here, but out there, I'll be just like everyone else, a simple soldier, trying to escape death.*

Chapter 68

Orazio held up his hand, "Ketrik, you know my sons. This is Durian, and that one is Webb."

"I know your boys, Orazio." He nodded at both young men.

"We aren't boys anymore, Ketrik." Durian pointed a bony finger at him. "In fact, I bet in a real fight, me and Webb could beat Kellen and Yen."

Ketrik rolled his eyes. "I have no time for this useless banter. Say what you mean or nothing at all." He stepped away from both young men.

"Don't turn your back on me, old man!" barked Durian.

Slowly, Ketrik turned to face him. "What was that...boy?"

Durian took a step towards him and stopped. Realizing his error, the fire in his eyes diminished. He waited for someone to rescue him from his own challenge. His brother complied.

"Ketrik, sometimes my brother gets overzealous with his remarks." Webb looked at Durian and stepped in front of him, "Forgive him. He often speaks without thinking first."

"That is a quality which can get a man killed in New Caporesso," replied Ketrik. "You should teach him to hold his tongue." Disappointed, he looked at Orazio. "They are here for a reason?"

"They will be in charge of the soldiers from Salvation. My sons will receive their orders from me, and then they will give orders to the other troopers. I have thought..."

"Wait, Orazio," Ketrik interrupted, "just wait." He held up his hands. "The only way this will work is if I am in charge of the expedition. If there are two leaders, there will be one outcome: utter failure. The people from Salvation will not be able to handle separate orders from Durian and from me, and they *will* receive orders from me. I know how to lead men." Turning towards Durian, he said, "Your son has no experience even leading men in training maneuvers on horseback." Ketrik looked at him with disdain, "He is ill prepared to control the lives of other men. Sending him is a bad idea; putting him in charge of soldiers is criminal."

"Shut up, old man!" yelled Durian. "Don't talk to me like that. My father is in charge of this village and could order your execution for talking to me like that." His brother restrained him.

A coy grin crossed Ketrik's lips, "You lose control over meaningless words. What will happen in the middle of a fight? Will you turn your horse and flee?"

"You would know all about running away from a fight..." Durian choked on his words, startled by Ketrik's reaction.

In three quick strides, Ketrik stood face to face with him. Glaring at Durian, he whispered, "You are no warrior, boy. How dare you question me, you miserable toad?" He spoke slowly, trying to keep calm. "Your recklessness will get someone killed." His tone was condescending, "You are irresponsible, and you always have been. Since we arrived in Salvation, you were always in trouble. Either your father or Webb has rescued you from your predicaments. That will not suffice on the trail. Each man must be accountable for their actions, including you."

Ketrik turned away from Durian, "Orazio, it would be better to let us go alone. Since you will not allow it, I hold you responsible for the lives of those who join us. Especially your sons. Any deaths are on your conscience, not mine. The cemeteries are full of boys like him," he pointed at Durian, "who cannot wait for a fight. Has he thought about what happens if he gets cut from his belly to his neck, with his innards falling out?" He traced a line. "No, of course not, he expects someone to watch over him and protect him." Slowing down, he sighed, "On this journey, everyone is responsible for their own lives. Our engagements must be kept to a minimum or we are doomed. Will your boys obey my orders and avoid conflicts? We are not returning to wage a war. We go back to gather information only."

Durian began to speak again, but his brother grabbed his arm, stopping him, "We'll follow your orders, Ketrik." He looked at his father, "He's right, Father. Ketrik is better suited to lead everyone on this mission," and nodded. Turning to Ketrik, he added, "You don't need to worry about us."

Throwing off Webb's hand, Durian walked over to stand beside his father. He leaned down, and the two shared a private word. Afterwards, Durian asked, "Are you sure?"

Orazio nodded yes, and Durian smiled.

Relenting, Orazio agreed, "All right, Ketrik, it will be as you suggest. You are in charge of everyone, and you are only collecting information at this time. I trust you will do your best to keep everyone safe, but I will not hold you accountable for any injuries," he looked at his sons. "Investigate New Caporesso. Discover what you can and then return to apprise us of the situation. From there, I release you from your obligations to us. You will be free to return, and we will proceed as we see fit." Conferring with the other elders, they nodded in agreement. Looking back at Ketrik, he asked, "When will you be ready to leave, and how long will you be gone?"

"I expect to leave by the end of the week. As far as the length of our journey, I cannot say. It will depend on what we discover and how quickly we do that. Our course is not known and it may be necessary to retrace our steps many times." He looked at Durian and Webb. "Both of you are under my command. You will follow my orders, or I will have you tied to a tree and left behind. Do you understand?"

Webb answered first, "Yes, Ketrik, I understand. You're in charge. Our orders come from you and you alone."

Durian took longer to respond. Webb slapped him on the back. "Durian!" he yelled.

The insolent young man spoke through clenched teeth, "I understand."

Oblivious to the tension, Orazio nodded his approval. "You see, Ketrik, my sons will do their best to follow your orders on the expedition. Good luck to you and your son on this journey. I will pray to the gods that you find whatever you seek." He nodded at Ketrik.

Ketrik replied. "I have planning to continue, so I take my leave. Your sons should plan for the journey as well." Turning to the two brothers, he reminded them, "Everyone is responsible for his own food and other supplies. Take what you need, but nothing you do not. We must travel swift and light if we are to succeed."

"Yes, sir," replied Webb.

Durian looked at Ketrik but made no sound.

"All right, I will decide who else joins us on this quest. When I return in a few days, be ready to travel the next morning. Understood?"

Both Durian and Webb nodded their acknowledgement.

"Then, Orazio, I thank you for your prayers, and leave you with your sons." He turned to leave.

"Ketrik," Orazio called after him, "your concern is expected, but do not be troubled. My sons will make me proud."

As Ketrik walked away, he could not help but think, *That is what I am afraid of.*

Chapter 69

Without a signal, their contest began. Effortlessly, Kellen advanced and slashed upward with his sword, and then sliced horizontally at Yen's chest. He thrust the blade straight and slashed diagonally downward. Each time, Yen met his sword with a solid block or parry.

Yen saw Kellen commence his attack and braced for the first impact. He deflected Kellen's sword to his left, then ducked under the horizontal cut. Next, he parried the thrust to the side of his head and stepped back. Blocking the next slash with a high hit, he stepped to the side, and followed with a low parry to knock Kellen's blade away.

Back and forth they went. They fought on the grassy area outside the smithy. For several minutes their weapons clashed and banged. Occasional kicks and punches were thrown, each trying to knock the other off balance.

After one such combination, Kellen stumbled.

Yen sensed him off balance and launched a new attack, slashing and lunging at his opponent.

Kellen regained his poise and blocked the ferocious attack.

It was a beautiful but deadly dance. They moved like a murmuration of starlings, changing course instantly, but staying in perfect rhythm. Their frenzied battle continued for over fifteen minutes. It was a breathtaking sight to witness. By now, a few dozen villagers had appeared to watch the spectacle taking place.

Hapco was amazed. He had never seen such a fine display of swordsmanship. Their speed was impressive, not even he and Ketrik were able to do that. He was watching something special.

Kyra returned to Hapco's side moments after the match began. She too was astonished by what she was witnessing. She believed Kellen was better than her, but that she could outmatch Yen with a sword. After watching this demonstration, she realized she was wrong. They were both much better than she was. Against an attack like that, she would collapse in a matter of seconds. It was an eye opening experience for her.

After twenty minutes of nonstop action, Yen and Kellen clashed swords, pushing them together. They held the position for several seconds and grunting, they jumped away from the contact. Both combatants stopped and stared at each other.

Yen held his sword with two hands over his head.

Kellen held his in his right hand, with the blade extending away from his body along his leg. His left arm was also extended away from his body, inviting a continuation of the conflict.

Sweat poured from their bodies as they panted heavily.

Before they could continue, Hapco jumped in between them and announced the end of the action. "Go-man. That is enough for today, you two. You fought like two warriors from some legend of old." Hapco was shaking his head in amazement, "I have never seen anything like it. Both of you should be proud. Bow to each other and end this sparring session."

Kellen and Yen were still breathing hard when Hapco finished speaking. Yen flipped his sword to a noncombative position, with the blade behind his right arm, and smiled at his friend. Kellen did the same. Bowing to each other, they stepped forward and hugged. They were done for the day.

Ketrik returned from his discussion with Orazio and the elders. He saw a crowd dispersing. Yen and Kellen were both holding their weapons and speaking to one another. Kyra was standing with Hapco; both of them had a wide-eyed look about them. Approaching, Ketrik asked, "Did I miss something?"

Kyra looked at him and chuckled, "Miss anything? I have never seen two people fight like they did for as long as they did. You and Hapco did an incredible job training them. They were amazing."

"They are better than we ever were, my friend," Hapco stated, still staring at the two young men. "Their techniques and endurance are unbelievable. Their skills are more amazing than even I imagined."

Ketrik looked dubious and shook his head. "Yesterday, Kellen beat you for the first time. How is he so amazing today?"

"I think he has been holding himself back, unsure how to handle the speed of his ability." He pointed at Kellen. "Before yesterday, he was afraid to unleash his power. Now, he knows how to control it." Then he pointed at Yen. "For Yen, he just needed someone to push him harder than anyone has before. They were incredible, Ketrik."

"Their minds needed to be set free from the fear of combat. They needed to embrace the energy of battle and wield its power. You have taught them well, Hapco." Ketrik placed a hand on his friend's shoulder. Raising an eyebrow, he said, "We need to talk; a situation has developed with the elders," he nodded for Hapco to follow.

Kellen and Yen were still talking and catching their breath.

Unnoticed, Kyra walked away from them. She kept walking away from the smithy, returning to the pavilion where they had been the night before. Kyra sat near the fire pit and held her head in her hands. The embers were cold, but the smell of smoke and ash still filled the air.

"What am I to do?" there was no one around to answer. "If we encounter enemy soldiers, I'm doomed. I'll let down my friends and family. My incompetency with a sword could result in our ultimate failure. Oh gods, help me. What can I do?"

Only the crickets answered her. The birds chirped, but did not pay her any attention. Kyra was disheartened by the skillful warriors she had watched. She felt her ability lacked the precision and intensity necessary for combat. Soon enough, she would be tested in New Caporesso, and she was not sure if she would survive.

Chapter 70

By the end of the week, Col and the Tu'nide were ready for their mission. They would leave for the western villages in the morning. Everything was in place for the journey. Today would be their last day in Cenkin for many weeks. Afternoon was dissolving into evening.

Col and Sed'la hurriedly walked to Trosho for a final meeting with Guan. They were a good distance away, and the meeting was supposed to start soon.

Cenkin's streets were still filled with activity. People passed them, carrying the goods they had purchased from stores, their baskets full. A few men nodded at Col and Sed'la, most simply ignored them.

"I can't believe he wants to change the riding orders the day before we leave, Col. Can you?" asked Sed'la, his tabard blowing in the wind as he moved.

A breeze blew against his face. "No, Sed'la, this is very out of the ordinary."

"He also wants to see Vee and your mother."

Both men were almost jogging.

Col only half-heard Sed'la's comment, "Hmm…Mother? That is strange." He was preoccupied with the details of their mission: to find assistance from outlaw rebels. *Are we crazy?* he wondered.

Sed'la realized Col was distracted. "Hey…you all right? You're not really listening to me."

Col glanced at the people as they passed by; they paid no attention to the two of them. "I'm fine; I just have some things on my mind." He abruptly stopped.

Horse drawn wagons passed them, taking their contents to Cenkin's shops. The normal commotion of Cenkin's streets was all around them.

Realizing he was alone, Sed'la turned around and retraced his steps. "What's the matter, Col?"

"You are a good friend, Sed'la." Col squeezed Sed'la's shoulder. "I may need to call on that friendship in the days and weeks ahead. I may ask you do things you never imagined. In fact," he paused, "you might think I've become the revolutionary utlagi we're searching for," he chortled. "Can I count on you?"

Sed'la's eyes narrowed, confused, he asked, "What are you talking about, Col?" He thumped his shoulder and saluted, "Strength of swords, honor in victory." His expression hardened, "You always have my sword; may it help you achieve that victory. Always." Sed'la faked being insulted, "Did you really have to ask?"

"No, I didn't," he grinned. "I know where you stand, but I want you to know I'd never involve you in anything without consulting you first. All right?"

Sed'la nodded his head in silence.

"I'm not sure what'll happen on this mission, but I need to know that you will support my sister no matter what happens to me," he said forebodingly. "If I'm gone, she'll have no support from the men. They will not consider her a brother in arms; she'll be alone. I need to know that I can count on you to stand with her and rally the men to her side. Can you do that for me, Sed'la?" Col asked earnestly.

"Sure, Col, but what are you talking about?" Sed'la knew his friend liked to be cryptic when he talked, but this was even more so than usual.

Col waved a hand, "Enough for now. Let's see what Guan wants. Then we'll attend to the men on our last night in Cenkin for a while."

They headed for Castle Trosho.

∾❦∾

As the guards escorted them into the throne room, Col saw his mother and sister. Guan was seated on his throne, but Mervekka was not beside him. Instead she was standing with Vee at the foot of the dais. Col glanced at Sed'la as they walked towards Guan.

When Col and Sed'la reached the base of the stairs, they both bowed and saluted.

"Hail, King Guan!" they shouted.

Guan's expression seemed more dour than normal. He looked up and spoke haughtily to Col, "How nice of you to finally join us, Captain."

Col was taken aback by the words, "I'm sorry, my king, for the delay. I didn't realize you wished to see me sooner."

"It's my fault, sire. I didn't understand the message to mean urgently," Sed'la admitted.

Guan snapped at him, "Was I talking to you, you miserable leican?"

Sed'la wilted, lowering his head. "No, sire. Forgive me."

Guan glowered at him, "Why does Col keep you as an officer? Did you earn that rank, boy, or was it given to you?" He jerked his head towards Col, "Answer me, Captain. Why is he an officer?"

Dejectedly, Sed'la peeked at Col.

Col only looked at Guan. "He is my friend and..."

"So, he is only a lieutenant," Guan interrupted, "because of your childhood friendship. Maybe the two of you should leave the soldiering to real men," he mocked. "I should let you play soldier with the other children of Cenkin."

"Sire, you did not let me finish. I..." *Why is he doing this?*

"Oh yes you are finished, Captain." Enraged, Guan slammed his fist down on the arm of his chair. "You asked to take your sister along on your next expedition, and I agreed. As a princess of New Caporesso, she is entitled to ride with the Tu'nide as an officer. She will be your second in command." He pointed at Sed'la, "You will take orders from her or be reprimanded severely for your dissent. Do you understand?" Not waiting for a reply, he continued, "You are not worthy to wear the uniform of the Tu'nide. Any woman could do what you do, and that will be proven on this mission." Scowling at Sed'la, he dismissed him, "You are of no importance you ignorant ass." Guan waved his hand as if swatting a gnat, "Leave immediately. Stay in the stables where you belong...with the other dumb animals."

Humiliated, Sed'la bowed and left the throne room. He walked away like a child scolded by his father.

Vee stood there speechless. *Me, second in command?* She had never commanded anything before, let alone a company of elite cavalry in hostile territories. What was Guan doing?

"Do you have a problem with that, Captain? Will he obey Princess Vitoria?" Guan tried to read Col's body language for a reaction, but there was none.

"No problem, sire. Vee is second in command. Sed'la will follow her orders." He answered matter of factly, with no additional emotion in his voice. Col was calm and under control. Whatever Guan was trying to discern from him would not be given away. This meeting was going to be more painful than he ever anticipated.

Chapter 71

Still angry, Guan questioned Col, "What course have you set for your expedition, Captain?" Before Col could answer, Guan stopped him, "No. Princess Vitoria, you answer the question." He turned to her, studying her figure. "What course would you set?"

All eyes in the room turned to Vee. She could feel them staring at her. She was not prepared to answer a question like this, and she stammered, "I ah…I ah. Well…" she glanced at Col, but he would not meet her eyes; the answer had to be hers alone. Vee took a deep breath and exhaled, "Sire, the Tu'nide will head west towards Werlo and Dreglo. We will ride a zigzag course to survey more land. Our path will take us west southwest from Cenkin, crossing the Paro River south of Castle Lau'damay. We will ride north along its western banks and scout the abandoned castle, making sure it still is. From there, we will head west towards Werlo and Dreglo.

"Once we are close enough to the villages, we will establish a base camp where we can support our scouting parties, while remaining hidden from the eyes of the villagers. We will gather information about the villagers concerning food stores, and any possible revolutionary agents. After learning what we can, we will return to Cenkin. I would estimate our time away from Cenkin to be about five months." Vee took a breath in through her nose and held it for a moment, then let it escape her mouth. "Yes... about sixty days to reach the villages, then roughly thirty days to gather information, followed by less than sixty days for the return trip." Her heart was pounding, but she had kept her voice even.

A grin crawled upon Guan's face. He was pleased with her response. She was learning faster than he anticipated and was almost ready to take her place. He had ambushed her with the question, and she responded with a reasonable plan. *She did well.* "Well done, Princess Vitoria. That was impressive. It was a test of your knowledge of the land and you offered a reasonable plan. I am satisfied."

"Thank you, sire. I only wish to please." She was not sure what had happened.

"Captain Col, what do you think of her route? Will it work?" Guan asked smugly.

Col knew he was trapped. If he agreed with Vee's plan, Guan would ridicule him for it. If he disagreed, Guan would chastise him for petty jealously. He picked an answer, "Her course will work, sire. I see nothing wrong with it at the moment."

"A simple 'yes' would have sufficed, Captain." His grin widened, and he addressed Mervekka. "Are you proud of your daughter, Milady? Her combat abilities are most impressive. I almost believed a woman could never master such a thing." He was baiting her.

Mervekka calmly replied, "Yes, sire, I am very proud of my daughter... and my son. They are both excellent soldiers. Each one is capable of leading men into battle, like Terikk. Vee has been ready for some time...even though you were unable to see it."

Instantly enraged, Guan kicked a footstool down the stairs, missing Mervekka by a few feet, "I have told you never to mention their father in my presence. Do not test me, Milady," Guan's snarl reappeared. "Do you question my ability to judge my men?"

She gave no reply.

He descended the stairs towards her. Stopping at the bottom, he slapped her across the face. "I asked you a question, witch. Do you question my abilities? You are nothing except what I allow you to be." He slapped her again, shoving her to the floor.

A guttural howl resounded in the great hall. Col sprang into action, charging towards Guan. He took five steps and launched his body through the air, trying to land a flying sidekick into Guan's side.

Sidestepping the attack, Guan kicked Col in the midsection as he passed, sending him sprawling to the ground. The guards rushed to assist Guan, but he held up a hand, motioning for them to wait.

Grunting, Col got to his feet, and ripped off his tabard. Stepping forward, he reengaged Guan, throwing wild punches and looping strikes at his head.

Guan effortlessly blocked Col's ineffective attack. He looked like a bear swatting away its playful cub.

Col's wild attack left him out of breath almost immediately. His emotions had gotten the better of him. With adrenaline coursing through his veins, the energy drained from his muscles at an accelerated rate. He was punching himself into defeat.

Realizing Col was losing his strength, Guan launched an attack of his own. He stepped forward, landing a crushing kick into Col's thigh. The blow dropped him to his knees. Then Guan slammed a powerful elbow into the soft flesh between Col's neck and shoulder, snapping his clavicle.

Crying out, Col pulled his arm to his body. He struggled to his feet again.

Guan pursued his wounded quarry. Seeing Col stumbling away from him, he stepped over and launched a jump back kick into Col's unprotected ribs, cracking two.

Collapsing in a heap, Col's battle was over. He had no fight left in him.

Mervekka looked empathetically at her battered son, knowing there was nothing she could do to help him.

Vee watched in horror as Col received a beating like she had never seen before. Guan was just too powerful. Not overly fast, but amazingly strong and powerful. How could they resist him?

Guan motioned for the guards to collect Col's body. "Take him to the dungeons. He is to be charged with treason."

Four guards picked up Col, carrying him by his arms and legs. He offered no resistance, whimpering from the pain in his abdomen and collarbone. They carried him away, leaving the throne room.

"Princess Vitoria, step forward. It looks like you are now promoted to commander of the Tu'nide."

"But, sire…" she shook her head.

"It will be all right, Princess. Lieutenant Maral, come here," he ordered.

Maral stepped forward, "Yes, my king."

"What is your rank in the Tu'nide, trooper?" he inquired.

"I was third in command, sire, behind Captain Col and Lieutenant Sed'la."

Guan nodded his head. "You are still third in command, soldier. Princess Vitoria is in charge, then Sed'la. Do you understand?"

Maral replied, "Yes, sire."

"Princess Vitoria, these are your final orders. In the morning, take Maral to the Tu'nide Prep Building and inform the men that you are in charge." He glared at Maral, "He will confirm your promotion."

"Yes, sire," Maral acknowledged.

Vee was torn; she wanted to ask about Col and her mother, but knew better.

Sensing her question, Guan asked, "Yes, Princess Vitoria, what do you wish to know?"

"Wha…What will happen to Col?" she hesitantly asked.

"He will be taken to the dungeons and," he tilted his head, "disciplined for his treachery."

"And my mother?"

"Your mother?" Guan repeated. "General of the Guard, come forward," he called out.

A well-built man stepped forward. He was several years younger than Guan and somewhat taller. He carried a single, red handled katana around his waist. On his right hand, he wore a black glove and on his left… there was nothing. There was no hand, just a black leather covering. Tyr responded, "Yes, sire, what is your command?"

"General, escort the queen to her chambers. Lock her in. She is to have no contact with anyone until I feel she is finished questioning me in matters in which she knows nothing." He waved his hand, "Take her away."

Tyr held out his hand and motioned for Mervekka to move before him.

Without a confrontation, she did as commanded. Her face was still aching from Guan's strike. She looked at her daughter and tried to smile. Knowingly, she nodded at her, *Stick to the plan, continue with the mission. Do not let this disrupt our plans to find supporters from the west. Without them, we are all doomed.* She hoped Vee understood what she had to do. Disheartened, Mervekka left the throne room and headed to her chambers.

"That is all for this evening, Princess Vitoria. Retire for the night; ride for the west in the morning. Godsspeed on your journey…may they bless you with a safe return," he added with a wicked smirk.

Bowing her head, Vee turned and exited the throne room. Maral followed behind her. Together, they left and headed for the Prep Building, hoping to unscramble the events that had just transpired. First things first, she needed to introduce herself to the men she was about to lead on an expedition into dangerous territory.

Chapter 72

Tyr led Mervekka to her room. He had not been there for almost ten years. The last time he was, was the day after the coup against King Terikk. His left arm had been wrapped in bandages from Hapco's amputation. He had been in tremendous pain, but assisted someone who needed it.

His injury made it impossible for him to keep a battlefield commission. However, Guan was so impressed with him that he made Tyr general of the Palace Guard. His duty was to oversee the protection of the castle. As a result, he saw Mervekka almost every day. At times, the sorrow she bore made him nauseous. She believed he had killed her husband and son, thus making him responsible for her anguish. Unfortunately for him, there was nothing he could do to alleviate it.

Terikk's parting words were to not tell anyone what really happened, not ever. Secrecy was necessary for their safety. If anyone found out their deaths were a fraud, Guan would hunt them down and execute them all. Tyr's burden was to carry the secret alone. Their wellbeing was more important than Mervekka's peace of mind.

When they arrived at the queen's chambers, he stopped and opened the door. Tyr stood at attention while he waited for her to enter. Without turning his head, his eyes moved to examine her new bruise.

She noticed the movement and quickly turned to face him. Mervekka glowered into his eyes, an intense hatred burned behind them. "What are you looking at, General?" she hissed.

Caught, he tried to apologize, "Nothing, my queen. I am sorry if I offended you." He always tried to steal a glance at her beautiful face to see if she had been crying, often wondering if he was the reason for her tears.

Her anger increased, "Yes it offends me. In fact, your very existence offends me. I know the truth…you murdered by family and destroyed my life." She was spitting as she spoke. "If I were strong enough, I would see you die in a most painful way." Grunting, she slapped him across the face once. She hit him again and again and again, trying to rid herself of the loathing she felt.

Tyr stood there, not protecting himself, absorbing her punishment.

When she stopped, she was exhausted and fell against his chest. She looked up at him and saw blood streaming from his mouth and brow. Breathing heavily, she straightened herself and backed away.

Tyr allowed the blood to flow, waiting for her to enter the room.

"Why do you not defend yourself?" she asked.

He opened his mouth and paused, "I know I've done a horrible thing to your family," he admitted. "Even the gods cannot forgive me for what I've done, and I will be punished. When I die, there is no chance the gods will welcome me. I know the Boatman will block my way and prevent me from joining my brothers. I will be cursed to roam these lands forever as a shapeless specter." Blood dripped from his lip. "My soul will know no peace, not that it deserves any. It would only further shame me to defend myself. I will never ask for your forgiveness, my queen." He choked up as he spoke, "I acted as a soldier from New Caporesso, loyal to King Terikk and honor bound, would've acted," he gulped. "I'm still honor bound."

Those words were strange to Mervekka, *still honor bound?* He was clearly delusional. "For ten years, I have lived with the horror of what you did to my family. My loving husband is gone. My honorable friend and general of New Caporesso is gone." New tears fell for the first time in years. "My little boy is gone. You murdered them and burned them. Nothing remains!" she sobbed. "I cannot even go to their graves and lay flowers at the markers!

You have taken everything from me!" she screamed. She pulled a large knife that was hidden in the layers of her dress and lunged towards Tyr, raising it to his throat.

He did not move or try to stop her, willing to accept her judgment.

She stopped, inches from his throat. A single slash and his life would pour from his body like a waterfall. Just a few more inches, and he would die by her hand. Revenge would be hers!

Staring into his eyes, she saw something that astonished her. She did not see remorse for the killing of her family. No, she saw something else. Mervekka dropped the blade and stepped away from him. They looked at each other for what seemed like minutes. Her heart was beating like it would explode.

Tyr remained calm. Bending down, he picked up the knife. Holding out the handle for her, he said, "My queen, you dropped this."

Slowly, she extended her hand and took it. Lowering the weapon, she put it away.

He motioned for her to enter the room.

As she passed him again, she stopped and looked at him, "What happened to my family, General Tyr?"

Averting his eyes, he backed away from her.

Mervekka grabbed his hand and forearm. "General Tyr, please tell me what happened. I beg you, I need to hear you tell me."

Tyr's eyes welled up with tears. He shook his head and tried to break her grip. "My queen, I cannot…" he paused, searching for the right words, "…tell you anything new about their death. You have heard the stories and…" another hesitation, "…know their fates. Why would you have me retell you of those horrors, my queen?"

She stepped closer and looked into his eyes, "Tell me you killed them, just once. I want to hear you say it while you look me in the eyes."

"My queen," he sputtered, looking away, "I cannot. Enter your chambers now or I will call the guards."

Mervekka released her hold of him and entered the room. Once inside, she turned and spoke again, "General Tyr, I have a question for you. My servant Abby said you granted her access to my room when Guan ordered it forbidden. Why?"

"You had just lost your husband and son. You were distraught and needed comforting. Who else but her could attend to you?" he replied.

"You disobeyed Guan by letting her into my room," she stated plainly.

"I do not remember it that way, my queen. I must have been hallucinating and not thinking clearly at the time."

"Do not lie to me!" she screamed, lunging at him again. She grabbed his shoulders and held on to them. "Tell me!"

His conscience was torn. "My queen, I have told you enough. I am sorry for my treacherous acts. You deserve a better fate, but there is none I can give you now." Tyr raised his arms and pushed her away. His stump touched her shoulder.

Horrified, she stumbled back into her room.

Before she could accost him again, Tyr grabbed the handle of the door and slammed it shut. Locking the door quickly, he backed away.

Mervekka grabbed at the handle and tried desperately to open the door. She screamed and sobbed, her words unintelligible. Tyr approached the door and whispered, "I am sorry my queen, one day I will tell you what happened. I promise, one day you will understand, but for now I cannot. I can't break my vow and tell you about that day," he stepped away from the door and looked around, again.

Tyr left Mervekka's room and headed for the throne room. On the stairs, he stopped and looked out a window. The sun was setting in the west. It was always beautiful to watch. Standing there, he wiped away his tears. Recomposing himself, he returned to the throne room.

Guan spoke to him as he arrived, "You were away longer than expected. Did she give you any trouble, Tyr?"

"She tried, my king, but I…" he waved his stump in the air, "handled it, sire." He chortled.

Guan smirked, and chuckled as well.

The two men continued laughing the hearty laughs of conquering soldiers.

Tyr was still hiding his secret from everyone in Cenkin, but it was getting harder to keep. His heart desperately wanted to tell Mervekka and rekindle her soul. His ego wanted to tell Guan of the lie, to prove he was capable of such a covert undertaking. For now, he was powerless to do anything, and his secret would remain safely hidden from the world.

Chapter 73

With much anticipation, the end of the week arrived. Ketrik and Hapco's preparations for the expedition were complete. In the morning, they would begin their return journey to New Caporesso. Tents and other supplies were stored in wagons or lashed to horses. Their weapons sharpened and the horses shod. Everyone was ready to face the paths fate had prepared for them.

The rest of their party had been selected. Ketrik and Hapco chose eight other companions to join them. Six of them were from the northern villages of Salvation, and two were from the south. The men from the south were brothers, Hasru and Esra. Those from the north were Minervo, Nagurum, Bitto, Wesne, and Eromo. Alecia, the only woman of the eight, was Eromo's sister. They were excellent warriors, trained extensively by Hapco.

Minervo and Nagurum were twins, resembling their mother. With short blond hair and blue eyes, they were a handsome set of boys. Strong jaws and deep set eyes made the girls swoon. These teenagers pretended not to notice the attention, but deep down, they relished it. Slightly taller than Kellen, they outweighed him by at least twenty pounds.

Bitto was the smallest of the group, being shorter than Kyra. A black ponytail reached halfway down his back. His black eyes were narrowly set in his round face. He had to work harder for everything, and that gave him an attitude. Proportionally, he carried the largest two handed sword of the group. Hapco always said he was compensating for his shortcomings.

Wesne was the most conservative, and quiet young man in the company. He seldom spoke, preferring to communicate with his actions. A faithful friend, he would follow his comrades to whatever end. His lanky frame belied his skill with his double axes.

Everything was ready for the journey. After sunrise, they would leave Salvation and head for New Caporesso. This was to be their last night at home for a long time, maybe forever. Ketrik's plans were complete, but he knew they were not perfect. Their success was not guaranteed.

The group gathered together for supper. They were all there, except Durian and Webb. Those two decided to spend their last night in Salvation with their father. For the rest, they ate their fill of cooked meats and fresh fruits. Sitting around several fires, they savored the meal and talked about what they hoped to discover along the way. Their desires were as varied as the trees in the wilderness. Everyone knew Kellen hoped to uncover the fate of his family, but the others had different ideas.

"I can't wait to return to New Caporesso. I want to see Werlo again," an excited Yen announced.

Kyra added, "I don't think I remember anything about it. It'll be like I'm visiting it for the first time, just like the rest of you."

"You were young when we left, Kyra." Yen pointed at the ground, "You've lived here almost as long as you lived in Werlo." He shrugged. "These memories have probably replaced your old ones."

"I guess so," she admitted. "After seeing Werlo again, I hope we have time to travel to Norkin. The way Ketrik describes the Mestoline Mountains...they sound breathtaking." Kyra closed her eyes as she imagined how they looked.

"What about the two of you?" asked Yen, "Hasru...Esra, what do you hope to find?"

The young men looked at each other and snickered. Esra answered for both of them, "We hope to find," he used his hands to make a wavy figure, "fine New Caporessoean women to bring home to Salvation and marry."

Hasru laughed louder, adding, "Beautiful New Caporessoean women, who are ripe for bearing children."

"I guess I'll have to show you how that works," blurted Eromo.

The two brothers stopped laughing, glaring at him. That made everyone else laugh harder.

"For me," continued Eromo, "I hope to explore the northern region of New Caporesso. I too want to see the Mestoline Mountains. I heard Ketrik's stories, and I desire to witness the beauty of those mountains myself. Then I want to climb over them and discover what's beyond." Looking at Kyra, he nodded at her, "Maybe together, we can travel there. What do you say, Kyra?"

Alecia slapped his arm.

Kyra blushed and looked at Kellen. Neither one responded to Eromo's comment.

Replying for both of them, Alecia insulted Eromo, "Has the ale gone to your head again, Eromo? A woman of her beauty can't be seen travelling anywhere with someone who looks like you." Laughter erupted again. "Ha ha," her fiery ponytail bounced as she described her desire. "As for me, I'd like to ride to Drador before returning to Salvation. Once I visit that fortress village, I will be able to say that out of everyone in Salvation and New Caporesso, I will have travelled farther than any man under the sun. What do you think about that, Eromo?" she chuckled.

He ignored her question, upset over her remark about his looks. Silently, he repeated her insults and bobbled his head.

The rest of the group had their own, still different ideas about what they hoped to find. The one thing everyone agreed upon was that this was an opportunity to find out what happened to New Caporesso. Was it a land worth returning to, or was it a desolate wasteland, destroyed by a decade of war? Soon, they would know the truth.

They spent the evening eating their dinner and sharing wild stories. Before midnight, they retired to their homes for a final night's sleep in a bed not on the ground. Only three of them remained around a fire. Kellen sat with Kyra and Yen.

Yen jabbed a long stick into the fire. He was poking the logs, trying to stir the embers back to life. "Are you ready for whatever we find, Kellen?" he asked without looking away from the smoldering fire.

"Yes," Kellen looked at his friend, "but I believe they're dead." Shaking his head, he said, "I don't have any hope of finding them alive; it's been too long. I'm only hoping to find their graves, so I know they're at peace. I'm going back so I can find out how they died." He sighed. "But that's not the only reason I'm returning. Father and I have a responsibility to the people. Ten years ago, we abandoned them to save ourselves. Now maybe we can restore order to the country." Shrugging his shoulders, he shook his head, "Maybe."

Kyra looked at him, "If you think they're dead, then why risk going back?"

Kellen turned to face Kyra; she was sitting beside him as usual. Her lips glistened, forming a frown. He wanted to lean over and... *This is our last night here. I should tell her how I feel, but...* Entranced by her eyes, those amazingly grey eyes, he caught himself and looked away. "I...ah...um, heh heh," he scratched his head. Flustered, he repeated his answer, "It's important that we go back for the people."

A corner of Yen's mouth turned up, and he chuckled to himself, continuing to stare at the dwindling fire.

Kyra kept looking at Kellen, unimpressed with his response. "Yes, you established the importance of going back for the people. But why? You don't owe anyone anything. I want a real reason."

Letting out a deep breath, he looked at her again. Her eyes beckoned to him. "My father has taught me a lot about New Caporesso over the years. The country was founded on the belief that everyone should be treated equally and allowed to live together in peace. For a time, the strength of a man did not determine his fate in the world; the more devious a man was, did not ensure his rise to power." He held her gaze. "It was a time when everyone felt safe in their own land. My family was entrusted with keeping that peace and protecting the people." He turned away from her. "We failed. This is our chance, I mean my chance, to go back and do something about it.

"If we can find support among the people, we can take back the country and return it to them. We can save them from Guan, or whoever is in power, and establish a new government that answers to the people." Shaking his head, he said, "It won't enslave or murder them. But understand, Kyra, this is not about revenge, it's about the citizens of New Caporesso."

Sarcastically, Yen asked, "Wow, that's kind of a big task for the fifteen of us, don't you think?"

Kyra shot him a glance. "Don't mind him; I'll deal with him later."

Yen opened his eyes wide, and raised his hands as if to say, *What did I do?*

The fire crackled and sputtered. A log hissed, releasing its pent up energy.

Looking back at Kellen, Kyra said, "That's a monstrous undertaking. I guess I never thought about it like that." She paused, "Do you really believe your family failed to protect the citizens?"

"Guan was revolting against my father, and we were forced to leave the country to save ourselves. You can't say we did a good job protecting the people, can you?"

"Nope, definitely not," Yen answered quickly.

"Yen!" Kyra scolded him, "Knock it off."

Yen sat for a moment, thinking about what to say. When it finally made sense in his head, he spoke, "Do you two know what the real problem is tonight?" He dropped his stick and crossed his arms, "I would tell you, but," he motioned at Kyra, "most likely she'd attack me, so I'll let the two of you figure it out." Moving to his knees, he started to stand. "But if in the morning you haven't discussed it, then I'll tell you." Getting to his feet, he added, "With the help of Ketrik and Hapco of course, but I will tell you." Waving at them, he headed for his home. "Goodnight." At least he would get a good night's sleep one last time.

Chapter 74

They watched Yen leave. He was not angry with them, but they knew he wanted them to talk about something. Kyra turned to Kellen, "What's he talking about?"

"I'm not sure." he tried to brush off Yen's comment. "What I said about my return to New Caporesso is the truth. If Guan is still in control, I want to free the people from his clutches and restore the government. I don't plan on doing anything so foolish that I get anyone killed in battle."

Kyra nodded her head in silence. "What did Yen mean about the real problem?"

Oh no. Kellen acted like he did not hear her clearly, "Hmm, what's that, Kyra?"

Asking him again, she leaned a little closer. "I asked, what do you think Yen meant by our real problem," she bit her lower lip, her eyes dazzling in the firelight.

She is so close to me. Kellen uncomfortably shifted his weight. "Kyra, Yen and I talk about a lot of things during the breaks in our sparring sessions. Some of the things we talk about should remain unsaid, but he brought something up tonight." He fidgeted more, trying to find a softer spot on the ground.

Kyra was intrigued. "What kind of things, Kellen?" She shifted her seat too, inching closer to him and putting a hand on his knee.

Uh oh, she's touching me! Gulping, he tried to remain calm, "We talk about…combat tactics…and…and…the weather." He pursed his lips and thought, *You idiot, think of something better than that.*

She mocked his response, "Yes, I can see why that's a big secret that only two *strong* men can talk about. Uh huh."

He sighed and dropped his head to his chest. *I can't get away from this. I'm gonna kill Yen when I see him tomorrow!* Raising his head, he gazed into her eyes again, "Kyra, we talk about things like…who we like…and…"

Kyra's heart started to beat faster. *Does he feel the same way I do?* "Well, Kellen, how do those conversations go for the two of you?" She squeezed his knee ever so gently. "I'll bet he likes Beth and you, Alecia. Right?"

Blood rushed to his head at the pressure on his knee, his face flushed. Kellen was not sure if she was playing a game or not. *Women are so confusing.* He spoke slowly and unsurely, "Yen talks about all the pretty girls, and I talk about…" his heart was pounding, and he began sweating. "You."

Her heart was beating faster too. Frowning, she asked, "Yen talks about the pretty girls and you're left with me?" Kyra's lip quivered; she pretended to be insulted, "Am I not a pretty girl, Kellen?" She removed her hand from his leg.

He was flustered, "No. I mean yes. I mean…" he threw his hands up in the air, "Oh, I'm not sure anymore." She was so close that he could smell her. *She's intoxicating!* "I mean, you are beautiful."

She gasped, and then in a half whisper asked, "You think I'm beautiful?"

He heard her gasp. *Is she mad at me?* Kellen let out a big sigh and stared at the fire. He whispered his reply, "I mean you're the most beautiful woman in all of Salvation." Kellen turned to face her, "You are so beautiful that there are times when I can barely breathe around you." *There, it's out; she knows.* "Yen wasn't supposed to mention that. I'm sorry if it offends you."

She flipped her wavy hair and twisted her tresses, trying to act naturally. "Why would it offend me?"

Kellen was confused now, more so than ever before. *Fighting is easy compared to this.* "I was afraid that if you knew how I felt, it might ruin our friendship."

Friendship? "You haven't told me how you feel. You've told me you think I'm beautiful and you talk to Yen about me. What do you say to him?" She needed to know what he said. "What do you say that could ruin our friendship?"

The last flames of the fire dwindled in front of them.

He was trapped. He had to tell her, "You're not making this easy, are you?"

Without a word, she bit her lower lip again and slowly shook her head from side to side.

"Kyra, I told Yen that I care about you. I told him that I..." he swallowed to try and keep calm. His heart was beating so hard, he could barely hear anything around them. "I told him that I love you." He was surprised when those words escaped his lips.

Her heart was pounding inside her chest like it was about to explode. She blinked several times and asked softly, "Why would that ruin our friendship?" Moving closer, she was right next to him. Their legs were touching for the first time in a noncombative way.

The fire was finally out, but the embers glowed red. A thin trail of smoke spiraled upward.

I can't stand being this close to her any longer! Kellen was uncomfortable, "I just thought knowing that might upset you, that's all." He wanted to move away, but could not. His muscles failed him.

"Kellen, I'm not upset or offended." Now she was feeling uncomfortable. She lowered her gaze momentarily and admitted, "I'm actually relieved. I thought I was the only one who felt this way." She raised her eyes, staring into his.

He looked away from the embers. "Wait...what? What do you mean?" Kellen tried to get up or move away, but his legs would not cooperate.

She whispered to him, "I love you too, Kellen. I have for a long time." Kyra let out a deep breath and smiled at him, her eyes twinkling.

Kellen smiled, bigger than he ever had before. His confidence returned instantly, "I love you, Kyra. I have since the first day I met you. You were so beautiful, dirty, but the most beautiful creature I had ever seen."

Kyra's smile vanished. "What do you mean dirty?" she joked, poking him.

The embers crackled, trying to reignite the blaze.

He laughed. "Back near Castle Lau'damay where we found you. You and Yen were both dirty." He tossed a log into the smoldering pit.

She laughed too, "You weren't exactly the cleanest person at the time either. Were you? You looked so…"

Kellen abruptly leaned into her, cutting her off with a kiss. He kissed her softly.

Surprised, she raised her hands to push him away, but stopped. Instead, she gently embraced him. He kissed her so softly that she thought it was like a kiss from the heavens.

Her lips were moist and perfect, he had dreamed of this moment for many years. Now, it was like he was in a dream he hoped would never end.

A light breeze blew across the pit. The embers ignited the wood, and its blaze burned intensely. The light illuminated Kellen and Kyra against the blackness of the night.

She was absorbed in the moment. His kiss was so tender and fragile that she thought she was going to cry. Kyra was frozen, unable to move. His kiss had stripped her of every defense. She was vulnerable, completely under his spell. Finally after what seemed like hours, Kyra moved her lips, kissing him passionately.

Holding each other, they stared into one another's eyes, caught in the fire of the moment. With their feelings for each other finally revealed, they rejoiced in the release. They only wanted to hold each other and feel the other next to them.

Remembering their journey in the morning, they decided rest was what they needed. But each time they tried to leave, they could not. They sat together as the hours evaporated. The fire burned itself out until only the glow from the coals lit their faces.

Before sleep overtook them where they sat, Kellen walked Kyra home and kissed her goodnight. As he headed for the smithy, he thought about the finality of the night. *This is our last night in Salvation.* He did not know if any of them would ever see it again.

Chapter 75

As the sun rose in Cenkin, Vee and Sed'la sat together on a fence rail in the corral. They watched as the grey twilight dissipated into brightness. Birds warbled the morning's arrival, shaking off the night. The grass glistened with the morning dew, reflecting the first rays of day.

"I'm glad we got to talk last night, Sed'la. Watching Col get pummeled by Guan was dreadful." She closed her eyes momentarily, reliving the memory. "Guan just toyed with him; Col was completely ineffective," she shuddered. "And then seeing my mother led away by Tyr was horrible." Shaking her head, she added, "And all of that the night before my first expedition." She humphed, repeating, "My first expedition...and I'm in command of it. Talk about shaking my confidence."

"I know. I'm sorry that happened, but you can't think about it on this mission. You have to be strong, self-assured, and only worry about the men." He looked in her eyes. "Vee, you're in charge; they'll look to you to make the right decisions."

She shook her head. "Sed'la, I think everyone knows you'll really be in charge of the Tu'nide. I'll just follow your lead."

"No, Vee." He paused, remembering Col's words. "Yesterday, Col and I talked about the mission. He talked about my friendship, and calling on me to do something I might consider crazy."

Raising her brow, she asked, "He really asked you about that?"

"He did, although, he wasn't specific about anything." He shook his head, "I have no idea what he meant. But," he raised a finger, "he also talked about, in the event something would happen to him, then you would be alone. He said the men would not trust you to lead them," he nodded, "and he's right about that." Holding up his hands in front of him, he said, "Not that you can't lead them, it's that you haven't earned the right to command them."

"I realize that too, Sed'la. I don't want this position, I never did. It was thrust upon me, and there is nothing I can do to be rid of it." Shrugging, she admitted, "I know I've never commanded anything, but here I am, in charge of the *legendary* Tu'nide; it doesn't make any sense."

"We aren't legendary, Vee."

"To hear the people talk about you, you are." Reminiscing, she recalled, "I remember Father's stories about the Tu'nide he served with in the Northern Kingdom. It sounded like they were immortal warriors from some epic poem." She shook her head. "How can I live up to those heroes, Sed'la? I'm not ready for this post."

"You won't be the first person assigned to this post who lacked experience. But believe me, Vee, there's nothing immortal about us," he scoffed. "As far as I know, your father's exploits were embellished to instill fear in their enemies." He grinned and nodded. Glancing at her, he said, "It worked well. They proved that fear of the enemy is worse than fighting the enemy; the battle is won or lost before the first sword is crossed."

They watched several starlings descend into the corral and drink from the feed trough. At first, they drank peacefully. Then the largest bird chased the others away, laying claim to the trough as his own.

"Besides, Vee, I told you last night, I'll help you whenever I can. I'll make my observations and give you my suggestions if I see something out of the ordinary. All right?" He looked in her eyes. There was no fear in them. "But as we leave Cenkin...you must make the announcement signaling our departure. I gave you the lines last night. Have you memorized them yet?"

"I think so, Sed'la. Why are they so important?"

"Tradition. In a word, that's it. Tradition means a lot to the Tu'nide. We are proud of our unit, and the men who have served in it, and the men who still serve in it. Commanders are promoted from within. Col was an exception, promoted at Guan's behest." He shook his head somberly. "We treated him like he didn't belong. We risked his life...I mean I allowed his life to be risked because I didn't feel he had earned his rank. Do you know how he repaid my disloyalty?" he asked, turning away from Vee.

"No, Sed'la. He never mentioned that incident. What happened?"

Sed'la jumped off the fence and walked away from her. Turning around, he recalled. "I allowed him to ride into battle alone, and he saved my life at least twice in that conflict. Our accounts hold that he saved almost twenty-five of us in that battle. He may have been the greatest commander of the Tu'nide...ever," he professed.

"Even better than my father?" she asked.

Sed'la bowed his head, "Vee, I can't say anything about that. I was too young to realize the kind of man your father was. I know the stories from Guan's historians are probably inaccurate, but I don't know the truth. None of us do." He exhaled fully.

The jovial Maral approached, interrupting their conversation. "Morning, Sed'la." He nodded at Vee, "Princess."

"Good morning, Lieutenant Maral," responded Vee. "Your report?"

His eyes went big, and they shifted to Sed'la.

Sed'la affirmed, "Maral, Vee is in charge of the Tu'nide. When you give a report, you give it to her. Do you understand me?"

"Yes, Sed'la. But..."

Holding up a hand, Sed'la stopped him. "No, Maral. Yesterday Col and I discussed this very situation. He said if something happened to him, Vee would be in charge." He pointed at her. "*She* is our commander; there is no one else." Stepping closer to Maral, he explained, "Listen to me, if Col trusted her to lead us, who are we to question his judgment? Hmm?" He shook his head. "We can't. Col would never leave us with an inferior commander. He would want us to be led by the best man, or woman, possible." Looking at Vee, he said, "She was handpicked by Col, and confirmed by Guan. She is our commander until Col returns. The loyalty we show to him is now hers. Do you understand me, Maral?"

"Yes, Sed'la. But, I was trying to say, there's nothing to report." He simpered, tilting his big head. "I was just wondering how soon until we leave? Everyone is ready to go and has been for some time."

Sed'la chortled, shaking his head.

"The men would never question Col's decision, Sed'la," Maral confirmed. "You know that."

"All right, Maral." Vee nodded. "If the men are ready, then it is time to begin our westward expedition. Tell them to mount up, and move to the assembly area."

"Yes, ma'am," he replied.

Vee and Sed'la looked at one another, silently nodding. They followed Maral to the stables and headed for their horses.

Several riders exited the stable and rode to the adjoining buildings. Within minutes, the entire Tu'nide was in the saddle and riding towards Cenkin's western gate. Vee and Sed'la rode side by side, followed by Maral; the rest of the men fell into rank behind them. They rode past Castle Trosho and continued through the streets.

The streets were lined with citizens cheering for their soldiers. They were grateful for the brave men who fought to protect the city, although, there was little to fight in recent months. The rebels were content to stay away from the cities and villages and avoid confrontations.

Vee hoped they would meet little resistance along the way. Her mission was to find men still loyal to Terikk, or at least men willing to fight against Guan and his oppression.

As they approached the gate, she spotted Guan, sitting on his golden Nisean. He was dressed in the royal robes her father used to wear. Vee thumped her shoulder and saluted him. Shouting to the men, she asked, "Riders of the Tu'nide, how many of us are there today?"

In unison, they shouted their reply, "Three hundred and ninety three soldiers, Princess! Three hundred and ninety three warriors of New Caporesso! Ah-ooh! Ah-ooh! Ah-ooh!"

Vee continued, "May the brave soldiers of the Tu'nide from New Caporesso return with glory and honor." She looked at Guan and shouted insolently, "Ride out!"

As Guan watched them leave, he smiled. Princess Vitoria learned her job quickly. She announced the unit and its men as they were leaving, *Impressive.* If everything went as anticipated, the Tu'nide would be caught in an ambush, decimating their numbers. After Princess Vitoria's safe return, the people would call for him to send the army to war and crush the rebels in the west. Soon he would unleash his army again upon the lands of New Caporesso.

If the gods favored him, his plan would be successful. Guan laughed at the thought. *Of course the gods favor me. How else could I have done so much? How could I have eliminated the rightful king and become king myself if the gods do not favor me. And soon Col will be dead, killed while trying to escape.* No, the gods had chosen him above all others, he was sure of it.

Two by two, the riders exited the city walls, embarking on their journey. They headed west, towards Werlo and Dreglo. They would travel about twenty miles this day. The light from their fires would still be visible from the city walls. It would be several days before they were safely away from the prying eyes of Cenkin.

As Vee escaped the mighty walls of Cenkin, she stared in wide-eyed wonder at the world around her. She had not seen the land from the ground for ten years, only looking at it from the parapet. It had been so long since she touched terra firma without walls, that it was like she was experiencing it for the first time. The grass beneath her horse was beautiful. She felt the breeze against her face, playfully teasing her ponytail.

She closed her eyes, inhaling the free wind. *I'm free now too.* Her thoughts returned to her mission. *How will I rally the people to support our cause? How will I convince them that I speak the truth, and want Guan removed from power as much as they do? How will I command these men who know nothing about me?* The possibilities were countless.

Sitting straighter in her saddle, she realized she would have to find a way. The time for her to be a kept child was over. She was the commander of the Tu'nide and it was her duty to lead them no matter the danger. Her whole life had prepared her for this mission, now it was her time to embrace her destiny. It was up to her to raise an army to free New Caporesso from Guan's evil grasp. Somehow, she knew she was up to the task; the possibility of failure was no longer in her conscience thoughts. Vee would do what needed to be done.

Chapter 76

The sun was rising in Salvation. Hapco greeted Ketrik at the horse pen. Everything was prepared for the journey. The wagons were filled and the horses loaded. The riders from Salvation were accounted for, tending their horses. Only Kellen, Kyra, and Yen were missing.

"Should I send for them?" asked Hapco.

From a stall, Ketrik replied, "No, Hapco, we do not ride for another hour. We are early; they are not late." He checked the gear on his horse, pulling and tugging at it.

"Everything is ready." Hapco paused, studying his friend. Clearing his throat, he remarked, "Yen came home hours before Kyra did last night."

Sighing, Ketrik acknowledged, "Ahh...I know Kellen was up late too, but I was not sure if he was alone or not. Now I know." Ketrik milled about his horse, not looking at Hapco.

"What do you make of it?" inquired Hapco.

Ketrik stopped, his expression tranquil. "I do not know what to think. They are the best of friends and have been for a long time. Are we to expect nothing more than that? Does love grow out of friendship, Hapco?" He shrugged and asked, "What comes next for them? Hmm?"

Before Hapco could reply, he spotted Kellen and the others approaching. "Ketrik, here they come. Should we ask them about last night?"

Shaking his head, he exited the stall. "No, we will let them broach the matter."

As the three friends moved closer, Hapco's mouth fell open.

Ketrik gawked at what he saw.

Kellen and Kyra were walking hand in hand.

Yen walked ahead of them a short distance. He turned to Kellen and assured him, "I'll handle this delicately for you. Don't worry."

The group of riders watched their approach.

When they got closer, Yen blurted out, "Isn't it obvious? They love each other and have for a long time, all right," He saw the surprised look on his father's face. "So…are we ready to go or what?"

Kyra and Kellen shook their heads. *Delicately.*

Kellen stepped forward, speaking to everyone. "Don't look so shocked. Are any of you really surprised that we fell in love? I love Kyra, and she loves me," he looked at her. "We have for a long time; we just didn't realize it." He looked from face to face, stopping at Hapco. Stepping forward, he addressed him, "Hapco, I love your daughter. I was a fool for not admitting it sooner." Clearing his throat, he continued, "I humbly ask for your permission to marry her."

Still in disbelief, Hapco was speechless.

Ketrik stepped to his friend and slapped him on the back. "Well, Hapco, Kellen just asked for your permission to marry your daughter. Answer him," he laughed.

Hapco looked at Ketrik, and then Kellen. A giant smile crossed his face. "Kellen, I would be honored to have you as a son. Of course you have my permission to marry her. May you live together for many, happy years." Hapco embraced Kellen.

Kellen turned to his father and the two men shook hands. "Congratulations, Kellen. I am happy for the two of you. This union is a gift from the gods. I am glad you finally realized what we could already see. The two of you were made for each other." Ketrik smiled at his son.

The other members of the expedition stepped forward and offered their congratulations to Kellen and Kyra. Everyone except Durian, he remained on the far side of the corral.

After several minutes of handshaking and hugging, the riders returned to their horses.

Webb walked over to Durian and asked, "What are you doing? Your absence was insulting. You should've congratulated them."

"Why should I?" growled Durian. There was a fire in his eyes. "I don't want the two of them to get married, ever. Father said if I prove myself on the mission, a world of opportunities will be opened to me." He ogled Kyra from a distance.

Webb grabbed his arm, talking into his ear, "Don't forget yourself, Durian. Ketrik is in charge of this expedition. We do as he says and answer to him. You must be careful of your actions," he half whispered.

With wild eyes, Durian responded to his brother, "Father said all I need to do is perform well on the battlefield, and then everything else will fall into place for me. Once we prove that Salvation's warriors are better than those from New Caporesso, we'll be able to return to our ancestors' homeland unafraid. We'll be able to reclaim Lau'damay as our home again." Looking around at Ketrik and Hapco, he barked, "Ketrik! When are we leaving?"

Ketrik studied Durian. In the excitement of the well wishing, he had not noticed Durian's deliberate snub. "Since everyone is here, I guess it is time to go!"

A chorus of cheers rang loud from the riders.

"To your horses everyone, we leave at once!" he shouted.

The young warriors from Salvation mounted their horses and waited for instructions. Two small wagons accompanied them, driven by Wesne and Bitto, their horses in tow.

Ketrik rode to the corral gate where he stopped to address the group. "Today we leave for New Caporesso. Today will be the last day you see Salvation for a very long time, maybe ever. You must clearly understand... this journey will not be easy." He looked at each face, *They are so young.* "Some of you may never return home." Their horses snorted and moved around the corral. "New Caporesso was in the midst of a revolution when we left, we have no idea what we will find. It may be more treacherous than when we left.

"In any event, it is important that we keep our identities a secret for as long as possible. Only reveal who we are if it becomes absolutely necessary." His horse turned and side stepped away from the others. "We must also hide the fact that we are from a place beyond the Western Wilderness." Leaning forward, he rested his hands on his saddle horn. "If Guan discovers another community beyond his borders, he will not rest until he finds it and forces its capitulation.

"If he is no longer king, then I fear we may face an even more sinister enemy." He paused, looking at each of his troopers, "Secrecy is our only advantage. There are not enough of us to engage in battle; therefore, we must avoid conflict no matter what. That means we will retreat before risking lives. Does everyone understand? Does anyone have any questions?"

Yen answered for everyone, "I got up early this morning to ride through the wilderness, on a quest to find New Caporesso. Can we go already?" he grinned.

Kellen responded, "Yes, Yen, you're right, it's time to go. Onward for New Caporesso!" he boomed from his horse, a muscular bay colored courser.

Ketrik rode over to Kellen on his leopard-spotted Nisean. "Who put you in charge?"

Surprised, Kellen replied, "I'm sorry, Father. I just echoed Yen's enthusiasm. It won't happen again." He bowed his head slightly.

"It is all right, Kellen," he assured his son. "In fact, at some point on this mission, you may be forced into making decisions for everyone. You must be up to the task. Understand?" Their horses blustered, shaking their heads. "We are going back to New Caporesso for you and me. The others are along to help us with that undertaking. They will look to us to make the right decisions at critical times.

"Our choices may result in the death of some of our friends." He looked closely at his son, "You cannot lose sight of our mission. No matter how hard we plan, there will always be casualties. The death of your friends must not be allowed to crush your confidence or confuse you. You will need a clear mind to react to the situations we encounter; you cannot be distracted by chaos. Do you understand me, Son?" he searched Kellen's face for a response.

Kellen smiled weakly, "Yes Father, I understand what you mean. I'll be ready when you call on me."

"All right, then let us head home to New Caporesso." Ketrik turned and shouted to Durian and Webb. "You two, lead us to the wilderness and through its great mysteries. Hapco and I follow them. The rest of you fall in place behind us. I want Alecia and Eromo behind the wagons to keep everyone together. Any last objections?"

The group remained silent.

"Then take us to New Caporesso, Durian," Ketrik commanded.

They steered their horses towards the edge of the woods. No one from Salvation came to see them off. No matter, they were leaving and soon would be inside the Western Wilderness and on the road to New Caporesso. Though they did not know it, their fates awaited them in a foreign land. Would they find what they sought?

Durian was anxious for a successful mission. *Determine the effectiveness of our warriors in combat; prove Ketrik wrong about our soldiers. Then discern if our people can repopulate Lau'damay and the surrounding area.* Those were Orazio's orders to his son, and he would do as his father instructed, regardless of Ketrik's orders. He would show everyone that he was a more skilled warrior than Kellen. In his distorted mind, his objectives were clear, find a New Caporessoean enemy and kill them. *Kill them all!* Durian smiled at the simplicity of his plan, *How can I fail?*

Kellen's heart was filled with hope. He believed they would find an account of his family's final hours. That was all he could hope to discover. *How could they still be alive after all these years?* He forced the thought from his mind, welcoming a destiny that would be revealed to him in New Caporesso. He was returning home to the land he had forgotten.

Ketrik's heart was heavy as he rode beside Hapco. The burden of leading men was his once more. The responsibility of keeping them alive was an instant reminder of why he loved his life in Salvation. There, his only concern was Kellen, but on the trail and in New Caporesso, the lives of fourteen other people would be in his hands. He said prayers to the gods to keep his comrades safe from harm. He said none for himself, understanding his fate would be sealed the moment he set foot in New Caporesso again.

After riding for several hours, the ragtag group stopped at the edge of the woods. They turned and gazed upon the beauty of the Salvation countryside one last time before plunging into the darkness of the wilderness. Durian and Webb were their guides now, it was in their hands to steer them through the forest and into New Caporesso. None of them knew how long they would be gone, but they were prepared to meet whatever challenges the journey presented. With steadfast resolve, the tiny band of warriors disappeared into the Western Wilderness, in search of New Caporesso.

Epilogue

The dungeon was dank and dark. Rats scurried to and fro. Torches were alight in the corridor, but did not provide much illumination in the tiny cells. The stone floors and walls were wet with moisture. The sound of dripping water was constant. Leprosy and dysentery were as much the enemy as Guan's perverted torture racks.

"Prince Col, don't squirm so much. I have to tie these wraps tightly or you'll never heal." Abby tried to tighten the bindings. "Stop fighting me," she ordered, her words echoing off the walls.

"Oww...Stop it, Abby. That hurts like hell," he yelled.

"Your mother complains less than you do, child." She quipped at him, "Why don't you toughen up a bit and do what's necessary to get better." Grabbing his chin, she yanked it upward.

Suddenly looking ashamed, Col stopped struggling. He glanced at her. "How is my mother, Abby? Is she still locked up?"

"Yes, my prince, she is. But don't worry about her. She's fine. Her bruises have healed and she's feeling better." She quickly tightened a wrap around Col's ribs.

He winced in pain, but did not vocalize his discomfort.

"That's better, my prince. Two more tugs, then we're done." She wrapped more bindings around his midsection, stabilizing his cracked ribs. Slowly, Abby helped Col put his shirt back on. Next she replaced a sling around his neck and laid his arm in it, alleviating the pressure on his broken collarbone.

"Thank you, Abby, for taking care of me. How long have I been here?" he asked.

Sighing, Abby replied, "Almost ten days, my prince."

"Ten days." His spirit seemed to sink. "Any word from Vee and the Tu'nide?" he asked, already knowing the answer.

"It's too early for any reports, and you know it," she offered a tight-lipped smile.

Col took a breath; then he took a deeper one. He choked on it, in obvious pain. "Oh...that feels much better today, Abby. Thank you for coming to see me." His expression changed to one of confusion. "But, how do you get in here? Who keeps letting you in?"

Instantly uncomfortable, Abby said, "I think that does it for today, my prince. I must leave before the guards come back."

"Abby, please tell me," he pleaded.

Getting up quickly, Abby crossed the floor and knocked on the door. It creaked open slowly. "I'll be back tomorrow, my prince. Do everything you can to get better. Eat what you can and save your strength for whatever comes next." Turning away, she exited the cell. The door moaned as it was closed behind her.

The iron bolt dropped back into place. Col tried to get up and look through the tiny opening in the door, but could not. The pain was still too much.

Abby walked to the end of the corridor and turned the corner. A man was standing there, awaiting her arrival.

Wearing a somber expression, she said, "He is healing, but it's very slow." She shook her head, confessing, "I don't think he'll be ready in a few days."

"In four days, he must ride," the man stated. "If he doesn't, he'll never catch them. Whether he is able to ride or not is irrelevant. He has no other option but to head west, and find the princess and the Tu'nide." Sighing heavily, he said, "He's there only hope. Only he can warn them of the danger they are riding into."

"Are you sure there's no other way, General Tyr?" she asked.

"I'm positive, Abby. Guan will not rest until all of New Caporesso is at war again." He sadly shook his head. "No, Abby. Col is our only hope."

www.ingramcontent.com/pod-product-compliance
Lightning Source LLC
Chambersburg PA
CBHW051445260626

47162CB00001B/252